LEGENDS OF HENOSIS I

BORN OF STARLIGHT

MARIET KAY

ISBN 979-8-9883005-0-2 (eBook Edition)

ISBN 979-8-9883005-6-4 (Paperback Edition)

ISBN 979-8-9883005-2-6 (Hardcover Edition)

November 18th, 2023

Mariet Kay

Born of Starlight / Mariet Kay

Editing by Britney Waldrop

Cover Design by David Gardias at bestselling-covers.com

Map Design by Alyssa Ruth

First printing November 2023

Published by Palm Lane Publishing LLC

3104 E Camelback Rd #2616

Phoenix

Visit www.marietkay.com

For those who feel stuck in the dark. Embrace your ability to light
the way.

AUTHOR'S NOTE

This book includes content that may be difficult for some readers. The intended reading age is 18+ years old. Within this book there is depicted violence, self harm, references to sexual assault and themes of oppression and war. This book also contains on-page sexual content.

Realm of Henosis
WASTELANDS
The Plateau
Warlock's Cabin
Kullworth
Kruthin
Lamoreaux
Belray
NORTH CORRIDOR
Helos
Brennac Ruins
North Tower
Central Tower
East Tower
WEST CORRIDOR
Luz
CENTRAL CORRIDOR
EAST CORRIDOR
Phynnic Ruins
West Tower
South Tower
Eros
Ikanten
N
W
E
S

PROLOGUE

LEGENDS SAY THAT TWO CENTURIES AGO...

The stars shone brightly over the Isle of Ikanten. The fishermen had returned to their families with nets bountiful and tales of sea monsters narrowly avoided. The village, tucked into the cliffs of the South Corridor, settled down for the night—lanterns were dimmed, and shop windows were hatched closed.

All grew quiet, save for the piercing shriek of Adelaide Bennett as she made her way out of the womb and into the cruel world. The child's cries could be heard a quarter mile wide. She was born at midnight, and she bustled with energy from the moment her lungs sucked in the salty night air.

The following morning, neighbors flocked to the Bennetts' door with loaves of warm sweetbread and meat pies to congratulate the growing family. The Bennetts were well-liked, hard-working Ikantens. Until the night Adelaide was born, her mother had worked selling fish at the market. Her father was a fisherman—like most men in the village—providing imports and exports to the main continent of the realm.

She was their first child, and in the weeks following her birth, they worried whether it was normal for a babe to cry so fiercely each night. The new parents coddled her and fretted and did everything they could to calm her. But not even a thimble of rum could ease their ailing child. Each evening, at sunset, Adelaide began to wail up at the sky in defiance until the break of dawn. Three long weeks passed with no reprieve—her father worried that the dear child was ill. But her mother knew what vexed Adelaide.

A year prior, while working the plum orchards of the North Corridor during the off-season in Ikanten, she had made a terrible bargain. The plump burgundy fruit had been too tempting to resist.

"Just this once. My dear husband will enjoy them," her mother had whispered.

She'd shoved a bushel of plums into her apron, holding the edges to capture as much of the forbidden bounty as possible.

"No one will notice them missing," she'd assured herself.

But when she'd turned toward the arched iron entry, the sorceress who owned the estate stepped into her path.

"Who steals from my orchard?" The sorceress' eyes had shone with sharpness.

Then she'd given Adelaide's mother a choice.

"You will pay for the fruit with your life today, or you will agree to your firstborn child's servitude as a debt. The choice is yours," the sorceress had bargained.

The Bennetts had tried for three long years prior for a child that had never come. Why would she expect one now?

Thinking herself clever, Adelaide's mother had responded, "Please, let me live—you should have what you ask. I swear it."

The picking season soon ended at the orchard, and Adelaide's parents sailed back to their family in the South Corridor isles. All the while, Adelaide grew within her mother's womb.

So, it seemed that dear Adelaide was the sorceress' to claim.

With each passing day, her mother's guilt for having made that dreaded bargain worsened. Her anxieties didn't cease when Adelaide was born—for weeks, she expected the sorceress to be waiting in every shadow and in every dark alley.

Then one night, Adelaide's father was running late, still docking his boat in the port. Her mother took Adelaide from her crib and walked with her, bundled in linens. The babe screamed to the heavens as her mother rounded the spiral steps to the stucco rooftop that jutted out stories above the village.

Sleep-deprived, hopeless and with tear-soaked cheeks, Adelaide's mother stood at the edge of the three-story building holding her daughter's tiny fingers in her own. The salted wind off the shores whipped through her dark hair, and she smoothed the bundle of soft fabric that entombed her inconsolable infant.

"Shhh, my dear girl…everything will be okay soon," she whispered into the wind. "I will make everything okay. She will not ever have you. I promise."

The sky above was clear. Planets, stars and mysteries opened as mother and daughter stood with nothing between them and the galaxies above. Then, as the clock tower of the nearby capital Isle of Eros struck twelve, Adelaide's mother calmly stepped off the roof—the babe was still cradled in her arms and screaming to the heavens.

They fell as one. The mother was a picture of calm resolution as she and the child plummeted down, down, down. But Adelaide fought and wailed, willing the sky to take action.

A beggar, awoken by the foreign sound of skin and bone hitting cobblestone, rose. Upon realizing what lay before him, he called out, "Help, help, someone has fallen!"

Lamps lit the windows of homes surrounding the Bennett residence. Neighboring families poured into the street, groggily appraising the commotion. Her mother had landed face up, her last moments of calm etched across her face permanently. A crowd formed before anyone noticed what she held tucked in her arms.

"There's a babe! She has a child," a woman gasped out. She knelt to the ground next to them, staining her nightrobe red. Three generations of Bennetts piled out of the building to witness the fate of their kin.

Gasps wrung out through the street as whispers carried from household to household. Mother and child lay unmoving. Men who had been ripped from their sleep leaped to action to gather others to help. But they knew their efforts were for their consciences alone. The mother and child would not be saved.

Myths were born from what happened next. Many said that a single star fell from the sky down to Ikanten. It fell to meet Adelaide's chest and willed the child's heart to beat again. The babe glowed in a bright silver-blue haze as the onlookers' eyes widened in disbelief. *"A miracle,"* they whispered. *"Magic,"* they hushed.

None of them noticed the strange woman standing in the shadows, watching. Then, when the star was fully absorbed, the babe was finally content—cooing quietly and reaching up at the night sky. As if she was waving up at someone looking down on her.

Her father returned from the harbor, shocked by the sight of his fallen love. "Cursed! She took her mother. The girl is cursed!"

As a crowd gathered to see the glowing child, thousands of stars streaked across the sky. All five warring Corridors looked up. The direction of the winds changed, and the tides ceased for a few rhythms.

That night, Adelaide's father set the babe he deemed a bad omen on a raft and let the tides whisk her away. An offering to the sea.

But the sea carried Adelaide safely to the main isle, where she washed ashore on the beaches of Eros. Word traveled fast from Ikanten across the narrow seas, and the people of Eros celebrated Adelaide's arrival—a girl saved by stars and protected by the moonlit tides, a promise that the Sources favored their progress.

Knowing that no other home would suit her, the High Enchantresses of the Corridors took the child up into their towers. No one ever beheld the face of the beautiful child of starlight again.

Some say the heavens intervened that night and sent the star to save Adelaide. Others say it was the Source Origin of the Stars herself that fell into the child's heart to resume its beating. The Sisterhood renamed the child in the Star Origin's honor—Asterie.

That is how the fifth High Enchantress of Henosis was thought to be born, lost and saved.

That night began two centuries of renewed peace in the new realm. Asterie's origins were retold and revised. The story bent and changed over the years to suit the storyteller. But our story doesn't start at the beginning of the Sister of the Stars' life. It starts at the beginning of the end.

PART ONE

WICKED WOODS

Chapter 1
FENRIS

A doe grazed in a clearing of tall grass. The night fog of the northern woodland tangled around the animal's hooves.

The docile animal didn't know it was being hunted. I watched the deer through Vangard's eyes as it stood calm against a backdrop of cricket song and pine trees. But judging by the angle, Vangard was lowered onto his canine-like haunches in the thick of the treeline. The deer had only moments before it would be wrenched from tranquility and shredded to pieces.

"Leave it," I commanded quietly through the bond.

Vangard growled in protest, and the deer's head shot up. With a quirk of an ear, it fled.

I returned to my own vision in time to see Van run across the clearing to my side. He let out a deflated grunt as I patted his shoulder. With only half of my power, it was sometimes hard to reel him back to me, as his will grew stronger by the year.

Van made horrible company—endlessly blood hungry and always thinking about food above all else as though he was deprived. But Van was company nonetheless.

"Oh, come on...I let you eat the rabbits back at the creek. That's plenty." I waved him away.

When we had lived amongst those in the courts, they had always been cautiously intrigued by our connection. I wasn't the beast, and he wasn't I, and yet in some ways, I would always be the beast. I shook that confusing thought from my mind, motioning to the field before us.

"Go and run—you're supposed to be stretching your legs."

Van gave me a whale-eyed sigh but soon bounded away to pounce and run around the clearing, snapping at lightning bugs and looking like a puppy out of his cage. A terrifying, bone-chilling, hair-raising puppy.

Finding a boulder to sit on, my eyes wandered to the night sky. It sent a chill down my spine. The vastness and depth glistened over us with promises of Sources and heavens no one could prove existed. *Bullshit.* I'd always been a skeptic. I had seen the conflict between those who idolized the Sources and those who did not.

Yet the stars continued to orbit while I was stuck in these damp, dark woodlands. *But I deserved far worse than this.* That repeated thought had eaten away at me for four centuries.

It was the damned truth. Here, in these woods, I was no risk to the world beyond the treelined mountains. Here, with the fog and the chilled air, was a peace that someone like me didn't, for one moment, deserve.

A comet streaked across the sky. Its glow was brighter than the rest of the stars as it plummeted to the South. Standing with a lump in my throat, I listened for a collision. A cracking of our atmosphere. Fire meeting ground. *Was I praying for the end?*

No sound came.

My blood ran cold as stars continued to fall; hundreds...thousands of silver threads streaked across the sky at once. Even Van stopped his frolicking and looked up at the illuminated skies.

Then a voice boomed through the clearing.

"Find her."

Eerie, otherworldly—while it sounded far away, I felt breath on the back of my neck. The winds seemed to change direction before the night sky returned to its usual twinkle and relative stillness. My heart pounded in my chest, and Van returned to my side once more, tilting his head.

"I don't know either. But it can't be good."

Chapter 2
Asterie

I was late—Firose hated it when we were late.

My hurried steps down my spiral stairway felt heavy against the wrought iron stairs. I'd overslept—it had been hard to pull myself awake. I hadn't been sleeping well and was gluttonous for any small reprieve. Nightmares wracked nearly every sleeping hour, and no amount of valerian root was helping.

The Sisterhood met each week; we gathered just after sunrise. *Far* too early for my liking. Not that I'd *ever* loved mornings. I preferred to sleep during the daylight hours, and when the stars were swept out of the skies, my body longed for dusk.

I shuffled across the foyer of my tower, not stopping in my kitchen for a tart or tea as I normally would. While the other towers had compartmented rooms, I preferred open space. The foyer connected to the sitting and dining rooms—the only separate rooms were the kitchen and a large greenhouse that I tended to daily.

The Egress was built into the lower balcony of my tower, just off the main foyer. I pushed open the door to step outside, and a bird's-eye view of the sparse woodlands of the Central Corridor was laid out before me. There was no time to admire the view.

As I stepped into the Egress, I cringed against the sun. Taking refuge against the abrasive rays inside the carved space in the stone wall of the balcony, my hand still shielded my eyes.

"North Tower." The words came out as more of a groan than a command. The Egress pulled me away in a dizzying gust of darkness that felt like both falling asleep and waking up.

Within seconds, my body was thrust into Firose's entryway, halfway across the realm. Incredible magic—Egresses. The only ones remaining for transportation from Corridor to Corridor after the Great Wars were those in our five towers. The others, I was told, had long ago been covered or destroyed.

I hurried into the hallway, nearly tripping over one of the many Lynx that lazed about cleaning themselves. *Nasty creatures.* Skirting around their feline bodies and snoring rat noses, I made my way toward voices bickering in the sitting room.

Everything in the North Tower was gilded, fit for royalty, fit for Firose. The hall was arched intricately with the finest marble, and nearly a dozen glistening gold mirrors lined the sides. During childhood, I'd told Amara that I imagined Firose stopping at each one to admire herself. Amara laughed but quickly scolded me to respect our Sister.

I caught a glimpse of myself in one of those mirrors. My robes were ruffled and unpressed, which was to be expected of garments you accidentally fell asleep in. If you could call tossing and turning sleep. *This was no acceptable way to look during a Sisterhood meeting.*

Turning the corner into the sitting room, I nearly ran headfirst into a kettle as it floated across the room to pour coffee into their cups. *Some Oracle I was—couldn't even see a kettle coming.*

My Sisters sat upright and quieted as I entered.

Wyeth of the West.

Cassidee of the East.

Firose of the North.

Amara of the South.

All four of them assessed me with raised brows and piqued curiosity. *Great.* I was the only one late. My cheeks heated.

I looked at Amara first. Finding warmth in her attention settled my stomach. But Firose's words cut through the air.

"Asterie—*precisely* who we have been waiting for." Firose's tone was always sweet in a sickly way.

Firose looked like a golden goddess—blonde hair plaited into a crown, blue eyes shining. She was the second eldest of us, only younger than Amara. Age did not rank us—though if it did, I was the youngest with my two centuries.

Though none of us outranked the others, within the tower walls, Firose dictated when we would have meetings, she decided when they started and ended, and she motioned nearly every vote. She held us together and kept us focused. I aspired to meet her expectations, always. And in that moment, my stomach sank to realize I hadn't.

Firose had taught me everything I knew. I had her to thank for my lavish life in those towers.

I nodded, taking my seat across from Amara and giving her a knowing look.

"I apologize for my tardiness. The time slipped away from me."

"Hmph." It was the only response Firose gave as she smoothed her robe. Below the robe, she wore a gaudy mauve monstrosity that one might call a gown. We were the perfect contrast—she with her floral hues and me in all black. Dark robes, dark tunic, gray breeches. *"Has someone died?"* Amara would often joke.

"Are we going to talk about the uprising at the northwest border now?" Wyeth spoke up, always eager to jump straight to business.

Wyeth's brown cloak hood was down now, allowing us to see her black chin-length bob. Wyeth was born into a royal family of the Old World. The ancient village her family once ruled was cursed to never tell lies. However, her family had made a bargain with a sorceress of the Old World. Instead of never being able to speak a lie, they could bend the truth—but at the cost of their hair temporarily turning a shade of green when they did. Therefore, she did not conceal her hair during our meetings.

Cassidee agreed with a wave of her hand. Firose's eyes narrowed on Cassidee's muddy boots that were kicked up casually on the coffee table. I would put coin on Firose having commented on Cassidee's tawny brown hair being uncombed before I arrived; she hated anything out of place.

Despite her impatience, the warrior of the East Corridor offered me a conspiratorial smirk and a wink. I tried to inconspicuously reach into my pocket for the small moonstone stowed there.

"That's a great question." Firose turned back to me. "What have we seen of the West?"

What have *you* seen, is what she meant.

"The West..." I flipped the moonstone in my fingertips. "I haven't felt any movement in the past week," I bluffed.

Firose let those pink-painted lips curl into a feline smile.

"Why then...have I heard reports of large camps in the West along the northern border? Hundreds of radicals."

I didn't physically react, but tightness gathered in my chest. It annoyed me to be put on the spot like this, but fighting venom with venom had never done me any good.

"Right, let me have a second look."

My palm sweated against the cold moonstone in my pocket as I withdrew it.

"If you are not an effective Oracle, we may as well train you to be a housekeeper or a cook," Firose jabbed.

It was a ridiculous statement—the towers did the cooking and the cleaning. Firose was trying to get under my skin and spark my power to life. It was a tactic she had often taken when I was a child. She would goad me just enough to allow the spite to overtake me, often succeeding in completing the task she had set out for me. Or she instigated my frustration enough that I'd throw blue flames from my palms. They didn't match her red flames, which we assumed was attributed to my star-born origin, but they interested her greatly.

"That is enough, Firose. She looks like she hasn't slept in days. What's wrong, Asterie?" Amara cut in.

Weeks. It had been weeks since the nightmares began. Now they claimed every hour of my rest.

Leave it to Amara to be the first to notice that my skin was too pale, the curves of my body and signs of health were waning, and my long dark hair was limp and without shine. I had always had ample weight to spare on my bottom half, but even my breeches were fitting more loosely.

Amara was the embodiment of fierce love and unrelenting kindness. She had raised me in the South Tower. The South Corridor was comprised of many isles—romantic, quaint, peaceful lands of sea cliffs and beaches. While living with Amara, she taught me to conceal every emotion—to master my anger. *"Face the sea, child, and count the waves hitting the shore. Count them backward. Ten...nine..."*

I shook my head. "Nothing is wrong. I have been struggling with headaches." My hand wrapped firmly around the moonstone, focusing on the conjuring.

Show me what might come of the radicals...

The path slammed into me with force—rage, oppression, anxiety. And then the whispers.

"He is her puppet—Mattock can't be trusted."

I focused harder.

"She doesn't belong in our courts."

I gritted my teeth, following that thread.

"That magical cunt is with him at all hours; she must be stopped. The North will squash us all if we do not act now."

I gasped as their bitter words evolved into traitorous plans. Rioters gathered at the border of the West and North Corridor—Firose's words were true. The radicals planned to cut through Kullworth and then travel through the Hussa mountain range to the capital city of Helos in the North.

When I came to, I found Wyeth, Firose, Amara and Cassidee at the edge of their seats, all staring wordlessly at me. It was eerie how one could command a room simply by going silent. I didn't allow my expression to reveal my worry. As an Oracle, it was important to not express bias.

Though my mind screamed one question—*why was Firose spending so much time with King Mattock?*

"The radicals are saying that Firose and King Mattock are disrupting the Order." My eyes landed on the accused. "You have been seen in the Court of Helos too frequently, and a group of western radicals has formed in fear that they will be your first target should the North Corridor decide to attack the West."

"That's preposterous." Firose's stare turned to Wyeth quickly. "You must get your Corridor under control."

"I shall handle the camps in the West." Wyeth appeased Firose quickly. Her hair remained black—truth. Yet her posture slumped.

Cassidee nodded. She seemed even less eager than Wyeth, but she always agreed with Wyeth. "The East will send our flying fleets to aid in squashing any unrest. Wyeth, you have my support."

The East Corridor armies were our fiercest, commanding air fleets of Griffiths. Through the centuries, the animals had been domesticated and trained for battle—a competitive advantage to attack from the sky. The creatures were winged like giant hawks with feline bodies, not much unlike the Lynx, only more useful.

"We must act quickly." Firose seemed pleased with their commitments. "What about the Central Corridor? Do they, too, feel anxious?"

I shook my head. "The Central Corridor is quiet."

Firose always dismissed the Southern isles. They were so distant from the main continent that she rarely asked Amara for aid and never deemed them a threat. Since joining the Sisterhood meetings on my eighteenth birthday, I'd often watched Amara and Firose go head-to-head. In recent years, their disagreement was near constant.

"Then we should vote—all in favor of eradicating the threat on the northwest border?"

Amara pointedly eyed Firose. "Can you first answer—what business do you have with King Mattock that you have been at the court so frequently?"

We all had to be wondering about it—we only left our towers if the ruler of our Corridor requested it. Amara had known Firose long before the rest of us, and though they often disagreed, they always came to an understanding that would benefit the realm.

"King Mattock is very ill. I have been tending to his ailments and helping the court's healer keep him comfortable. Unfortunately, there is nothing more they can do. I was going to share the news last meeting, but he requested discretion until his prognosis was known."

We all stilled—no one sipped their coffee, and no one spoke for what felt like minutes. In my two hundred years, I'd seen more than one transition of power. But the North had been under Mattock's rule for centuries before my time, and Mattock was immortal. No illness could take him.

True Source magic, a descension of ancient bloodlines, was rare. And that type of power died out long ago. Except for within the towers and, I shuddered to think of it, in the Wastelands if anyone still remained there.

The Sun King was one of the last people with Source magic remaining in the realm. He was grandfathered in due to his royal standing. Mattock never married, nor had he sired an heir before the Order and the bans on immortal conception were decreed.

"That's impossible." Amara scoffed, but I saw something akin to fear glisten in her eyes.

Firose shook her head. "It should be—but he's been blighted by magic that I can't undo. His mind slips away more and more each day."

Amara's back tensed, and her golden-brown eyes seemed far away.

"So the rising from the West—" Cassidee started.

"Could be a coup," Firose finished for her. "It's possible word has begun to spread—it's been hard to contain that an infallible King has struck ill. So we must appoint someone to power."

Amara cleared her throat, and sunlight from the window gleamed against her brown skin. For someone who had taught me to control my emotions expertly, she said so much with her eyes. They were drenched in sadness and unshed tears.

"We will *all* need to weigh in on that matter." Amara's voice was strained.

What was I missing? It was so unlike her to appear moved in any way in front of the others.

"Of course," Firose answered with mild annoyance. "But the King hasn't even gone cold. We will discuss the next steps for finding his replacement during our next meeting. For now—shall we vote to handle the more pressing matter of threats on the northwest border? I vote that we quell the unrest with force. Those in favor?"

"I second," Cassidee confirmed.

"I," Wyeth added.

Firose loosed a smile—she had a majority. While it took all of our votes to make any decision, we tended to make decisions as a unit.

Amara seemed conflicted before she sighed and agreed. "I."

"I." The word felt as wrong as the energy in the room.

Amara watched a bird that was perched outside the gilded window frame. She seemed to grow removed from the conversation.

"Is the news from the West all we have to cover today?" Wyeth's foot tapped against the marble as she spoke.

"Yes, the meeting is adjourned." Firose paused. "Asterie, do stay a moment, dear."

I fought the urge to grimace. This might be the reprimand for being late I'd been waiting for. Despite the Order, Firose had allowed me to stay, and I hated disappointing her.

Firose had taught me all of my spells, enchantments and charms and how to read both the Brennac and Phynnic languages of the Old World. Most importantly, she had taught me how to manipulate the moonstone to conjure visions, paths and prophecies.

As Henosis' last remaining Oracle, I had essential work to do for the realm.

Sometimes I wondered where I would be if I hadn't ended up in the hands of the Sisterhood. I'd read so many storybook versions of my origins that I'd long ago stopped inquiring about the truth. *What if my mother had never stepped from that rooftop? Would I be slinging fish at a market in Ikanten? Begging on the streets of Eros? Worse?*

Dealing with an outburst from Firose was all in a day's work. I served the realm, the Central Corridor, and by the Order, I would keep it safe.

Amara squeezed my shoulder gently as a goodbye before she left the room. Cassidee swung her feet off the table and stalked out with a grunt of dismissal and a waved hand.

Wyeth trailed behind her, murmuring, "Good day." Then she quickly caught up to Cassidee.

Firose poured herself another cup of coffee. When she offered me some, I shook my head politely.

"Asterie, you seem distracted lately." She sipped the coffee innocently, looking concerned. I wasn't buying it. *She wanted something.*

"The headaches, as I mentioned." I forced my body to relax back into the seat. "They can be intense."

"You must ask Wyeth for some feverfew." She set down her cup and examined me.

"That's a good idea."

"Can I ask something of you?"

Here it was. "Of course."

"King Mattock...he keeps having night terrors of the Wastelands rising against Henosis. He is fever-ridden and confused but claims dark magic is roiling again in the realm. That it will soon break free."

My eyes widened a pinch.

Firose continued, "Have you felt anything? I seek your opinion before I worry our Sisters."

An eerie, ethereal voice whispered right into my ear. It was so close that I could feel breath on my ear lobe.

"Lie."

It took all of my nerve to remain in my seat.

"Did you hear something?" I asked.

"No, did you conjure something?" Firose pitched forward with eager anticipation.

"Oh." I backtracked quickly, shaking my head. "No, it must have been a strange bird call. How odd."

What was *that voice?*

Why did it want me to lie?

Why did I want *to lie?*

I cleared my throat. My blood ran cold, and the hairs on the back of my neck stood. The truth was I had felt something similar to the King during the nightmares that visited me each night. Dreams of wars, pain, darkness and ruin. But I thought them to be dreams—they *were* just dreams. *Right?* That inner voice had told me to lie—maybe it was because those dreams were meant to throw us off course. I wasn't confident in sharing my experiences yet.

And so...I lied.

"Sorry—no. I have not felt what the King speaks of. Do you think there is merit to his claims—that the Wastelands will rise, that the realm...Henosis will fall?"

Firose eyed me carefully as she stirred sugar daintily into her cup. "I never said the realm would fall."

I didn't lie often and it didn't come easily.

Luckily, when speaking to Firose, my words were often clumsy.

"My apologies, I shouldn't have made assumptions...but do you worry his night terrors may be something more? Something to worry about?"

Firose seemed satisfied with my deflection as she sat back in her chair and shook her head slowly.

"I have no reason to think any magic will rise in the realm. The Wasteland wards have been strong for centuries. He is an old immortal growing weary with death." Firose stood. "Thank you, Asterie. I do appreciate that we can speak openly like this."

I was dismissed. *Thank the Sources.*

Before I got to the door, Firose spoke. "Asterie"—she waited for me to turn—"it would be best if you do not tell the others about this. I don't want to worry them unnecessarily."

I nodded my commitment. Firose smiled sweetly back at me as if to say, "You've done well." My heart sang with her unspoken praise.

I quickly left the room, dodging the sleeping Lynx that still dozed in the hall before launching myself into the Egress. My hands grasped the cold stones as if they might bring back my sense of balance.

The thought of the dying King of the North Corridor plagued my mind. I was unable to shake the feeling that maybe the Sun King's night terrors mirrored my own. It was enough to solidify one decision.

I needed to find the right path—a way to avoid whatever darkness loomed over the realm of Henosis.

CHAPTER 3
FENRIS

It was a clear-skied afternoon. The humidity had finally let up, and a warm breeze swayed the canopy of trees in the woods. A rabbit sat a few yards away, whiskers flickering, unknowingly awaiting death. My bow was raised—string pulled taught.

A rustling in the trees beyond the rabbit startled it, and the rabbit bounded off into the dense forest thicket.

"Fuck," I growled.

I didn't *need* the rabbit. I had venison that was not yet spoiled back at the cabin, but I was just so damn tired of eating the same thing daily. Plus, it was rare to find pheasant this deep in the woods, and fishing was so tedious. Not to mention, I was never a skilled fisherman—which is likely why I hated it so much. Petty as it was, failure left me in a foul mood.

When the rustling in the trees didn't subside, my aim turned to the treeline—something was back there. *Something big.* Taking shelter behind a giant redwood, I kept my bow pointed in the direction of breaking branches.

Dark creatures had been breaking free of the Wastelands with greater frequency. It was becoming a weekly occurrence. The screams of a Banshee had awoken me late last night. I'd lain awake until it had passed, unworried. Its howls into the night couldn't signal the death of my loved ones, as no such people existed.

When the rat-like nose of a Lynx poked from the brush, my blood ran cold. The Lynx wasn't alone. Three more feline forms prowled behind it. Lowering my bow and flattening myself to the tree, I faced away from the direction they were traveling. Not because I feared the beast but because I feared why it might be here and who might be trailing it.

Shit.

Their noses were to the ground, rustling the leaves. I hoped they would not pick up my scent and made quick work of whispering a cloaking charm.

Hearing those guttural snarls brought me back to my days spent in the Brennac Court. Those fierce creatures protected the gates of the palace. Children feared them enough to take the longer route home to not pass by the palace guards.

There was only one person who might still keep Lynx.

I steadied my breathing and remained utterly still. The Lynx's senses were dull compared to most predators—poor eyesight and low-tracking abilities. Their hearing, however, was impeccable.

Their steps grew farther away into the brush.

The Lynx were headed toward the Wastelands. *What the fuck for?*

In four hundred years, I'd not seen Lynx in these woods.

My body relaxed only after the creatures had long disappeared into the thick of the woods. Van could take on dozens of Lynx. I could let him out now, but to risk even one of them carrying a vision of me or Van back to its master wasn't worth it.

There was no desire in my heart for a reunion.

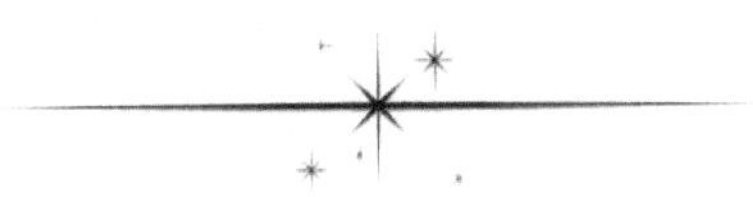

Still reeling from the encounter with the Lynx, I returned to my cabin. In moments like these, I wished there was a way to contact Amara. She would doubtlessly tell me I was overthinking their significance.

Maybe they got free of their own will. Lynx are fickle creatures, she would say.

And I would answer, "Or maybe I'll finally get a sword through my heart as I deserved."

I'd spoken the words out loud.

Conversations with yourself. Great, Fen—you've truly lost it.

I reached the cabin porch and kicked off my boots before placing a hand on the doorknob.

"She's coming…"

The whisper hit the back of my neck like a cool breeze. Gooseflesh rose on my skin.

I spun around on the rickety steps with my bow raised. That voice—where had it come from? Realizing I was alone, as always, my bow lowered. *No one.*

It flooded back in a flurry of frantic memories—being in that clearing two centuries ago, looking up to see stars fall. *"Find her."*

That voice was impossible to forget.

She's coming.

For fuck's sake, who was the "she" *it referred to?* The Lynx sighting and the dull burning in the ink on my arm where Vangard rested made me question if I even wanted to know. A bad omen, I was sure of it.

"Come on out, Van."

A familiar gust and kicking up of dust greeted me as Van's hulking canine body filled the porch, tail wagging softly, awaiting my command. It was too coincidental, and something told me that voice and the Lynx sighting were connected. There was only one way to find out.

"I need you to track those Lynx. And you must remain unseen."

Chapter 4
Asterie

My mind pressed against an invisible barrier. No matter how hard I strained against it, no paths formed, no images revealed themselves and not even a whisper graced my ears. Unable to maintain the effort, I gasped. My heartbeat elevated and the room spun. *How long had I been at the orb?*

My reflection in the large moonstone sphere greeted me when my mind returned to my body. Instead of the milk-white coating that usually overtook my eyes while conjuring, my irises were ominous, inky pools of swirling black rimmed by an eerie iridescence. Dark hair had loosened from my braid and stuck to my forehead, which was wrinkled with exhaustion.

My eyes continued to regain focus against the dim candlelight dancing across my tower's foyer.

Ten...nine...eight...

My mind was exhausted from trying to conjure any path that might lead away from the night terrors that had plagued my dreams for weeks. The dreams were too vivid, too clear. Too real. Since

Firose had revealed the dying North King shared my visions, peaceful sleep had not found me.

Without a clear prophecy, it would be near impossible to find any path that might lead away from the destruction of the realm. *If that's even what I was seeing.* Yet I continued to try.

Show me the prophecy my night terrors foretell of. Show me a path to prevent them.

Darkness crept through the windows in the atrium, telling me it was not yet morning. Hundreds of candles lit the foyer and highlighted pointed arched iron windows as shadows ebbed across the dreary room. The flame's jovial flickering mocked me, licking toward me instead of the ceiling as they should.

How could an Oracle protect the realm if they couldn't even effectively command a moonstone? It should be easy for me to conjure a prophecy—like heating a kettle or lighting a match. *Why was this one so difficult to find?*

The moonstone refused to respond when asked about the night terrors. It was as though a tall wall was built around any revelation that might protect the realm from what my nightmares warned of.

Seven...six...five...

As my breathing slowed and I prepared to try again, the moonstone began to ripple with light. *Was I doing that?*

"It would be best if you did not tell the others." The voice startled me stiff and filled every corner of the room. Yet when I looked around, I was still alone. The voice was feminine, but not. Kind, but not. It sounded...old, otherly. A warning.

I rolled those words over in my mind—they were familiar. That was what Firose had said in her sitting room. I was not to tell the others about Mattock's fears.

My chest constricted as though a weight was being pressed to it. *Did the voice mean my Sisters too?* The other High Enchantresses of

Henosis were the only people I *could* tell anything to. But I'd never dreamed of disobeying the Sisterhood. I'd never dreamed a danger might lurk ahead that we could not solve together.

Crackle. Flash. Smoke swirled around the stone as it sputtered to life with images more vivid than I'd ever conjured before. Typically, a prophecy only showed me fragments—a picture, a conversation, a feeling, a direction, something small that I could form a path to or away from. I'd never been able to conjure all parts of the whole at once. This was something new, and it pulled me in with force.

The city of Luz was below; I stood atop a high wall of what seemed to be a palace. It looked to be the highest point aside from a bell tower at the far end of the city. I'd never seen Luz before but knew it from intuition alone. Buildings of white limestone and blue slate rooftops and cobbled streets stretched for miles. It put all other cities to shame. Not that I had *seen* any other cities, even in my visions.

The scene below soon turned to gruesome, gut-wrenching chaos. Blood, smoke, screams and fire permeated every one of my senses—it was unbearable. The bell tower fell. Women and children ran from the city gates only to be met with the swords of armed soldiers cutting them down. The palace walls crumbled below as cannons rocked the ground. There it was, as it had been in all my night terrors—the fall of Luz. Seeing it then, awake, left goosebumps on every inch of me.

Four...three...two...

Bile rose in my throat. I could no longer calm myself by counting.

"You will not survive this war. Do what you must, starling." The voice echoed through the chamber of my mind that I was now trapped in.

The vision was overwhelmingly clear, all-consuming and severe, like oil had been poured into my ear and settled into my mind. It was unsettling, violating. It sucked the breath from my lips and the energy from my limbs.

This was no night terror. The moonstone did not lie. This was a prophecy.

The rest unfolded in a rush of whispers and words—all of the realm would fall. Towns and cities would burn to ash. Each would meet a demise more grisly, more heartbreaking than the last. *Peace Prevail, make it stop.*

I cried out, "Stop it! Stop...please!"

But the vision still gripped me. I couldn't get out.

My eyes slammed shut, but the screams and heat of fire still accosted me. Then the smell of something distinctly evil invaded my senses; it raised the hair on the back of my neck and smelled of whale oil from a lamp but deeper, sootier, and rancid. I'd read that dark magic came with a stench—*was it the smell of burning flesh?* I'd never smelled either before, so I couldn't be sure.

I held my hands over my ears but could still hear those gut-wrenching shrieks.

"Stop!"

Then everything quieted.

When I opened my eyes, the streets were empty below, save for debris, blood and ash. I sunk to my knees before the orb.

"It is time to act, Sister of the Stars. Go to the young Queen."

My vision cleared of the horrendous scene, and I was back in my tower. Every candle in the tower blew out as though the air was sucked from the room. The light of the orb sputtered out and left me in the pitch-black room. Being alone in the dark was a reprieve from the visions I'd experienced.

Crumpling to the ground, I let my tears fall to the cold stone.

Ten...nine...eight...seven...six...

Exhaustion took hold, and I hoped for peaceful sleep to take me.

I awoke on the stone floor and began pacing the space like a caged animal.

Despite the immensity of the space, the tower had never seemed so confining as it did now. Walls lined with shelves of ancient Phynnic and Brennac texts stretched twenty feet to the ceiling, and arched iron windows laden with overgrown ivy towered above.

Every part of my tower's construction and design was to my liking. Amara had teased, *"Are you sure about all this dark iron and stone? This is meant to be your home, not a fortress."*

The tower still felt like home, yet something stirred in me to leave—to do as the prophecy told me to.

"Go to the young Queen."

But *how*? I couldn't get far alone. Navigating the woods below and the highlands between here and Luz wasn't an easy task for even the most well traveled, or so I had read. With so little experience, I'd be lost in a night.

The Queen hadn't requested my presence. By the Sisterhood's rules, I was not allowed down to the courts without a request from the ruler of my Corridor.

No request had ever come for me. My face wasn't yet known to the people—two centuries of service, and yet I was unrecognizable to the masses.

I have to write the Queen.

The thought came so easily, making me pause in the middle of the foyer. Corresponding with the ruler of the Central Corridor without consulting the Sisterhood first left a pit in my stomach. But the prophecy had been very clear—

"Don't tell the others," I whispered, not trusting my resolve to keep the promise.

I stepped over to the spiral iron staircase, which circled up to my bedchamber on the second story of the tower, and ambled into the bathing chamber. The tower was already running a bath for me. It knew that when my mind was ailing, my body longed for a good soak.

"Thank you," I murmured to no one. The tower knew how to care for me lavishly, yet no companionship could be found in charms and spells.

I stepped into the bath and attempted to calm my nerves.

What could be the harm in requesting an audience with the ruler of my Corridor, the woman I was duty-bound to protect?

CHAPTER 5
FENRIS

Through Van's eyes, I could see the Plateau—a place where the trees of the northern woodlands abruptly ended and the land seemed to drop off into nothing. A great cliff descended into a seemingly endless sun-soaked canyon. The entry to the Wastelands.

The harsh contrast of evergreen against the brown sand and rust-toned rocks still shocked me despite having known what lay there. I'd only traveled there once since my binding to the woods didn't allow Van and me to leave the treeline. Plus, nothing in those vast wastes looked enticing enough to venture further, even if I could.

Van had tracked the Lynx, staying out of their earshot and sight. I was sitting in my favorite suede chair in the cabin as I vicariously watched, and my hands gripped the tufted armrests.

Their feline bodies were pacing on the cliff's edge as though searching for something. Rat-like noses inhaled dirt and expelled snot, wetting the ground. Van's instincts were taking over, and he emitted a low growl.

"Shhh, Van," I said to him through the bond. "Do not draw their attention. Just watch, stand down."

The low growl ended, and Van sunk further down into the brush, stalking closer to the treelined edge. I'd instructed him to roll in a clay-banked river miles back. His black fur was undoubtedly dulled and caked in mud to help him blend better into the woodlands. Van's eyes remained trained on the Lynx as they paced and howled.

One of the nasty creatures snapped its jaws at the others, a chittering sort of sound like a house cat that had caught sight of a bird.

We watched as the Lynx gathered around a particular point in the Plateau. There was what looked like a rippling in the air, like a seam of invisible curtains flailing in the wind and capturing the light of the sun.

"What in the Sources' names..."

The Lynx continued to chitter and back away from the slash, which seemed to extend up to the sky. A rip. It was iridescent—only when the wind blew did I notice the slight shift in light.

The Wasteland wards were compromised.

An ache formed in my chest. *Was it hope or dread?* Part of me longed to see how those exiled had fared.

People crested the cliff's edge on foot, along with carts pulled by horses. My excitement was laced with horror as they peeled back that rip to step right through. Nearly fifty men and women, all armed with broadswords, stepped up onto the Plateau and out of the Wasteland wards.

One man on horseback yelled out, "Follow the Lynx from here!"

He then turned his mount back toward the rip.

"There must be switchbacks in the canyon walls..." I mused to Van, not that he could piece together what was happening. By all shows of his intelligence, he was canine.

The horses pulled large carts stacked with crates—supplies? Weapons? The Lynx began to lead the Wasteland escapees east. I breathed a sigh of relief. The Lynx didn't seem intent on traveling back the way they'd come.

My heart was pounding as I gave Vangard his next command.

"Stay put until they've left. Then slip away and run back."

There was no explanation that made sense for why Lynx would be collecting Wasteland exiles and leading them east. *Are they headed to the Brennac ruins?*

More importantly, *how much longer could I hide away from whatever trouble was brewing in the realm?*

Chapter 6
Asterie

After my soak, I entered my study in nothing more than a bathrobe and found a loose piece of parchment. My hand shook as the pen hit the page.

This was punishable.

I could be cast out of the Sisterhood for inking the words onto that page. Cast out to the Wastelands. But I needed to understand what the prophecy wanted from me meeting the Central Queen.

To My Queen Sybilla Wymark of Luz,

Do handle this letter discreetly. I write not as your High Enchantress but as a hopeful ally in difficult times ahead. I was delivered a prophecy that spells ruin for the Corridors as we know them.

I witnessed the fall of Luz. I have yet to find a path to stop it, but I see no clear one. So I warn you to be wary of the other rulers in the realm, as I do not know how the war will begin—only that it will.

The prophecy came with an instruction to seek you out. I do not know why. It also asked that I not share my visions with my Sisters, hence my request for your secrecy. I need your formal request to leave this tower.

That is what I ask of you—please request my presence in your court if you see fit to heed my warning.

I will do everything I can to protect the city and its people once there. I make no promises that we can stop the war ahead, but it feels imperative that we should try. Together.

Writing this letter is the only thing that may bring me to sleep tonight. It also could condemn me to a fate too wicked to fear. I am at the mercy of what you choose for me.

Accept the assurances of my highest regards,

Asterie

I rolled the parchment quickly and hastily tied a ribbon around it to secure it. The faster its contents were concealed, the easier it would be to forget the traitorous message within. Then, stepping to the window, I whispered a Phynnic charm to draw the attention of a nearby hawk.

When it landed, the predator eyed me carefully.

"No biting," I warned as I tied the parchment to its taloned foot.

"You will take this to Queen Sybilla Wymark of Luz. Please, make haste."

Its wings pounded the air as it carried my message away to the capital city of the Central Corridor. With every flap of its wings, the raging power within me quieted. *This was the right path...it had to be.*

In the week that followed that terrible prophecy, my stone facade was cracking. My nerves and emotions were resulting in inconvenient side effects.

During this week's Sisterhood meeting, I'd barely been able to hide the blue flames ebbing from my palms that refused to be snuffed out. My magic was acting out in ways I'd never felt before. The charged blue light threatened to burn anything that I touched while in the presence of my Sisters. So I clenched my fists at my sides during our meeting.

Amara seemed to sense something was still wrong. I felt terrible for withholding the truth from her. I had reached out to Queen Sybilla Wymark; I had broken so many of the rules in doing so.

Yet the worst thing to hide from my Sisters was that the moonstone no longer responded to me. No matter what I tried, the stone remained cold. No paths, no images, no whispers. Since hearing that prophetic voice in my foyer, it seemed my gift as an Oracle had been *gone.* I'd read once that an Oracle's power could wane if their fate was tied too closely to a prophecy. Given what that voice had told me, that seemed likely.

I thanked the Sources that the discussion centered on who would take Mattock's seat as ruler in the North, and my gifts hadn't been required. Yet.

But Firose had asked me to prepare to use the moonstone during our next meeting. I feared the look of disappointment in her eyes when she realized that I couldn't.

I was sprawled across a chaise on the balcony in the shade, deeply caught up in reading. I was engrossed in a text that hovered inches from my nose—a common sight at this time of day.

All the discussions of power transitions in the realm had sparked my reading selection. This volume detailed how the Great Wars had begun.

The Old World had been a united land, much like Henosis. Then, the Kingdoms of Phynx and Brennax slipped into a civil war that divided the lands into two opposing forces. Brennac rulers grew weary of the fast-rising civilization in Phynx and attempted a failed coup that turned the realm against them. Once Brennax fell, the Order was enacted—magic was no longer allowed in the realm.

The Order still held strong.

Reading about it made something churn in my stomach.

A dove on the balcony railing let out a jovial coo that startled me upright. The history volume fell to the ground next to me as I noticed a scroll attached to the dove's delicate claw.

"What do you have there?"

It flapped its wings with excitement, feathers fluffed, as I approached. Carefully, I untied the rolled parchment from the bird's leg.

"Thank you, off you go." The dove flew up into the canopy of trees.

I unraveled the scroll—it had a faint scent of lilac. That sweet floral smell was a welcome contrast to the herbs and leather of the foyer as I stepped inside.

Dearest Lady Asterie,

Accept my apologies that this note is brief and comes by dove instead of hawk. I didn't want to draw attention, and this seemed a fitter way to honor your request for secrecy. I have only told the most trustworthy member of my court about the contents of your letter. He will arrive soon to escort you on your journey. Pack only essentials—and do arm yourself.

Your escort carries with him a request I cannot put in writing for the risk that it will fall into the wrong hands.

I look forward to the honor of meeting you,

Queen Sybilla

P.S. I wish I could say differently, but I believe your words. I know it to be true.

My mind raced as I re-read the Queen's penned words silently no fewer than ten times.

A request. *"Pack only essentials."*

And then, more cryptically, *"I know it to be true."*

Was the young Queen an Oracle? It couldn't be. My kind had become so rare after the Great Wars—it was one reason Firose insisted that I stay in the towers unless as a last resort.

But this was a last resort, wasn't it? What good would I be in this tower if the realm crumbled?

"Pack," I repeated. Then, finally, the reality of my actions took hold.

I was leaving the tower. I would pack and *leave the tower.*

The world outside didn't frighten me. I'd read countless books and learned everything possible about the dangers out there. But that was all hypothetical. It felt wrong to be excited at such a time—so much was at risk. But my mind wandered to what the city of Luz would be like, to its people, to its palace. My duty was to the Order. And, *Peace Prevail*, I'd serve the realm to my dying breath. But at least I'd get to see a sliver of the realm I'd served first.

The voice of the prophecy echoed through my mind. *"You will not survive this war."*

Already contemplating which weapons to bring, I held the Queen's letter between my palms. Blue flames formed there and seared the scroll to ash.

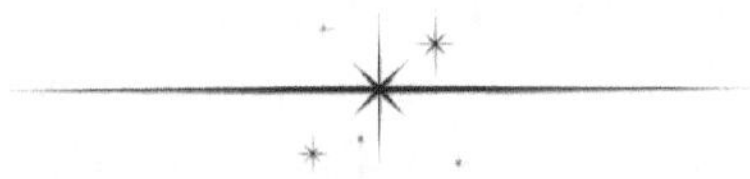

The Queen was true to her word. That afternoon, hoofbeats confirmed that a traveler approached. An enormous figure rode a large black horse with feathered legs into the clearing, ponying a smaller red horse behind him. *Did they expect me to ride that?*

My heart jumped into my throat, and my thoughts raced. *Maybe this was a bad idea.* Allowing no part of my appearance to show worry, I stood on the lower balcony with my hands neatly folded on the railing. The giant figure dismounted onto the grass clearing below before tying the horses to a nearby tree.

He wore leathers and armor. The crest across his chest plate bore the Luz emblem—a crown of acorns. It was a symbol of prosperity and resilience.

A Knight? No, he was more than a Knight by his looks and how he carried himself. It puzzled me why the Queen would send a member of her guard—*what was happening in Luz if a man of war was her most favored advisor?*

His eyes skimmed up the tower before finding me. One hand casually settled on his sword hilt and the other shielded his eyes from the sun. He seemed to glow under its rays—standing tall and unmovable like he belonged there.

"Lady Asterie, High Enchantress of the Central Tower," he shouted. "I am Sir Emmerick, Constable to the Court of Luz."

Ah. A Commander.

His deep bow heated my cheeks. No one had ever bothered to bow to me before—it made me feel uneasy.

"It's just Asterie. You may come up, Sir Emmerick."

His eyes scanned the tower as if looking for a way up; when he found none visible, he yelled back up at me, "There are rumors in court that you throw down a rope made of your hair. Is that how I climb up?"

I had to stifle a laugh. When you'd lived as long as I had, it was humorous to hear of the legends surrounding your existence. In my case, there were many—this one was one of the more bizarre. Yet I had never once told a man there was a door. *No,* I let them climb the tower wall.

"No, there is a door around the back facing South." Despite my amusement, my voice remained measured.

He wasted no time. Sir Emmerick's large frame stepped across the lawn and around the tower, where he would find a heavy iron door. Judging by his sheer size, he'd have no trouble with it.

Whispering the Phynnic uncloaking enchantment to lower the ward, I entered the foyer to meet him at the stairway door.

"Watch your step around the middle—the stones are loose," I called down the spiral staircase, hearing the groan of his armor as he climbed.

He rounded the last turn and reached the landing, not seeming an ounce out of breath. Up close, he looked exquisite—young, no more than thirty, clean-shaven with a strong jaw, and black hair kept short in neat coils. I'd never considered myself short, but he towered over me by at least an arm's length. He barely fit through the doorway and needed to duck so as not to hit his head. Once inside, he looked in place against the high ceilings of the foyer.

"It is nice to make your acquaintance, my lady." He gave another low bow.

"Just Asterie will do."

The formality of the courts wasn't going to come quickly to me. *Nothing* would come easily to me beyond these tower walls—I could only guess how to act based on the texts and stories in my library.

"Can I get you a cup of coffee or tea?"

"That is very kind. Tea would be great, thank you."

He followed me into the kitchen. When he saw a kettle floating over to the hearth, he balked.

In the courts, this type of magic would be banned. Even immortality was growing less and less common in the realm with the conception bans. And any dark magic that could have once created immortality was long forgotten with those in the Wastelands.

"Am I the first immortal you have met?"

He seemed surprised by my abrupt question. *Was that too forward a thing to ask someone?*

"No, there are members of my army who lived during the Great Wars."

"Ah, so older than me even."

The kettle hissed, and the tower lifted it, pouring two cups that floated to us. Emmerick took his cup, looking around uneasily. He'd barely stepped into the room.

"Thank you?" he said unsurely.

"It's charmed, this place—there is no one to thank. We are alone."

That seemed to relax his enormous shoulders.

"Let's sit out in the foyer." I motioned toward the exit.

Emmerick followed me—taking in the space as if planning an escape route with every step. His hand never left the hilt of his sword. *He doesn't feel safe*, I realized.

"Come sit. I won't harm you." I pointed to the chair across from mine as I sat. My voice was more reassuring than I thought myself capable of. "I know this is unusual—my requesting an audience with the Queen—but my intentions are pure."

Once settled, he eyed me from where he sat and nodded slowly, not looking entirely convinced.

"I have instructions from Queen Wymark"—he reached into a pocket of his leathers—"to give this to you before I explain her request."

His fingertips brushed mine as he handed me the parchment. His hand jumped away as if my magic could burn him. Or worse, jump to him, like it might be contagious. His attention was trained on me as I began to read aloud.

"Dearest Lady Asterie, if you are reading this, it means that Sir Emmerick has made safe passage to you. For this, I am glad."

I raised my eyebrows as I looked at him over the page for a moment, letting no other show of emotion touch my face. It only occurred to me then how awkward it felt to read the letter aloud, but it seemed too late to stop.

Clearing my throat, I continued, *"He is my most trusted advisor when it comes to matters of the Court of Luz. He will escort you here, but first, I ask for your service with an important task that I feel only the two of you might hope to accomplish successfully."*

The Commander shifted uncomfortably as though bracing for the next words.

"Sir Emmerick carries with him the nature of this request, along with maps that I hope will benefit you in your travels. While this is a request, and you have every right to decline, I'm compelled to believe this may be our only option to secure the safety of Luz. I write to you with the greatest hopes that you will accept. Please remain unseen and do not draw attention. My best regards."

The signature on the letter was not *Queen Sybilla Wymark of Luz*, not *Your Queen.*

Just *Sybilla.*

My fingers ran across the name—it was how one might write a friend. *Was the Queen wise to consider me such when friendship wasn't something I could offer her?* Forming bonds with anyone outside the towers was forbidden, and even within tower walls, we were meant to keep matters professional.

Meeting Emmerick's eyes, I spoke first. "It seems you have details of the task at hand."

He nodded stiffly. "My Queen requests that we find a warlock in the north woods." He cleared his throat. "A powerful potential ally," he added.

A warlock...one that lived *within* the realm. My cheeks sucked in as I gave thought to that anomaly. "Why not write him to come to Luz?"

"He is *bound* to the woods," he answered. "He is believed to be dead, but my Queen believes that he is alive, bound and hiding still."

"What crimes has he committed?"

"Sybilla would not share." There it was again, that slight grit of his teeth between words. "We need your help to unbind him and ensure that he arrives safely in Luz, where the Queen requests his presence with yours."

"Will he travel with us as a prisoner?"

That struck a nerve. Emmerick's pronounced jaw jerked while he shook his head. "No." He strained through the words as though not quite believing them. "As a guest."

No judgment passed my features. *Very interesting and seemingly unwise.* "Why does Queen Sybilla think he will come willingly or quietly? That seems like a dangerous gamble."

Emmerick's posture softened in response to my shared concern. His hesitation was blameless, and yet, *what other hope was there?* "We will promise him his freedom in exchange for helping us—the Queen says, with conviction, that he can be trusted and will accept."

"You do not think so." It wasn't a question.

"I think he was bound to those woods for crimes that none of us remember...so no, I do not trust him. But I trust my Queen and will do as she wishes."

Sir Emmerick's commitment was endearing. It seemed he would do anything to keep his Queen and court safe. Anything, including escorting a High Enchantress into the northern woodlands to look for a dangerous warlock. Even if he didn't want to.

"I did at least convince her to allow me to bring magic binding cuffs—at first, she didn't want even that," he finished.

"You have them now?" Concern was hidden from my voice.

"No—I left them on my horse. I am no threat to you," he said. His hand left the hilt of his sword, and he placed both palms up as though surrendering before attack.

"Sir Emmerick, you are safe in my home," I reassured him. "I am committed to helping her, our Queen." My words were flat but heartfelt.

"You are sure?" He eyed me. "You don't sound sure."

"That is just how I sound."

A wide smile spread across the Commander's face—any attempt to match it would be feeble. Instead, I allowed the corners of my mouth to rise ever so slightly.

"But it sounds like I have a curse to break," I added. "I need a night to research binding curses. We must prepare for whatever magic ties the warlock to those woods. So if you agree not to put those cuffs on me in my sleep, then I agree not to turn you into a newt. Deal?"

His cheeks grew rosy for a moment before his smile faded.

"That was a joke, Sir Emmerick." Clearly, it hadn't landed. Interacting with people was *exhausting*.

Emmerick nodded, but only a fraction of his smile returned—I missed the rest of it. He seemed kinder than the men who had ambled into the tower's clearing before him. I shuddered at the thought of those other men's hungry gazes.

"Guest quarters are upstairs. You can roam the tower, but don't open any books."

He looked confused, as I turned and headed for the library.

"My lady?" He stopped me.

I corrected, "Asterie."

"Asterie, do you think it will work—Queen Sybilla's plan?"

"I have seen no paths where Luz remains standing." I'd conjured no paths in weeks.

But that was for me alone to know. If we left the next morning, I could narrowly avoid the next Sisterhood meeting and having to tell them. Despite every rule I was breaking, it felt right.

Emmerick's face fell.

Wanting to comfort him, I added, "But meeting you isn't a path I've foreseen either. So maybe, Sir Emmerick, we have some hope."

I left the room, unnerved by my inclination to give him false hope in order to appease his worries—such a stupid mortal thing to do.

Binding curses were fickle magic. I thought back to the first time Firose had told me about them.

It was my eighteenth birthday. I was finally of age to join the Sisterhood's ranks officially. Firose invited me to tea in her study after our weekly meeting, my first ever. No one was allowed in Firose's study—it was always off-limits. Which was why I was so surprised she'd invited me there.

When I entered, Firose pulled me into a warm embrace—warmth she rarely extended—and her eyes beamed with pride as she drew me in. She stroked the back of my head like I was prized. My heart swelled under her affection.

"Your strength knows no bounds, young Asterie. Welcome to the Sisterhood—you will be our strongest."

She peeled herself away from me, rounded her desk and motioned for me to sit across from her.

Her study was large, and gilded windows spanned up to the ceiling. Sunshine leaked across every pore of the lavish marble, making me want to draw my feet away from its rays.

Every detail was manicured. Plush pillows topped tufted yellow sofas, and a tea set of the finest gold sat on her desk. It could be a throne room—not that I'd ever seen a throne aside from in books.

"This is usually when we would have your portraits drawn and sent to the courts...a time when you would be presented to the Court of Luz. But my dear, we've decided something..."

Reeling in excitement to finally see the courts and leave those towers, I sat at the edge of my seat.

"The people, they should know you for what you are—their Central Enchantress, a legend amongst us, the receiver of a grand miracle from the stars. Sister of the Stars..." She spoke wistfully.

My hands were tightly clasped in my lap. I didn't like where this was going. I was no more a legend than any of the other Sisters.

"But to be an idol of the realm, you must be Henosis' best-kept asset. You must not be revealed to its people, or their wonder will dissipate."

Asset. My mind swam through other assets one could own—a pair of shoes, an estate, a sword. Such a harsh choice of words from such sweet-spinning lips.

"I don't understand." I spoke softly.

Firose's feline smile spread. "The courts won't know your face. You will not be making an appearance in the Corridors. You must stay in your tower until a time comes worthy of revealing your gifts."

My stomach dropped. My dreams were washed away with her words.

I tried to sway her toward a different decision. "Surely, it wouldn't hurt if I wore a veil. So that the people cannot see—"

"It has already been decided," she said, cutting me off. "You will not leave unless a request comes from the Central King. We must conceal

what you are. Asterie, they would never *accept the dark magic that burns under your skin, my dear. You belong nowhere but here, up in the towers. If they should realize that your magic is unpure...well, I can't protect you then."*

"We have no proof that the star left me with dark magic." I tried to argue.

"Ah—but we have no proof it didn't. You have dark tendencies, my dear. The Brennac texts call to you, don't they? You live in shades of gray and black. Death has laid its mark on you. No one rises from the dead without dark magic playing a hand. It is safest this way...I do hope you will understand and be dutiful to the realm—to the Order."

Guilt gripped me. The acquisition of my immortality and powers might be something to be feared by the courts. *I'd never thought of it that way.*

"You will be the most respected in our realm; no one will dare cross the High Enchantress of the Central Corridor. You are our most protected weapon. For you can only fight darkness with darkness."

She made sense. She was waiting for my answer with an expectant painted smile.

"By the Order, I agree to these terms—agree to be bound here," I promised, awaiting Firose's praise.

It didn't come.

"We will not need to bind you, will we?" Firose's smile faded.

"What do you mean?" My words sounded meeker than I had intended.

"Binding curses allow you to attach an object and an entity. For example—a Jinn bound to a bottle. It is painful and hard to reverse," Firose explained. "Do you want to be bound there, like a Jinn? Or can we rely on trust between us?"

"No, I don't want to be bound—like that—I will stay. It's my duty," I promised. *Curiosity got the better of me.* "But why would someone be bound like that, to something or somewhere?"

"Well"—Firose tapped her painted fingernails on the desk—"sometimes an entity..."

Firose was struggling, which felt odd.

"Sometimes an entity doesn't belong in this world. So the most humane thing is to ensure they are kept somewhere they can do the least damage."

"Like those bound to the Wastelands," I mused.

She nodded. "Yes, very good."

I reveled in her praise.

Pleasing her gave me a giddy sense of accomplishment.

Surfacing from my memory, I flipped to the next page in a Brennac text about the ancient curse that binds Jinns to bottles and lamps.

There was a tap on the doorframe.

Emmerick began to greet me, "Lady—"

"*Just* Asterie."

He restarted. "*Asterie*—I prepared some dinner. The tower seemed...upset that someone else was cooking."

"It cooks every night." My nose was still down, looking at the page.

"Do you want to join me?"

I looked up from the text and blurted, "What binds the warlock is the same magic that binds a Jinn to a bottle."

"That was quick. How do you know?"

"This text. It says the curse is the only known one to bind a person or being to an object or place *'with any hope of permanence.'* So, by that logic, if our warlock is truly a threat, they would have used the strongest binding possible. Wouldn't you think?" The question was entirely rhetorical, but Emmerick nodded along.

He clapped his hands together with jovial enthusiasm. "Good work, then."

His praise was so genuine, so easy to attain, that it made me pause and realize he'd offered a meal.

"Oh." My cheeks heated. "Dinner sounds nice too, thank you."

He showed me his winning smile. At least the Queen had sent me a man handsome enough to bear looking at for the weeks of travel ahead. The young Commander motioned for me to follow him to the kitchen.

A hen carcass was picked to the bone before us, a pan of roasted potatoes was depleted next to it and only one fresh roll remained. The kitchen and hearth were in disarray—the tower had stopped trying to pick up after Emmerick. Flour still dusted most surfaces, and dishes were piled next to the wash basin.

"Where did you learn to cook so well, Sir Emmerick?"

"If you are going to insist on informality, then it's *just* Emmerick." He thought for a moment. "My ma taught me. She has this saying: 'No one deserves a good woman if they can't cook as a good woman can.'" He waved an arm around. "'Or clean as a good woman can.' Or any variation of that line which suits her."

I smiled at that. "She lives in Luz?"

"Yes, she and my father."

We drank a bottle of wine over the next hour as Emmerick told the most endearing stories of his upbringing. It made my heart long for the type of family he had.

His mother was a baker at the palace—that explained the cooking. His father was a palace groundskeeper. His parents worked two trades that made them commoners yet were still able to provide a comfortable life for Emmerick. They still lived in the palace walls that he was sworn to protect and happily served the Wymark family despite Emmerick urging them to retire.

"Is it normal for someone of your upbringing to rise to the ranks that you have?"

His expression hardened slightly. I'd struck a nerve, again. *Peace Prevail*, it was hard making small conversation.

"I'm sorry—I don't know what is proper to ask."

"No, it's okay." He raked a hand over his chin. "Before Sybilla's father died, he took an interest in me. Queen Sybilla and I used to sneak into the woods behind the castle grounds and hunt squirrels as children.

"He found us one day—saw that I had been teaching her to use a bow. I thought for sure I was going straight to the pillory. But, instead, the King began to come find me to give me lessons in swordsmanship and hand-to-hand combat. He took me under his wing—but made me promise I would keep teaching Sybilla every-thing I learned. She never knew about the lessons. I was her guard full-time by the time I was a teenager."

He looked wistfully at his empty wine glass.

"Looking back, it's easy to see why—the King was sick. He knew he wouldn't be around to protect her forever, and in our unlikely friendship, he saw an opportunity. I wasn't noble-bred or a threat to the throne. She had plenty of cousins she should have been able to trust, but he feared they would betray her. Growing up as royalty is a vicious thing—she had so few people in her life that wished to see her succeed."

I nodded along, completely enthralled by his stories. "She seems to have a good friend in you."

It was easy to imagine why the Queen would trust someone like Emmerick. Suddenly, I was saddened that this couldn't be an everyday occurrence—to have *company*. Conversation—it was lovely. Talking to him was completely different from discussions with my Sisters.

"It's getting late," I mused, not wanting to convey my warring emotions. The tower began picking up our plates to float them into the kitchen for washing. I rose and pushed in my chair.

I wasn't sure what type of dismissal was customary, so I settled for simplicity. "Goodnight, Emmerick."

"Goodnight, Lad—" He caught his words. "Goodnight, Asterie." He headed to bed, and I headed to my library.

CHAPTER 7
ASTERIE

My library was in disarray. The smell of old pages and leather surrounded me, and the stained glass windows allowed only fractured light of sepia and the deepest burgundy into that quiet sanctuary.

Books had been pulled haphazardly from their shelves and discarded in piles around the room where I'd left them. The tower knew me well—there was no point returning anything to the shelves until the place was thoroughly ransacked.

My finger skimmed over the page of a thick, dusty, leatherbound text. It settled below an ancient potion called the Skei remedy. I double-checked the ingredients to ensure that I'd not missed adding anything essential.

"Lavender, pig's blood and grated birch bark," I read quietly. "To unbind the power of an entity from a place, object or person. One vial—ingested."

It seemed simple enough. The warlock would need to ingest the nasty concoction, and then, with all hope, I'd be strong enough to break the bond with the Brennac spell I'd found earlier. The text had been clear that the spell was a difficult one, and faulty.

Pocketing the vial, I left my library and descended the tower steps.

Emmerick had headed down to the grounds below the tower at dawn to ready the horses and secure our packs. He'd made pleasant company at dinner—respectable, well-mannered.

In recent years, most of the men I'd seen were in charge of deliveries or were lost travelers. Some sought me out to meet the *fabled* enchantress, to have her. To have *me*.

As a younger woman, it was thrilling to watch them climb with lust-filled eyes. The version of men that I'd learned had been nothing like the young Commander.

Every step down the spiral staircase felt like liberation. I was leaving. I trailed my hands over the staircase's cold gray, windowless walls. I'd be back...*why did that not bring me any comfort?*

The morning sun peeked over the horizon as the iron door swung open and laid the world before me. My hand gripped the door frame. Seeing the towering trees and the size of the horses up close made me feel small and vulnerable.

You are Asterie, the High Enchantress of the Central Corridor. Sister of the Stars. Legendary miracle. One of the most powerful in the realm...

No amount of repeating reassurances removed the pit from my stomach as my boots met the lawn. The earth gave beneath my feet. It was an odd sensation—soft, welcoming. When I reached Emmerick, the towering structure above us commanded attention. I'd never seen it from this angle—it was daunting, hostile and sharp from below.

"Good morning," Emmerick said as he offered his hands to hoist me up into the saddle.

My blood flashed cold, and I braced. "I've never ridden," I admitted.

"Not once?" He didn't hide his surprise.

The anxiety that must have crept onto my face softened his expression.

"Okay," he said. "I'll lead you. You won't have to steer—you can just hold on. Does that sound alright?"

"I would like that, thank you." Giving him a shaky nod, I took a deep breath.

He leaned over and motioned for me to step into his hands for a boost. He counted to three before easily propelling me up. The reins were braided, and my fingers were clumsy with them as I found the seat. Emmerick kept his promise and attached another rope to the horse's bridle before mounting his own.

New emotions clashed against each other—helplessness, a lack of control and unease paired with excitement and levity. A giddy sensation overtook me. I was on a horse, on the *ground*. I combed the mane that hung in wind-whipped knots across the red gelding's neck.

"You'll be good to me, won't you?" The hushed words made the horse's ears turn.

Emmerick began to lead us away from the tower. The movement of the horse's stride was smooth, and yet I felt unbalanced. I allowed myself one final look up at my tower—*it didn't look like home.* I shivered at the intrusive thought.

The tower was soon erased from view when we entered the forest treeline. Onward toward a forgotten warlock, onward toward hope for Luz.

Emmerick had planned a route using the maps Queen Sybilla had provided him before arriving at my tower, and he shared the plan as we rode.

"If we travel straight north and then west just before reaching the Plateau, we won't have to climb the Hussas," he explained.

We would camp at night and avoid any towns along the way. I'd noticed all of the Commander's weapons bore the Luz emblem. I'd also caught him *talking* to them this morning—calling them by names as he packed them. We were abundantly armed—my short dagger was tucked into my boot, and a broad sword was strapped across my back.

I was decent with a sword. Cassidee had made sure of that by beginning my training as soon as I was old enough to hold the weight of a blade. She was ruthless in the arena—she fought dirty and hadn't been afraid to knock me down *many* times until the bad habits in my form were corrected. I had my magic too, of course. However, breaking the Order of Henosis would not fit the Queen's "don't draw attention" instructions.

We rode wordlessly for miles before Emmerick spoke over his shoulder. "How long has it been since you've been down here?"

"I've never been down here."

His head swung around, and he twisted in the saddle to look back at me. "Never?"

"No," I answered with a shrug. "I can effectively serve the realm from my tower."

"So, you've never been down here, never been to the courts…" His voice trailed off in wonder, like I was some mesmerizing specimen in a jar.

"Correct."

One thick eyebrow rose. "Am I the first man you've ever seen?"

At that, I burst into laughter, surprising myself, and the red horse's ears perked up. I covered my mouth to stifle it.

"No. The towers receive visitors." *Some unwelcome.*

He smiled over his shoulder. "Well, I'm glad. I wouldn't want this mug to be the first man's face you saw," he joked.

I shook my head. "You have a very nice face. I am sure your wife is happy with its symmetry. I read once that women like that in a face." I could have grimaced at myself. In all my years studying spells, charms, curses and potions, why hadn't I read up on *casual* conversational skills?

It was his turn to laugh. "You say whatever you mean, don't you?" When he composed himself, he answered, "No wife."

"Well then, I am sure you have plenty of women back in Luz awaiting the opportunity."

He shook his head, answering simply, "Only one that matters."

I smiled despite myself. Emmerick was so amicable and effortless—he wanted nothing from me beyond our shared mission. My shoulders relaxed. I hadn't realized the tension I'd held there.

"You talk to your weapons—why?" I asked.

He shrugged, facing forward but speaking loudly enough to be heard over the whispering winds. "Why not?"

"Are you sound of mind? Talking to inanimate objects seems odd."

"Pot to the kettle." He turned in the saddle again. "I name them after the people I care for. When I'm away for extended periods, it helps me feel like they're close to me."

He reached into his boot and withdrew a dagger that was embellished with rubies. "This one is Angeline. My mother's name. I carry it with me everywhere."

The thought of Emmerick, the picture of force and power, carrying a dagger named after his mother was charming.

"And your broadsword?"

"Enough questions." His tone was light but clearly deflecting. "We need to pick up the pace to make better time."

Emmerick led us until the sun descended. We'd rode into thickets of trees denser than the woods by my tower.

Sunset was always my favorite time of day. I'd hoped we might be in a clearing so that I could see it from this angle. The forest floor at dusk offered me its own beauty, immediately dispelling that disappointment. Golden specks of light peeked through gaps in the tree canopy to cast a glow over the ferns and brush below. That mix of green and gold sang to me. Every whisper of wind, every drop of dew falling, became a mantra that I'd hold onto forever. Emmerick looked entirely unmoved—*was nature always so beautiful down here? Why didn't he notice it?*

Emmerick dismounted and helped me down. "How are you feeling?"

"That doesn't matter—my duty is to serve Luz." My voice was barely a whisper as I soaked in the golden glow of the forest.

He contemplated me. "You're not what I expected."

"What did you expect?"

Emmerick tied the horses to a highline he'd created between two trees, allowing them enough rope to graze and lie down.

"Can I be honest?" He rubbed the back of his neck.

"I always appreciate honesty."

"I expected horns and sharp teeth—far more hair," he said nervously. "There are rumors in Luz that you are...ghastly."

I placed a hand over my mouth to suppress a smile, but it must have shown in my eyes because he returned it.

"You are odd...but pleasant. And you don't have hooves—someone told me you would have *hooves*." He was rambling now, and his light brown cheeks turned a shade of mauve.

At that, I couldn't help it. I laughed at the young Commander trying so hard not to offend me and yet be honest. His innocence was refreshing. No man had ever entered my tower and walked away remembering what I'd looked like the following day. So, in a way, he was not the first man I'd ever seen, but he was the first to truly see me.

My fingers clumsily helped him loosen the packs before we set up camp. We had a meager canvas tent strapped between trees within half an hour. He, thankfully, told me when and how to help him. He unrolled two thick rugs and placed them on the ground before offering me a wool blanket from his pack.

"It's not much, but without pack mules—"

I waved away his concern. "It's just enough."

It *wasn't* enough to keep me comfortable. I barely slept due to the hard ground and the howl of wolves in the distance, which fueled my already rampant nightmares. But if I looked directly up, traces of the stars between tree branches winked down at us.

Under the stars, at ground level, of my own will, all of that was enough.

We'd been riding for seven days before I stopped counting. My dark robe and breeches were dirtied beyond hope of laundering. My hair had caught twigs as we passed under trees and tangled into knots that there was no time to comb.

Despite every lack of luxury, I didn't wish away the experience. Every creek we passed, every woodland creature we startled, my mind logged them all, and I wished to forget nothing about this journey.

We set up camp each night where we could find refuge from the elements, but I rarely slept. When I did, the nightmares persisted. I'd woken Emmerick up a few times with my screams, which was a feat since he slept like a bear. Being a heavy sleeper seemed a terrible quality for an army Commander.

While my mind longed for the experiences of nature, my body revolted. Emmerick was a good enough cook to make even a foraged and hunted meal edible. Still, my stomach was unused to wild game, and I constantly felt queasy.

I was not conditioned to travel, and every muscle ached, but it didn't matter—we needed to find the warlock. To my relief, since we had started this journey, the voice hadn't spoken to me again. I could only view that as a good omen despite the night terrors persisting.

It was the right path.

Yet the moonstone in my pocket remained a decorative, useless rock. Not seeing a solution could mean I wasn't a *part* of the solution.

A lump grew in the back of my throat. It could also mean that my death would come before this war ended, as the prophecy had predicted. My hope was it wouldn't be in vain.

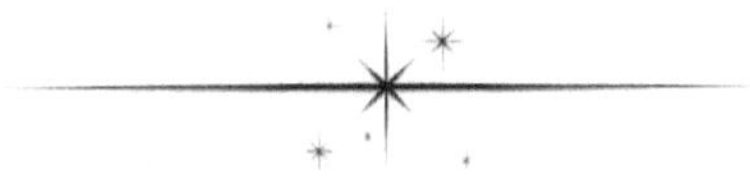

We passed into the North Corridor, avoiding any run-ins with beasts of the night or criminals. We'd been fortunate to that point. Unfortunately, the further into the northern woodlands we traveled, the more fog hung in the air, making it harder to see.

We were finally traveling westward when the canopy of trees grew even thicker and the forest floor darker. It was quieter here, eerily so. The trees were primarily redwoods and pines, and the brush was replaced with tangled roots of red and brown that threatened to trip our horses with each step.

"The right path," I whispered to my steady red gelding as we neared a clearing of tall grasses, and the horse's ears perked at the opportunity to graze. We'd become fast friends because I often had snuck scratches between his ears while Emmerick led us. Mounting and dismounting on my own had become easier, and I even steered myself for a few days.

We had to be close to the warlock. The Queen had marked where the cabin should be on the map, and we were within a few miles of the mark.

The sun had just set. Only shadows remained against the entwined root forest bed, a recipe for disaster on horseback after dark. Before I could tell Emmerick we should stop, there was rustling in the trees. Emmerick's hand quickly found his sword's hilt over his shoulder.

"Shh..." I cautioned with a raised hand.

Emmerick dismounted, and I followed.

Whispers carried in the wind—hushed, blurred sounds mixed with laughter and cries of despair that grew louder. It sounded like thousands of voices approached. The air grew so chilled our breath could be seen despite it being late spring. The dew on leaves around us froze.

Then the smell hit me. It was a mixture of lamp oil and raw meat—putrid and musky. All the hair on the back of my neck stood. I had smelled it before. It was the same scent the air carried during my prophecy of Luz falling. It *had* to be the smell of dark magic.

Dark magic could only be created of two things—death or shadows. *What could possibly be in these woods that commanded either?* Searching the catalog of creatures in my mind, only one made sense.

"They are Specters," I whispered to Emmerick. "They cannot hurt you. Hold your ground and face the same direction *no matter what.*"

"And you know this how?" he whispered back uneasily.

"Books."

He let out an unconvinced "hmph."

We continued walking with our horses in hand. Emmerick's body was stiff, and he'd drawn his sword.

"If it is Specters, they simply aim to confuse travelers."

"Why would they do that?"

"We're more likely to die in these woods if we lose our way. That's when we join them. Death likes company," I answered, yelling over the sound of the approaching voices.

Then, the cacophony of shrieks burst from the treetops, descending from all directions. There were at least twelve of them. The red gelding reared and pulled back, threatening to set me off course. I let go of the reins and let him run. Emmerick's horse broke free as well. *There went our packs.*

The Specters' appearances were ghastly—tattered skin and bone. They were only human in shape, and their edges blurred and bent like shadows. Their semi-translucent bodies darkened our view. They would add to my nightmares for weeks to come. They darted toward us and away, around us and over, taunting, screaming.

Ten...nine...eight...

The moment the Specters descended upon us, Emmerick attempted to strike, but his blade found nothing. He swirled and swung wildly.

"Emmerick, stand your ground. Don't swing!" I yelled.

I forced my feet to remain in the direction we traveled, not moving them an inch. *Focus.*

The Specters passed through us as though we were nothing to them but toys to be played with. Cackling, screaming. Each time one passed through me, I was chilled to the bone, and the smell was enough to make me want to vomit.

Emmerick fell to the ground, growling, as his sword continued not to find purchase with flesh or bone.

Seven...six...five...

The screaming and voices suddenly stopped—the Specters were gone. I heard Emmerick get to his feet with a grunt and a slew of profanities that I wouldn't have thought he was capable of saying with all his courtly manners.

"I told you not to try."

Emmerick seared me with a scowl as he stepped beside me. He was winded and catching his breath. "I don't understand how you *didn't* react to those things." He wasn't hurt, at least not physically, but his pride seemed bruised. "And yet the sight of a horse made you pale."

I shrugged. "Belittling my fears won't change that you just tired yourself fighting air."

He grunted in response before waving toward the clearing to our right. My feet were no longer pointing to it. The Specters had altered the appearance of the woods.

"We were headed this way," he said, heading to the clearing.

I shook my head. "No, we go into the woods. My feet never moved, and they are facing the woods now. They tried to throw us off course."

He pulled out a compass and let out a drawn-out sigh as he realized I was right.

The horses were nowhere to be found. We were on foot, heading deeper into the northern woodlands, without our belongings.

This is the right path. I kept repeating the mantra.

I patted my robe pocket in order to ensure the vial of Skei remedy was safe within. That was all we needed.

We were too on edge from our encounter with the Specters to sleep. Getting comfortable without a pack would be challenging, so we decided to carry on into the night. The northern woodlands at night somehow grew even foggier. Luckily, our eyes had adjusted to the moonlight.

We walked for a few miles before hearing a low growl from the treeline to our right. I placed the source of the sound immediately.

What are Firose's Lynx doing out here? Have they come to bring me back to my tower?

"What now?" Emmerick growled, clearly not wanting another encounter like the last. He kept close beside me and unsheathed his sword.

"Lynx," I answered him, stepping forward.

Emmerick halted, scanning his surroundings. The growl was low, and it was impossible to tell which direction it came from. *The Lynx won't attack us as long as they were under Firose's orders to be here.*

"Don't worry—they belong to my Sister. They likely just can't recognize me yet through the fog."

The rustling continued, as did the growling—there was more than one.

All would be well. I stood tall, awaiting their approach.

Emmerick yelled out from behind me.

"Your left!"

CHAPTER 8
FENRIS

Dusk cast shadows on the woodland surrounding my cabin. I stepped out onto the rickety front porch to await Van.

"Come home," I commanded through the bond. *What was taking him so long?*

The sound of a horse's whinny alerted me that someone was approaching. I stood, and fire spewed from my upraised palms, ready to meet the threat. Through the thick of the woods, hoofbeats pounded. As two horses burst from the brush, my body relaxed. At least they were without riders. No one had found me here, *yet*. Though, apparently, someone had been close.

Van crashed through the trees behind the equines, cutting right and left to keep the prey animals in front of him. I ran to follow them around the cabin. The horses pressed themselves against the fence line that had been built to keep deer out of my garden.

"Van, stop that!" I scolded. "Are you *herding* them?"

As usual, no response came, and Van's eyes hungrily fixed on the horses. He paused as though displaying them to me, waiting for my permission to eat the majestic creatures.

"No. You remember horses—they are useful. Not food."

The horses were slicked with sweat, pasterns scratched from galloping through the thickets but they seemed otherwise unharmed. I fisted my hands to snuff out the flames from my palms before jogging down to where the horses trembled by the fence.

"Whoa, whoa, now." I captured the reins of one horse, a large black draft with feathered fur on its legs. The smaller red horse stayed alert but nearby.

I unfastened one of the saddles and packs and allowed Van to sniff it.

"Go on, go track where their riders ended up. Do *not* eat them either, and stay out of sight."

I stood on the porch and closed my eyes. Van let me into his vision easily.

Our visitors were not far. Vangard tracked them a mile or so south. In the dark, I could see a large male form who looked to be in armor and a smaller female form in dark robes.

"Stay low," I told Van through the bond.

Another pride of Lynx also slinked nearby.

Has she come back to kill me? Two Lynx sightings in twenty-four hours was unsettling.

Under the cover of night, it was hard to see the trespassers clearly, but my sense of curiosity won out over my sense of logic. After unsaddling and tying the horses, and dragging the packs inside to rummage through later, I ran to follow Van's trail. I knew exactly where they were—just a couple miles north of that clearing where I'd heard a strange voice call to me two centuries ago. *Coincidence,* I told myself.

By the time I ducked down beside Van, I was breathing heavily. I wasn't sure what had my heart racing more—the threat of visitors or the running.

At first, I thought the intruders were paired with the Lynx—allies. However, it became evident quickly they weren't.

We looked on as a Lynx launched from the shadows of the trees toward the female figure. *Move.* I didn't know what compelled me to root for the mystery woman. Her dark hair hung in a braid, and it was clear now I recognized neither her nor the behemoth of a man next to her. The woman ducked right, withdrawing her sword just in time to slash the neck of the animal before it could take her down. It fell into a silent heap beside her.

Five remaining Lynx stalked them—that was a lot for two mortals to attempt to take down, no matter how strong. *If* they were mortal. To get out of this alive would take a strike of luck—I wasn't willing to reveal myself to give them that strike.

One of the Lynx pounced, this time catching the woman by the shoulders and taking her down swiftly. The large male's blade met the bone of another behind her, downing the creature as he scrambled to get to her aid.

The woman's back was thrown against tree roots, and her sword was knocked from her hands. I saw a flash of blue light beginning to form in her palms—*interesting. Not mortal then.*

I looked on as she kneed upward in an attempt to wiggle her arms free and use her Source magic. I had every impulse to jump out to help her. Fighting that urge was near painful.

Her elbows scraped against the ground below her as the creature's rat-like mouth snapped and snarled, opening wide to expose a double row of teeth. *Fuck.* I'd hesitated too long.

The Lynx lunged at the woman's head.

No—I stepped forward, still in the shadows of the treeline. My arm reached out toward her, and fire formed at my fingertips. My heart seized and my eyes slammed shut. I expected to hear crunching bones and screams.

I heard a loud yowl. Allowing myself to look, I witnessed the man pull his blade from the Lynx's skull as the creature slumped to the woman's side. He was swift for a mortal of his size—*he might not be mortal after all.* The man grabbed the woman's elbow and pulled her to her feet.

"Thank you." The woman's rasp was just barely in earshot.

As the strange woman rose, three Lynx still circled them, deterred only by the armored man's pointed sword. The two strangers were back to back now and had retrieved the woman's sword.

The Lynx seemed to be calculating their approach more carefully now that they knew they weren't dealing with vulnerable prey. They had power in numbers and hunted as a pride.

I could help them.

Don't be an idiot—no matter how much my heart had just tugged at the thought of that Lynx killing the strange woman. No, it wasn't worth the risk. Yet I had started to step forward. The next time a Lynx charged her, I wouldn't hesitate to intervene.

Something pulled me toward her—it felt inevitable, it felt alluring.

"You should not be in these woods," the dark-haired woman shouted. "Return to Helos. Return to your master."

Your master. My blood ran cold.

CHAPTER 9
ASTERIE

We were surrounded.

"Return to your master!" I commanded again. I could imagine Firose's rage when she learned her Lynx had gone rogue and harmed a member of the Sisterhood.

They would stand down—they were loyal to her.

The largest Lynx eyed me with curious intent and tilted its head. Drool pooled down its snarled lips. For a moment, the Lynx looked like it might turn away and lead the others.

Instead, it rocked back on its feline haunches, ready to leap at me. Emmerick grabbed my arm and spun me toward him. He tucked us together, shielding my head as we hit the ground and rolled.

While I appreciated the chivalry, it delayed my ability to bring the blue flames to my palms, ruining our only chance of fighting them from a distance.

The Lynx landed where we had just stood with an angry hiss. We only had moments before it launched again. I was sure we were about to be eaten alive when we heard a crash through the trees. The biggest Lynx yowled as it was picked up by something much larger. The cracking of teeth against bone filled the air, a horrid chomping sound.

"What *now*?" Emmerick ground out.

We rose to face whatever beast was fierce enough to make the remaining two Lynx yelp and scurry away into the dark woods.

Brennac superstition claimed that bad things happened in threes. We were about to meet our third opponent within twenty-four hours. Emmerick's non-sword hand steadied me by my scraped elbow as a creature with black fur and the face of a wolf towered over us.

It was no wolf. For one, it was too large. For another, its head was spiked with two sharp horns, and its great paws struck the ground with talons like a falcon scraping at root bark.

We slowly backed away with our swords drawn.

It was a creature that didn't exist in any book I'd come across. I had an awful impulse to reach out and touch its hauntingly beautiful black coat. The beast shook the Lynx in its powerful jaw—the last signs of life faded from the Lynx's eyes, and its body went limp.

"Drop that. It's too foul to eat," a voice drawled casually from behind the beast.

The creature released the Lynx from its mouth reluctantly, letting the lifeless body drop with a wet thud.

As blood ran down the beast's chin, it prowled toward us.

"Who are you?" That same smooth voice spoke to us.

A figure emerged at the beast's side—a man of average height. His features were hidden under a dark green cloak hood.

"I am Sir Emmerick, Constable of Luz. We mean you no harm. We are just passing through."

The young Commander had enough bravery for the both of us—I was frightened mute. My hand trembled, betraying my otherwise stoic expression. While the thought of being eaten alive by the Lynx had been unpleasant, the horror of what was before me was worse.

"There is nothing beyond here but the Wastelands. What about the girl? Who is she?"

Girl. I was too frightened to be offended by that slight.

The creature grew closer.

Emmerick tensed beside me, still clutching my elbow. This wasn't a beast we had any hope of defeating on our own, and it seemed to be at the command of this man. While he did just save us, he also wasn't calling his beast back.

A lump grew in my throat—*Sources, tell me this isn't the warlock we're trying to find.* The Queen had been foolish to think me and Emmerick capable of this, if so.

I finally found words. "I am Asterie, High Enchantress of the Central Corridor."

The man laughed at that, an odd response. His deep-bellied laughter would have sounded jovial and pleasant in other circumstances.

"Oh, a *High Enchantress.* Now *that* is ironic."

The irony was lost on me.

The creature grew so close that its nose touched my ear and smelled my hair. The iron scent of Lynx blood hung heavy on its breath.

"We mean you no harm. We are looking for a warlock that is bound to these woods. The Queen of Luz has sent us." Emmerick spoke for us again.

The beast pressed its nose into my shoulder, further bloodying my dark robes. Meeting its gaze, I stared into one of its beady dark eyes and pleaded in a hushed whisper, "Peace Prevail. Please, please, don't hurt us."

I'd never begged for my life before—it was against the Order to put my life above the needs of the Corridors. The creature's eyes seemed to soften. Then, it laid down at my feet and put the tip of its huge, bloodied nose over my boot. The only thing holding me upright on my shaking knees was Emmerick's grip on my arm.

"Intriguing," the mystery man mumbled.

He stepped closer and pulled his dark green hood down. It wasn't easy to make out his features in the fogged darkness, but the soft glow of the moon revealed a handsome face with an amused smirk. Given the beast before me, I'd expected someone equally as grotesque.

"I believe it's me you're looking for then. At least, I don't know of any other poor saps living in these woods," he said with nonchalance, as though he hadn't just witnessed his beast tear apart a Lynx in a single shake of its head.

Emmerick and I stepped away from the warlock—keeping our distance as he continued to approach. Then, dropping my sword, I allowed blue flames to ignite in both of my palms and prepared to throw the flames if he grew too close. A better defense than any blade. The use of magic was forbidden in the realm, but something told me the warlock wouldn't fight by our rules. There was a reason he was exiled here, after all.

The warlock didn't look phased by my use of magic. Instead, he continued to step toward us and spoke to the beast. "That's enough—come." He tapped his arm, and there was a sudden gust of wind and dust. The beast had vanished.

"Don't come any closer," I warned.

The warlock eyed the burst of light in my hands, and the pompous smirk remained.

"You're a unique one," he mused. "How are those old crones in the towers doing? Do they miss me?" His tone was playful—a predator playing with his prey. He continued to approach, and we continued to silently retreat.

Only Emmerick's sword and my lit palms stood between us and the still-approaching warlock.

"Listen, we can play this little game all night. But something tells me that if you and I went at it"—he motioned between himself and me with a hint of flirtatious insinuation—"neither of us would walk away alive. I've got my weapons put away—now *extinguish* yours."

The warlock's palms rose in mock surrender. The beast was nowhere to be seen, but I was still hesitant. *Weapons.* Plural. He could still have something up his sleeve. As we continued to step back, the warlock stepped right over my sword as though it was no use to him.

"I take it the two horses I found were yours? They're safe at my cabin." The warlock pressed on. "So, why don't you share what you need from me?"

Eyeing him wearily, I stopped stepping backward. Undoubtedly, he could have allowed that *thing* to kill us if he'd wanted to. He still could.

"Emmerick, lower your sword."

I could feel him tense beside me. "Are you serious?"

Closing my fists, I snuffed out the blue flames in my palms. I heard Emmerick sheath his blade with a slew of profanities under his breath, but my eyes never left the warlock.

The warlock lowered his hands to his sides. "Oh, I do love a woman in charge. So it *is* you who leads this little expedition? You were shaking in your boots so violently that I thought maybe it was the boy."

"Neither of us leads the other." My voice was measured. "We will share why we have come—but first, swear in blood that if you refuse to help us, then we walk away from these woods unharmed."

His smile waned. He seemed to lose interest in toying with us. The warlock reached into his robes, and withdrew a small hunting knife, and nicked the inside of his palm. Blood dripped down his hand and hit the forest floor.

Firose had once told me— *"Blood oaths are flimsy magic—binding, and unbreakable, yet how they are worded matters greatly."*

I awaited the warlock's words, ready to listen carefully to their meaning.

"I swear, in blood, that I—*we*—will allow you both to walk away from these woods unharmed—whether I choose to help you or not."

My shoulders relaxed slightly. I could find no hole in his oath.

The warlock had drawn close enough for me to see his features better in the moonlight. He was less than an arm's length away now.

He had unkempt facial hair and a head of tousled dark auburn waves that were just as disorderly. A scar ran from the warlock's left cheekbone down his neck, creating a gray streak in his otherwise copper-threaded beard before disappearing under his shirt collar. He had an athletic build yet he was not imposing. My eyes roved down him before I caught myself and forced myself to meet his gaze.

I could see a thread of gold in his eyes. Despite wanting to look away, something compelled me not to.

"Plus, I would never harm a face like this." He tilted my chin up with his bleeding hand. It was as though he was purposely marking me. Emmerick stiffened beside me.

The warlock stepped closer. He smelled of leather, cedar and smoke. Surprisingly pleasant.

"No, a face like this"—he released my chin, looking down at me with an infuriatingly confident smirk—"should be *worshiped*. So now, what is it you two seek from me?"

Ignoring every impulse to launch a venomous response, I turned to Emmerick, nodding to prompt him to speak for the Queen's Court.

"We come to ask for your aid in a war to come. Should you accept, you will be escorted to Luz as Queen Wymark's guest. We offer your freedom from these woods and refuge in the Central Corridor."

The warlock's flippant demeanor hardened. I swallowed hard. Seeing the lines of his face grow harsh, I retracted any thought of him not being imposing.

"I will not fight in any war. Our gifts will not be used on any battlefield. You've wasted your time."

Great. A pacifist with a bloodthirsty pet. I noted to myself that he said *gifts*, plural, again. I wondered what Source magic he possessed.

I stepped forward, mere inches stood between us, this time meeting his eyes of my own volition.

"The intent is not to fight or conquer on any battlefield. The intent is to reinforce the Central Corridor's defenses. I have seen a prophecy. The city of Luz will fall. *You* are among our last hopes to stop it."

He held my gaze intently, expression softening. *Hazel.* His eyes were hazel and ruinous behind thick dark eyelashes. Glints of gold and green almost distracted me from continuing. I had an odd impulse to reach up and touch his cheek. I physically shook my hand at my side to dismiss it.

"Innocent women and children...no one will be spared. This isn't an attack on soldiers. It will be an attack on the *people* of Luz—civilians. We want a fighting chance to save as many as we can."

His lingering gaze unsettled me as it trailed down my face and settled on my lips. "And who is the aggressor in this supposed attack?"

A sigh escaped me. I hadn't foreseen *that* critical detail—and the moonstone not responding now made it impossible. Mattock thought it would be the Wastelands rising, but it felt foolhardy to reveal too much to the warlock.

"We don't know. The prophecy didn't reveal it. But it led me to the Queen, who led me to you. That has to mean something."

I didn't break eye contact—we needed him. The people of Luz needed him.

Meeting him felt right.

His demeanor was no longer playful or light-hearted. Instead, his eyes seared me with quiet intensity and something akin to confusion.

"I believe you have good intentions."

"Then you will join us?" Emmerick asked eagerly.

The warlock shook his head, turning to look at the Commander.

"I'm a firm believer in sleeping on big decisions." He motioned for us to follow as he began to walk away from us. "My cabin is just a mile north—unless you'd rather sleep out here and get eaten by something."

Emmerick eyed me, clearly uncomfortable with staying under the warlock's roof for even a minute. However, the other options were limited and we had no packs. I shrugged with raised brows.

I wouldn't let the warlock out of our sight now that we had found him. The idea of sleeping under a roof and between four walls was simply a worthwhile bonus.

"After you." Emmerick sighed, holding an arm toward the retreating warlock.

CHAPTER 10
FENRIS

There was no reason to help the trespassers. If it had just been the boy, then I may not have. But seeing the enchantress in peril had struck a nerve. Something about her—I couldn't help but intervene.

The enchantress and the boy trailed me, keeping close together as we neared my cabin.

"Those things, the giant rats, belong to one of your Sisters?" the boy Commander whispered.

"Yes. They're one of my Sister's...companion animals."

"Not very companionable."

"If you knew her, you would understand."

The boy scoffed. A smirk crept across my face at her slight. When we arrived at the cabin, I held the door for them before snapping to light the fire and lamps. Even in late spring, the woods grew cold at night.

I hung my cloak on a peg by the door and offered to take the woman's bloodied cloak. *Asterie.* She seemed to be taking in my space—the hearth, the sofa, the one-chair wooden table where I ate my meals alone. Some items were crafted with magic, and some were handcrafted to pass the time. It was better than what I had started with, which was *nothing*.

When first bound here, I was thrown into a jarring, rustic existence. Considering most of my life had been lived amongst the court's pampered nobles, the first ten years were fucking miserable. But I deserved misery. For nearly a century, I allowed myself to wither away, wishing they had just killed me as planned.

Learning how to *want* to live again came slowly, but never fully. Time has a way of dulling pain. One hundred forty-six *thousand* days had passed. But my guilt would always be there, a dull ache in my chest.

"Boots off," I requested, not wanting to deal with the mud they would track in. Plus, I liked my pelt rugs.

They both looked uneasy about removing their shoes. Warranted. They reluctantly untied their boots anyway. I reveled in the sight of the enchantress bent over. *For fuck's sake*—it'd been way too long since I'd been with a woman.

I could see more of her now in the light of the cabin, and Asterie was fascinating to look at. Strong-featured and full-lipped. She was classically beautiful—like a painting in a gallery or a sculpture in a museum. If they painted her, then she would wear that same neutral expression that she wore now but in her eyes...there would be fire like the lustrous blue flame that flickered from her palms earlier.

Asterie peeled the bloodied cloak off, revealing more dark garb beneath it—she wasn't in skirts, but dark breeches and a black tunic that hugged her frame. She winced as the fabric of the cloak pulled away from her back.

Asterie turned to warm her hands at the fireplace—the fire seemed to reach toward her long, slender fingers to kiss her fingertips. A rip in the back of her tunic revealed deep claw marks on her shoulder from when the Lynx had downed her. Blackened bloodstains seeped through the thick gray fabric. *Fucking Lynx.*

"You're hurt." My teeth ground—chest tightening into a knot. My reaction to her marred skin shocked me.

She shrugged. If it hurt badly, she wasn't allowing it to show on her face. "It will heal by dawn."

That didn't suit me. "Why suffer? Allow me..."

My hands hovered over her shoulders impulsively. She looked like she might refuse, but she hesitantly pulled her thick braid to the side to give me a clear view. My jaw tightened. *What did I care if this strange woman was hurt?*

The heat of her shoulder warmed my palms as they pressed to the bloodied tunic. Mumbling the healing charm I had learned from an old Brennac healer centuries ago, I focused on the wounds beneath my fingers. The heat grew more intense. She hissed so quietly it was barely audible as the lacerations closed. An unpleasant feeling, but it guaranteed she would remain unscarred, though I doubted the wound was deep enough.

An odd urge to continue touching the enchantress overwhelmed me.

She turned to me, before running her eyes down my torso as though appraising me. *Maybe that was wishful thinking.*

Plus, the last thing I needed was to get wrapped up with an enchantress. *Bad idea.* No matter how lonely this existence was, I refused to make the same mistake twice.

Asterie pointed at the inked image of Vangard on my bicep. "Is that"—she paused—"is that where you keep *it*?"

I nodded. "*It* is a he. And, yes, he rests there. He's not always so ferocious—he just really hates Lynx. But what's to love about them?"

Her neutral expression didn't falter. Drawing a smile out of her seemed like a difficult task that I inexplicably wanted to challenge myself with.

The boy Commander seemed to be creating an inventory of everything that could be used as a weapon in my cabin. He skeptically ran his finger over a set of whittled bone crochet needles. I almost laughed, but the enchantress' voice regained my attention.

"They shouldn't have been there. The Lynx."

"Yet, they were..." I drawled in response.

Asterie had moved to the log mantle over the fireplace, and she brushed her fingers over the dust that coated the jackets of the few history volumes there.

"I have the same ones," she mused. "How did you get them?"

I'd only had one visitor in four hundred years, about three decades ago. She'd left a pile of history volumes, thinking it would help me pass the time...I didn't *care* what happened out there. What kind of world *she'd* built. I'd skimmed the books once and contemplated using them as kindling a few times.

"A friend passed through—she thought I'd like to know what I'd missed."

Her dark eyes grew glazed and contemplative; I took her moment of distraction as an opportunity to admire her. *Fuck, she was beautiful. Strangely so.*

It was likely that any woman would appear so beautiful, *wasn't it?* But those odd blue flames. I'd never seen anyone with Source magic wield flames of blue before. And something about her reserved, enigmatic nature sucked me in.

"Let me get some tea started—in the meantime, do you want to...clean that off?" I motioned to the dried Lynx blood on her face and then pointed to the doorway of my bedchamber.

The boy nodded his approval but she hesitated.

"I'm making him tea, not challenging him to a duel—your boy Knight will live another day. After all, I swore in blood that neither of you is in danger."

Emmerick ground out through his teeth, "I am a Constable, not a Knight."

"What is the difference, anyway?" I knew full well the difference. But the boy's outraged expression entertained me.

Asterie's interest peaked as she noticed the packs I'd lugged inside from their horses. She let out a held breath. *Relieved.* I logged that emotion and how it changed her face.

It was my new favorite expression of hers. My mind wandered to other ways I could relieve her.

I needed to get a fucking *grip*.

"You have a bathtub?"

A lump grew in my throat at the thought of her disrobing entirely *in my cabin*. Given the circumstances of our meeting, I would have thought she'd barely want to step inside my bedchamber.

"Yes. There's running water—you'll have to heat it with magic."

I'd meant for her to wash her face, but I wouldn't deny her a bath. I'm not sure I could have denied her anything.

"Good. Emmerick, guard the door." She swirled a finger at me. "He's odd."

Her stoic bluntness and utter disregard for propriety had me choking on a laugh.

"Right, *he's* the only odd one..." the boy grumbled.

Asterie disappeared behind the door to my bedchamber. I could only imagine every detail of what was happening behind that door. The boy Commander sat at the kitchen table and cleared his throat. A distraction for my own good.

The boy was massive, both in height and weight. He looked every bit like a Constable should. His face still held youth, but a few smile lines told me he was likely to be nearing thirty. After moving to the hearth and brewing the tea, I set a cup in front of him. He grunted his thanks.

The boy sniffed his tea for poison—smarter than he looked. I smirked.

"What is your name, Warlock?"

"Fenris." I accentuated the syllables like he should know them, *Fen-ree*. Evidently, neither of them was polished on their history of the realm. There was something comforting in the knowledge that they had no idea who I was.

The bath began to run, and I forced myself to focus on spinning a spoon in my tea. "You've traveled a long way to find me."

Emmerick took a sip. "I've traveled farther."

I pointed toward the bedchamber door. "Has your friend? She looks...tired."

And absolutely breathtaking even still. But I left that observation out.

"She's never left the towers. Lived a pampered life up there—I bet this journey hasn't been easy on her, though she hasn't complained once, which is a relief. She barely sleeps because of the nightmares—" Emmerick grabbed his throat as though the flow of his words caught him off guard.

I smirked. *Ah-hah. It has kicked in.*

The first time the strange enchantress has left her tower. *Interesting.*

Emmerick glared as he set down his tea. Of course, no harm would come to him—but I didn't swear in blood that I wouldn't mark the tea with a truth charm. They were staying under my roof, after all.

"I'm sorry—I wanted to ensure that I'm safe. Am I safe?"

Emmerick gripped his knees with paled knuckles, his taupe face growing red with fury. "Yes, you are safe. The Queen would like you to arrive *alive*. I, on the other hand, couldn't care less either way."

I smiled. "Do you want to hit me right now?"

"Very much so."

"Do you think I want to hurt you?"

Emmerick paused. "I'm not sure."

I shook my head. "I don't. I charmed my tea too."

"When will it wear off?"

"In a few minutes. I'll make a normal brew for your friend in there. Are you and she...romantically involved?" It was a throwaway question, but it burned in me to know.

Emmerick crossed his arms over his chest and shook his head. "My heart belongs to another."

Though I could have pressed the question, I wasn't petty enough to inquire further about who his heart belonged to. Emmerick nodded toward the bedchamber. "My Queen asked me to escort Lady Asterie to you. Asterie thinks she can unbind you."

Unbind me. The thought made a shiver run down my spine—I deserved no such luxury.

"And how did you two come to find me?"

The boy rocked forward and back, seemingly trying to avoid sharing more. "We didn't find you. You found us."

Clever boy. I smirked. "How did you know I was alive?"

"Queen Wymark believed you to be still alive. Asterie's prophecies led her to contact the Queen, who sent us to find you. So, here we are—running the Queen's errands and narrowly avoiding being eaten alive twice in one night..."

Prophecies were untrustworthy. They'd always given me goosebumps.

So the enchantress did have Reverist bloodlines. I'd guessed it when she mentioned a prophecy earlier. Oracles and other mind magic-wielders were rare even when I'd still been in the courts. To possess Source magic and abilities as an Oracle—now that was strange. I could understand why they felt the need to hide her away.

Even with an Oracle involved, they were grasping at nothing. Their prophecy had not revealed enough. If it had, they would know to stay far away from here.

"Do you trust that was the right choice—seeking me out?"

"I warned that it seemed risky, but Queen Sybilla convinced me that it was worth the risk for even the slightest chance at saving the Corridor."

"You aren't wrong to distrust me," I noted. The Commander's shoulders relaxed in response to my validation. "As a Constable, do you think a war is coming?"

The boy ran a hand down his face. "I've heard rumors from other courts that radical groups exist in all the Corridors. Some of those groups believe we should open the Wastelands."

My brow rose. "'Open the Wastelands.' As in allowing who is beyond their borders out?"

That rip in the ward, and the men stepping free, suddenly made sense. If my suspicions yielded true, the realm was in imminent danger.

When the Commander nodded his response, I grimaced.

"I am afraid that even I couldn't protect you against the forces bound there." I sighed. "Who leads them?"

"No one knows. But as tensions grow, trust in the Order is dwindling."

"What is the Order you speak of?"

"You're aware of the High Enchantresses?" Emmerick expertly answered my question with a question as he pointed to my history volumes. *I probably should have read those more carefully.*

"Vaguely, yes...though I was never in the courts while they ruled."

Emmerick nodded and paused as if trying to calculate something in his head.

"I'm five hundred—give or take," I answered the unasked question. "I've been here for four hundred of those years."

The boy straightened uneasily before nodding.

"Well, the High Enchantresses maintain peace and order. They ensure nothing threatens the realm. They're among the last remaining wielders of Source magic in Henosis, with the exception of King Mattock. The Order was a law established hundreds of years ago that prevents magic from growing strong in the realm again."

"So Source magic—it's almost vanished entirely under these orders?"

The boy Commander gritted his teeth. *What's the boy trying to hide?*

"Yes. Banned for all but the five High Enchantresses and the North King."

My heart pounded as the boy continued talking.

"The teaching of magic is outlawed entirely. Anyone who wields *any* magic ends up in the Wastelands. So the understanding of magic is waning in all Corridors. And immortals are not allowed to conceive." The Commander sighed. The charm would be fading any minute now.

The bitch had really done it. Remembering when magic had flourished through the Kingdoms of Brennax and Phynx sent a pang to my chest. *Gone.* All of it banished to the Wastelands. A land no one knew much about other than its notoriety for being a harsh and unlivable climate and its volcanic shores, sealing those exiled there to a miserable fate.

No one thought it possible to survive there—yet I knew people lived there. I'd seen those Lynx leading some of them away.

"The decree against immortals reproducing in Phynx happened long before these orders." My jaw tightened. "It's one of the many disagreements that drove Brennax and Phynx to war."

"Which side of that war did you fight on?" Emmerick asked.

I curled my lips into a smirk. I knew I couldn't say much more truthfully. "That's an interesting story," I answered.

I needed to change the topic quickly as the charm wore off.

"So, you have a lady back home. But have you ever imagined what's under the tunic while you..." I threw a thumb toward the bedchamber door and made a crass pumping gesture with my hand, unable to help but provoke him.

He met my eyes with a glare and no response. My time was up.

"Just testing you, of course."

Emmerick's attention turned as the door creaked and Asterie stepped out—freshly clothed and no longer looking like a butcher. She wore a black tunic and long black skirts. Disappointing. I liked the view of her curves in those breeches.

"Feeling better?" I asked, and she nodded.

"Yes, thank you." A grateful expression crossed her face, only momentarily. Then, I remembered the boy's words—*her first time out of that tower.*

"Careful. Fenris the Warlock here gave me funny tea that made me only able to speak the truth," Emmerick revealed.

"Fenris." My name on her lips and the tempting rasp to her voice made my senses flare. "Is that so? A truth charm? That's clever."

Asterie crossed the floor to the hearth. Her woolen socks caught some of the upraised wood splinters on her way to smell each kettle. She set out two mugs and lifted the charmed tea.

"That's the wrong one," Emmerick warned.

She gave us both an impassive look as though unamused. Still, the corners of her lips tilted up, betraying her show of indifference. A trace of dimples indented her cheeks—an unrepressed smile would reveal them.

"Is it?"

Emmerick rubbed his hand down his face again. "You are completely insane."

A flash of her front teeth in response to the boy's worry caught my breath. A slight gap between them—a wildly interesting imperfection. *Why did I find so much about her wildly interesting?* She crossed the room with two mugs of charmed tea and handed one to me, meeting my gaze.

Her hair was wetting her tunic, causing it to stick to her shape. *Distracting. So very distracting.*

Strange beauty—dark and ebbing with power. Yes, she was pretty, but there was a certain dangerous allure about her that both excited and frightened me.

"We'll travel a long way together if the warlock sleeps on it and agrees to help us. So we may as well speak openly." Asterie's expression returned to its impartial mask, but her gaze never left mine. She seemed so self-assured for someone with so little knowledge of life beyond tower walls.

She looked confused when I outstretched my cup to hers.

"You touch your cup to mine—it's a gesture of celebration."

She tapped her mug to mine. "But what do we have to celebrate?"

We both sipped. "We can cheers to the truth, to new friends. There is always something to celebrate."

It was something my father used to say.

"I am not allowed friends but having them seems pleasant." The tea had taken hold of her.

I swallowed the second sip of tea harder than the first—that raw, unfiltered statement left my heart bruised. To be condemned to loneliness for what I did was one thing, but to be lonely for the sake of some stupid *Order* just seemed cruel. I motioned for us to sit on the sofa.

She sat, pitched forward and inclined toward the fire with her still-wet dark waves over her shoulder. Out of the braid, her hair hung impossibly long—nearly to her waist.

What would it feel like to run my fingers through those locks?

The boy Commander stayed seated at the table, cautiously allowing us privacy as he began to clean his weapons.

I opened my mouth to speak.

"So, Fenris." She didn't let me get a question in. "How long have you been bound to these woods?"

"Four centuries."

Her eyes widened, but I spoke before she could ask more.

"Why is it that you have never left your tower?"

She glanced over my shoulder at Emmerick before returning her attention to the fire.

"I do leave my tower. I can travel to the other towers, and I'm here, aren't I?"

I chuckled quietly—she wasn't going to make this easy. "You know what I mean. Until now, why didn't you leave?"

"None of my Sisters leave the towers unless the rulers of their Corridor request it. Mine never requested it. The others frequent the courts more regularly—a few times a year. I am not missing much. I'm told."

"Your Sisters, they know you are here?"

With a spotted history with a certain enchantress, I needed to know where her allegiance lay. I couldn't risk falling into the wrong hands—couldn't risk *Van* falling into the wrong hands.

She shook her head. "No. I could be cast out for my actions. But the prophecy spoke to me alone. It told me not to share it with them."

Her attention turned from the fire to sear me with a narrow-eyed gaze. "You speak of them as though you know them. How do you know my Sisters?"

My teeth ground—how could I answer that honestly?

"I have old friends and old enemies in those towers. Don't you enjoy your work? Why risk your position of power?"

Lines etched into her forehead as if she had just realized something.

"I don't enjoy it." Her fingers raised to her mouth as though the words could somehow be put back. "But enjoyment isn't important. I must keep the Corridors safe. Luz and the Central Corridor are mine to protect—I serve the realm, and I won't stand by and let innocent people die. If it makes me a traitor in the end...so be it."

Then, she asked what I knew I couldn't answer. "Why are you bound to these woods?"

My mind warred to tell her the truth. *Fenris the Destroyer. Fenris and his Beast.* I'd put a stain of darkness on the Old World so big it couldn't be erased. That darkness seemed to have spread its poisoned veins through the lands if magic was truly gone.

"My actions warranted exile. My hands have the blood of many on them, and I deserve worse than this fate." My admission seemed to surprise her, but she said nothing, not pressing me.

Instead, Asterie nodded and combed her fingers through her still-damp hair. She pulled her knees to herself on the sofa and smoothed her skirts down around them. She was so hard to read.

I'd spent years philandering through the Courts of Brennax and Phynx, dallying with women who wore every thought on their faces. Women who swooned. I'd pay good coin to see her swoon.

I asked, "Does that scare you?" I'm unsure why that mattered to me.

"A little."

Her lips downturned ever so slightly—*good*. She *should* fear me. "It seems you have power of your own—that little show of blue light. Which Source do they say your magic is from?"

"The Stars. I feel my strongest whenever the moon rises."

"I might have guessed that." *Bullshit.* But not quite a lie. I *might* have guessed she had starlight in her. Certainly, she did. I *might* also have guessed she was a Siren or a figment of my imagination.

I knew one thing—I could feel her fire calling to mine. She may have thought the stars alone marked her, but I grew uneasier by the minute just being near her. It was like she held a piece of me. But that *couldn't* be.

She asked, "Why would you guess that?"

I flashed her what should have been a winning smile. "Because nothing but the heavens above could have created such a beautiful creature."

The boy Commander cleared his throat in warning. Which was laughable, really. All the brute force in the world would never save him from Van's locked jaw or the fire in my veins.

She leveled a skeptical look at me; her dark eyes seemed to swirl with iridescent smoke.

"Flattery isn't going to win you anything with me."

"And yet, you've leaned closer."

She looked down at her body in disbelief, as if it had betrayed her. A dark chuckle escaped my lips. I swore she blushed as she straightened. Seeing her lean away was disappointing, but it satisfied me a little to see her flustered.

"What about you—what is your Source magic?" She changed the topic.

In response, I held my fingers to the fire and let it grow out of the hearth in a blazing roar.

"Fire," she mused softly, watching the flames die down in the fireplace to their usual flickering glow. "Firose commands Fire too—one of my Sisters. Do you know her?"

"Yes." I ground it out too quickly. This wasn't a topic of conversation to have on a truth charm. Not when her loyalties to them were so strong. "Do you find me handsome, Lady Asterie?"

The distraction landed perfectly. She was mid-sip of tea.

She choked out, "Of all things—you want to know if I think you are attractive?"

Emmerick quipped from the corner, "I think that's enough tea for you two."

She set her tea on the wooden side table and surveyed my face with interest. Those glistening dark depths consumed me like a black hole.

"You are handsome..." she admitted. "My mind screams that I should stay away from you, fear you, but my body betrays my mind."

"Your body has the better idea," I drawled quietly.

Her gaze darkened for a split second as she placed her feet carefully back on the floor. *Fidgety.*

"Just reminding you both that I *am* still here," Emmerick chimed in from the corner. He was mumbling something about the absurdity of immortals as he continued to sharpen his blades.

Asterie's lips quirked up at the sides. She seemed grateful for the buffer, amused even. On the other hand, I would do anything to see her look at me the way she just had for a second longer, including having Van drag the boy Commander out into the woods.

"Don't worry, Sir Emmerick, you are still more handsome than any man I have encountered." Her words were not seductive in the least. They were spoken as if it was simply a fact, but envy struck me fast anyway. *Fuck.* But I couldn't deny that the boy looked like he had stepped off a storybook page.

"That's enough tea." The boy Commander groaned. When I glanced over the sofa, he had reddened at the ears.

Despite her companion's interjection, she leaned over me to speak into my ear.

"We have no time for distractions, Fenris. No matter how gratifying those distractions might be for fleeting moments." Her voice was quiet and her words were only for me.

My breath caught—she had to know what she was doing to me. The brusque rasp to her voice, the intentional closeness, her slender fingers braced on the sofa beside my head. She was no innocent fawn to be snared by some pretty words and pleasantries. I'd need to try harder—*but why did I want to? Why was winning her suddenly the most important thing to me?*

The offer she brought should worry me, given her loyalties. My freedom—of all things. In exchange for using me, using Van. I should never have let them come here.

"I assure you it would be *much* longer than fleeting moments, my strange beauty." The words were an intentional purr. She raised a brow while looking at me with smoldering intensity.

But that delicious expression was quickly erased from her face. *Disappointing.*

She dragged a finger over the ink on my bicep. "You, and whatever this beast is, have a purpose to Henosis. I hope you'll agree to come with us to Luz. But first, put any philandering thoughts aside. Save your flirtations for the women of the courts."

The cool touch of her finger lingered on the ink. She was so close—full lips beckoning me to taste them. But then, she leaned back.

"By the way, the charm wore off minutes ago. I have been backwashing. That was simply from the heart."

A sigh escaped my lips. I was a fool for even contemplating this.

"I know of an Egress that will make the journey shorter. It's in the township of Belray—a little over a week of travel on foot if you know which way to go."

Emmerick cut in, "They've all been destroyed—we'll need to travel on foot."

"I assure you this one is well hidden," I answered.

"So you agree to come with us?" the boy Commander asked from behind the sofa.

"I agreed to sleep on it," I drawled, glancing over at the tempting enchantress next to me before physically shaking the lust from my head and standing.

Asterie had returned to the infuriating muted version of herself—her hands were folded in her lap and her expression neutral.

I couldn't go back to any court with her. No matter how long it had been, I still was not fit for the realm. Letting her step across my doorstep tomorrow would be hard. This strange beauty, who willingly charmed herself to the truth to prove her cause, would haunt my fantasies long after she left. But, by all logic, I needed her to go. I needed her to go *badly*.

Yet I could kneel before her and beg her to stay. *What, in fuck's sake, was wrong with me?* I avoided looking at Asterie for a second longer and turned to the boy Commander.

"Would you two like to take the bedroom?"

"No, I'll take the floor. Asterie, you can take the sofa," he answered.

I nodded. "Goodnight, then."

I'd sleep on it.

But what I really needed was time—time to understand what this connection was that made it so difficult to think about her walking away from here.

I'd spend the rest of the night thinking of a way to stall them.

"You found her." The ethereal whisper shook me awake.

I needed to see her.

Asterie. Where was she? My pulse rose and my heart thumped hard in my chest.

When I slammed the bedchamber door open, there was no sign of her on the sofa. Blankets were neatly folded and draped over the armrest. Emmerick sat at the table with a cup of tea and some flat cakes on a tray—there was a second empty plate on the table that told me he hadn't been alone all morning.

"Where has she gone?" My voice sounded erratic, panicked even, and Emmerick eyed me cautiously.

He set down his cup. "She went down to the river for some fresh air."

In seconds, I pulled on my boots over the woolen socks I'd worn to bed and threw my cloak over my shoulders.

"She's rather moody in the mornings. I wouldn't do that if I were—"

His warning was snuffed out by the sound of the cabin door shutting behind me. The sun was just breaking over the horizon, casting limited light into the depths of the forest. Dew drops made the grass slippery under my boots as I hiked the quarter mile down to the river.

When I approached, she was barefoot in the shallows. One of her hands held her skirt above the water. The other hand was delicately outstretched toward the bubbling current.

She was forming glowing orbs of flickering pale blue light. At least three orbs floated down the darkened riverbank, creating a glow illuminating it from all angles. Golden rays of the morning sun began to peak through the trees.

She looked angelic, tranquil and at ease. Content with setting eyes on her, I immediately regretted my intent to interrupt her. Before I could retreat, she spotted me. Her expression was neutral—not surprising. She didn't *emote* much. I stepped down to the riverbank.

"It's beautiful here," she said evenly.

"Yes." I watched her wading in the river. "Yes, it is."

When offered a hand, she whispered a quiet thank you before taking it. I hoisted her up onto the bank. Her hand stayed in mine. She seemed too distracted to notice; I was too selfish to retreat.

"That sound…" Asterie paused with a finger pointed at the river below, and I listened to the bubbling trickle of the river. "It might be the greatest magic I've ever witnessed."

She squeezed my hand.

"How do you not spend all day here? I would…"

For once, I had nothing charming to say. So I settled for the truth. "I think the prophecy spoke to me too."

Her brow creased, and her mouth hung open, exposing that slight gap in her teeth. *Surprise.* I logged that emotion as my new favorite. She turned to meet my gaze before looking down at our bound hands. I gripped her fingers gently so she wouldn't pull them away.

"Two hundred years ago...it told me to '*find her.*' I had no way of leaving here, but since that day, I've felt...restless." It was illogical, but it all poured out of me as fast and erratic as the river below us. "I think you are '*her*'..."

Her surprise settled back into that infuriating, indifferent expression she wore as a mask.

"The moment I saw that Lynx attack you in the woods, it was like something *snapped*. I don't know what it means or why I was supposed to find you. But I woke up this morning panicked, thinking you'd left without me. I couldn't settle until I saw you," I finished, almost out of breath.

This connection, this feeling, like a taught rope that pulled me near.

I'd felt this before. It was a nagging thought that I wanted to dismiss.

Her tone stayed even as she reasoned, "Surely it's just the prophecy's way of swaying you to come with us. What if '*her*' is the Queen? She was the one who knew where to find you." She sounded so sure of herself.

I shook my head. "Don't you feel it—a pull between us? It feels dangerous."

She withdrew her hand forcefully and shook her head. "We all have a purpose. You have a great one, Fenris—with or *without* me. We are connected only in our service to the Queen. To Luz."

Without Asterie. What an absurd thing to fear after knowing her less than twenty-four hours. My attention caught on the blue glimmering orbs floating peacefully down the river to attempt to calm my irrational anxiety.

No good could come of our alliance, not while she remained loyal to the cause she set out for. And yet, I didn't know if I'd be strong enough to give her up.

"Fenris." Her voice was reassuring. "If you are compelled to come with us out of some odd, misplaced affection toward me, I won't stop you. It doesn't matter to me *why* you join us so long as you do."

Her rejection felt like a bruise being pressed and a relief all at once. I was glad the boy Commander wasn't here to witness my humiliation. Needing to recover some sense of my pride, I changed the subject.

"What are they?" The blue orbs continued to float further down the river.

She smiled sadly. "Memorandums."

"I'm familiar with the term, but I've never seen them created like that." Usually they were magically set into stones, sometimes buried with the dead in their graves.

These memorandums were as beautiful as the hand that created them—bright blue orbs of pulsing energy that seemed to flicker like water catching starlight.

"If we do not make it to Luz, they will hopefully make it to my Sister in the West Corridor. I left without explanation. They document my journey so far." She paused. "In case I don't get the chance to tell them myself."

"What if they make it into the wrong hands?"

She looked me in the eye with a determination that couldn't be swayed. "What if they make it into the *right* hands?"

I raised a brow because our definitions of right and wrong hands seemed slightly different.

"I've charmed them to only be unlocked by my Sisters. It will be fine."

Nothing about that would be fine.

That voice had told me to find her. My only wish was that it had been clearer about *why.* Did it mean I should go to Luz to fight a war that was not mine? Should I follow her into the fray, whether we belonged together for some higher purpose or not?

Something told me that this woman was going to change the realm in irreversible ways—for better or worse was still to be decided.

I needed time to decide.

Chapter 11
Asterie

"Absolutely not." Emmerick dismissed the idea immediately, with arms closed over his chest.

Fenris had just casually dropped an ultimatum onto the table.

"Emmerick," I warned.

"No, Asterie, no. You won't be staying here *alone* with this lunatic."

Keeping my expression neutral, I couldn't help but sigh. Since this morning by the river, the warlock had kept looking at me like I might grow three heads—like he was waiting for something.

"The trek to Belray is more of a climb—better to go on foot than risk injury. Your horses will be food for the wolves here. It's only a few days' travel to and from Shelten Falls, where you can board them. But it's in the opposite direction," Fenris reasoned.

It still sounded like a poor excuse to get alone time with me, but I'd grown fond of that little red horse. Not wanting him to be food for wolves was reason enough for me.

An added benefit was avoiding four unnecessary days sleeping on the forest ground if we accompanied Emmerick. For some reason, in this cabin, no nightmares haunted my sleep. Last night was the first peaceful night of rest I'd gotten in weeks.

"Exactly—a few days' travel that you both will *join me* on." Emmerick straightened his posture, unyielding. He towered over Fenris.

The warlock just smirked, running his fingers down the ink on his arm with a tilt of his head that had Emmerick deflating.

"Why?" Emmerick demanded.

"I'd like to understand the enchantress' intentions better before agreeing to come along and fight a war for her that's not mine."

His answer seemed genuine and honest. Though I didn't like what the "for her" implied. This wasn't something he was doing for *me*.

"Also—she looks like the Source of Death himself. We wouldn't want our enchantress' youth to wane, now would we?" His teasing erased any sympathy. His possessive *"our"* had not gone unnoticed by me or Emmerick, who glared.

"It's fine, Emmerick. Take the horses...it's only a few days, and I've fended without you long enough." I refused to admit that I could genuinely use the rest. "The warlock and I will reach an understanding." My words were a dull threat that only seemed to make Fenris' eyes light with interest.

He was incorrigible, yet spending a few more days with him would allow me the chance to fully assess whether unbinding him *was* a good idea after all. Not that, at this point, I had a choice.

Emmerick slammed a palm down on the table before storming onto the cabin's porch.

"Your Commander is so *protective* of you," Fenris remarked as he rounded the table to where I stood, "but something tells me you don't need his protection."

"I don't." My words were flat.

My assurance only deepened Fenris' infuriating smirk, and his gaze trailed down to my lips. My cheeks heated, and I bit their insides, leveling what I hoped was an unaltered look into those hazel eyes.

Damned mesmerizing green and gold. His irises looked like the morning light hitting ferns on the forest floor, like that first morning that I'd witnessed the forest sunset.

"You will come with us if I spend these days with you." It wasn't a question. "And what exactly will we be doing?"

Bile rose in the back of my throat thinking of what so many men had climbed the walls of my tower seeking. How many bloodied fingertips had grasped at me. Yet I wouldn't refuse whatever he asked, just as I'd surrendered to so many before.

He chuckled darkly. "We *talk*—my strange beauty. Do you think I'm a monster?"

Yes. No. I said nothing. I glared at the pet name he had no right to give me, but even that show of emotion made the light in his eyes brighter and the smirk on his face deepen.

I supposed I was to find out. *It would be a long few days.*

Emmerick galloped away that afternoon, eager to return as quickly as possible, leaving Fenris and me alone. I stared wordlessly at the venison stew in the wooden bowl in front of me.

"So talkative." His voice was light and jovial.

My shoulders shrugged. "I'm not very used to being in the company of others."

He'd pulled a stool over to sit at the table with me and set down his own bowl. That infuriating smirk returned as he kicked his feet out with unnerving nonchalance.

"Well, you see, it's been about four hundred years—give or take—since I've courted a woman—"

"You are *not* courting me," I sharply corrected him.

"All the same." His brow quirked upward. "I'm not sure how to converse with you without your participation."

I held the bowl up off the table for a moment. "It's rude to talk and chew," I noted.

He huffed a laugh but our meal went on in silence.

When our bowls were dry, he moved to gather mine, and in doing so, his hand skimmed over the top of mine. The heat of his touch startled me, but it was gone just as quickly, leaving me disappointed in a confusing way.

"I wouldn't know how to help you carry a conversation if I tried," I admitted.

"But will you try?" He'd risen to put the bowls in a wash basin and now leaned against a shelf, looking down at me.

I nodded. "That was the agreement, wasn't it?"

"Yes, but will you do so *willingly*?"

He seemed to be fishing for an answer I couldn't think clearly enough to deliver. So I simply said, "I'm here, aren't I?"

"Will you answer every question with a question then?"

"Will you keep asking useless questions?"

He chuckled, a devastating smile flashing across his face before he turned to wash the bowls. The silence burned between us again—somehow, his fight for conversation had let silence feel like abstinence from our agreement. *Peace Prevail*. He'd somehow won because I *wanted* to talk to him. I just had no idea where to start.

"Do you regret it...what you did to be exiled here?"

He'd be sorely disappointed if he expected sparkling conversation skills. Fenris' back stiffened at my question.

"Yes."

It was nearly a whisper, and he turned back toward the wash basin. Apparently, I had a knack for striking nerves.

"Then I won't pry again into what it was. But can you make me one promise?"

I'd piqued his interest enough that he looked at me over his shoulder with a reluctant nod.

"That when you're ready, you'll tell me about who you were before?"

He smiled weakly. "I'd like that." He turned around and leaned back against the basin. "You'd want to know that?"

I nodded.

"I'll tell you about him someday. But I warn you, he was a fucking fool."

"Ahh, so—the difference being?"

His weak smile cracked into a full one. "Was that a *joke*? From the stone-faced Enchantress of the High Tower? A joke." He pretended to be in deep thought. "Huh. Who knew she was capable of such a thing?"

His smile was contagious. I bit the insides of my cheeks. But behind his playful intent lurked something dark, something haunted. I wouldn't let my defenses go completely lax around him.

"And you'll tell me"—he thought about his words for a moment—"who you might *like* to be—if you weren't holed up in that tower?"

All traces of a smile left my face. He seemed to notice my shift, for his smile fell too.

"That won't be necessary." My words were measured. "There will be nothing of me beyond the Sisterhood. Beyond upholding the Order. That I'm sure of."

If the prophecy spoke true, my life was likely just a pawn in whatever resolution lay ahead. *Why wonder what could have been?*

"That's a shame." That darkness lurking in his eyes flared as he leveled a glare at me that could melt iron. Then he stalked off to his bedchamber and slammed the door so hard behind him it rattled the rafters.

He didn't come back out that evening.

Infuriating, volatile man.

The riverbed called to me the following morning. I perched myself on a rock with my feet dangling in the cold rushing currents below. Under the canopy of trees, with the morning sun peeking through their branches, I breathed deeply for a few moments of peaceful reflection.

The golden glow of morning didn't feel oppressive in the woods as it had when the sun cut through my tower windows. Instead, there on the riverbank, it brought me joy.

I couldn't remember the last time this light of a feeling brushed my heart. Specters and howls in the night were forgotten. The wicked woods were not wicked at all—they were beautiful.

Fenris found me in that space of tranquility. He sat beside me, drawing in his knees and resting his forearms on his legs.

"Good morning." His voice was low, as though he did not want to disturb the peace of my moment alone. Yet he was there—interrupting it.

"Mhm," I answered. I wasn't in the mood for his hot and cold conversation—jovial one minute, brooding the next.

Judging by the lack of ink on his arm, the beast was roaming somewhere in the woods around us. He seemed cautious of allowing me to see the wolf-like creature again. Whether that was for my comfort or his own, I couldn't be sure.

"I owe you an apology." His blunt words caught me off guard; I'd expected a reprimand. "I'm sorry. I forgot my manners last night."

Unsure how to answer that, I shifted to allow one leg to cross beneath the other and faced him. *An apology. Had anyone ever apologized to me? Felt the need to? Maybe Amara on occasion.*

"I don't see why you should be sorry." At my words, his face contorted into a wince, and his brow wrinkled. I wanted to reach out and smooth those worry lines. Instead, I sat on my traitorous hands.

"When someone's a prick to someone else, they tend to owe them an apology." He broke my gaze and stared out at the running water below us.

I only shrugged.

"The man I was before...he hated authority figures," he started before relaxing back onto his hands. "I don't think that man ever took the weight of the world very seriously. Idealistic—and not in a good way..."

The way his lips turned down and his eyes grew glassy and contemplative intrigued me. *Guilt? Regret?* I couldn't pinpoint what he might be feeling, but either way, it affected me.

I didn't want to sympathize, didn't want to build an attachment to the warlock. *What would be the point?* I kept my face emotionless despite my warring thoughts.

"I grew up in an estate here in the North Corridor. My parents were Brennac. Magic-wielders."

I nodded. Given his power, it didn't surprise me that his parents were gifted with Source magic too. Outside of the High Enchantresses and the North King, he was likely the last remaining wielder of Source magic in the realm.

"Phynx began to regulate that magic. They exiled those who wielded dark magic to the Wastelands. Execution for more extreme cases—like my parents who aided dark magic-wielders." He finally looked at me again.

"I am sorry that you lost your parents in that way." I truly was, though I could not relate.

"So you see, it's hard for me to trust someone raised to uphold an Order created on the same foundations. To oppress, to rule with no absolution. It is so close to the old Phynnic ways. And yet—"

I interrupted, "The Sisterhood is not Brennac or Phynnic. We came after the ways of the Old World had failed."

"Right. Yet, by stifling *all* magic, you take a stronger stance than Phynx did. You are still an authority over the realm that isn't needed. Wielders of Source magic lived in peace for thousands of years. The Phynnic let mortal fear cloud their judgment, and the Brennac gave them a reason to have that fear. No one side was right. But your views are awfully one-sided, Asterie." He breathed deeply, seeming to try to quell the temper I'd already stirred within him.

"I understand." I didn't.

I'd never thought of the Sisterhood's role in the world as being anything but positive. But it seemed like the right thing to say. For some odd reason, the warlock's disappointment in me mattered. That unnerved me more than his words.

He bumped his shoulder into mine playfully.

"So tell me, Enchantress, how are you feeling right now? Because your expressions are infuriatingly unreadable."

My hands wrung in my lap for a moment as I gave that some thought. "Afraid." It was the honest answer. "Mostly of the things I haven't seen coming that I won't be able to control—the unknowns. And a little bit of getting close to you…I'm not sure if freeing you is the right thing to do. I fear you might be manipulating me."

He bowed his head at my words with a smirk as though my honesty amused him. "I can't tell you the future. Not like you can see it. But trust me when I say...I have far more to fear in you than you do in me."

If only he knew that I could see nothing, including *why* I should fear him. I felt helpless without the moonstone to guide me at such pivotal moments for the realm. But for some reason, he didn't truly frighten me—perhaps it had simply been the Phynnic fanaticism he alluded to that condemned him here.

I wasn't sure why my heart wanted to think the best of him.

Fenris rose, and I took the hand he offered to help me up. In the process of rising, I stumbled and teetered precariously toward the river bank's edge. I braced.

Before crashing down, I felt an arm wrap around my stomach. Fen pulled my back to his front, steadying me there. Heat rose in my cheeks as his beard tangled with my hair. For a split moment, every nerve in my body relaxed with an impulse to lean all of my weight into him.

He seemed to regain his wits and stepped back to put an arm's length between us.

Thank the Sources. His effect on me was dizzying. A dangerous warlock, hidden away in the woods for crimes he wouldn't speak of. That *shouldn't* be of any interest to me.

I stubbed out the flame that grew in my stomach—the longing I felt was just curiosity, just inexperience. That had to be all it was. Admitting any differently wouldn't make the decisions ahead any easier.

Outside of his purpose to the Queen and how he could help us, he should be nothing to me.

We spent the remaining nights that Emmerick was gone sitting by the fireplace and making small talk.

Fenris knew my favorite color was dark blue, like the night sky. His favorite was green, though the constant onslaught of the forest had him thinking twice about it. I told him about the legend surrounding my name—of the star and the miracle around my origins. I told him of my upbringing in the South Tower, of my studies and rise to power.

He told me of his time in the courts, grand feasts, balls and debauchery. He scoffed at my suggestion that the debauchery may have simply been due to *his* nature and not the courts.

We kept a physical distance, though the familiarity of him was already giving way to buds of affection that I desperately tried to stomp out.

I could imagine living in the cabin. Life here with Fenris would be beautiful, quiet and uncomplicated. My stomach sank at that realization.

Something about the cricket song and distance from the rest of the realm set my mind at ease. I'd gotten the best sleep of my life on that tufted sofa next to the roar of the fire that Fenris never let die. Not a single nightmare had roused me awake since coming here.

The night before Emmerick was meant to arrive back on foot, I was sprawled across the couch, about to drift into sleep. Fenris sat on the ground, facing the fire and letting his back rest on the sofa next to my hip.

"I'm going to come with you, you know."

I forced open my heavy eyelids before placing a hand on his shoulder. He patted my hand with his. "I know."

He rose and pulled a crocheted blanket from the back of the sofa. Before heading to his bedchamber, he draped the blanket over me. The sound of the closing door between us felt wrong.

A wiser woman may have asked to stay there hidden away, forgotten the realm and lived a quiet life away from the imposing threat of war. But I wasn't a wise woman—I was a righteous one, and it would be my undoing. Maybe his too.

"So I drink this awful-smelling mixture, and then you'll snap the bond to these woods? That sounds awfully painful." Fenris shook the vial of Skei remedy and eyed its contents. "How do I know this isn't all a ruse to poison me?"

The blade of my dagger met my thumb, and blood hit the cabin floor. "I swear it in blood. I won't harm you unless you threaten others."

"I was joking. That was unnecessary—and you stained the rug!" Fenris looked down at the streak of red on the pelt below.

Emmerick let out an impatient huff at him. "Get on with it."

Fenris had not made a single flirtatious comment since the Commander arrived. Instead, he had spent the night showing us various maps of the North Corridor and the best way to get to Belray, a town nestled into the Hussa mountain range.

The easiest way to Belray was through the smaller northern township of Kullworth along the western border of the Corridor. From there, we would Egress into my tower and could make a quick passage to Luz.

"Ready?" I asked.

"As I will ever be."

Fenris laid down on the sofa, and Emmerick held his arms, anticipating his body's reaction. The texts said there was often a struggle when unbinding an entity from a place or object. The subject might act to reinforce the bond and fight the unbinding.

"Whatever you do, Fenris. Do not let *him* out." My eyes trailed down his arm.

"I'll try..."

"Do more than try," Emmerick warned as I raised the vial to Fenris' lips.

As I poured the potion, Fenris' eyes met mine with resolve. He only grimaced momentarily at the taste.

My hands met Fenris' bare chest. I'd never broken a curse this strong before. The scar from his left cheek down his neck didn't stop there—it spanned down his toned torso. *Focus.*

"Untether this heart," I began the curse-breaking spell. My Brennac was sloppy at best, but beneath my hands, a soft blue glow formed on Fenris' skin. The warlock's body convulsed against Emmerick's hold, eyes rolling back and showing their whites.

That was fast.

"Don't fight it." Emmerick's voice was an even, reassuring whisper.

My hands found the sides of Fenris' head at the temples, leaving glowing blue imprints wherever I touched his skin.

"Liberate this mind, free it of this confinement—"

He kicked and writhed against Emmerick's hold as I took his shaking hands in mine.

"Release these hands from the ropes that bind them here—"

A picking up of dust and a rush of air hit my back. A shadow formed over us. *Not good, not good at all.*

"Fenris...don't..." Emmerick pleaded. "Is this normal?" Worry laced his words.

I stayed focused. Grabbing Fenris' ankles, I knelt on the sofa beside him. A low growl rumbled.

"Unshackle the legs weighed to this place—allow them to roam free."

The growl grew louder, the shadow over us bigger and Emmerick met my gaze with horror written across his features as his grip loosened.

I shook my head—we needed to keep going. Emmerick tensed but obeyed and tightened his grip again.

It was unclear what spooked Emmerick more, the creature that stalked behind us or the ferocity of the magic running its course through the warlock. My hands rested on Fenris' torso again; everywhere I touched glowed brighter now, battling the bindings within him.

"Sever the ties holding this body to these woods."

I kept focus; the beast didn't attack. *Yet.*

"Release him!" I commanded the magic beneath my fingers. His torso grew hot to the touch, and he cried out.

The beast's jaws snapped behind me—my work on the warlock was done. I scrambled to flip from a kneeling position to face the beast. Fenris stopped convulsing, but he cried out in pain, still behind me.

The beast approached Emmerick, seeming to place the blame on him for his master's pain. Emmerick began to reach for the dagger that he always kept concealed in his boot. *Angeline.*

I shouted at the beast, "No!"

The creature's ears pricked toward me with a snarl of discontent.

"Do not harm Emmerick." The beast recoiled. He was *actually* listening to me. "Return to Fenris. We are not here to harm him."

A gust of air rattled the windows before the ink returned to Fenris' arm. Emmerick looked at me wide-eyed. Then, the warlock's seizing calmed—his body lay limp on the sofa, and he stopped crying out.

"You can let go. It's done." My hands shook, and my breath hastened as I hovered over Fenris. Tapping into Source magic was an exhausting feat.

"Asterie, he isn't waking up."

Fenris looked lifeless—I couldn't tell if the blue of his lips was from my imprints or a lack of air. The Commander tapped the warlock's cheek without gentleness.

Had I killed him? Panic set in. I threw myself up onto the couch to reach his pulse point below his jaw. His heart beat, and he was breathing. *Peace Prevail.*

"Mmm…If this is how this spell works, bind me and unbind me again, my strange beauty," Fenris drawled groggily with enough seduction that hairs raised on my arms.

Pompous ass.

His eyes fluttered open to meet mine, and I became keenly aware I was *on top* of him.

However, against my will, a smile touched my lips to see him awake. *Why had my heart constricted so much at the thought of him dying?*

Surely, it was because killing him would be a failure in my promise to the Queen.

"Hilarious," Emmerick ground out as he helped me up.

The Commander seemed shaken by all he'd witnessed. I'd forgotten how jarring it must have been for him.

Fenris propped himself onto his elbows, looking down at the blue handprints fading from his body, and mused, "Now, if only I could remember all of that."

"Enough," I warned. "It was part of the spell, and I was checking your pulse—we thought we killed you." My voice wasn't as even-keeled as I'd intended. "I am glad to see you awake. How do you feel?"

"Utterly unbound."

Emmerick let out a long, slow breath. "You could have *killed* us—"

I leveled a glare in the Commander's direction and shook my head. Emmerick stopped speaking. Whatever had happened with the beast, we would keep the fact that the beast responded to my words between us. Fenris had given us no reason not to trust him, but his words stuck with me. *"My hands have the blood of many on them."*

Fenris was too enamored with the blue light fading from his body to notice the discretion between Emmerick and me.

"I hope you two have shoes designed for climbing in those packs," the warlock said.

I didn't.

The journey to Belray would be treacherous, but we were so close to fulfilling the Queen's request. Traveling to Belray, where Fenris assured us there was an Egress, would cut weeks from our journey to Luz.

Once Fenris had a few moments to dress, we reviewed our route once more—through Kullworth to Belray, then a quick Egress to my tower and a short carriage ride to Luz from there. The only potential pitfall—we'd need to enter my tower. My stomach soured to think of what might await me there.

Seeing the Corridor and capital city that I'd protected for centuries was right at my fingertips. I wondered if the Sisterhood would try to stop me.

I wondered if I would let them.

PART TWO

FATEFUL FRUITS

CHAPTER 12
ASTERIE

We'd been walking, climbing really, for at least a week uphill toward Kullworth. We would reach the town tomorrow. With each pine passed, the night grew closer and the mountain air grew colder. The Hussa mountain range was known for its low temperatures at night, even in the late spring, and this night was particularly cold.

My feet began to dissociate from my mind. I'd tripped over countless roots and rocks all day, and my hands had been scraped raw from catching myself so many times.

As if my thinking about falling had summoned a rock to form in front of my toe, I stumbled once more. Fenris grabbed me by the elbow to prevent my fall.

"You can make it further," Emmerick encouraged me over his shoulder.

Each day, he'd pushed me for one more hour when I'd grown tired from riding—he was a hardened soldier. While traveling with him, he treated me as one too. Despite my exhaustion, I'd refused to be the reason to slow him down.

Fenris stopped Emmerick with a cuffed hand on the Constable's shoulder. Emmerick had insisted on using the binding cuffs on Fenris to restrict his magic while traveling. The warlock's wrists were loosely bound together, allowing for enough mobility for him to be able to climb.

I thought the cuffs were unnecessary. We'd already made Fenris swear in blood that he wouldn't try to escape or harm us after we had unbound him.

"She should rest," Fenris said wearily.

The two of them bickered over whether I should or shouldn't carry on, like I wasn't present.

I huffed impatiently at their squabbling, unable to hide my boiling annoyance.

"Enough!" I groaned.

They both turned to look at me, and my back straightened.

"I would like to stop for the night." I couldn't deny my exhaustion. My legs felt heavy, and I feared I couldn't force them to carry me further with any sense of reliability.

Fenris smirked at my words while Emmerick sighed up at the sky where the sun was beginning to set.

We walked only until we found refuge from the mountain winds in a shallow cave and settled for the night. Our breath was visible, and the whir of the wind outside the cave made me thankful we had found some, albeit meager, shelter from it, unlike the past few nights. If it were the winter months, we likely wouldn't have made it this far.

After eating a meal of stiffening bread and cured venison, we hunkered down for the night.

A fire crackled, and a flurry of embers scattered above toward the cave's low ceiling. Emmerick was already snoring from the corner. His ability to find sleep anywhere was enviable. But I, on the other hand, still wasn't used to sleeping in such conditions—I longed for Fenris' sofa.

Luckily, in Belray, we would stay at an inn. The thought of a bed, pillows and warmth lightened my mood. The stability of Henosis was at risk, and I longed for material things. *Pathetic.*

Yet, even sleeping on the forest floor in those mountains, I had no nightmares. Not since we were united with Fenris.

My knees drew into my chest as I stared into the feeble fire. I willed my eyelids to grow heavy. It wasn't working. Instead, my mind restlessly rolled through the what-ifs and what-thens. *Who awaited me back at the tower? What had the Sisterhood done when they realized my tower was empty? Would they let me leave once more to go to Luz?* Shivering at the uncertainty, I slid my hand into my pocket to clutch the useless moonstone.

Amara often reminded me, *"Conserve your power or it will rule you."*

So many Oracles of the past had gone mad. Driven crazy by not knowing what paths led to where—not knowing what version of events was reality and what was merely a possibility.

It was easy to get lost in a conjecture. Each path pulled at the fabric of your mind. Just like a body could grow tired from the use of Source magic, a mind could be exhausted all the same.

I wondered if my inability to conjure anything was simply exhaustion.

Fenris lay by the fire, his legs stretched out and his hands behind his head—wrists still bound by the cuffs. The light danced off his features and accentuated the beauty in them. My gaze trailed down to where his scar disappeared beneath his shirt collar. I now knew that it ran down to his pelvic bone. Immortals rarely were left with scars, so I grimaced to think about what he must have endured to keep that one.

I hadn't realized that he was watching me until I looked up—he had the audacity to wink at me. *As if his ego could get any bigger.*

"You're shaking. Can I help you?" Fenris whispered.

I answered, "That depends." My flat tone warned him that I wasn't in the mood for his flirtatious antics.

He motioned to the ink on his arm. "He seems to like you...and he makes a comfortable pillow. Plus, he's warm."

It took me a moment to realize what he was offering. He wanted to let *him* out to sleep with me. My mind snagged on his words—*had he somehow been able to see what happened after I had unbound him?*

He continued, "Also, I can tell he needs to stretch and relieve himself..."

Confinement. The beast was restrained when he didn't want to be.

Caged in a tower. Never seeing the world, never wading through rivers or climbing the Hussa mountains. Was I much different from the beast in his arm? No, the beast had it better—Fenris cared about his wishes. But who truly cared about mine?

That raw emotion shocked me. Bitterness, anger, sadness...

I snuffed the emotions out. I didn't get *wishes.* That wasn't part of my duty. My mind felt at war with itself, and Fenris' quizzical stare told me he noticed.

"Fine, but he stays away from the Constable. And...I don't need a pillow."

"Suit yourself."

I looked at Emmerick once more before turning back to Fenris, who sat upright and was reaching his cuffed hands toward me. If in contact with the wearer's skin, the cuffs prevented any use of magic. They were designed using ancient spells that even I didn't understand.

I warned, "Don't think for a second I won't kill you if you, or *he*, moves to harm us or run."

"I'm in such lovely company. Why would I run?" That infuriating flirtatious smirk spread across his face. I leveled an unamused look at him, though my heart skipped.

Reaching into my robe pocket, I retrieved the key and unlocked the shackles. Fen's gaze seared into mine with quiet intensity as the metal thudded to the dirt ground between us.

The idea of being shackled without my magic made my throat constrict. *How could he bear being so helpless?*

Yet nothing in his demeanor indicated he wanted to flee—he appeared content and relaxed to be where he was.

"They were Emmerick's idea. I thought you would be more useful without them," I stated flatly.

He shrugged. "The boy is justified in wanting me cuffed."

"I told you I wouldn't ask you *why* again. But *who* exiled you to those woods?"

His shoulders stiffened. It was the first time I had seen him look somewhat vulnerable, and his arrogant smirk slipped away. It appeared like he was straining against his thoughts, like a wolf fighting the impulse to kill. The hair on the back of my neck stood. Maybe uncuffing him wasn't a great idea.

He sighed. "Telling you who would make no difference."

Such simple words and yet the sorrow in them filled the cave like a somber melody. The hairs on the back of my neck stayed on edge as I began to hear whispers. It was uncommon for this to occur without me trying or a moonstone in my hand.

It seemed I was at the mercy of whatever my magic wanted to show me.

"Foolish...Damned...Traitor...Murderer..."

The words were an onslaught of vicious hisses into the night air between us. Each accusation hit my mind with painful angst.

Fenris looked unaffected—he couldn't hear them. But he seemed to notice the shift in me.

"You just saw something..." Hope laced his voice.

"I don't always see things—usually, it's whispers or fragments of images. Sometimes, a heightened sense of what path is best. It's hard to tell sometimes whether what I'm experiencing is the past or the future. This time, it was whispering and it was in the past."

The fire danced and seemed to grow brighter. "And what did the whispers tell you?"

"Foolish, damned, traitor, murderer."

His shoulders deflated with each word.

"All of that is true. There you have it." There was no underlying charisma in his voice.

And despite his confirmation that I should fear him, I wasn't afraid. *That* was the more frightening fact.

I felt the tug of something—the wants and needs of another being calling to me. To roam, to stretch. My eyes met the ink on Fenris' arm...I was feeling *his* wants. *The beast.*

Then something else snapped into place like a tugging on a harp string. I felt *it*—the connection Fenris was so confident about at the riverbed. When plucked, he and I would bend within our confines and make a beautiful, sweet sound.

I wanted to be near Fenris, *needed* it. *Sources, this couldn't be a good omen.*

It wasn't rooted in logic. There was no way we could be connected. We couldn't be more different—born on opposite sides of the realm, of different Source magic, and in different centuries. But it was undeniable.

"Are you going to keep staring at me like I have multiple heads now?" Fenris' levity returned.

"No," I answered. "You can let him out."

I nodded to his arm, welcoming the distraction.

"Come on out, boy." As soon as Fenris spoke the words, a quick burst of dust and wind kicked up before the beast took form. The first thing the creature did was stretch dramatically with a yawn. Then, the beast let out a low whine. "Yes, you may go out."

The beast sprinted out of the cave joyously. He was in a smaller form than what we had seen in the woods and Fenris' cabin—still larger than a wolf.

"Does he have a name?" I asked.

"It's Vangard—I call him Van. He's like family."

"Vangard. That sounds familiar."

He eyed me as though he was contemplating something. "Do you have any family?"

I thought hard about that, and moments passed.

He cracked a smile. "It's a simple question."

"Not in a true sense, no. You know about my Sisters. But they are more like...colleagues. Except for Amara. I suppose she is something like family." For some reason, I kept sharing. "I will spend my life serving the Sisterhood. I have no natural place in this world, no family and no friends. I was meant to die as a child but was spared for this purpose alone." As they left my lips, the words felt hollow.

"Who says you have no other purpose?"

My stomach dropped. I'd been fed those words my whole life. *If I was meant for no other purpose, why did leaving my tower make me feel so alive?* "Well, I suppose the Order dictates that." My voice wavered.

"You suppose, or you know?" When I leveled a glare at him, he conceded with rolled eyes, "And Amara—she's your family?"

The thought of Amara's warm voice singing hymns at her piano in the drawing room of the South Tower filled my mind and made my lips turn up at the corners.

"She was the one who took me in as an infant and saw my potential. I didn't call her mother, but she felt like the closest thing. I seek her advice more often than the others."

He hung on my every word as he rose to his elbows before pitching onto his side. It closed the distance between us, making the conversation feel more intimate than it should.

"The others." His voice grew slightly hoarse and strained. "What are the others like?"

The weight of his burning stare unnerved me, but I didn't dare look away. I answered, "When I was young, they were skeptical. But they accepted that I could be an asset. Firose led my education—she can be intense, but it helped me become sharp-minded. My Sister Cassidee taught me how to wield a sword and protect myself in battle, should it ever come to that. And I learned my way around potions from Wyeth, who is a talented healer."

Fenris seemed haunted by my words as he looked away from me and into the fire, offering temporary reprieve from the heat of his gaze. "And they're all family too? You call them sisters."

I hesitated at that. It was easy to call Amara my family—*why was it harder to say with the others?*

"They have the best interest of the Corridors in mind. I am their ally in that," I said.

He seemed to grow very still. I had an odd impulse to reach out and touch his face, to redirect his gaze back to mine. We were close enough that it would only take leaning over to brush my lips against that scar on his cheek. The impulse was jarring.

Vangard, luckily, interrupted me from acting on any odd impulses by padding back into the cave.

"Van, keep the lady warm." Fenris leaned back on his elbows, putting distance between us again.

Vangard skulked over to me and rested his massive head on my knee as though asking for my permission. His eyes were soft and wide. Despite my pulse growing quicker in his presence, that look was hard to resist. When he let out a low whine, I could almost feel my heart soften—the pitiful creature seemed nothing like the beast that almost ate Emmerick back at the cabin.

Was he begging for affection?

"Okay, fine. But only because the ground is freezing and the fire is dwindling."

A slight wag of his tail preceded Van circling me to curl up against my back. His body created the perfect nook to lean into and rest my head on.

"You two don't share...physical feelings, do you?" I asked.

Fenris let out a low, deep-bellied laugh as he collapsed onto his back with his arms above his head. "Not exactly. I can feel through our bond what he needs—when he's hungry or hurt. Occasionally, I can see through his eyes if he chooses to let me. He has some of his own free will. He just chooses to listen to me...most of the time."

I let my body slacken. *Was the thought of cuddling up to Fenris worse?* I hated my mind for taking me to a place of wanting. Loneliness wasn't an uncommon feeling—that's *all* it was.

"How did he become bound to you?"

"Centuries ago, I was a bounty hunter for a powerful man. He set his sights on Van, so I retrieved him from a ruin in the East Corridor jungles. Afterward, my allegiances shifted..."

"Hm…" I wanted to ask more, but the steady rhythm of the beast's breathing was lulling my tired mind and body to sleep. "He does make a nice pillow." It was all I could manage.

"Sleep tight, Lady Asterie, High Enchantress of the Central Corridor. Friend of Beasts." Fenris' voice held a note of amusement.

"*Just* Asterie. Goodnight, Fenris."

"I prefer just Fen."

"Then goodnight, just Fen."

I fell asleep to the sound of the crackling fire and the slow, steady breathing of the warlock and the beast.

CHAPTER 13

FENRIS

"Leave her be!"

The boy Commander pointed a sword at Van, who was still happily curled around the enchantress.

Asterie's eyes shot open.

I'd been watching her all morning as the young Commander slept like a rock until sunrise. She'd been peacefully nestled into Van's black fur—like a dark angel, fallen from the heavens just for my eyes to behold.

Now, with Emmerick waking up on the offensive, I watched with amusement from the corner of the cave.

It took her only a moment to assess the situation—she grimaced at the sun.

"Enough, Emmerick. Emmerick—I'm fine." Asterie held a hand out, signaling the boy to stop.

The Commander didn't put down his sword. Van's posture and position changed. His upper lip curled as he raised his head around Asterie. His hackles rose. He was protecting *her*. His eyes turned to me with the same look of defiance. *Shit.* A knot wrenched in my stomach.

"Emmerick, put down the weapon!" My voice held more panic than intended.

During my unbinding from the woods, Van had ripped from my arm. In those moments, I had seen through his eyes. The moment Vangard obeyed the enchantress' demand to return to me was disorienting. It shouldn't have been possible—the fact that she was hiding it from me, well, that was just plain worrisome.

The boy reluctantly lowered his weapon before Van's head protectively rested back into Asterie's lap with a *hrmph*. I envied his closeness to her. My mind wandered to that look she'd given me last night. *Desire.* I had added that look to the short log of emotions she'd shown me. My new favorite, by far...

I am so fucked. This woman seemed to already have command of Vangard, and she definitely didn't realize she was dual-sourced. Plus, she had shit allegiances in this new realm.

"You took the cuffs off him? Are you ins—"

Van's low growl interrupted Emmerick's outburst.

"Emmerick," she said calmly. "It's fine. I've seen that it will be fine."

I had not seen her use her moonstone before freeing me of the cuffs. She was lying to appease the young brute.

In fact, I hadn't seen her use the moonstone at all since I had met her. *Interesting.* I supposed that I wouldn't like to know what would happen at every step of my life either.

She looked down at Van and gingerly touched one of the horns on his head, seeming to contemplate something. Seeing them together made me realize how idiotic it was to let her near him.

"Van—come." A familiar gust of wind swept through the room as the ink returned to my arm.

"You're impossible," Emmerick muttered to her as he stomped out into the sunlight.

"He's touchy this morning," I murmured to her.

She lifted herself off the ground and dusted her breeches before gathering her pack. I admired the view of her bending over. Four hundred years had done horrible things to my already debaucherous mind. I shook that feeling off quickly—the enchantress was off-limits.

Off-limits.

Off-limits.

Maybe if I repeated that truth, it would make me want her less.

She answered finally, "He likes order and safety—like most Constables."

"Have you *known* many Constables?" Insinuation slipped into my tone.

She leveled an unamused look in my direction but didn't answer me.

"Isn't order and safety your job too? Why not use that moonstone to see what unknowns lurk ahead today, Asterie?" I asked.

"Yes, it is my job. But I'm an Oracle. I exist in a thousand versions of chaos that could happen at any instant or simultaneously. I would go mad if I feared them *all*. I do not need a moonstone to lead my every decision."

Strange, beautiful liar. Yet my heart warmed a bit at the fact she looked well rested and eager to carry on.

Good boy, Van, I thought, despite the dread that couldn't be eased in my stomach over his reaction to her.

The moment we arrived in Kullworth, a town three miles south of Belray, something felt eerie. Most of the shop windows were closed, and there was a heavy presence of Helos guards stopping people as they passed. *Not good.*

I'd visited Kullworth plenty while living in the northwest region of the Old World. Once a territory of Brennax, the town had a prosperous farming trade. They had grown crops on the hillside meadows surrounding the town.

Lord Kullworth had made it possible—his Source powers were derived from the Soil itself. But the people left here were without magic. Lord Kullworth likely had been exiled long ago. Turning my eyes up to the hillside beyond the town, all that was left of the farmers' cottages were shack-like structures with busted windows and faulty roofs.

The hills no longer burst with green crops. Dead weeds and brown soil surrounded us in their stead. We'd stepped into a bleak township. No plants graced window sills, no flags flew, no children played. I turned to Emmerick quickly.

"The cuffs. You need to cuff us. Pretend you are passing through, taking us as prisoners to Luz," I instructed.

A crease formed on Asterie's brow—*concern.* It was not my favorite look on her. I shot her a pleading expression.

I added, "Trust me."

She hesitantly nodded and pulled her black robe's hood up, and I did the same. It would be strange if anyone recognized us, but I had no desire to be sent to Helos. There was someone there I'd never be ready to face again.

Asterie and I each held out a wrist, and Emmerick bound us together without question just before a Helos guard turned to approach us.

"What brings a Commander of Luz to our Corridor?" the guard asked Emmerick. He poked a stubby finger to the crest across Emmerick's chest plate.

For the love of all things, please lie, you giant oaf.

"Hello, sir." The boy's courtly manners would do him good. "There is a bounty for these two—I'm bringing them to Queen Wymark's Court for sentencing."

The guard lowered his head to look at my face and then Asterie's. "What is your name, girl?"

I could feel her brace through the cuff that linked us.

"Adelaide…" She paused. "Adelaide Bennett." Her words were so certain. *Fuck.*

The boy had done well in lying. But the enchantress would get us sent to rot in some dungeon.

Emmerick stiffened. The guard laughed a hearty, full-bellied roar. Asterie visibly flinched at the noise, though her expression remained dull, emotionless.

"That's a riot—she claims our fifth Enchantress' birth name. The mystery hag. What cruel parents."

I wanted to punch the man's ruddy face. But that would surely draw attention, and we desperately needed to *not* draw attention. The guard pointed in my direction.

"And you?"

I hesitated. Damn racing thoughts. *Speak.*

Emmerick spoke for me. "It's an unfortunate married name, isn't it?" He glared at Asterie—as though to ask what she was thinking. "His name is Dario Bennett, her husband. He's been mute since I captured them. They stole from the Central Palace—we're not sure if they used magic to do so—the cuffs are precautionary."

He spoke like this was no news at all, like it happened all the time that a Constable would be sent to catch petty criminals. He then placed a hand conspiratorially up to his mouth as though speaking in confidence despite the fact we could hear every word.

"The woman—she only stole some silver from the kitchens. But the male—he was caught stealing the Queen's undergarments. So, it's sort of a personal errand."

Emmerick exaggerated a conspiratorial wink at the guard. Now I wanted badly to slap the boy on the back of the head.

The guard hollered with laughter once again, showing off his yellowed teeth—what was left of them.

"Alright to pass through, then?" Emmerick asked jovially as he gave the guard a hearty slap on the shoulder in camaraderie.

"Carry on," the guard said as he fought back laughter.

I kept my eyes on the ground.

The guard muttered as we stepped away, "Undergarments, what a riot…"

We ventured further into the lifeless town.

"Very funny," I whispered.

My teeth gritted, but when I looked at Asterie, her free hand was to her mouth, stifling a laugh. It was the most beautiful thing, and my anger with the boy vanished instantly. If he could make her laugh at my expense, then I'd continue to let him rake me over the coals to see her smile.

"You hesitated." Emmerick shrugged, not looking an ounce sorry.

"Clever, really," I admitted begrudgingly.

Asterie's eyes scanned the rows of abandoned shops. The gray cobblestone was grimy and blackened. Smoke stacks from tattered row homes left soot an inch deep on the ground. It smelled of piss and other bodily excrement. Kullworth had become a slum.

There seemed to be one pub open, and people filed out of it and toward the town square. With steins in their hands, their faces were red from drink and thin from malnutrition.

It wasn't how I remembered Kullworth—always a small town but once a lively one. *What had happened?*

"Is this how all the towns and cities look?"

Asterie's words interrupted my thoughts. She'd never *seen* a town. Her face was not trained in its usual expression of indifference. She frowned, her brow furrowed and her eyes crinkled—*disappointment.* I hated that look.

"No," Emmerick answered. "Kullworth didn't fare well after the Order was enacted. The soil here wasn't fertile enough for crops, and they had relied on growth charms. When those charms were banned, the wealthy moved on, leaving those remaining in row homes—or without shelter at all. Others who refused to stop the charms were pushed out to the Wastelands."

"What of Belray?" I asked.

"Belray still prospers—they could afford shipments in winter months and have better growing conditions."

Asterie walked stiffly beside me. I couldn't imagine how seeing this world for the first time felt—being introduced to darkness before ever seeing the light. Selfishly, it was a relief to see her facing the realities of the Order that she so vehemently sought to uphold.

We walked into the town center, where a rowdy crowd began to gather. A platform had been set up in the square, and a man was yelling to anxious onlookers. Helos guards surrounded the onlookers as if ready to shut down the event. The air was thick with tension.

"What good has the Order brought to our Corridor?" the man yelled above the crowd. The scene made my stomach drop. The man looked like a commoner—a tattered tunic and holed shoes.

The man on the platform spat words down at the crowd. "Yes, there are no wars—'*peace*' they call it. But that's all for show! When will they turn on us like our friends in the West faced? When will they cut us down too?"

Great. A righteous idiot about to get himself killed by well-armed soldiers. The crowd was growing more and more restless with every word.

A boy, no older than ten, brought the man a lit torch.

The preaching man raised the torch toward a figure rigged upright and hanging from a rope. It was a cloaked human-shaped form made of straw.

"We have dying crops with no magic to aid the soil. We have children dying of sickness and plague because the remedies to cure them require the art of potions that they keep locked in those fucking towers! And what do our Kings and Queens do? They continue to allow it!"

As the robe burned, I recognized the emblem patched onto it—an eye, a scale and a ring of thorns. I looked down at Asterie's robe, and there it was, right on her shoulder sleeve.

The symbol of the Sisterhood? Fuck.

I reached out and ripped the patch off her robe as quickly as possible, thanking the Sources it only left a few frayed threads. Glad that the guard earlier, and no one in this crowd, had noticed it, I shoved it in my cloak pocket.

"Time to go," Emmerick whispered.

For once, me and the Constable agreed. We needed to get Asterie *out* of there. I tugged on her sleeve to try to pull her away from the growing crowd, but she was rooted to the cobblestone.

Asterie stared wide-eyed at what unfolded on the platform. The straw within the robe burst into flames. Embers and ash scattered over the crowd.

"They must burn! Down with the Order, down with those magical bitches!"

The cuff around my wrist tugged. Asterie trembled—whether it was shock, fear or anger, I didn't know. Her eyes were pitch black, irises swirling and inky but with an iridescent shine—mesmerizing but eerie. It was the same effect that overtook her irises as when she'd heard whispers in the cave the night prior.

That couldn't happen here. Grabbing her hand, I turned to put myself between her and the platform.

Her grip found mine and she squeezed back, but her attention never peeled from the burning robes on the platform behind me.

"Look at me, Asterie. Count with me. Ten...nine...eight..."

Her eyes shot to mine in recognition. An old friend had once helped me learn how to cool down when my anger had overcome my emotions. I suspected that my friend had taught her the same.

"Seven...six..." She mouthed the words with me. The whites of her eyes returned, and her irises glistened warm brown by the time we got to one.

The people around us were shouting their agreement. Their anger was palpable, like the smoke settling in the air. They began throwing whatever they could find at the guards—a bottle, a rock, a shoe.

"You back with me?" My whisper was tender enough to surprise me—and her.

I became acutely aware that both of our hands were now entwined as she nodded. Her expression softened. For a moment, it looked as though she was going to kiss me right there in the chaos.

"You two need to get it together. Come on," Emmerick said quietly over his shoulder as the Helos guards began to violently break up the assembly.

It was growing more dangerous by the minute.

Shields were used to shove people away from the square. A guard stepped up onto the platform to wrestle the man who spoke to the ground, beating him mercilessly as he cried out.

"They will kill us all! Let magic reign!"

Emmerick pushed through the crowd. I let go of Asterie's unbound hand and dragged her by our cuffed hands to follow him.

Two soldiers now restrained the man on the platform, continuing their battery. Each strike drew more blood, and the man's screams of defiance rang through the town square. His shrieks were silenced when one of the guards slit the man's throat in one swift, exact motion. Asterie gasped and stilled. It took force to uproot her from the spot.

"They...they killed him." She gasped. "Fen, they killed him."

I pulled her through the upheaval of rioters and soldiers colliding.

"I know..." I tried to keep my voice reassuring, but my heart was in my throat.

We finally reached the edge of town, headed East. By our luck, it was the same guard we'd encountered upon entering Kullworth. He waved us through, giving Emmerick a gentle nod of approval as we passed.

"Safe travels." The guard's voice was too cheery—*asshole.*

I stayed silent, mute, as I was supposed to be. Asterie looked haunted—her hand trembled in mine.

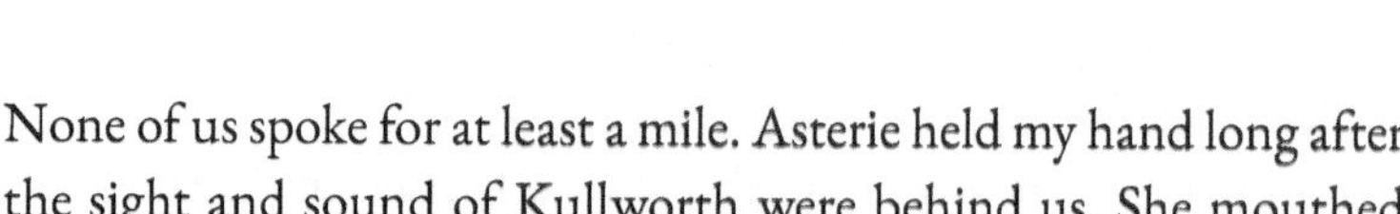

None of us spoke for at least a mile. Asterie held my hand long after the sight and sound of Kullworth were behind us. She mouthed numbers quietly to herself.

"Only a couple miles," the boy said before he tilted his head to meet Asterie's gaze.

"I'm fine," she said in return. That metered tone irked me.

Emmerick shook his head. "*Why* would you use that name?"

Asterie paused and then pulled her shoulders to her ears in the weakest shrug. "They were royal guards. I thought surely if they just knew who I was, they might help us. I didn't understand—"

"No. You didn't and that was foolish." Emmerick cut her off. Asterie's mouth momentarily hung open.

"Why were the people so angry? I have heard of small uprisings. But that was a *whole* town."

The boy sighed and stopped. He looked between us before he ran a hand through his dark curls.

I watched as Asterie grappled with a truth I'd already known. The Order was a calculated way to oppress people into submission under the guise of peace rather than a way to make any real compromise or progress. It was precisely the type of world I had imagined *her* creating.

Yet here I was, holding hands with one of her allies. Asterie's heart beat so hard that I could feel it in her palm. Maybe that was my pulse. I couldn't tell—they were tangled.

"The Sisterhood puts the principles of a peaceful realm above all else." Emmerick frowned. "You just witnessed *above all else*. Give me your hands." Asterie let go of my hand to allow Emmerick to unbind us—losing her touch felt wrong immediately.

"What do you mean?" she asked him bluntly, voice incredulous.

"Some weeks ago, a radical group was killed at the northwest border town of Kruthin. Kullworth is on the other side of that border. They watched as hundreds of Kruthin townspeople gathered along the West Corridor border. The Kruthins were killed by attacks from above—eastern soldiers on Griffiths. A hundred more were slaughtered by western soldiers on horseback.

"The town of Kullworth saw firsthand what happens when the Order is enforced." Emmerick paused. His expression grew grave. "But the Kruthins...they were not armed."

I watched as Asterie's back stiffened.

Guilt. Regret. Horror. Self-disgust? Whatever expression was on her face looked like pure torment and was my least favorite by far.

"Not armed?" she parroted back at him as though it couldn't be possible. The boy nodded.

Her face crumpled. Emmerick shook his head.

"Surely, you are wrong." She looked between us.

My heart ached for her, but I longed for her to realize the consequences of blindly following orders. Another part of me was so angry with her and hated her by proxy. *How could she not see it?*

"What part did you play?" I was unable to control the accusation plaguing my tone. It came out harsher than I meant it.

She looked at me with wide, pooling eyes. *Fuck, not tears.* Seeing a woman cry was always my downfall. Seeing a woman who didn't seem to have emotions at all cry would be torturous.

"I'm their Oracle...I told the Sisterhood what I felt, what I heard—the radical's thoughts were so violent. I heard their whispered conversations. When I told them, Firose initiated a vote to take out the threat."

The threat. Such a cruel way to view it. My teeth ground, and I was thankful that the boy Commander spoke first. I couldn't look at her.

"Yes," Emmerick confirmed. "But they were *peaceful* protestors, not a threat. Angry, yes, but armed, no." His tone was venomous. He was losing his composure too. Apparently, me and the Commander had found common ground in our anger.

Asterie's eyes turned to a dark swirl again behind the welled tears.

What the boy had said to her had to come as a shock. She didn't strike me as a good actress. I tried to remember that none of it was entirely her fault—it was hard not to be angry even still.

"Count..." I said quietly before I turned to the Commander. "Clearly, she didn't know. Lay off for now."

Was that my guilt defending her?

I'd been used as a pawn once too. I had destroyed and set ablaze any claim to my innocence with one idiotic act. *An act of love.* Asterie was suffering the same manipulation, and from experience, I knew facing it head-on was a bitch.

"We should keep walking. We'll be able to rest in Belray. The Egress is at an estate outside town. It would be best to travel in the daylight, and we could all use a night's rest." My words were flat.

We walked away from the setting afternoon sun toward Belray and tried to put the horrors of Kullworth behind us.

CHAPTER 14
ASTERIE

We arrived in the township of Belray during summer commencement celebrations. A crowd of people dressed in vivid emeralds and blues had taken to the cobblestone streets that wound through the town.

I stood, a wallflower, against the brick of a blacksmith shop as a quadrille of dancers whirled about the town square. The musicians that accompanied them played a cheerful tune. I barely noticed Emmerick and Fenris slip away to secure our rooms at an inn nearby.

Dusk settled on the bustling town, and men were lighting oil street lamps, but music still played in the square. Bunting banners with an emblem of a rising sun were strung from lamp to lamp.

Tucked into a valley among the evergreens and pines, the township of Belray was built of low-roofed stone shops and cottages that surrounded a great lake. Insulated by the Hussa mountains surrounding it, Belray seemed a hidden gem—an oasis of the North. Even the winds were not as chilled here.

Groups paraded past me, traveling from one doorstep to the next, lighting a candle on each and singing songs to the Sun Source as they went. Amara had once explained that it was not uncommon for some towns to be devoted to both the Sources and the Order. The people here were of that unique combination. By Emmerick's earlier explanation, Belray was prospering. I wondered whether this was where the wealthy and fortunate families of Kullworth had ended up migrating.

I'd read about the summer traditions.

Light for light. The ceremonious act was meant to ask the sun to shine bright and let the days grow longer. A simple ritual with Brennac origins.

As the dancers passed in graceful sways and spins, the image of that man on the platform wouldn't leave my mind. I replayed it repeatedly—*the rage in his eyes as he lit that robe, the blood running from his throat.* With every passing smile and laugh, it seemed more and more unfair.

A simple "*I*" of agreement had condemned a peaceful assembly to death. No one else was to blame for the events that unfolded in Kruthin and Kullworth.

While the people of Belray emanated happiness to welcome the sun season, their neighbors were being slaughtered and brutalized. For fighting the Order—fighting against the constructs I'd spent so long upholding. Constructs that had doomed their town to poverty.

Emmerick and Fen found me still staring blankly at the dancers. We hadn't spoken during the rest of the walk to Belray. The weight of their words and their anger hung heavily on me.

"I'd like to walk down to the lake. I will find my way to the inn later." I forced my feet to move away from the square.

The new bonds I'd formed with Emmerick and Fen seemed to have broken so easily. *How could they* not *hate me?* I caused what we'd seen in Kullworth—my *visions*, my words.

"I'll join you."

Emmerick's words surprised me.

"Stay out of trouble," he warned Fen, who grunted a response with a dismissive shrug. Emmerick seemed to be warming to the warlock—at least he hadn't suggested the cuffs again. Maybe their hatred toward me was what they needed to get along.

Fenris didn't follow us down to the water. Instead, he walked toward a footbridge over the river that fed into the lake's depths, toward the direction I'd watched them take to the inn.

"I didn't know," I said quietly as we neared the water.

"I understand." Emmerick glanced over at me. "I'm sorry for *how* I told you. It was unfair. I could have warned you what you might see..."

"You don't need to apologize for how you speak to me or what you withhold. I deserved the reproach of those people."

"Regardless, I didn't need to be an ass about it." He offered me a weak smile that quickly faded. "My Queen... she's worried about your Sisters' decisions recently. She wouldn't put it in the letter—she was afraid to. So, when you reached out to her, it gave her hope. That maybe you were different, that maybe you could change their ways."

Afraid. My mind snagged on that word. *Afraid of us—people who were supposed to protect the Corridors and uphold an Order to maintain peace.* But I'd just witnessed what it actually was doing to the realm.

"How are you feeling?" He seemed genuinely concerned as he looked away to observe a flock of waterfowl gracefully floating across the water.

"Confused…" I answered. "Angry, and if I'm being honest, sick with myself."

"The fact that you feel that way…that truly is hope for us."

The music from the band in the square poured out over the lake in a rhythmic, hypnotic tune. The melancholy warmth of the violin, married with an uplifting flute, made me sway. I imagined the quadrille dancers. The thought of their movement calmed my mind, and I found myself swaying to the sound.

"Do you want to dance, Lady Asterie?" Emmerick must have caught my muted movement in his peripheral vision.

Still with the formality. "Asterie," I corrected.

"Do you want to dance, *Asterie*?"

"There are stories about what happens when you dance with an Enchantress of the night sky under the moonlight. Unfortunately, those stories are all very true—or so I've been told."

I pointed at the moon that peaked above the treeline.

"Plus, who could dance at a time like *this*?" I added.

"I am aware of the stories," he said unwaveringly. "And my mother has a saying—'Look for the brightest sides of your darkest days.'"

He outstretched his hand.

My lips quirked into an involuntary smile, and I shook my head.

"C'mon." He impatiently fluttered his fingers.

I had never danced before, but Emmerick seemed an honorable choice to learn from. The wary look in his eye told me he might need a distraction too.

"Alright, but you will need to keep your wits about you," I warned. "The texts say everything will shift, except my voice…so, if you get confused, let go and listen to my voice."

He rolled his eyes and matched my measured tone. "I will know who I am dancing with and who I am not."

"Very well." My heart skipped a beat—to *dance.* It seemed such an absurdly normal thing to do after everything we had witnessed that day.

Upon taking Emmerick's hand, my own hand grew slightly smaller. If Emmerick was surprised by my features contorting in the moonlight, he didn't show it. Instead, he pulled me close enough to position my left hand at his waist and took my other hand in his. It felt unnatural and incredibly awkward.

"Just follow my feet..." he said reassuringly.

While he wore no expression, he could not hide the ache that crept into his eyes at the sight of whoever's face I wore. Whoever it was that he truly desired.

"Remember, listen to my voice," I reminded him. "I'm sorry if I step on you. I've never danced before..."

Emmerick seemed like an excellent dancer, but maybe he was simply an excellent leader. He did not allow me to stray too far or stumble over myself. His traveling steps were hard to keep up with, but I kept thinking of the quadrille in the square, the laughter, the joy.

"Do you want to tell me about her, Em?"

He smiled and swayed me closer and away from him again. "That's what she calls me. Em." His tone revealed a hint of sadness.

"Focus on the *differences*," I warned.

Interesting that I not only adopted a new face but some mannerisms that weren't my own.

He nodded. "Your voice is much raspier—stronger—not in a bad way. Hers is sweet, smooth. Unless she's provoked or angry, then it can turn from honey to daggers. She's loyal, and she can be ruthless if those she loves are threatened. Swears like a damn sailor in private."

He turned me into a spin. I enjoyed the dizzying feeling of it. My impulse was to keep spinning until the events of the day were just a blurred memory.

"Do you often find yourself a recipient of her anger?"

He threw his head back gently with a chuckle. "Yes."

"What do you do to deserve it?"

He contemplated that as he took my other hand, and we began to move in the other direction; the grass tickled my ankles, and I admired the moon glistening off the lake over his shoulder as he continued explaining.

He answered, "I have a habit of being overprotective. She hates being coddled. I know I shouldn't compare you, but she's like you in that way—fiercely independent."

How wrong he was. There was no independence within the Sisterhood. I wouldn't have been able to navigate this world without him and Fen for the past weeks.

I was trained to be a concealed weapon, hidden away in that tower. A tower I would have to return to tomorrow in order to travel to the only Egress left in the Central Corridor.

What if the Sisters were waiting there for me? Would they bind me there before I could make it to Luz? I shuddered.

"I think you would like her, is all I mean," he said carefully.

The dancing grew dizzying, but my mood grew lighter with every step, spin and sway—it was fun. *Have I ever had fun?* Surely, as a child. But I couldn't think of a time recently when frivolity overtook me.

When Emmerick stepped in a circle, his palm against mine guided me to turn with him. I looked into those golden-brown eyes that now shone with life, laughter and a glimmer of happiness and familiarity. *Hope.*

His smile was wide—eyes creased. Then he tripped over an up-raised tree root, nearly falling into the lake. I barked out a laugh. It was a guttural, uncontrolled sound that surprised me.

I held his hand still, helping him regain his balance, but was buckled at the waist in laughter. Emmerick matched my laughter's intensity as he regained his balance.

In the reflection of the lake below, the woman laughing back at me was petite, with honey-colored curls. She had large, green eyes and a smattering of freckles over her nose.

When Emmerick let go of my hand, it was only a moment before my face was my own again. My pale, sharp features and long dark braid cascading down to my waist returned.

"Well, *Asterie.*" He made a point not to add formality. "Now you can say you have danced. It has been my honor. But, of course, you'll have to do a lot of dancing in the Court of Luz, so I hope you enjoyed it."

"I like dancing," I acknowledged, surprising myself.

He took in my changed features. I was glad he did not look dazed. "I need to send a hawk to the Queen about our arrival. Can you make sure the warlock gets to the inn without trouble?"

I nodded. "Of course." He was already walking away.

"Em"—at my words, he looked back—"thank you. I needed that. And whoever she is, she's lucky to have you."

He smiled and swatted away my words, seeming bashful of the praise. Then, when Emmerick had disappeared around the east side of the lake, I saw Fen waiting on the footbridge. It appeared as though he'd been watching.

CHAPTER 15
FENRIS

As Asterie danced with the boy Commander, it took all my restraint not to intervene. It would have brought me great pleasure to cut in and show her how someone with a century of experience dancing through every court of the Old World could lead her. Instead, she stumbled around with that big oaf.

The worst part? She wore a face that wasn't hers. *Fucking moonlight trickery.* I'd forgotten about that mark of the Star and Moon Source magic. It confirmed one thing—she *did* actually hold starlight in her veins. It didn't explain why her fire called to me like a beacon upon a hilltop.

I was too far away to hear her voice, and the thought of her essence being *gone* made me lose my breath. *Was it anger or fear?* I couldn't tell the difference when it came to her.

Then she laughed, and that lovely sound carried across the calm lake. It washed over me like the warmth of fire caught in the wind. She was there, and she was *happy*. Even after such a horrible day. Even after the pain my words had inflicted.

Why did it make me so angry that it wasn't me who summoned that heart-wrecking sound from her?

I feigned lazy indifference and leaned against the railing as she approached the bridge. Moonlight reflected on the water below, and I tried to focus on that and not her nearing.

"I'm heading back to the inn. You should too." Her words were clipped, and she wore a blank, mile-deep stare.

I pushed off the railing, falling into stride next to her.

Was it the boy that plagued her mind? Was I jealous? Hating that train of thought, I searched for words to poke her with.

I'd bring that fire out to play with me one way or another. I knew it was in there because it *called* to me. Loudly. My every impulse was to embrace her, guard her, hoard her to myself. It was a primal urge that could only be the Source magic within us mingling somehow.

"You shouldn't indulge him like that." The unwelcome advice left my mouth impetuously.

That faraway stare zeroed in on me as she stopped short. While apparently Emmerick earned dancing and laughter, I was earning ice and hostility.

I could work with that. It would just take one little spark.

"And why not?"

She was so close—it would only take leaning in to capture those full lips with mine. She smelled of sweat mixed with vanilla and herbs—warm, sensual, so at odds with her cold facade.

"Well, what if he should desire *her* to dance right into his bed next time?"

Her brow turned down and her chin lifted. "Noted." She began to walk again and I trailed her.

Letting her walk away would be wise. Nothing good could come of lusting after this woman who stood for so many things that I hated. "Unless that's *precisely* what you wanted. So the High Enchantress likes men in uniform?" It was a petty thing to say, but the game was to see if I could get a reaction.

"Maybe it is..." Unnatural calm spread across that pretty face. *Unacceptable.*

I'd seen a glimpse of what she was capable of—the blue flames in her palms, those swirling iridescent dark irises. "Ah. So you are jealous that it wasn't *you* that he saw."

Every muscle in her body was stiff, and her fists clenched as though aching to react, to erupt. Yet she kept calmly walking toward the inn. "Considering I am two centuries older than him, of course not. Emmerick is a valuable ally," she said over her shoulder,

Brainwashed *still*. Asterie couldn't even admit that the boy Commander was her friend. He made her laugh and put her at ease. "That's no issue—all the great immortals of legends have fallen in love with young men and maidens. The bigger the age difference, the better."

She bristled visibly but said nothing.

I goaded on, "Do you think he's a virgin? You'll need to be gentle with him."

She finally spun on me with the ferocity of a cornered animal. I'd put the final nail in my coffin.

Yes, a reaction. The shell of a person the Sisterhood had created was of no interest to me.

"Enough!" she barked.

When she saw my coy smile, the swirling darkness in her eyes sputtered out and her eyes returned to their warm brown stare. Her clenched fists loosened and her shoulders slackened. Here I was playing foolish games while she faced the weight of this world for the first time.

Damn it all. I'm an ass. I'd never meant to hurt her. I caught her arm gently as she tried to turn away.

"I'm so sorry, Asterie. Look at me."

She glared past me, but she didn't pull away. "Why are you acting like this? One minute you're talking me down from a panic in Kullworth, and the next, you're being…" She struggled to think of a word.

"A prick?" I answered for her.

She nodded unsurely, seeming surprised by my candor.

"Your laugh." It came out a raw whisper. "It wrecked me. I have no idea why. It's the most beautiful sound I've ever heard."

She stilled and finally leveled a glare that held all the fire I knew her capable of. "Are you *flirting* with me now after implying I wanted to take Emmerick to bed? And implying that it is somehow *my* fault—for simply laughing—that you are so mad? Hot, cold, hot, cold—pick a version of yourself to be, Fen."

Her outrage was warranted. I stepped closer to her. "It is not your fault that it got under my skin. He made you feel joy, and yet I wanted to rip his head off. None of that is your fault. It's mine for being a selfish ass."

There were no longer daggers staring back at me. "Are *you* the jealous one?"

Her question hit my chest—*I was.*

"I am."

We were in front of the inn now, and its gabled stone structure shadowed us there on the lawn. To leave me there, she would just need to take a few steps and walk through the wooden double doors. *That would be smart.*

Getting my feelings tangled up with an enchantress that would, without doubt, stomp on them. *What a lovely idea.*

"You have no reason to be jealous."

"But, don't I? He makes you happy. He will stay your friend." My teeth gritted. "I'm a war criminal that you're dragging around until

I can aid your cause in Luz. Then you'll be on your way." To be used and discarded again. It would ruin me.

Her shoulders fell, and her expression softened further. *No—not pity, anything but pity.* "I hardly think we've dragged you. You came willingly," she retorted.

I shook my head. "*That* is not the point. What comes of us after we finish whatever higher duty we serve? Will you and I be friends then?"

Her hand reached out as though she wanted to offer me comfort but stopped halfway. "Fen, this isn't an issue with who you are. It's an issue with who *I* am. You will get to live in this world freely after the realm is safe, but I won't. You will not see me. That's not my place in this world."

"Don't go back to them." My voice was strained. "You've seen it first hand—the work you're doing is hurting people. Have you never thought about not going back?"

She stood there, mouth agape—like it truly was the first time anyone had offered her that choice. "You need to put that out of your mind. This infatuation might feel real now, but..."

Her voice was growing raspy, and her sentence hung unfinished. She was unsure, which gave me the confidence to take one step closer to her.

I could feel her heat and the rise and fall of her chest through our robes. *Far too much clothing between us.*

"Then tell me, Asterie." I leaned down to whisper the dare into her ear. "Tell me now that you feel no connection to me. That you want to go back to your Sisterhood because there is nothing out here for you..."

Her breath warmed my cheek. *Stupid, wishful words.*

She said nothing, which was the answer I needed to know that she felt it too.

As I straightened, she pitched toward me, like a string was pulling her chest nearer to mine. Her flushed cheeks compelled me to whisper more pretty words to her. I had plenty of those.

"Asterie, my strange beauty. If you would just stop fighting this...I would give you all the gratifying distractions that your body could take. Those 'fleeting moments' of intimacy you warned me against back at my cabin? If you let me, I'd make fleeting moments feel like an eternity."

Let me. The words were bold, forward, and yet not a stitch untruthful. She could lay me bare in more ways than one. I'd always been a sweet-talker, but this was one of the very few times I had meant it.

Her pupils dilated at my insinuation, and her lips parted. We were so close now that my breath mingled with hers.

I expected her to pull away.

Abruptly, she leaned in, grabbed my tunic and pulled my lips to hers.

One of my hands found the back of her neck and dug my fingers into her impossibly long hair to tilt her where I wanted her, needed her.

Savoring the taste of her, I let myself consume as much of her as she'd allow. It wasn't gentle—it was wild, frantic, hurried. Like she might change her mind at any moment.

Finding the small of her back, I pulled her up against me to show her how painful my need was. My hard length pressed against her waist. She was absolutely intoxicating. If she would let me, I could have laid her down and taken her on the inn's lawn and had no shame about it.

A carriage clambered past, and Asterie seemed to regain a sense of her surroundings.

Judging by the shock in her expression, it was a crushing realization. With a gasp of air, she pushed me back just as abruptly as she had pulled me in. Her cheeks and neck were flushed.

When she backed away from me, each step felt like a mile between us. Disbelief haunted her expression, and she shook her head.

"That..." she said as she touched her fingers to her lips. "That can't happen again."

"Why?" An edge entered my voice. To be so quickly rejected after *she* had kissed me so eagerly. It sent me spiraling.

Casual relations with women had once been a game I relished playing, and rejection was part of that game. But hers cut me down to nothing.

Fleeting moments were what I had offered, yet there was no way that would ever be enough.

"That just isn't how this story ends, Fenris."

I'd gotten so used to hearing my familial nickname that my name sounded sharp on her tongue.

It sounded like a conclusion rolled into one. Final. *Had she conjured something?* Whatever she may have seen of our future, she didn't share it.

Instead, she turned and was through the inn's door faster than I could shake away the lust. When I reached the door, she was already stepping up the stairs two at a time. She didn't look back.

Every impulse told me to race after her, but she'd made it abundantly clear that she wanted me at arm's length. I stood there dumbfounded and torn.

This could never be a casual dalliance. I should thank her for ending it when I was too stupid to.

Emmerick entered the inn. *Excellent.* Just the person I wanted to see.

He glanced around, confused.

"Did you truly scare her off *that* quickly? We haven't even had dinner."

"It's a personality defect, I'm afraid." My self-deprecation seemed to take the boy off guard.

"Can you do me a favor? Get her to eat something tonight—she listens to you." I sighed the words, and Emmerick's skeptical expression faltered.

He contemplated. "I will do *her* the favor."

Semantics. That was good enough for me.

I needed to put distance between me and the enchantress, so I waited until the boy climbed the stairs before slipping back out into the streets of Belray.

Pubs were always a great place to lick wounds. The liquor loosened conversations, the music lifted spirits and a card game or two could change my luck. Shantey's Pub turned out to be just the place for my mood—a divey establishment where the carpet smelled of piss and so did the ale.

The pub had sticky floors, scuffed furniture and worn seats, but the clientele looked mostly respectable. Locals posted themselves up at the bar, and those traveling through seemed to commandeer the tables closest to the band. It was easy to tell them apart since the travelers seemed to simply clap when a song ended and the regulars amicably heckled the band from across the room.

Three steins of ale had not been enough to relax the tension in my shoulders. *Women—it would have to be women, then.* I sidled up to a rickety table beside a pretty brunette. Soon I learned she was traveling through Belray to meet her sister in Helos. My propensity for small talk came back quickly—shallow conversation had never been difficult for me. It felt hollower than usual tonight.

The brunette was everything I would have once loved in a woman—outwardly beautiful and showy about it. Her breasts were hiked high in a low-cut dress, and her sultry eyes told me it would be easy to get her out of it. She was the type to whisk you away to a coat closet or alley and hike up her skirts. She'd let me take her from behind—impersonal, physical bliss. No commitments.

Yet the idea of it brought me no excitement at all. Damn that dark-haired enchantress for making me want something deeper than light-hearted debauchery. After just a taste of her, my senses were blind to any other.

"Do you want to see a magic trick?" I let fire dance across the back of my palms before catching it in mid-air and snuffing it out with a fist.

The brunette's cry of delight made me feel empty. "How is it done?"

"A magician never reveals his tricks."

A wink, a hand on the small of her back, a couple more rounds of ale. Turns out my charm had come back quickly too.

The woman hung on my every word as I tried to shake a certain dark-haired enchantress off my mind.

Then, Asterie stepped into the pub with Emmerick. Seeing her felt like having the air sucked right out of my lungs. Her hair hung clean and free of its braid, cascading over her shoulders in long waves. A simple blue linen dress hung loose from her body, which did nothing to showcase her figure but everything to excite my imagination.

The musicians played loudly from the corner stage, washing out what Asterie was saying to the boy Commander, but she made him laugh. I was grateful that he had gotten her there, at least, to eat as he'd promised. But the inn's kitchen was likely closed by now.

When Asterie looked around the pub, she took everything in with the same wonder I'd seen that morning on the riverbank. Emmerick elbowed her playfully as the song ended to prompt her to clap, which she did unsurely. She looked overwhelmed, yet her foot was tapping below the table.

Asterie's gaze landed on me. My arm was lazily slung around the brunette's chair. The enchantress stilled and her back went rigid. Then something interesting overtook her features. A slant in her brow and her lips ever so slightly downturned.

Disappointment. In this context, that expression was glorious.

Feeling giddy, I tilted my glass in Asterie's direction. She looked over the edge of her wine glass and raised one brow in response. An unspoken question.

Emmerick was going on about something. When she finally returned her attention to him, I knew that she hadn't heard a word.

Her fingers touched her lips. *Did she imagine how mine had felt against hers?*

Her presence spelled failure for sleeping with any other woman that night, though I had been kidding myself to think I would have gone through with it. If there was a chance she could be disappointed for even a second or was rethinking her rejection, then I might be the luckiest man alive.

The woman beside me, whose name had already escaped me, whispered into my ear, "Do you know her?"

"Hm?"

She narrowed her eyes. "I am feeling like a change of scenery."

"Perfect, let me walk you back to your inn."

When we left, I made a show of tucking my arm around the woman's waist and leading her out of the pub. In my peripheral vision, Asterie seared me with a glare. It was petty, but I soaked up every bit of her dissatisfaction.

I'd be back. In the meantime, she didn't need to know my intentions.

CHAPTER 16
ASTERIE

"Have you heard a word I've said?"

My attention snapped back to Emmerick with a feigned smile. My stomach groaned; it was empty and warmed with wine. The Constable had insisted we come to eat, but the service was slow since the celebration was in full swing. I didn't know whether I *could* eat with so much anxiety twisting in my core anyway. I'd never felt so off-balance, so erratic. Emmerick had Angeline, the dagger he kept hidden in his boot, out. He spun the blade on the tabletop. It seemed he was always active—maybe that was why he slept like a bear.

"Of course," I lied.

He didn't look convinced, which was justified. I hadn't heard a thing he had said. Instead, my eyes had been fixed on Fenris, who was charming the dress off of a woman across the pub. It burned a pit in my stomach to see his arm around her.

That's silly. I tried to quell the raging feeling—I held no claim over him. In fact, earlier that evening I had rejected him so wholly that I had no right to be angry. If he should seek the warmth of someone else's bed, then it was none of my concern. Yet envy was an ugly, unfamiliar beast rearing its head inside me in ways I hadn't known I was capable of.

Wine. I angrily poured myself another glass.

Emmerick let out a low "ahhh" just audible over the music. Then, a playful grin washed over his face.

"Why are you smiling so widely?"

"Because you are about to tell the funniest joke."

"I am?"

"Asterie, catch up here—play along." He pointed at me and laughed as though I'd just said something humorous.

"Are you drunk?"

"Not yet, well, not *too* drunk yet."

He raised his glass to touch mine, and we drank to that. *"There is always something to celebrate"*—Fen's words the night we met.

Maybe I'd had too much wine with too little to eat. *That must be why the pit in my stomach lingered.*

The music grew louder. Barmaids stood on the bar stomping their feet and pouring ale from steins into the mouths of drunken men below.

Music was a temporary distraction. The way it was played out here was something I would miss. It sounded so warm and authentic when mortals played instruments compared to when the tower piano or harp played for me. Missed strings and keys created perfect imperfections in the sound.

"He's flaunting that woman to get a rise out of you. *Whyever* would he want to do that?" Emmerick's tone was light and taunting in a good-natured way.

My fingers touched my lips, and my mind raced back to how Fen had kissed me. I initiated the kiss but hadn't expected his reception to be so *consuming*. It was a foolish thing to do, but I'd been so overtaken by the moment. The way he had kissed me set every nerve in my body aflame. It had felt *right*.

"I kissed him," I groaned. "It was such a stupid, stupid thing to do."

Emmerick smirked knowingly. "Ahh. He looked disheveled and dumbfounded when I found him earlier."

"It can't happen again."

"Why not?" Emmerick balanced his chair back on two legs. It was the first time I'd seen him look truly relaxed. "Aside from the fact he's a war criminal and has been alone in the woods for far too long? But...no offense, you're not entirely *ordinary* yourself."

Emmerick was awfully blunt when he drank.

Why not? There were a thousand reasons—weren't there? Only one mattered—there was no point in leaving loose ends behind.

What I hadn't shared with Fenris and Emmerick weighed on me—my inability to see any path ahead, anything at all in the moonstone. That this was because my fate was tied somehow to the prophecy.

Whatever choices lay ahead, making them without emotional ties would be easier. When the time came to greet death again, I needed to be ready to do so quickly. I needed to be unattached.

Yet, as Fenris walked out of the pub with his arm around that woman, I wanted nothing more than to stop them.

"You're a Constable—isn't the war criminal part reason enough?"

"Deflecting isn't going to make you feel any differently."

"And how do you think I feel?"

"Well, if looks could kill—your eyes would have shot daggers into the back of the warlock's head as he left with that woman."

Hating that he was right, I sighed. "And what do I *do* if you're right? If I am attracted to the insufferable man?"

"I'm the last person you should be taking advice about men from. I don't know."

Emmerick looked sympathetic, which only made me feel more pathetic for allowing any of these emotions to surface.

This was an unwelcome distraction.

I sighed out, "Well...I have a headache and could use a bath. You'll be alright if I head back?"

"Of course." He smirked conspiratorially as I rose. "Asterie—if he breaks your heart, I will delight in breaking every bone in his body."

Emmerick's eyes went lethally dark. The jovial boy who had swung helplessly at Specters, taught me to ride a horse and saved me from a Lynx would no doubt defend me.

I was not without attachments—Emmerick was a friend.

"How brutal, brotherly and completely unnecessary." My tone became playful and lighter than I'd ever heard. I stole one last sip of wine before standing. "If it comes to it, I have a few tricks for that up my sleeve."

"I would put a good coin on that."

"Goodnight, Em."

The song of passing light-bringers greeted me as my boots hit the stoop outside the pub. I stepped down into the crowd and was ushered by the flow of bodies moving through the streets. The night air cleared my mind, and the hymns of those celebrating were a welcome contradiction to my warring thoughts.

My muscles ached from the full day of travel. I'd rushed my bath earlier and was eager to return to the inn for another. Yet the celebrations looked so joyous—*just a moment would be good for me.*

I happily fell into stride behind a young family. Baskets of candlesticks were worn on each of the children's arms. One child was tucked sleepily to their mother's side, and a smaller child sat atop his father's shoulders, eyes ablaze, staring with wide-eyed bewilderment at the glowing streets. My wine-softened vision followed the child's eyeline. Thousands of candles lit the doorsteps of shops, flats and establishments. It *was* mesmerizing.

A tug on my dress made me look down.

The older child, a girl no more than six, grasped the dark blue linen of my dress and held a candle up to me. My eyes widened—I'd never actually been around children, and I didn't know how to react.

Crouching down to her level, I awkwardly asked, "For me?"

Her tiny curl-topped head nodded. "For the Source of Sun, Astros—to win his favor. He rests at night only because it isn't bright enough, so we must wake him up. He and the stars protect us from the Black Moon Prince."

Her words made a lump grow in my throat—such steadfast belief in forgotten idols that no longer gifted them immortality or Source magic. Everyone could learn a simple spell or two, but for mortals, magic was always faulty, fickle and risky. It took years of training for a mortal or immortal without Source power to master even the simplest of charms.

"Thank you. I will leave it somewhere special for the Sun," I promised.

The Black Moon Prince was not a name used in the towers.

"But who is the Black Moon—"

The child was pulled away by her mother, who cast a wide smile over her shoulder at me as they continued along and began a new carol into the night.

The chorus of celebration traveled east, past what looked to be a temple. It surprised me that such an old house of worship still stood—it looked ancient. Something made me stop at the temple and look up. Its spires were five stories tall and covered in intricate details of carved limestone embellishments and statues.

Practicing the old religions of the Brennac or Phynnic, or believing in the Sources, was not outlawed in the Order. Yet. But the old religions had grown less common over the centuries as magic waned.

The crowd continued, stopping at each doorway, each lit candle adding to the glow. My feet were rooted as I continued to study the temple architecture.

"Enter."

I flinched.

That voice again.

My hand was on the temple door before thinking twice. I'd never entered a place of worship before. Each step against the slick marble ground echoed against the ornate domed roof. The stone ceiling was carved with the same rising sun symbol I'd seen on the celebration bunting banners. The space was mostly empty save for kneeling stools around the perimeter and a large sunstone at the center of the room on a pedestal.

As I approached the sunstone, it began to glow a golden hue as though responding to my nearness. *A defense, maybe? Interesting.*

"It has been a long time since a descendant of the Stars has been in this temple."

Sources, save me.

I reached for the dagger in my boot, in a house of *worship* of all places. I met the silver stare of what I assumed to be a Divine. His skin was dark, a contrast to the gray hairs that framed his face at the temples.

His kind eyes showed amusement. "You are safe here, High Enchantress. Welcome to the House of Astros."

So he knew who I was. I shivered to think of how.

He lifted a finger to a darkened stained glass window. I could make out the picture of a man holding up the sun. "Did you know that the Source Origin Asterie was thought to be Astros' sister?"

I shook my head. "I haven't heard that one," I answered. "But I've heard of this place. It is an old myth. It was said to be where the Source Origin of the Sun lived."

The Divine chuckled. "So you believe the place where you stand now is a myth?"

My formality was exhausted. "That wouldn't be possible," I blurted. "This place would have stood before the Old World. And that assumes the Source Origins *ever* walked the lands."

"So you believe they did not?"

Was he going to keep answering my questions with questions? That was *my* strategy. He seemed to sense my hesitation and smiled warmly as he approached the sunstone.

"For the millennia the Sun has granted me, this building has stood," he said with unnerving calm.

For an immortal to age at all past their thirtieth year, they had to be *old,* and he looked to be in his late fifties, healthy and mobile. *Thousands of years old.*

He took my silence as a reason to carry on. "Before Henosis or the Corridors, before Brennax or Phynx, this was a land growing into its magic. The Sources once walked the lands, embodying the sun, the stars, the sea, the soil and more. They were called the Origins."

My brow creased.

He cleared his throat. "The Source Origins' magic was tethered to the elements. They were beautiful and vibrant. But they were also wild and feral folk, lawless and fickle. They toyed with mortals for fun and gifted their powers only to the noblest and most loyal of them.

"But the Source Origins could only give so much magic before they could no longer hold a human form. So, rarely did this gift fall onto humans. To be disembodied, pushed into a place *in between*—that frightened them."

My eyes widened. This was not what I was taught, what the Sisterhood preached. The Sisterhood acknowledged the Sources only as vast pools of power, not at all sentient as the Divine described. But I found myself drawing closer to him, awaiting more stories woven from his beliefs. He held a hand to me and led me to a series of etched stone drawings on the walls.

"What do these tell the story of?"

Each of the drawings grew more morbid and gruesome than the last.

"The Reverists were another set of magic-wielders, a different bloodline. Their magic was not drawn from external elements but from the mind itself. They were mortal only in lifespan, and they are the originators of your gift as an Oracle."

His tone grew so impassioned that the hairs on my neck stood.

"The Reverists were a strong lot. Dream Walkers, Empaths, Oracles...but a Reverist, a pure-blooded Reverist...they could completely control the mind and bend it to their whim and desire. To simply be near one put you in danger of their influence."

Swallowing hard, I allowed him to lead me down the row of images. One carving stuck out as particularly violent. It showed the

Sources being placed under a large slab and the Reverists standing upon the slab as those below were trapped and crushed.

"There was peace for a long time, but the Reverists craved immortality, something only the Source Origins could grant them. After centuries of quarreling, the Reverists attacked the minds of *every* Source power in these lands."

My heart was beating quickly, on edge from the story—I'd never had an explanation for how one could have both Reverist abilities and Source magic. It was as though something fell into place in my understanding of my own magic.

"The Reverists used tricks of the mind to get the Sources to give away all of the power in their veins. Thus, ridding this world of the Source Origins and casting them into that in-between place they feared.

"The Reverists were granted the gifts of the Sources and immortality. But with each generation, their Source magic diminished."

I tilted my head. "But Source magic was strong before the Order."

"Nothing compared to what it used to be."

"Because the Origins no longer walk the lands to gift their magic onto others?" I asked

He shrugged. "Some of them don't."

I balked, "What do you mean *some* of them?"

"The rarest Source magic is water because the Source Origin Aquas escaped his ill fate by sinking to the bottom of the ocean—so I suppose he doesn't walk, he swims. The Death Origin survived as well, of course. And then some say the Shadow Origin struck a bargain with his half brother Death to live as well."

My mind rolled around the information that he shared.

Origins walking the realm, the rise of the Reverists, the peculiar words of the young child outside.

"The people outside think they protect this place from a Black Moon Prince—who was he?" I asked.

The Divine's face fell. "The Black Moon Prince led the Reverists. He was both the Source Origin of Death *and* a Reverist. The only known warlock in history to be purely both. After the Reverists defeated the Sources, he turned on them, killing every pure Reverist. He was never seen again."

I stared at that image of the Source Origins beneath the slab, being pressed out of this world. My heart hung heavy.

I could not imagine a world where Source Origins still walked the land, commanding mortals. Nor could I imagine the chaos the Reverists' power could bring to Henosis.

"Thank you for sharing this with me, are you—" My breath sucked in.

The Divine was gone—without a sound, without feeling him move. *Vanished.*

With one last look over my shoulder at the pictures carved in stone, I ran out of the temple as fast as my feet would carry me. But, before running toward the inn, I halted with a strange urge to look up.

There was a single candle burning in the top spire, and a dark figure stepped up to the window.

It was just a trick.

I tried to tell myself that there was no importance to a story told by a man of worship, in a temple. It was just another legend of Henosis—*just another tale woven to offer an understanding of our existence.*

Though just in case the Source Origin of the Sun was watching, I knelt down and lit the candle that I'd been given and placed it on the temple steps among the other glimmering flames.

"May you protect those who need the light," I whispered into the night to no one. Though maybe Astros truly had once walked the lands, maybe he listened now.

The three stone tubs of the communal bathroom at the inn were empty. *Thank the Sources.* With what little strength remained, I dragged a wooden divider over to the tub. Even though it was late enough that I doubted anyone would enter.

My stomach growled, reminding me that most were getting heavy with food and drink. The wine, paired with my experience at the temple, still made my head spin. I kicked off my linen dress and knotted my already clean hair above my head. Baths had always helped me feel centered—like the water could wash away the troubles of a long day.

Someone had left a bushel of dried lavender behind. As the tub filled, I sprinkled the dried petals into the swirling pool and lowered myself in. Only the light from a few dim lanterns lit the room, and it was the perfect place to reflect on what mattered.

Get the warlock to the Queen.

Figure out where the threat was coming from.

Save Henosis.

It wasn't a simple checklist.

Did the Black Moon Prince have something to do with this? I shook that thought—*just a tall tale.*

More intrusively, the thought of Fen touching that woman, leaving with her—it was making an uncomfortable tightness grow in my chest. It didn't make sense why I was so upset. He wasn't mine to be jealous over. Who he spent his time with was none of my concern.

My mind quickly wandered to places it shouldn't. *What was Fen doing with her now? Where was he touching her, kissing her? Would he have the same desperate passion he had when he'd kissed me earlier?*

And his words burned into my mind, filling me with heat and longing. "*I would give you all the gratifying distractions your body could take.*" My fingers had just slid between my thighs when a knock came at the communal bathroom door.

CHAPTER 17
FENRIS

After walking the no-name brunette back to her inn on the other side of Belray, I said goodnight at the door. She offered me a few choice words that felt fitting. *"Dallying asshole"* had been my favorite.

I walked back to the pub, thinking of a dark-haired enchantress that I could not shake—that hungry look beneath the veil of her lashes before she kissed me, her full lips sipping wine as she glared at me over the glass. I'd take her passion and her fury and everything between them.

'Dallying asshole'—indeed.

Emmerick sat alone at the bar, sipping ale and chatting up the barkeep. I approached him and gripped one of his obnoxiously broad shoulders—the boy was built like a giant. Before I had a chance to speak, he turned.

"She said she felt like a bath. Something about a headache." He raised his eyebrows. "You were going to ask me where she was, right?"

I gripped the boy's shoulder even tighter before releasing him. "You're sharper than you look. Most brutes I know are dumber than you."

"Most immortals that I know are taller than you."

I grunted a laugh at his jab. "Fair."

I couldn't deny him some satisfaction in figuring out my buttons. The boy was insufferable, and yet I couldn't help liking him. Just an ounce. Just because Asterie seemed to.

"And, speaking of intelligence, aren't immortals supposed to be wise from their *years* of experience?" Emmerick taunted.

I let my forearms rest on the bar, waiting for his next blow. "Get on with it, boy *Knight*."

He shot me an unaffected smirk. "Flaunting pretty women on your arm while trying to win someone else over seems counterproductive. She left upset before she ate anything."

Fuck. I nodded slowly, finally fully comprehending what a prick I had been. The Commander hunched over the bar—his eyes glassy.

"If I could hold the woman I love for even a *minute*." Emmerick took another chug before offering me a seat next to him. "I wouldn't be so stupid as to pull a stunt like that—you half-wit."

More name-calling. "No one said a thing about love. We've known each other a few weeks." I reasoned that was the right answer, though none of my thoughts concerning Asterie felt casual either.

The Commander was right about one thing, though. I'd gone too far in making Asterie jealous and playing stupid games. She'd been locked away by the Sisterhood without ever experiencing the games of selfish, stupid men like me. It left an ugly feeling in my gut that I'd hurt her.

Asterie represented all the things that made my blood boil in anger. *Oppression. Fanaticism.* Yet my blood heated in her presence in unwholesome, idiotic, longing ways.

"A bath?" I filled the silence. "She looked pretty clean to me."

"I'm not her keeper."

Emmerick lifted his palms in defense. Seeing him with ale-hazed eyes and a loose tongue was entertaining. If not so eager to find Asterie, I might have stayed and had a drink with him to see his mannerisms change further.

"I should go and apologize," I said

"It's your funeral." The boy patted my shoulder. "But sure, go ahead and try. Maybe wait until she's out of the bath."

A smirk crept onto my face. "Where would be the fun in that?"

The Commander rolled his eyes. "Like I said...your funeral."

When I returned to the inn, a light was still on in the kitchens. I caught a kind maid who was baking bread for the following day. At first, she refused, but after a couple placating compliments and a dazzling smile, she relented.

She made me promise to return the tarnished silver tray, lest I want to lose a hand, before supplying me with an abundant array of bread, still warm from the oven, and an accompaniment of hard cheeses.

By the time I knocked on the communal bathroom door, I'd nearly lost my nerve to apologize. There was no answer, so I pushed open the wood door, which creaked on its hinges. My feet stayed planted outside while I whispered into the dimly lit room.

"Asterie?" I heard the water splash. "It's Fen."

"I'm bathing," she hissed.

"I'm aware. I won't look—I promise." I paused, reeling for anything to explain my sudden urge to see her. "Can we talk? I brought you a cheese tray—Emmerick said you didn't eat."

"You want to come in while I'm bathing...to talk?"

There was no answer to her skepticism that didn't make me sound completely insane. "That's a normal thing to do—it's a communal bath. There are multiple tubs in there, are there not?"

"Fine."

Relieved, I slipped through the door, my back to her, and placed the tray on a vanity. I knew where I'd heard her voice come from—it was as though my body knew exactly where hers was without setting eyes on her.

I stepped backward until the stone hit the back of my legs then slid down next to the tub. Letting my knees bend, I draped my arms over them. There were such delectable smells of warmed lavender behind me, and I could feel the warmth of the water kiss the back of my neck.

"You're sure you are an enchantress and not a Siren?" I asked.

The water shifted behind me. "Yes. Why?" She'd taken my words seriously—they had offended her.

"It was a joke. Since Sirens lure sailors to their death."

I let my shoulders rest back against the stone tub, trying not to think about the fact she was nude, bathing, inches from me. Somehow, it felt more vulnerable to be fully dressed next to her and unable to successfully land a single flirtatious line.

The water shifted again. My imagination ran wild.

"I didn't lure you here. You let yourself in to speak your nonsense."

I cracked a smile. "My 'nonsense'..."

She shifted again. The beautiful sound of water dripping and rippling off her was enough to make my throat tighten.

"Do you think it's nonsense that I am drawn to you?"

She was quiet momentarily. "No, I don't think that's nonsense."

"Then what is?"

"Your talk of Sirens—I'm not one, and you're no sailor. And I'm not going to drown you."

I swallowed. Hard. "What is this game we're playing?"

"What do you mean?" she answered in that voice of damned false neutrality.

"You kissed me like you wanted me. Then you pushed me away."

Was this line of conversation a smart idea? She'd already rejected me once that day. Regardless of one interested look across a crowded pub, that fact remained.

She had made it clear she wouldn't let anything happen between us.

"Wanting isn't something I should do. And I'm not playing any games," she said.

"*'Should'* is the keyword, but do you or don't you?" I pressed her.

"What are you asking me, Fen?" The rasp in her voice was sultry yet restrained. She was still holding back. Still *pretending*.

"I think you want me." My words landed boldly. "But you're scared to let yourself. Why?"

"I already told you at your cabin—I find you attractive. But my loyalty will always lay with what's right for the realm." Her voice was less sure this time, less measured.

"Well, that feeling is very mutual. You're the most beautiful woman I've ever seen. But I didn't ask you what the realm needs."

She should tell me to go, to get out of that bath chamber and leave her alone.

"What do you *want* from me, Asterie?"

There was a pause as though she was thinking, and the water went still. "I want you to look at me."

I stilled, losing the ability to draw breath. "Is this a figurative request, or are you asking me to look at you right now?"

The water shifted.

Torturous, tempting sound.

"Now." Her voice was soft but sure.

My torso pivoted. My eyes met hers, and I didn't dare let my gaze wander further down. *Not yet.* The lamplight danced over her face, and every captivating feature radiated in its glow.

"Now, I want you to tell me what you did with her." It was a quiet rasp.

"Who?" No one existed but her.

"The woman earlier." She tried to suppress a wounded tone. Guilt settled in my chest again—toying with her had truly hurt her. "I'd like to know what you did together. Explain it to me."

"As much as I would like to say that I maintained my reputation as a rogue, I have to admit that I did nothing with her."

"Why?"

"Because she wasn't you."

There it was, bare, flat in front of her, to stomp on if she pleased.

"And I'm not too much of a 'dallying asshole' or 'half-wit' to accept that I want *you*."

She contemplated that momentarily, only a hint of curiosity shining in those darkly alluring eyes. *So hard to read.* "Then tell me what you would have done? If it were me." She captured her bottom lip with her teeth.

It was a challenge. She was flipping my games back on me, and I would happily play along. I answered, "If it had been you...I wouldn't have been able to keep my hands off you. For starters."

Her head tilted, lips parting in thought before she spoke again. "Then why are your hands not on me now?"

I swallowed my last ounce of doubt. Asterie did want me, regardless of how unworthy I was of her desire. "You want me to touch you, Asterie?" At my drawl, the corners of her mouth upturned slightly, and she nodded.

Look at her. Touch her. Oh, the places I could let my mind wander to.

I lifted myself onto a footstool that was topped with soap. The sweet-scented blocks tumbled to the ground with a clatter. It was a better angle to see her from, *to touch her* from. Water droplets hung from her still-parted lips—I longed to kiss them away. Instead, my thumb wiped them gently, and her eyes fluttered closed at the simple touch.

As I took her in, nothing was obstructing my view of where her body met the water. The peaks of her breasts were just above the surface—nipples taught. A lump grew in my throat, and my breath sucked in when I saw where one of her hands had wandered. She palmed herself with delicate fingers between her thighs—*how long had she been touching herself?* The corners of my mouth twisted upward.

"Now, I'm going to need you to *say it*...tell me what you want from me, my strange beauty."

All the reasons to leave tumbled through my head. Starting with the power that burned in her—I recognized it. No good could come from me touching her except the satisfaction of seeing pleasure wrung from her body.

But that seemed like enough reason to stay because I *was* a "dallying asshole" and a "half-wit," after all.

"I want you to touch me." Her breathy plea was all it took to break my resistance—it broke all reason and logic. *You can touch her. It wouldn't mean anything more than it would have with that brunette from the pub.*

I let my hand trail down her chin. Her lips parted, and her gaze softened—*how could she want me?* I didn't feel remotely worthy of putting my hands on her. Her head relaxed against the tub's edge, and she looked at me expectantly.

My finger trailed further down the soft skin of her neck and chest. She gasped quietly when I cupped a breast in my hand. Her rapid heartbeat beneath my palm betrayed that infuriating calm she showed the world.

I gently rolled her nipple between my thumb and index finger. She arched toward my touch in response and released a torturous whimper. It made me want to do it again and again. She moved to brace her hands on the sides of the tub.

"No, no. Keep touching yourself for me." It came out as a purred demand. When she complied, it took all my restraint not to intervene.

I didn't care about my sleeves anymore. I let my other hand dip under the water to rove over Asterie's torso. I wanted to memorize every inch of her. She was entirely exposed to me—curved waist, a tousle of dark hair between ample thighs distorted in the ripples of the water.

"You look perfect. But we can stop—tell me if you want to stop." *Please don't tell me to stop*—is what I wanted to say. But I wouldn't press this any further if she told me to leave.

"No, don't stop." She shook her head with another short-breathed gasp as her fingers worked in tight circles.

"Tell me, Asterie—where else do you want me to touch you?" I watched her work herself up.

"Down there," she whispered.

"Oh, I'd gladly let you ride my hand, my beauty," I drawled. "But I'm going to need you to beg me first...you don't want to have to keep doing that yourself now, do you?"

Her eyes widened, but they lit from within. It excited her. *I was a fucking goner.*

One of my hands began to trail down further. Asterie's legs readily parted for me, and I didn't complain when she reached for the tub's edge to hold onto it this time. I trailed my hand over the dark hairs at her center and stopped—she let out a low whimper, making me smirk.

"*How much* do you want me to touch you there?"

"Badly."

The impatience in her words only made my smirk deepen.

"*Fine.* Please, Fen. Please."

At those words, I finally let my fingers part her. She sank back, eyes closed and hands gripping the tub's sides. It gave her enough leverage to rise to meet my touch as my fingers worked against her.

"No, no, Asterie...you're going to need to keep your eyes on me." Her eyes popped open. "I want to watch you come undone."

She writhed against my hand. Seeing her like this caused me to harden painfully against the seam of my breeches. To enjoy her hands on me, to taste her, to be inside this woman—it would all be a mistake, but one I'd happily die to make.

When one finger slipped inside her, I wanted to swallow the delectable moan she let out. I could burst in my breeches just from the sound alone. I slowly worked in and out, still holding one breast firmly.

She bucked against the motion with parted lips. I slipped in a second finger and curved them up toward her navel. She seemed to grow more desperate and hurried. *She's close.*

She held my gaze with desperation as she gasped, "Fen, I'm going..."

She was going to alright, and it was fucking beautiful. Her expression cracked as she constricted around my fingers. She couldn't stifle the guttural cry of pleasure. I'm sure the nearby rooms heard it, too. But, shamelessly, I wanted them to.

I let her rock against my hand until every muscle in her body relaxed. She seemed disoriented and satiated.

"I could watch your release all night."

Those full lips were still parted and showed the slight gap in her front teeth. Yet she said nothing, which had panic rising in my chest.

"Talk to me..." I urged softly.

Abruptly, Asterie grabbed me by the front of my tunic. I caught the tub's sides to avoid being pulled in. The front of my shirt slapped the water as she captured my lips with hers, claiming me for the second time that day. Her lips parted mine—she tasted of red wine and *power*. Her kiss felt electric, like the blue flame she yielded.

She could pull me in and drown me like the Siren I'd joked she was, and I'd die happy having seen her release every ounce of tension.

"One of you will surrender to the other..." a voice that was not Asterie's hissed into my ear, startling me stiff. Judging by the fact that Asterie's kiss grew deeper, she hadn't heard it.

The voice was meant for me alone.

I lifted away from her hastily, to my disappointment and her confusion. The voice had been so close, the same one I'd heard in the field, the same one I'd heard at the cabin after meeting her.

Surrender. I had already surrendered myself to an enchantress once, and it had been the wrong choice. My blood ran cold at the thought of doing it again.

"Goodnight, Asterie." It came out with strangled finality.

She was out of breath and wordless, staring up at me and looking devastatingly wounded by my sudden dismissal. My mind screamed—*get out, get out before you end up in that tub with her.*

My legs couldn't carry me out of the bathing chamber quickly enough, and I let the door slam shut behind me.

It was best to leave before doing anything more stupid than I already had.

Her words from earlier that day echoed back to me.

"That just isn't how this story ends."

CHAPTER 18
ASTERIE

The sun rose the next day with agonizing brightness. Its rays cast light through the mud-colored curtains. My night had been spent with my head buried under the covers, wholly mortified by my actions. The things I had *said* to him, what I had *asked* for.

I barely knew him and yet had easily opened myself up to him. *Such a damned fool.* Yet the feeling of his hands on my skin had lingered and made my toes curl. He'd left me there, flustered and confused. I should have known he was more interested in the conquest than in me, but I couldn't dispel the hurt that grew in my gut.

Stupid, stupid, stupid.

I was no genteel maiden. Men had taken me before. But he hadn't *taken* anything from me—he'd given me release without expecting anything in return. That was the most mind-boggling of it all. *Was it a display of power, of will?*

I dreaded traveling with him today. This was precisely the reason the Sisterhood had a stringent no-fraternization policy. No bonds. No connections. No friends. No *lovers.* Not that Fen was any of those—*no,* he was a war criminal and in our charge to be escorted to Luz. That was *all.*

Curiosity and wine wouldn't make a fool of me twice.

I braided my hair over my shoulder in an intricate fishtail then dressed in the breeches and tunic that I'd been able to launder at Fenris' cabin. While slipping my black robe over my shoulders, I noticed the frayed edge where my Sisterhood patch had once been. I hadn't asked for it back after what I witnessed in Kullworth.

My pack was ready, but I paced the small quarters for another twenty minutes to compose myself before finally deciding it was time to go downstairs and face him. *There is no way out of this now.*

A knock startled me out of my worried thoughts.

"It's just me." Fen's voice was cheery and bright. *Just him.* Panic rose as I flung the door open.

"My behavior was inappropriate last night," I blurted.

He raised his thick auburn brows. *Why did he look* so *good today?* He was dressed in a dark green tunic and black breeches that clung to his athletic frame. His waves were combed back to perfection, and that infuriating, knowing smirk made my cheeks flush. He had even tamed his beard—it was now neatly trimmed tighter to his face. It reshaped his jawline in the most appealing way.

"Oh, it was *very* inappropriate, wasn't it?" he teased, seeming to enjoy every second of my squirming. "These are for you—you missed breakfast." He lifted a checkered cloth napkin containing sweet bread and a scone and placed it in my hands.

He eyed the desk behind me where the tray sat, empty. I'd indulged in the breads and cheeses after he'd left me reeling in anxious disbelief.

"Also, I promised a kitchen maid I'd return that tray. She said she would take my hand for the theft if I didn't." My cheeks were hot as he brushed past me to retrieve the tray. "Now that you know what these hands are capable of"—he wiggled the fingers on his free hand—"I'm sure you're in full support of me not losing one."

My mouth hung open at his lax choice of words. His nonchalant and chipper behavior this morning began to add up. *I was just a conquest.* He knew he could have me, which took the fun out of the chase. My lips drew into a line, and my body straightened.

Disappointment slipped easily into anger—it was a kinder emotion than the one that had me recognizing something I didn't want to. *I liked Fenris in ways that I should not. I am the realm's biggest fool.*

It should have brought relief that what transpired the night before was simply a game to him. It should mean nothing—it *did* mean nothing. But there was a tightness in my chest as he stepped out of my bedroom, turning back to look at me. I hated that my eyes roved over him.

"Never again," I ground out between my teeth.

Fen chuckled and made a point of trailing his stare down my body, as though telling me that he'd caught me doing the same. "Whatever you say." The flirtatious drawl was thrown over his shoulder. He'd already headed down the stairs before I could fully master my composure to respond. It seemed the warlock and I were back to the start.

Playing games.

The inn's carpets were grayed in high-traffic areas, and a drunk lay asleep at the door with a stein still in hand. The morning sunlight cracked through the window, casting shadows on the wood paneling. I missed the stone and iron, the strength and stability, of my tower. But I didn't miss *living* in the tower. *I would take hundreds more nights in a meager inn like this one—worn curtains, lumpy mattress and all.*

Traitorous thoughts.

Emmerick was at the bottom of the steps, appearing a bit more disheveled than I'd seen him look before. His eyes were red, and his clothes rumpled.

"Get a good night's rest?" Emmerick asked with amusement.

Was there no propriety or shame among these two? "What did he tell you?" I snapped.

"He didn't have to—your defensive tone tells me everything I need *or want* to know. Plus, he returned late last night and spent the morning preening himself."

Fen rounded the corner and slapped the Commander on the back, not casting me more than a glance.

"Has the ale made you a bit groggy this morning?" Fenris spoke loudly into Emmerick's ear. The Commander winced.

I fought the sting of Fen's dismissal. I could not allow more cracks to form in my foundation, and I could not let him seep into my emotions.

"I've got us a carriage ride to the estate—the roads are still relatively intact. I'm told that the ruins and orchard are somewhat of a visitor's attraction nowadays," Fenris explained as we left the inn.

Emmerick stepped up into the passenger seat of the carriage first and held a hand out to take my pack. I handed it to him but ignored Fenris' offered hand to help me up into the seat.

Letting an icy calm wash over my face, I pulled myself up and scooted around Emmerick to seat him between us.

Two hours later, the carriage stuttered to a stop in front of an arched iron gate that read "LAMOREAUX." The driver banged on the roof to signal we'd arrived. We piled out of the carriage with our packs before Fen waved the driver off.

Beyond the gate and down a tree-framed path stood a behemoth limestone estate. The right side walls were decayed and crumbling, and the roof was barely present—but otherwise, much of the outer structural walls stood. Ivy crept up the stone—when left untrimmed, the harsh plant could overtake even the strongest structures.

There was nothing but vast countryside and orchards to look out upon, along with a large pond on the east side of the property fed by a quaint waterfall. In its prime, this place would have been a secluded paradise just close enough to town.

I glanced over at Fen, who seemed transfixed on the estate.

"What is this place?"

"Home," he answered. My eyes settled on the name curled into the iron archway.

"Your surname?" I asked.

Emmerick stepped behind me, helping to secure my pack over my shoulders.

"Fenris Lamoreaux...quite a mouthful," Emmerick teased.

Fen only smirked. It seemed the Commander had grown on him—when that had happened was a mystery.

"Interesting. I never use my surname," I mused before looking at Emmerick. I hadn't heard him refer to himself with a surname either and now I wondered.

"Except when it was least convenient for us," Emmerick teased.

I grimaced. "What's your surname?" This time, my question was directed at Emmerick, who rubbed the back of his neck uncomfortably.

"Faulker."

Fen laughed heartily. "No," he said with a slap of his knee. "How did you survive as a schoolboy?"

Emmerick raised an eyebrow of challenge in Fen's direction. "I got *bigger* than everyone else. But that's why I go by Sir Emmerick."

"And not Sir Faulker." Fenris howled—his amusement couldn't be contained much to Emmerick's dismay. "No wonder you're such a fucker, Faulker."

I left them to their light-hearted quarrel, compelled to enter the gate. It was as though the wind urged me toward the orchard of plum trees that spanned for miles. Fruit hung from the trees, plump and ripe for picking. My fingers stilled before touching one of the tree's burgundy offerings.

"These trees, who maintains them?" I yelled the question over my shoulder. "Plum trees only live a few dozen years at most..."

"My family charmed the orchard. The fruit from the trees never rots, even when picked. The trees are forever bountiful—it's an ancient spell. Lost in the purges of scrolls during the Great Wars."

Fen continued, "They were lords, my parents. They were both powerful enough to be threats to this new world. They wielded dark magic...but they were peaceful."

Dark magic-wielders who used Death or Shadows for good? It hadn't ever been done. At least, not to my knowledge.

"My mother used to make sacrifices every year. Usually, a cow from our herd. Each time, using dark magic to help feed the needy. She enchanted this orchard to feed Belray one cold winter when food stores ran very low. Hundreds would have died. It took a herd of twenty cows to wield this much dark magic. She didn't care about the cost if it helped someone. She didn't care whether it would pose a risk of becoming a target for the Phynnic either. Which it did ultimately."

"She sounds like a lovely woman," I mused.

"She was," Fen corrected. His sadness was potent. "An old friend visited me once. She told me my parents had lost their heads for these trees, for their use of dark magic here. Before then, I had always hoped they had made it to the Wastelands after the Great Wars and found some way to survive."

The weight of his words struck me. I had spent many years trying to counteract the use of all magic in the realm. Controlling the spread, doling out judgment to those who disobeyed the Order, to ensure it never grew strong in the Corridors of Henosis as it had been in the Old World. It may not have been me who killed his family, yet I would have condoned it as necessary just weeks ago. *My Sisters would have deemed it necessary.*

That thought sent a chill down my spine.

The weight of my own guilt made me dizzy. My hand found the tree trunk between the bountiful branches of plums to balance myself. When I touched the rough bark, my body crumpled under the strength of a conjured image so vivid it flooded every crevice of my senses.

I sat clutching that tree, but Fenris and Emmerick were nowhere to be seen.

"Fen? Emmerick?" I called to them, but my voice sounded like a ripple through water. I could only wander and observe in this unwelcome vision.

Getting to my feet, I stepped around the tree to see an ivory-skinned woman clutching a branch on the other side. She stood there with the grand estate behind her in its former glory, making a beautiful backdrop of ivy-laden stone. The woman had long dark hair like mine and a similar frame—wider than average hips, tapered waist, narrow shoulders. Was that me? No, she wore a torn tunic and tattered skirts with an apron. A farm worker. She was shaking the branch and capturing fallen fruit into her apron pockets.

The woman glanced around nervously.

A sweetly poisonous voice called to her as she stepped away from the tree. "What is the name of the thief who steals from this orchard?"

The dark-haired woman stilled as Firose's petite figure approached from the estate's arched gate. A golden silk robe trailed behind my Sister, her hair was braided into a crown, her small nose tipped up and her rosy lips curved in a cruel smile.

I wanted to ask her why she was in Fenris' family orchard but had no voice.

"Adalasia...Addie Bennett. My lady, High Enchantress Firose."
Adalasia Bennett.

I was looking at my birth mother; how did I not see it immedi-ately? *Our matching chin, nose and eyes. I was a portrait of her, only she was more beautiful than I'd ever imagined.*

Adalasia fell to her knees. The plums fell from her apron and scattered to the ground around her tattered skirts.

"My lady, I apologize. My husband, he is growing weak with hunger. It will never happen again. I promise you. I promise—"

"I could have you hung in the town square." Firose circled my mother like a Lynx. "You will pay for the fruit with your life now."

"No! Please," my mother begged.

Firose looked down at her with calculation and interest. It was the same expression she sometimes gave me when I showed her my blue flames or conjured something from the moonstone.

"If you are unwilling to die for your crimes, then let's make a bargain," Firose cooed. "You will agree to forfeit your firstborn to me, or you meet Death today. The choice is yours."

My mother's hands met the ground at Firose's feet. "Please, I will work more hours for no pay—I will do anything you wish."

Firose only deepened her smile. "I told you my conditions."

Adalasia's shoulders crumpled as she heaved out a teary question. "Is there no other payment you will accept? What do you need with the child of a commoner?"

Firose tilted her head. "We have never met, Mrs. Bennett. Nor does anyone know that I took ownership of this estate. Yet you called me by my name. Did you not?"

My mother stilled as if realizing her own mistake.

"Reverist abilities are quite rare nowadays." Firose shrugged. "Rare enough to be worth my interest."

My mother looked up at Firose with tear-soaked cheeks. "You should have what you ask. I'll swear it in blood. My husband—he's ill and needs me now, but my child shall serve the debt."

Firose crouched before her and handed my mother a dagger. "Very well then."

Adalasia made a small cut in her palm and let the blood drop to the grass below their feet. "I swear to forfeit my firstborn child and her power to the owner of the orchard I have stolen from." Adalasia sobbed.

Firose smiled. "Congratulations, Mrs. Bennett...you are expecting."

My mother's mouth hung open, her eyes were bloodshot and her tear-soaked cheeks turned red.

"Ah, you did not know yet."

Firose stood. Then she laughed down at my mother like it was all a wicked game to her. The whole ordeal—doling out a punishment so cruel for such a minor crime.

I began to step away from them as my mother bawled. Firose looked right at me as though seeing me there. My heart pounded. A vision, it's a vision...she can't see you.

But Firose's face contorted into a look so blood-chilling that I was convinced otherwise. She didn't look like my Sister any longer. For a flash, she wore the face of another—male, cruel, with a power that reached out to me like an all-consuming wave of oil.

Out, out. *I needed to get out of there, away from those fateful fruits and the horror of my mother's bargain with Firose or whatever this being was.*

My return to consciousness was abrupt. It felt like pieces of me getting stitched back together. With a gasp, my hands scrambled to find hold of something real. The first thing they found was the front of Fen's shirt. He sat with his legs splayed out in front of him in the grass and was cradling me across his lap, supporting my head from lobbing backward.

Emmerick knelt beside us and let out a relieved sigh. "Peace Prevail, woman...we thought you were dead. You were so cold."

I regained focus, letting my attention settle on Fen's face. Panic, fear and relief washed over his features and outweighed any feigned indifference he had shown me that morning. Van paced nearby; *had I drawn him out?* The beast approached and laid his head between his front feet at my boots, wide-eyed and awaiting direction. His tail wagged gently.

"Asterie." Fen's voice was soft and pulled me back to this reality—where my mother was dead and this orchard stood amongst ruins. My head buried into Fen's shoulder, and tears poured onto his cloak. My breath heaved out unevenly as the emotions choked away my ability to intake air. I sobbed and relaxed into the warmth of his body.

The sorceress, from the legend—she was real. She was *Firose.*

It was a real story. My mother's story. My story. The Sisterhood hadn't rescued me...they'd *taken* me. Firose had a claim on me, on my power.

Fen stiffened at first, but then his arms wrapped around my shoulders and drew me closer to him. Neither of them spoke until my sobs subsided.

"Where did you go?" Fenris whispered gently into my hair, still holding me to him. It somehow felt more intimate than the night prior—with my expelling tears like rain and unable to compose myself.

Through my tear-blurred vision, I could see Emmerick over Fen's shoulder, his brow creased in concern.

"She was here...my birth mother. She worked here." I knew it sounded crazy.

"This estate would have been abandoned four hundred years ago. Your mother wouldn't have been alive yet." Fen reasoned gently into my hair before letting his lips rest there. The beat of his heart was a rhythmic reminder that I was not alone.

"She was not working for your family. She worked for Firose. Firose owned the orchard—my mother, she made a bargain with her." The words were hard to get out. "For me, she agreed to give me up, and my power."

Fen stiffened, causing me to pull back and look at him as he turned ghostly white. Emmerick's face contorted with confusion.

"What do you mean?" The worry in Fen's tone shook me.

I explained everything my vision had shown me. His face grew paler with every word.

"What exactly does the legend say?" My question was aimed at Emmerick. "What do people think happened to me?"

The Constable cleared his throat. "Your story was one my mother told me often..." He looked out into the orchard and wove the old tale. Most of it I knew.

A sorceress made a bargain with a woman who stole from a plum orchard. She bargained for a life of servitude from the woman's firstborn child. To avoid her debt, the woman jumped off a roof in Ikanten with her child in her arms. The Star Origin opened the heavens and saved the child. The babe's father claimed the child was cursed, so the same night, he set her on a raft and let her drift out as an offering to the sea. But the sea carried the babe to Eros, where the people celebrated her. She was a child saved by stars and protected by the moonlit tides.

Emmerick continued, "The High Enchantresses took pity on the child and took her into the towers, where she was raised to become the fifth and Central Enchantress of the Corridors. Sister of the Stars. Born of starlight itself to serve Henosis. The public has never beheld the face of the child of starlight again. Until now, of course."

I had heard various versions of the story—in texts, from my Sisters. All just as far-fetched as this one. Fen looked haunted—his face had slackened as he stared out into the orchards.

"What's wrong?" My voice sounded weak from the exhaustion of crying.

Fen shook his head slowly. "Did she ever claim you, to your knowledge?" His words were soft, curious, but not prying.

"I don't know," I admitted. "If she had, couldn't she have prevented me from leaving or called me back? Firose invested so much time in my learning. Maybe she condoned this journey—maybe I needed to see this world to truly understand her plans for me."

Fen shook his head, but he didn't respond or look at me.

"Where is the Egress?" I lifted myself upright and out of his arms and dusted my breeches and robe.

"You still want to go *back*?" Fen gawked up at me from the ground. A look of betrayal crossed his features before Emmerick stood and offered him a hand.

We'd come too far now to go back, too far to let my fear of the Sisterhood lead us astray from our mission to get to Luz.

"How else will we make a quick passage to Luz? And how else will I get *answers*?" I asked.

Fen seemed uneasy, but after I took Emmerick's offered hand and got up, Fen motioned us to follow him toward the estate door. When he pushed, the rotting wood creaked on its hinges before opening in a burst of dust.

Rays of sunlight peeked through crumbled holes in the ceiling. Inside, it wasn't much to look at—furniture had long ago been removed. Structural features like fireplaces and staircases remained, but not much else discerned it from any other ruin.

Fen approached a seemingly solid wall and placed a hand against the stone. The wall glowed red beneath his fingertips and suddenly began to move.

"It only opens at the touch of members of my family," Fen explained. *No wonder he had been so sure that this Egress would not have been destroyed.*

Stone by stone, the wall opened to reveal a depthless space—a hallway so long that the eye couldn't meet its end.

"After you," Emmerick said as he leaned away from the moving brick with a furrowed brow.

I stepped inside, creating a blue flame in my palm to light the way for us.

"The 55th door on the right side," Fen said quietly. He still looked uncertain, calculating something. His posture was rigid, and any trace of warmth was gone from his demeanor.

So many doors—the hallway seemed to go on for miles.

"What were they all for?" I asked.

"During the Great Wars, when dark magic was coming under scrutiny, my family housed those looking for refuge here."

Emmerick's brow furrowed deeper. "On the night we met, you told me that you feared what would happen if those in the Wastelands were to get out—why? If dark magic-wielders weren't truly a threat, why fear them?"

"Not everyone sentenced to their fate in the Wastelands was a monster. Not everyone deserved it. Some have every right to be angry. I don't fear them for them using dark magic—I fear for you, being defenseless against it. Any form of magic can be used for evil. Just as any form can be used for good."

My mind wandered back to the plum trees outside, charmed to feed the needy, to the endless row of doors that housed refugees. *Good people, magic-wielders helping their own.* My head spun.

Luckily Fenris knew the way, and stopped when we reached the 55th door on the right, because I'd lost count.

I opened the door to reveal a small space big enough for only two of us. It would be best if I went first in case my sisters awaited on the other side. But leaving the warlock to the Commander felt risky. Fenris had agreed in blood not to run, but that magic was flimsy. *If I left them here, would he be obligated to follow?*

"I'll go first, and you two follow. Alright?" I said.

Fenris refused to meet my gaze but nodded, adding to the pit in my stomach. I turned to Emmerick.

"It will just feel like the blink of an eye, like falling into a brief sleep and waking up somewhere else."

Emmerick assessed the closet-sized room uneasily. I stepped inside, looking between the two of them. Fen was standing stiff with unreadable intensity. *Do not let this be goodbye.*

"Central Tower." Once commanded, the Egress pulled me away.

Leaving the ruin of Fen's childhood home and the charmed orchards beyond its walls, my breathing grew shallow.

I thought of Firose stepping through those orchards as though she owned them—*what connection did she have to Fen's family in order to take ownership of the estate?*

The night we had taken the truth charm together, Fen had shared that he had old friends and old enemies in the towers.

It begged me to question which enemies he kept within my ranks.

The balcony of the Central Tower seemed smaller than it once had. When I stepped into the foyer, my cheeks heated at seeing the disarray I'd left behind.

I wasn't used to having company in the tower, at least outside of the Sisters and the occasional delivery of necessities or a stray traveler.

"Didn't think to clean up without me, did you?" I mused to the tower.

The tower began shelving books quickly, sweeping away dust from shelves and blooming fresh red roses in a vase on the table at the far end of the foyer—the hue brought color to the otherwise dark space.

My heart pounded. Awaiting Fenris and Emmerick to appear on the balcony, I left the door open for them as I tidied the foyer.

Fen had hesitated in that long hallway. It had been minutes since I had arrived. They should have stepped onto the balcony only moments after me. *What was keeping them?*

The thought of Fenris being so far away cast an uneasy feeling in my gut. It felt wrong in some unexplainable way. *What is the worst he could do?* Ward the Egress so that I couldn't return and run for it. Emmerick would be no match to stop him, try as he might.

A gust of wind swept across the balcony. I turned toward the door as boots crushed dead leaves on the stone landing. My heart skipped a beat as Fen appeared in the doorway, but he hadn't seen me yet. He glanced around, assessing his surroundings and looking out at the view of the central woodlands before stepping inside. When Fen's eyes found me standing by the fireplace, his whole body relaxed. *Had he felt it too, that* wrongness?

Emmerick trailed him, looking a bit green—he stood on the balcony behind Fen with his hands on his knees as though dizzy.

"I was waiting for Van," Fen explained as he leaned in the doorway and rubbed the ink on his arm. I remembered the beast in the orchard and realized he hadn't followed us inside.

My lips curved upward. Having him here—it brought me joy. What an odd sensation to want someone in my space.

"This is where you live..." As he entered the foyer, Fen's gaze trailed up the ivy-covered iron arches and then into the greenhouse. "It suits you."

Emmerick stayed on the balcony.

"I'm sorry for the mess." I shuffled a few texts that the tower hadn't yet picked up into neat piles and lifted them off the dark leather sofas to provide sitting space.

A book slipped from my grasp and landed open at the spine. A fierce blue flame burst from its pages.

"Oh, Sources." I kicked the book shut with my boot. "Don't open any of the books. Some of them have...*experimental* safeguards."

Familiar female laughter filled the air, causing me to spin on my heels. *We weren't alone.* My blood ran cold.

"And from whom, exactly, are you safeguarding your incantations, my girl?"

Amara stood halfway down the staircase to my bedchamber with crossed arms, leaning over the curved iron railing. She leveled a skeptical yet amused look in my direction. Her hair had been left to coil to its own will instead of pulled back as she usually styled it. Her appearance was somewhat haphazard, with a non-matching robe and skirt—neither looked neatly pressed.

I felt the blood drain from my already pale face. I hadn't thought about what I would tell the Sisters when I returned. Especially Amara, who now nodded at our two guests as she rounded the steps down. She was going to need an explanation that I didn't have.

Worse yet, I didn't know whether I could trust her. The person who lovingly raised me from a babe into my adolescence in the South Tower seemed a stranger to me.

"Fenris, it's nice to see you, my old friend."

My eyebrows rose. "You two know one another?"

Amara. She was his friend. Did that bring me relief? I couldn't be sure then, but it did take an edge off of my anxieties.

"Quite well," Fen said as he crossed the room to take Amara's hand and kiss her knuckles. "Always a pleasure to see you, Amara. Just as beautiful as always."

Amara smiled warmly at the compliment, but she batted away his hand with a roll of her dark eyes. Despite that, her gaze remained soft—*she truly regarded him amicably.*

I was trying to hide my surprise, too stupefied to feel any flutter of jealousy.

Amara answered, "Still a relentless flirt, I see."

Fen gave her a playful wink. "My charms still haven't worked on this one." He threw a thumb in my direction and seared me with a wanton look, trying to make me squirm, I was sure of it. My back straightened, but my expression was unyielding.

"Well, she is a smart woman," Amara teased before placing her slender dark fingers on his shoulder. "I am happy to see you well, nonetheless."

Emmerick finally entered the foyer, and Amara's attention turned to our other guest. Her expression changed but was unreadable. *Was it pain?* Emmerick stood up straighter before realizing he should bow, and he did so with grandeur.

"High Enchantress Amara of the South Corridor, it is an honor to meet you."

"Oh, the formality…" I grumbled, throwing my head back in exaggeration but allowing them their introductions. Amara's hand dropped from Fen's shoulder before she extended it to Emmerick.

"Sir Emmerick of Luz," Amara said, suddenly turning serious. "The honor is all mine. I have heard many great things about you and all you have accomplished for the Central Corridor."

Emmerick's eyes widened at her compliment, and he bowed again.

"A baker's son, then a Knight, and now Constable—great things are in your future."

She took his hand between hers, seeming to hold it too tightly. Amara assessed the metals that adorned Emmerick's armor. Emmerick looked uncomfortable, but he allowed her to hold him there until she released him.

Unable to think of a single intelligent way to explain myself, I stalled. "I need to attend to the greenhouse. The tower can only keep up with so much."

"I will come help, Lady Asterie. We can give Lady Amara and Fenris some time to reunite." Emmerick seemed to want a moment away from the intensity of Amara's stare.

"Seriously, we're back to the formality?" I teased.

I crossed the foyer to the double glass doors that led to the greenhouse. Emmerick hurried behind me, without responding, into the glass-topped antechamber. Only a narrow path allowed us to amble through the flora.

Before I could shut the door, Amara stopped me.

"Asterie." Amara looked at me without malice. "I've been warding your tower since we realized you left. I came straight here and waited to allow you through. The others can not Egress in."

The others. "It would be best not to tell the others." Those were the words the prophecy had chosen. *Was Amara ever part of the prophecy's wishes?* I wasn't sure, but the tightness in my shoulders slackened in the hope that my dear friend was genuine.

Maybe I could trust her after all.

CHAPTER 19
FENRIS

As the boy and Asterie exited, I watched Asterie pick at her cuticles with a faraway gaze. That wall of indifference was cracking, and I wanted to know what she was thinking, to ease some of those worries somehow.

Amara and I were left alone in the foyer as the atrium door clicked shut. It was hard to hold back all the questions burning through me. When we'd worked together centuries ago, it was to even the odds—we never picked a side. We tried to keep the peace between two opposing kingdoms. Brennax and Phynx were at odds, and neither side was willing to compromise.

I wondered how my dear friend had gotten woven into this new political structure. But that was not my first priority.

"I sense something in her that I haven't felt in a very long time." I nudge my chin toward the atrium. "Care to explain?"

Amara's smile dimmed. "I feared you might. You aren't going to like the explanation."

I gave her my best 'try me' smirk and allowed myself to collapse into the oversized leather sofa, kicking my legs out. I might as well be comfortable for the blow she was inevitably about to deal me.

Amara carefully sat down next to me, hands in her lap. She turned to face me and spoke quietly. "After the attack, the rulers of Phynx decided your power should be destroyed. They ordered me to destroy the half we possessed."

"And yet," I mused, "here I stand. If you'd destroyed that part of me, then we wouldn't be having this conversation. Now, would we?"

Amara glanced toward the atrium. "I couldn't follow through. I couldn't kill you, Fen."

She looked down at her shaking hands, a frown cutting across her features.

"You were my dearest friend. If I put those powers to rest, I would lay you to rest with them. And I couldn't do that."

My heart broke as a tear slid down her umber cheek. She'd saved me.

"I let Firose think your power was destroyed, that you were dead. Let the whole realm think that. But you know I'm talented with binding spells. Instead, I bound the other half of your power to a star. It seemed the safest hiding place—out of reach even to me. Lost amongst billions, irretrievable in endless heavens."

I drew a deep breath before reaching over and wiping away the tears streaking her cheek with my thumb.

"I deserved to die, Amara." I shook my head. "I did not deserve the mercy you showed me."

Glancing toward the atrium, I watched Asterie show the boy Commander how to correctly prune the botanicals they were crouching near.

"So, how did those powers end up within her?"

My voice was even, but everything inside me was cracking. I could understand Amara's motivations for hiding my power in the stars, from Firose, from even me.

But I couldn't understand why she would give that burden to Asterie. As Amara continued to tell me what had happened, I gripped the sofa cushion.

"A young mother in Ikanten wrote to me. She was weary and exhausted in the weeks that followed labor. She was sleepless, afraid, and she told me that Firose demanded her child for a debt...I am no Oracle, but at that moment, my intuition told me I needed to go to her. So I traveled to Ikanten, against the Order."

Amara's voice had lowered to a whisper. "When I got to Ikanten, I was too late to stop the woman. I watched her fall, take her own life and attempt to take her child's with her. On impulse, I pleaded for a bargain with the Sun Origin to help rouse the Stars to help. By some miracle, my request was granted, but I was only able to send a single star. The chances of it working were one in billions. I'd never bargained with an Origin before—I didn't even know that type of magic was still *possible*."

I'd always been skeptical of whether that type of magic existed at all.

My mouth hung open at my friend's admission.

"What did you bargain?" I asked as a pit grew in my stomach.

She combed her fingers through her curls. "No price was named. No debt has been collected."

I shook my head. *That didn't sound good.* My throat felt too dry. "Does she know we are bound?"

"Asterie or Firose?"

"Either of them," I ground out.

"Neither. Firose always suspected there was something *more* to Asterie—she didn't know about her mother writing to me. Or that it was me who sent the star, or that your magic was not destroyed. I don't think she ever intended to call in the debt for Asterie, but once she realized the *miracle child of Ikanten* was the very child she had claim over...well, she claimed her. Or so we thought—until Asterie left. Firose was livid—she began having her Lynx patrol the Corridors looking for her."

Rage flooded me. "So you let her brainwash and imprison a child because..."

At least if Firose hadn't been able to claim Asterie, then my powers weren't at risk of falling into the wrong hands. *Yet.*

Amara's pained gaze met mine. "She had Corric."

Shit. "Had?" I asked.

"She's killing him"—Amara's eyes pooled—"but she stole his mind decades ago. She holds his life over me even now, telling me that if I can't get Asterie back to her, she will end him and take full control of the North. He truly is a puppet for her now."

King Corric Mattock, an immortal, dying. A chill ran down my spine.

What was Firose up to now?

I tapped my fingers on the armrest. "Why has no one else stopped her?"

"You know her, Fen. Until recently, she was a beloved figurehead of justice. Of peace and stability—something people were so eager to grasp after the Great Wars. But the people...they are starting to turn on her. It needed to happen before anything could be done. I've stuck around to fight her more aggressive policies, to be a voice of reason, but she's snapped. I'm not sure when it happened."

I knew exactly when it had happened. My fingers tapped against my thigh in thought. Pulling strings, wearing masks and playing multiple sides of political favor. It was a Firose specialty.

But Amara didn't know about the first time, and *I* couldn't fucking tell her. So, instead, I changed the subject.

Glancing at the ink on my arm, I shared what I'd withheld from Asterie and Emmerick.

"I let Van follow a pride of Lynx that passed my cabin. They went to the Plateau, to a rip in the wards. They were escorting men from the Wastelands away. Traveling east..."

Amara's back straightened. "How recently?"

I squinted, contemplating that. Time was so relative. "The same day Asterie turned up in the woods and was nearly eaten by *another* pride of Lynx wandering toward the Plateau."

Amara let her head fall into her hands with a sigh. "I believed that she was building an army in the North. I didn't know magic-wielders would be among them. The rest of the Corridors—we'll be sitting ducks."

Amara had never been one for commanding armies or planning warfare. I watched as she recovered her posture.

We both stared at one another, lost for words—it seemed like it was just yesterday I'd last seen her. Yet that was decades ago.

"The blue flames"—I pointed at the atrium—"those don't come from me."

Amara smiled. "A gift from the Stars, maybe."

"You've kept a lot from me, old friend."

Amara was the only one to speak to me after the fall of Phynx, the only one to look at me like I wasn't a monster.

"And the boy, how does he fit in?" I asked.

"You've met him before. They can't know—it's unsafe for them to know."

She stared hopelessly out into the atrium.

Thirty years ago...

A knock sounded at my cabin door; I immediately shot to my feet and formed fire in my hands.

"Who is it?" My voice boomed.

"Amara." Following her voice was the soft coo of a child.

It could be a trap, but I didn't care. I flung open the door to see her there and nearly sobbed at the familiarity of Amara's face. In her arms, a child was bundled in blue—tanned skin and golden eyes beamed up at me.

"I don't have long—I need your help." Her voice was laced with a fear that I'd never known Amara capable of. Amara didn't reveal much. "It's better the less you know. The less anyone knows, the harder he will be to find. The conception of immortals is now outlawed—they'll kill him, Fen. She'll kill him."

She explained it all quickly in jumbled sentences.

"All of the magic-wielders have been forced out into the Wastelands," she told me.

"All of them?"

"The realm is entirely without magic. Only immortals who weren't gifted Source magic were allowed to stay. But they aren't allowed to conceive."

Her words were frantic. I'd never seen her so affected.

"I need to hide him," she pleaded. And, so, I helped her.

That night, we cast a spell to stunt the babe's magic, to suppress it until he was ready.

"Odd how they found each other," I said.

Had nearly thirty years passed so quickly?

"Indeed." She paused. "Stranger still is how they both found you, the one who saved them both from horrible fates."

My hand ran down my face. In the atrium, Asterie showed Emmerick how to feed a giant carnivorous plant a dragonfly. The plant snapped around the insect with force, and Emmerick flinched. Asterie's lips turned up as though amused by his reaction.

"I see how you look at her—and I don't condone it."

"Like a mother hen." I rolled my eyes. "Isn't she centuries old? Old enough to consent to my affections if she chooses."

"It's not that." She gave me a stern look. "I don't condone you lusting over the power within her. I fear you will use her heart against her to get to it."

I'd been seen as the monster for four centuries—unforgivable even to Amara, my dearest friend. I understood why she doubted my intentions.

The beast that had destroyed a city was under my ward—men, women and children laid out in the streets. Ancient temples fallen, artifacts lost and landmarks laid to rubble. It *was* my fault. I let Amara's unease wash past me, attempting to keep calm about what I'd just learned.

"I still don't understand it, Fen. When I found you that night in Phynx, you looked...shattered. You had so much control over him before then." She couldn't help but look down at the ink on my arm. "When Firose told me what you had done...I just, I never believed you capable of it. Will you ever speak of it? I want to understand why."

I cleared my throat, feeling the familiar constriction there.

A threat.

"I can't."

Her gaze met mine with sad familiarity as I continued, "But I'll make you a promise. Asterie is safe with me. Besides—killing her would just kill me too, right? So my incentive to keep her alive is very high. After all, who loves me more than me?"

My old friend chuckled, and I smiled back. It used to be so easy between us—when I could tell her anything. When she didn't look at me with sorrow and disappointment.

As Asterie's strangely beautiful figure flitted about, toiling with the foliage, it struck me that being bound to her didn't feel wrong.

"Oh. I don't believe you could kill her if you tried," Amara quipped as Asterie and Emmerick approached the greenhouse door. "She would bring you to your knees before you ever laid a hand on her. Even without your power in her veins—she was born of something fiercer than even you can handle, my old friend. When you are ready. When *she* is ready, tell her you are bound. It's a matter to be handled between the two of you."

I could see why Asterie never considered this place a prison—the food alone might make me question ever leaving.

The tower prepared a dinner of roast chicken and potatoes so mouth-wateringly delicious I almost took thirds. It had been a long time since any meat but venison had touched my tongue.

"So you will travel to Luz tomorrow then?" Amara asked Emmerick.

The boy nodded. "Yes, I've sent word to the Queen to expect us. She'll send a carriage to the nearest road."

Stiff conversation continued—I watched Asterie push what little remained of her potatoes around her plate with a fork.

After dinner, Asterie led Emmerick and me to our separate bed-chambers wordlessly. She seemed fatigued. She and Amara had not spoken much throughout dinner—a tightrope seemed to be pulled between them, each waiting for the other to give. While they didn't seem uneasy with one another, it was as though the ground was being reshaped, and they were trying to understand their foot-ing—dancing around topics of conversation.

I empathized with the exhausted feeling of too much information all at once, but I still lingered in the room's doorway. Hopeful.

"I've kept something from you." My words echoed heavily in that stone antechamber. "I had Van follow Lynx to the Wasteland borders. There is a rip in the wards...Amara believes Firose is raising an army from Wasteland defectors."

Her eyes met mine with a hint of betrayal gleaming there. I should have told them sooner. I'd had a dozen chances, but only when my dear friend confirmed my fears did I feel confident enough in my suspicion.

"Goodnight, Fen." She turned away abruptly.

I grabbed her tunic sleeve gently, pulling her back to me. I should have clasped my hands behind my back to keep from reaching out to her. But, even after everything I'd just promised my dear friend, I couldn't help it.

She turned back toward me willingly before melting into my arms as I embraced her.

"I'm sorry," I whispered into her hair. "For how I acted this morning, for all of it."

When I moved to pull away, she held onto the back of my shirt. Her head was tilted just right, and I leaned in to let my lips brush hers.

It wasn't fair to play games with her, but I wasn't sure what game I was even playing anymore. Maybe the one where my heart gets roasted over a spit.

"See you in the morning, my beauty." I spoke the words between our mingled breath before placing the gentlest kiss on her lips and then stepping back out of her grip, unwinding my limbs from her.

She looked confused but offered me a tired smile before she backed away and turned to walk down the iron steps.

As I settled into bed, Amara's words returned to me. *"She would bring you to your knees."*

What would I give to see Asterie from that angle? In my imagination, I dropped to my knees before her, tasting her, making every muscle in her body tense before I brought her to release. I couldn't help wrapping a hand around myself at the thought.

After completing myself like a lusty teenager, I buried my head under a pillow. *This infatuation is nothing.* It was simply my power within her, tempting my ship toward the rocks.

No amount of lying to myself could veil that my fondness for the enchantress grew beyond whatever magic bonds threaded our fates.

CHAPTER 20
ASTERIE

Amara awaited in a worn leather chair by the foyer fireplace. I was exhausted and wanted nothing more than to curl up under quilts and let sleep carry me away. Being awake meant facing how the Sisterhood had taken me and how Firose had a *claim* over me. *Did she own the power in my veins, my free will, my actions? Then how did I leave?*

Amara owed me as many answers as I owed her, so I sank into the chair next to her, facing the flickering flames of the grand stone fireplace. Its mantle was laden with candles and botanical specimens that Wyeth had gifted me for winter solstice through the years.

"I saw it all fall. The Corridors..."

Amara stared blankly into the fire and nodded. Then she turned to the table beside us, where a bottle of dark liquor and two glasses sat, and poured a generous amount into each glass. "I'm not upset with you."

She offered me one of the crystal tumblers, which I graciously took.

The liquor burned as it went down. I preferred wine, but this was an occasion for something harder.

"You should be. I left my tower without telling the Sisters. I kept a prophecy from you." I swirled the amber liquid in the glass before taking another sip.

"You assume any of that matters to me more than your safety and happiness." Amara shifted in her seat. "The visions, have they continued?"

"The nightmares continued until we got to Fen's cabin." I paused. "I've struggled to conjure anything since though. The moonstone, it will not respond to me."

"Nothing at all?"

I shook my head, staring into the embers of the fire.

Surprise spread across Amara's face, and she set down the glass. She knew as well as I did what that might mean for my fate. We'd always been free to speak when it was the two of us. Free to express ourselves.

"Fenris told me that Firose had Lynx patrolling the north woods. They seem to be collecting Wasteland defectors."

I nodded. "Emmerick and I were attacked by a pride—we killed two of them before Fenris arrived, and they scurried off after seeing Vangard."

"The Lynx. They *saw* Van?" Amara stiffened.

Her reaction made me uneasy. "Yes. He killed one of them."

Amara gripped the glass tighter and raised it to her lips. "Fen hadn't told me that part." It took a moment for her to speak again. "And the moonstone, before it stopped responding to you, it showed you no way to stop it? The coming war?"

"No." I let my head sink back into the leather chair. "I tried to conjure path after path. I found no success for us as a unit, the Sisterhood. Then I tried alternate routes—eliminating elements and people. Each time, it just ended in war. It wouldn't show me anything else. When I'd stopped trying—that's when the prophecy came to me. And, this prophecy, it *spoke* to me."

Amara pitched forward in her chair. "What do you mean it spoke to you? Prophecies don't speak *to* Oracles. Oracles conjure them. Are you sure it was a prophecy?"

I sighed, running a hand through my knotted dark hair, realizing how much it needed combing. "It specifically said, 'Don't tell the others.' Which, I'm sorry...I thought it meant you too."

Amara said nothing as she shook her head in disbelief yet waved a hand at my apology, her golden-brown eyes wide.

"And then, the prophecy told me, 'It is time to act, Sister of the Stars. Go to the young Queen,'" I recounted. "I didn't trust the voice at first. But it was so alluring. I didn't know what else to do."

"I understand," Amara spoke softly. "Cassidee and Wyeth are coming around. But Firose, she will try to make an example out of you. It would help if you appealed to the Central Queen's good graces. Seek refuge there—stay in Luz."

I nodded my agreement before looking around the foyer. So much time had been spent here. Nonetheless, it no longer felt like home.

I was eager to leave for Luz, toward whatever damned fate lay ahead of me there.

"How do you know the warlock?" Too much curiosity bled into my voice.

Amara cracked a smile. "Have you never picked up any of the history volumes I gave you, dear? I had a life down in the world before the Sisterhood." She motioned to the bookcases around us.

I rolled my eyes, allowing my lips to crease into a smile.

"I haven't read *every* one. Regardless, he's an insufferable flirt. But he seems especially fond of you. I wondered if it might be something more?"

A lump grew in my throat at the thought of it, and I hoped she didn't press me on why I asked.

"No, no." She waved a hand at me. "Handsome though, isn't he?"

My cheeks grew hotter. "If you like men with egos the size of the Hussa mountain range, then yes, I suppose he is."

Amara chuckled. "He used to be very popular with the ladies of both the Courts of Brennax and Phynx until Firose got her claws into him. They were together for some time—if you could call the volatile nature of the two *together*."

Every hair stood on my arms. I stilled, and Amara noticed. The thought of Fen and Firose together sent spiders down my spine. "And were their ties broken?" My voice went rigid, pressing. Amara's brow creased—she knew my tells when withholding information. If Fenris still had ties to Firose, then bringing him to Luz could prove dangerous.

"What do you mean?" Amara asked.

"Firose met my mother in an Orchard—in Fen's family orchard. She bargained for me...why was she there?"

Amara's eyes clouded. I wanted answers. Amara was my only hope of getting them.

"Firose took ownership of the Lamoreaux Estate after all prior tenants were condemned to the Wastelands and Fenris was thought dead," she explained.

I nodded but my brow furrowed in thought. "In the memory, Firose was interested in my mother's Reverist abilities." I shook my head, unable to piece it together.

"She'd grown intrigued in finding what Reverist magic still exists in the realm. I thought it was out of a personal interest in studying the magic, but it seems it may be more sinister." Amara paused for a moment. "Your mother—she wrote to me when you were born.

She was so afraid for you…I regret getting to Ikanten a minute too late."

My back straightened. "You were there? The night my mother died?"

"I was." Amara swallowed hard. "I sent the star that restarted your heart."

"You?" My head was spinning.

"It nearly killed me to use that much of my Source magic—but some instinct told me to protect you." She paused, eyes glistening. "Your father was convinced you were cursed. He begged me to take you away and threatened to offer you to the ocean tides. I thought the safest place for you would be by my side—where I could protect you."

So the legends were part truth and part myth. The stars didn't save me. Amara had. The tides didn't carry me to Eros. Amara had. She was the stars and moonlit tides. She was the sun like her Source magic, music and joy to all of my darkness and midnight.

"I'm sorry. I have kept so much from you…It seemed safer for you if you didn't know. Safer if Firose didn't know I'd had a hand in saving you. Despite her, I tried to fill your upbringing with as much laughter as I could. Asterie, I still believe you will be the one to right the wrongs we've rutted into this realm."

My attention fixated on the amber liquid nearly drained from my glass. "If you knew she was so cruel, why did you stay? Why not take me somewhere else?"

Amara was quiet for a moment before speaking again. "We were friends once—Firose and I. At first, I thought we were doing good things together—that feeling was lost along the way. Like the moral ground we had built was crumbling. And one day, I realized that she held all the cards. That she could take everything I've ever loved from me. That she could turn the Corridors against each other with a snap of her finger."

Turn the Corridors against each other. Was that her plan?

"The radicals at the northwest border," I mused quietly. "They were unarmed when struck down by the eastern air raids and western soldiers."

She nodded.

"You knew? How?"

Tears slid down my friend's cheeks. "I received a letter from the North King that Firose was, in fact, pushing for the North Corridor to seize control over the West. The Kruthins were right."

She'd let innocent people die. "How could you not have stopped her?" My mouth hung open in quiet disbelief.

Ten...nine...eight...

I breathed deeply, trying to let the edge of my violent rage simmer into a low boil instead of fiery depths. My irises were likely lit from within, with iridescent inky swirling.

"Firose is a Lynx in sheepskin—the people love her because she's never the one who wrongs them. But she's grown bolder these past months. It was the catalyst the realm needed for its rulers to begin pulling away from the Order. After the last meeting, Wyeth and Cassidee finally approached me, wishing to break ties with Firose...the Sisterhood is crumbling, Asterie. And the Corridors are vulnerable—she ensured that.

"She plays her cards well. Firose will always make sure she has something that you want. She always ensures the stakes of the game she is playing are high. It was the only way to make them see it..."

Seven...six...five...

A pit grew in my stomach. Amara was willing to let blood spill to *prove a point*. I only hoped it wouldn't be in vain. It was easy to imagine the Wastelands rising against us. It was harder to comprehend that the threat might come from within. It had already begun, and it began with us.

Four...three...two...

Amara allowed me time to restore my composure and said nothing more. Then, after a few deep breaths, I looked at her across the side table between our chairs.

"Why is she like this?" I was still grasping for an explanation. *No person could be so evil—no person could exist just to hurt others.*

I needed to understand how the person who shaped my view of the world could be so cruel, needed to believe my foundations hadn't all been a lie.

If there was some good somewhere in Firose even long ago, it might help me hold onto the belief that there were pieces of myself that were good too.

"Has she ever told you anything about her upbringing?"

I shook my head.

Amara continued to explain, "It was six centuries ago. She was born into a poor Brennac family, barely above beggars. As soon as Firose was old enough, she was pushed to sell the one thing men would pay top dollar for from her.

"Before the Great Wars, the kingdoms had warred once before, the Midpoint Battles—Brennax and Phynx fought for the midway lands between their kingdoms. The Hussa mountains and the lower North Corridor were once in that midway. In the early raids, Firose and other women from her brothel were captured by Phynnic soldiers—passed around like cigars. When Brennac soldiers attacked the Phynnic camps, they *left* the women there. Not worthy of saving even by her own kingdom's forces."

My heart ached, and I nodded. "So, how did Firose survive it?"

Amara sighed. I braced for what she might tell me. "She made it to the shores of the northern countryside—on foot, on her own.

When she reached the north shores, her rage had grown so fierce she accidentally set acres ablaze—created a brush fire for miles. She became the 'girl aflame.' She leaned into the world from that point flames first. Overtaking, manipulating, charming."

Amara's eyes were glassy and contemplative as though remembering something fondly.

"She became a maid to a noble house in western Brennax. Somehow, she rose to be the lord of the estate's advisor. She had him wrapped around her finger and owned half his estate before he even realized he'd signed over everything to her."

"How did you come to work together?"

"I was an advisor to the lord of a neighboring estate. When I met her, she was a scared girl with a sharp mind. I got her the job as a maid. It intrigued me when she rose to be a formidable ally. We were young, beautiful and able to make powerful connections in the courts. It took centuries, but we grew to influence political structure more and more."

"Until the fall of Phynx, when movement toward the Order began."

She nodded. "It was well meaning. I didn't agree with some of the Order—the conception bans, the exile of magic-wielders. But it cascaded out of my control, and Firose's silver tongue made it impossible for me to reverse the course we had set."

It felt like I'd become one with the leather chair cushion. *Firose wasn't trustworthy.* She was owed empathy, but no amount of personal suffering should lead one to make others suffer.

"I don't suppose you're able to come with me to Luz?" I asked.

Amara reached over to squeeze my arm with a sad smile.

"I must go to Eros and prepare our fleets for war. None of the rulers know the extent of unrest in the towers yet."

"And King Mattock?

"Corric is nearing death." Her eyes glistened with the words.

"Amara—you cared for him deeply. Didn't you?"

My dearest friend simply nodded through her tears. Her reaction during our meeting that day when Firose revealed he was ill made more sense. It suddenly felt unfair to keep what I suspected of my own fate from her.

"There is a real chance that my death is a part of righting our path. I'm sorry to leave you if that's the case. I wish we had the chance to know one another outside of these tower walls."

"I wish that were not true, my dear. But I trust what you must do. I trust in you. I have always trusted *you*."

Pressure grew behind my eyes. For the second time that day, I was crying. *Was showing emotion becoming a new habit for me?* She squeezed my hand across the side table. We sat like that, hands held, turning back to stare at the flames for a long while.

"I have so many questions," I mused finally. "But I fear their answers will have come too late."

"Me too, love. Me too," she answered to the flames.

My mind raced through all the information she had just unraveled. After our glasses were drained, Amara pulled me into a tight embrace.

"Goodbye, Asterie. I will come to Luz as soon as the Southern isles are secure from attack."

I nodded, sniffling back my tears. Neither of us was ready for a goodbye so final, so we attempted to treat it as any other farewell.

"See you soon," I said with a weak smile.

Once Amara left through the Egress, I began to blow out candles before retreating to my bedchamber. Before my feet hit the steps, a particular set of history volumes caught my eye on the bookshelves. Tip-toeing, I pulled the volumes from the shelf, dusting them off before I lugged them up the winding iron stairs with me.

I awoke with a history volume tented over my chest. It was a miracle that I'd slept through the night, and without nightmares. *Why dream of horrors when there was one sleeping right under my roof?*

The stack of volumes was littered around my bedchamber. The otherwise gray wood floors were colored in a rainbow of dusty-hued spines—a haphazard mess of texts.

Upon waking, I opened the volume once more. *Would the light of day help me read something different?*

The dark crimson curtains were pulled tight and blocked all but a sliver of light, which taunted me by illuminating the passage.

The volumes were chronological. Fenris' name was four centuries back. Four centuries ago—when he'd been condemned to the northern woodlands. It wasn't a long passage.

"The Three" were magic-wielders whose powers were feared and respected amongst both courts of the Old World. The vigilante group was composed of Amara Odili, Firose Van Gran and Fenris Lamoreaux. The Three were once a neutral party, siding with neither Brennax nor Phynx and instead prioritizing the protection of the vulnerable during the beginning of wartime.

I flipped to the next page.

"Fenris the Destroyer." Fenris was the strongest among The Three and commanded a great beast named Vangard. The origin of this bond is unknown. During the fall of Phynx, Fenris betrayed The Three

by aiding Brennac forces in their attack. He and Vangard destroyed the city of Phynx in a single night and allowed the Brennac to siege the court. The fall of Phynx is said to be one of the most significant losses of civilian life in all of the Great Wars. The attack began on the armed forces surrounding the city, but once white flags were flown and Phynx surrendered, the Brennac onslaught did not end. Instead, the beast continued to destroy the city. Krait Darvanda, then King of Brennax, never called his troops back.

Historians have long speculated over the motivations for the attack that night. Many hypothesize that Fenris' actions were spurred by jealousy of a budding romance between his then lover, Firose Van Gran, and Gauvin Wymark, the then King of Phynx. Others speculate that his ties to Brennac's beliefs and prior employment with Krait Darvanda had radicalized him enough to aid in the attack.

In an act of heroism, Van Gran stopped Fenris' destruction by casting an enchantment to strip him of half his power, thus gaining control of the beast. Odili and Van Gran then destroyed half of Fenris' power, condemning him to death in the process. It is said that the fall of Phynx's capital city sparked the rapid fall of the two kingdoms and the rise of the Order of Henosis.

Thinking that I offered Fenris *any* kindness in the preceding weeks sickened me. Worse yet, I'd let heat into my veins at the thought of his touch, which now made my skin crawl.

If history thinks Fenris is dead, how was he sleeping in my guest chambers? How did Queen Wymark know precisely where to find him? Why did she want him?

There were so many omissions they *all* had kept from me. Fenris didn't just have blood on his hands—he was responsible for one of the most horrific acts in the history of the realms. *And for what? A lover's quarrel with Firose?*

If I hadn't been sick at the image of them as lovers before, I was now. My stomach churned thinking of what he'd done—killing women, children, innocent civilians. He was no better than whatever evil approached Henosis now.

The story in the text was so different from the man that I thought I'd grown to know. *He couldn't have.* Yet he'd told me the night we met that he had the blood of many on his hands.

Stupid, stupid, stupid. I'd been so naive. My mind raced further.

Amara knew about that night.

How could she stand in the same room as him without wringing his neck? She hadn't been ill at ease with him the night prior. They had regarded each other as friends.

Can I truly trust Amara, or could the text be wrong?

I was so sick of cryptic half-truths and accepting the words of others at face value. My veins burned, and my heart pounded.

I stormed into my bathing chamber and tried to soak in the tub, but it didn't ease my growing wrath. Instead, it made me think of Fenris' hands on me. That feeling was burned into my memory in painful detail.

After deciding a bath wasn't what I needed after all, I hurried to dress. A pair of supple leather pants and a dark linen tunic were quickly pulled on, and I didn't bother with a braid.

There was only one place where my fury could be released without leaving the tower in a pile of rubble. I had to keep my hands clenched shut to curb the involuntary blue flames growing there as I rounded my way up to the arena.

"One of the most significant losses of civilian life in all of the Great Wars."

The arena was a large square platform built on the tower's upper level, open to the sky. The sunlight cascaded across it, and my eyes squinted against the abrasive light. I pulled a blade off the weapons wall, which had been built under a large awning. The morning dew darkened the smooth paved stone beneath my feet.

I began practicing movements with the broadsword. Each movement became more violent than the last, each strike more unhinged.

"White flags were flown. The beast continued to destroy the city."

The anger burned through me like oil ignited with a match. Before long, the blade glowed an iridescent blue and trailed licking blue flames in the wake of its movement. *Good.* I needed to let some of that energy out.

I knew Fenris *the Destroyer* had entered the arena before I laid eyes on him. I knew it from the surge of power I felt in response to him.

CHAPTER 21
FENRIS

The door to Asterie's bedchamber was cracked open. I approached it with an irrational desire to see how she looked well rested, with mussed hair and eyes softened with sleep.

I poked my head in only enough to see that history volumes littered her bedchamber and that she wasn't there. A lump grew in the back of my throat as I pushed the door in further and stepped into the room.

The volume on her bed lay open, and my whole body stiffened to see my own name on the page.

I turned quickly back toward the door—I needed to find her. *Had she left without me?*

On my way out of the room, something else caught my eye on her desk. An old Brennac text. I stopped to peek at the section she had stopped at. *Unbindings.* A particular spell was circled—its roots in dark magic, the Lacero curse.

Did she truly intend to bargain with Death to unbind herself from me?

I hurried out of the room and hit the stairs at a run.

Asterie tracked me as though waiting for me to strike. Her irises were gone as soon as my boots hit the stone of the arena entrance. Black depths swirled in their place, threaded with an iridescent sparkle like stars orbiting.

The predator before me had long waves kicking up in the wind and sticking to her full lips. Those damned leather pants—I had half a mind to just lay down and let her torture me for the view alone. Seeing her look at me with such disdain was torture enough.

Underestimating this woman, or her Origin-gifted power, could be deadly—for both of us. She white-knuckled the hilt of a long blade that shined silver-blue, so bright it burned my eyes like staring into the sun.

Stepping into the middle of the arena unarmed was possibly the stupidest decision to make. But kissing the enchantress hadn't been wise either. We were bound in more ways than she knew. *She needed to know.*

Fuck Amara for not telling Asterie where that power came from. My friend had many lovely qualities and talents, but she'd never been a direct communicator when it mattered most.

"I take it you did some light reading last night."

Asterie didn't respond as she approached a stone wall where weapons hung and grabbed a second broadsword. She spun it in her palm. It looked like she would raise both swords against me. But, instead, she threw the dull weapon at my feet with such force it cracked the stone.

Her skin began to glow, a faint but noticeable hint of blue that charged the air around her. That raw, unhinged power. I bent carefully to take the offered sword, not wanting to use it in the least. Asterie's sword was still aflame, a blue inferno pointed directly at my head across the arena.

"How could you do it?" She spat the words—they filled the arena in a way that sent a chill down my spine.

She stepped to the left, and I circled to the right. She launched at me, wasting no time. A skillful assault that took me by surprise, but my blade kept pace with her onslaught of strikes, only blocking. *Amara was right—all this power couldn't be from me alone.*

"I don't want to fight with you, Asterie." My voice remained measured.

"What? Am I not vulnerable enough for you?" She snarled the question before throwing another strike with precision. "Do you just get off on killing those who *can't* fight back? Maybe you should let your pet come out to fight me so you can keep *your* hands clean."

I didn't move to allow Van out.

She knew so little.

Her blade nicked a hole in my shirt sleeve at the shoulder, and warmth dripped down my bicep and forearm. Her feral smile at the sight of my blood running over the ink of Van chilled me.

My jaw tightened, and my defenses became more hurried and fueled by my growing anger. Her righteous disregard for the truth was infuriating.

Open your eyes, I wanted to scream. Fire meeting fire. It mingled in the air between us. We were charged and ready to ignite.

"If the Queen hadn't asked for you alive, then I would kill you right here."

Frustrated, I barked back, "Have you ever killed anyone?"

Getting a taste of what it felt like to have someone look at me without disdain only to have it ripped away over a bullshit passage in an old book ate at me.

"Have you?" I shouted.

Our blades clashed again, hers sparking.

When she did not respond, I thrust her back with my next block with as much force as I could muster. My own blade flashed with fire before I quickly extinguished it.

Asterie lost her footing and landed with a thud as her blade came out of her grasp and skidded across the arena floor. She seemed to glow brighter—her whole body flickered like a star. I pointed my blade at her heart, having no real intention of hurting her. I was simply out of breath and out of patience.

"No, you haven't, have you? If you'd ever killed—saw the life leave the eyes of someone at your hand, then you wouldn't throw the threat around so fucking lightly."

She glared up at me. "I didn't mean it lightly. You can hide behind the actions of *that thing* in your arm, but you're a pathetic wretch. A stain on this land...and I would be doing the realm a favor to be rid of you."

She closed her eyes as though bracing for me to pierce her heart. Her glowing skin flickered out like a candle. She honestly thought I'd hurt her—that struck me deeper than her words or any blade could. I threw the blade away with force and knelt in front of her.

I could feel her breath on my cheek as I said, "And you mean to tell me that you don't feel '*that thing*' calling to you too? Keep pretending that you don't know exactly where your fire comes from. That you have no idea why you can't keep away from me. Why you can control him too. Admit it—even now, you don't want to stay away. Even knowing what a monster I am."

She swallowed hard. She was trembling—*was it out of fear or rage? My guess was the latter.* "What nonsense are you spewing now?"

"You are bound to me!" My shout made her flinch, making me wince against the unintended malice in my voice.

I need to rein this in.

"What you have, Asterie—what saved you two hundred years ago. It was *my* power. My fire. And you have it. Half of my Source power. It was given to you."

She didn't deserve to face the truth over a fool's temper. I watched as her brow wrinkled and her face fell. When she looked up at me, her dark eyes dimmed. Undoubtedly, every moment of her life was being assessed and checked for maleficence or goodness. Every outburst, every infraction. But her gaze was still full of hate. I'd never learned when to shut the fuck up. *Why start now?*

"You sit up in here in these high towers, playing Sources." I scoffed. "So righteous about it too—but ask yourself, Asterie, what good have you done? You saw those people in Kullworth. Your precious Order is a facade. Don't act like you don't have just as much blood on your hands as I do."

She stilled. I felt a strong pull at the ink on my arm.

Shit. I fought it, not allowing her reaction to draw Van out of me.

"How dare you ask me what good I have done?" Her voice had grown even darker. Blue flashed in her palms—she didn't have control. "What right do you have to question me? You, who wouldn't be free of those woods if not for my mercy? You, who murdered so many in cold blood?"

She finally noticed the flames in her hands, which seemed to startle her.

My resolve to be angry with her quickly diminished as her face fell. It was as though she realized then that she could break me so easily. I didn't lean away.

"You feel it…" It wasn't a question. It was a quiet plea, needing her to acknowledge the pull I'd felt so strongly from the moment I met her.

My power must have been warring within her. I could almost feel her urge to tear me limb from limb, to burn down this tower, to leave nothing but ash. I'd seen the way half of my flames had changed someone before—I wouldn't let it happen to her.

"That feeling, you cannot let it consume you, Asterie." I quieted my voice further, still begging.

"Says the Destroyer. You know nothing about me and have no grounds to tell me how to feel."

True, and not. *I knew her.* In some depth of my soul, I always had. "You have a kind heart. But you know now what my power is capable of. You read the text. It doesn't care about you or your heart. Or them." I motioned out to the woods toward Luz.

The dark swirling in her eyes began to calm.

"You told me yourself—you don't know what direction this supposed war is coming from. Do you not fear at all that you could be the catalyst? That I could be?"

If her eyes could throw fire, then they would have been, but her irises had returned. She didn't speak, and her chest heaved as though she was trying and failing to catch her breath.

"I would sooner kill you, killing myself in the process, than see you go down in a field of flames with the people you love," I admitted. I meant it—however well meaning her actions seemed, I wouldn't let her judgment become clouded by my flames and wrath.

When she looked up at me, her warm brown eyes were pooling. *No, please, anything but tears.* Give me anger—give me fire and fury.

Falling to my knees beside her, my hand instinctively reached to wipe away her tears.

Amara's words rushed back to me. *"She would bring you to your knees before you ever laid a hand on her."*

A dagger pulled from Asterie's boot met my neck—the blade erupted into blinding blue flames. She stopped just before drawing blood.

"Beautiful," I whispered, taking in every detail of her face as the flames licked at my skin. Any anger I'd felt was replaced by a desire to kiss her, *still a damned fool.* Yet I'd done far stupider things for women who didn't make me feel half as alive as she did.

"I should kill you," she said as her dagger hand shook.

"You should, but where would that leave you?"

Her posture slackened, but the knife remained at my throat. "I don't want to see you," she breathed, seeming to struggle with the words. "After we meet the Queen and do her bidding—I don't want to see you again, ever." The anguish in her words tore me open.

"That was always the plan, wasn't it?" I managed a weak smirk. "I will live in the shadows of your mind alone...but this power will still exist in you. So you need to be careful with it, Asterie."

She sheathed her dagger and got to her feet. *"Careful with it?* Like you were during the fall of Phynx?" She threw the words over her shoulder as she walked away with lethal grace.

I flinched against them because she was right—I had not been careful then.

My back fell to the ground, exhausted by the energy ripped away from my body.

This was a nightmare.

I cursed Amara for not destroying my power in the first place, cursed Asterie for her righteous rage and cursed myself for ever trusting in an enchantress' well-meaning actions again.

This may not have been how it had happened before, but I felt damned to repeat a vicious cycle of regret.

CHAPTER 22
ASTERIE

At Emmerick's request, Queen Wymark sent a carriage to the road nearest the Central Tower. Fenris and I hadn't spoken a word to each other since our argument in the arena.

We rode silently in the carriage for just over an hour. The central highlands came into view as we exited the woodlands and headed southwest toward the city of Luz. Sprawling fields, bogs and centuries-old rock formations passed through the carriage window. My eyes stayed fixated on the world outside—it was as mesmerizing as the northern woodlands and almost distracting enough to quell my anxiety.

While my exterior was guarded and silent, internally, my mind shouted at me to face what Fenris had told me that morning.

He and I shared his Source magic; he and I were bound to one another.

I could feel the flames. I'd always been able to feel them.

I'd never glowed like I had in the arena that morning. That was new. Was it due to his nearness, our bond? Was it a defense against him? I was left with more questions than answers.

Amara always warned me to control my emotions. *To hide my power.* She had often said, *"Count backward from ten, my love."*

She made sure I was never idle. My days were filled with training, reading, practicing my potions, tending my greenhouse and using the moonstone to monitor for disruption in each Corridor. Forever busy, forever toiling away at something of "great importance."

I chanced a glance across the seat at the murderous stranger that I'd let touch me in irrevocable ways. Emmerick stared between us and let his fingers drum against his thigh in discomfort.

My eyes lingered for a moment on the ink on Fenris' arm. Van's response to me and my commands could not be denied. It unnerved me.

Much to the driver's dismay, Fenris allowed Vangard to run alongside the carriage. Part of me wondered if Fenris was allowing him to spook the horses to antagonize me into saying something or commanding Van back to his master's arm. It all seemed like a game to the warlock.

Yet there had been something akin to agony playing across his features when I'd accused him that morning. He'd looked gutted.

Was I simply wanting him to be a better man than he truly was?

I would sooner kill you than see you go down in a field of flames."

He was right. I had not considered that my role in wartimes ahead could be anything but good for the realm. This whole journey was a march toward my inevitable death. But that didn't mean I would die a martyr. I sucked in my cheeks.

Emmerick interrupted my thoughts, looking uneasy as he stared between us. "Either of you care to explain what's going on here?"

"No." The answer came in unison with mutual glares.

He mumbled something along the lines of "typical immortal bullshit."

When the carriage halted abruptly in front of the city gates of Luz, a stone archway accompanied by two watchtowers loomed over us. *The city gates.* My breath caught at the sight of them.

We climbed wordlessly from the carriage. Emmerick paid the driver, and Fenris stalked ahead of us—every muscle in his body tense as he stepped through the archway. He called Van back to him before anyone could see the beast.

My hand found Emmerick's elbow, holding him back.

"I need to speak with you." I paused, allowing Fenris to walk ahead. "Privately."

Emmerick's interest peaked. "What happened? Did he hurt you?" He was jumping to conclusions. "I'll have his head on—"

"No, Emmerick—listen." The Commander now held my elbow too as though our braced arms could prepare him for whatever I was to say. "I am bound to him. It's why I can control Van. Why he is so...interesting to me. It isn't wholesome, and our connection may be a danger to the realm."

Emmerick's mouth hung agape, but he said nothing.

"I need you to make me a promise. An important one." I tried to think of the best way to put this very difficult request. I chose the bluntest words for lack of time. "When the time comes, and I ask you to, I need you to kill me."

His head tilted. "Asterie, kill you? I can't do—"

"Stop. You can, and you will." It was unfair to ask this of him, and yet my shoulders pulled tall and my chin tipped upward.

Emmerick stepped back, unlinking our arms, like I'd just dealt him a physical blow.

"I need you to promise to kill me when I ask you to. If I ask, then it is the only way forward in which Luz stands a chance. Please."

His nostrils flared and he looked paralyzed. It surprised me too, how much it pained me to use him as a fail-safe.

"When you ask"—his teeth gritted—"I will do as you wish."

"In blood," I demanded.

He reluctantly took Angeline out of his boot and nicked his finger, only letting a few drops escape. "I vow to kill you *if* you ask me to, not when."

As soon as his blood hit the cobblestone, every muscle in my body relaxed.

His jaw tightened. I threw my arms around his neck in a rushed embrace that nearly knocked him from his feet. He only grunted in response before awkwardly wrapping his arms around me.

I stepped back with my hands still resting on the sides of his forearms, hating the burden I had dealt him. But it could be no one else. "Thank you, and I am sorry. When the time comes, do not hesitate."

"*If*, not when," he reiterated. "This better be a last resort. Because I hate it."

"Of course."

We followed Fenris and quickly caught up with him since he had stopped to look up at a grand structure. The building's large half-circle windows were crafted of beautiful stained glass. In the glass were depictions of five women—I quickly recognized them.

"That's the Temple of the Order. Every capital city has one," Emmerick explained.

I gazed up at the pictures of us commemorated in glass. Firose with her locks of gold next to a Lynx, flames ablaze behind her. Wyeth with her hair covered by a green hood, holding a vining plant. Cassidee in armor and sitting atop a Griffith with her sword to the wind. Amara wore a crown of sunlight.

I stopped in front of the last pane. It was of a woman in black robes and black hair, not unlike my own. Dreary, dark. Atop her head were horns that spiraled. From what abstract detail the glass offered, it seemed sharp canine-like teeth jutted from her mouth. She held a star in her right palm, and her left clawed hand gripped a broad sword held to the night sky.

"Is that supposed to be..."

I put my hand over my mouth.

"That one is you—I told you that you weren't what I expected," Emmerick answered over his shoulder, seeming to want to put distance between us after my ask of him. As if I would ask him to kill me there on the streets of Luz in broad daylight. He walked ahead, greeting a Luz guard and falling into a conversation that I couldn't hear.

Fenris' mouth twisted into an infuriating smirk as he stepped beside me to see the glass more closely. He spoke the first words between us since that morning in the arena. "The all-feared High Enchantress of the Central Corridor."

Peace Prevail.

"Horns...They remembered the horns." I paused. "And the teeth and claws...like a wolf." *Like Van.*

I glanced at the ink that contained him on Fenris' arm before turning back to the glass imagery. Fenris stopped observing the glass and turned his attention to me. It made my stomach flip in a way that infuriated me just as much as that smirk. He was a monster—my heart needed reminders of that. *No, not my heart, my body—my traitorous, stupid body.*

"Who remembered horns and sharp teeth?" he asked quietly.

My lips quirked upward. "The men I've let into my tower, my bed..."

I couldn't kill him, but I could at least kill his ego. I was foolish to ever think that he wanted me for more than the power below my skin.

He bristled. "You bedded men while sporting horns and sharp teeth? I would pay *very* good coin for that experience." Sarcasm coated his voice, but his fists clenched and his jaw tightened behind his smirk.

Let him think what he wanted. Yet my tongue betrayed my thoughts, unable to stop myself from correcting him. "No, I didn't."

He braced as if waiting for me to continue, and his brow quirked upward in expectation. I owed him nothing, but the words fell out with a sigh.

"Stray travelers sometimes made their way into the clearing of the tower. Usually looking for a hot meal or place of refuge—so I would invite them up. If they could scale the walls, they would be rewarded. So it became a game of sorts."

"So you slept with all of them?" There was an edge to his voice.

"Some, not all of them."

His shoulders stiffened.

"I was starved for conversation. I knew so little of the world below...Those men offered a glimpse into that, however small. I would have given anything for it. Some only wanted food and respite as a reward, others...wanted something different. It was tolerable—mostly."

My own words weakened my point.

He took a deep breath, glancing back up at my ghastly depiction in the glass as his jaw grew more taut. I snuck a glance at the profile of his face, which had been made more handsome by his recent grooming.

"I understand the longing for company. I know I have no right, but it doesn't stop me from wanting to dismember anyone who took advantage of you. Intimacy like that isn't something to be *tolerated,* Asterie."

There was silence between us before his eyes widened, and his neck snapped to look over at me.

"You didn't...in the tub. You know that you didn't have to..." He was jumbling his words, but I understood his concern.

"I asked you to touch me. That was very different. Foolish, but of my own will." My response took no thought at all.

It didn't seem to dissuade his concern because he was scanning my face for any fault. I pulled my attention back to the glass.

Being in those woods as long as he had been couldn't have been easy. He could relate to my starvation for company. Only his was earned. He deserved to rot away in those woods. It didn't make us friends again to empathize with him.

"That doesn't explain the teeth and horns," Fenris mused.

It was my turn to grow still and stiff. "After my first *encounter* with a man, he was not—" I struggled to explain it. "He was a brute and not gentle with me."

"He forced you?" I could see him heave a deep breath in my peripheral vision. *Was it the magic within him calling to protect me? Or something else?*

"Yes."

I chanced another glance at him. There was no amusement in those hazel eyes—only lethal intent. He looked like he could set fire to the man who had undoubtedly died decades ago of old age.

Fenris' attention returned to the figure of the half-woman, half-beast etched in the glass above us as though bracing for the rest of my explanation.

"In the morning, he demanded I make us tea." I spoke up to that version of myself as though trying to remind her. "In those moments away from him, I charmed the tea. Instead of seeing my face, he would see and remember only a beast so gruesome and fierce that he would never think of returning. He soiled himself when he took the first sip. He never attempted to climb the tower again."

"I am sorry for what you went through." His tone was sincere, but he still looked murderously angry.

Fenris' interest still lit a fire inside of me—*stupid bond*. "He's good and dead by now, I'd guess."

"Then give me a name because I want to piss on his grave."

"I don't know it." I frowned. "From then on, all men—even the pleasant ones—were sent away with the same enchantment. It was the easiest way to ensure no attachments and no return visitors. It was risky enough to allow them up at all—if the Sisters found out I'd let them in..."

What would have happened? I suddenly found myself not knowing.

Every ounce of stiffness in his body left him. He cracked a smile before releasing a quiet chuckle. With my vulnerable details laid bare to him, my mouth hung open at his audacity to laugh. He really *was* a monster.

"Oh, I can see it now. The fools scrambling from your bed, breeches around their ankles, pissing themselves." Fenris' laughter was gaining momentum. "Too scared to remember their boots."

My lips involuntarily quirked upward. He was bending at the waist, too overcome with laughter to stand straight.

"Did they even use the stairs or just fling themselves off the balcony?"

His laughter was smokey and magnetic—his breath caught in a cough. My lips curved further in response. When I thought about it, it was a comical deception, no matter how dark its origins.

"It is brilliant. You're brilliant."

He grew intense when he looked at me. He could say so much with that gaze—*forgive me, kiss me, want me back*. I needed to keep my wits—he was a charming war criminal. Deadly, dangerous.

"You're so damn beautiful when you smile. Has anyone ever told you that? I'll miss it." He seemed unable to control his words as he blurted them between catching his breath.

My face fell into an expression of smooth tranquility. "No." It was all I could muster.

I didn't recall anyone ever calling me beautiful in any context before Fenris. *Sources be damned.* The disappointment that spread across his face tugged at some deep thread within me—I wanted to reach out to him but kept my hands at my sides.

"I still hate you." My words didn't sound convincing as they left my tongue.

He nodded. "Get in line."

He didn't sound like a man who wasn't remorseful.

Why had he done it? There was a piece that I was missing.

Fenris interrupted my thoughts.

"We should catch up with Emmerick."

Twenty minutes later, Emmerick led us into the city's heart.

Gray cobblestone streets snaked through tall buildings. The city buzz was mesmerizing and overwhelming—so much noise, clamber and activity. It was so much taller, so much more congested than Belray—but lovely all the same.

I could see why Emmerick had made the driver stop at the gates. Navigating the bustle of Luz by carriage would have proved difficult on such narrow roads. The various spires and rooftops made for a towering sense of belittlement. The city spanned for miles—all built into the temperate, fog-coated hills of the Central Corridor.

The cobblestone we stood on extended up to the palace. From this angle, all that was visible of the Queen's home were great stone walls and a tall barbican. Though from here it looked small, the walls jutted out taller than any other building on the horizon.

We walked uphill past marketplaces, pleasure halls, taverns, shops and schoolhouses. There was so much *life* here of every sort. From beggars to bailiffs, craftsmen to courtesans.

The smell of bread wafted from a nearby bakery, and the sound of children playing in a schoolyard nearby sweetened the air further. All of my senses were overloaded—so much to experience. So little time.

But something felt *off*.

In the prophecy, Luz's buildings all had blue stone rooftops and were constructed with white limestone. Yet all the buildings in this city seemed to be constructed of granite—still beautiful, but with gray roofs and not a flicker of white limestone. No bell tower stood anywhere either. I'd seen a bell tower fall.

There may be other parts of the city. My mind reassured me that conjuring visions was not a science. *This may simply be a city district not seen in my visions.*

As we continued through the city, I found nothing familiar. *Had I been wrong?* It was growing harder to breathe. *This is all new. You are just overwhelmed.*

Fenris' hand found the small of my back, tugging me gently out of the way of a horse passing. He quickly backed away from me once I was safely to the side, as though the touch stung him.

I hated that I wanted to sink into the warmth of his palm. Instead, I looked over my shoulder at the city we had just walked through to get to the palace gates.

"It's wonderful." A smile tugged at my lips. *Mine to protect.* That smile quickly faded because I wasn't sure if I could.

With Emmerick's signal, guards raised the iron gates of the barbican leading to the Court of Luz. There was more space between the city and the castle itself than it seemed from the outside. Surrounding us stood fortified battlement walls that insulated the palace grounds.

The grounds were sprawling with gardens of blooming roses and wisteria and acres of pristine hillside. In the middle of it all, a palace stood—a behemoth granite structure with many turrets and towers.

As we approached, I steeled myself to meet the young Queen.

Guards opened the silver-trimmed double doors of the throne room. It took all of my self-control to not spin around to take in such a room.

The domed ceilings were painted with murals of the night sky, deep hues of sapphire against silver foiled stars with the constellations mapped in silver lines. Emmerick tapped my shoulder gently to catch my attention before he stepped away. My gaze turned to the throne at the center of the room. It was enormous and looked to be made of solid silver and bore Luz's emblem of a crown made of acorns.

The young Queen watched us as we moved further into the room. Her hands were neatly folded in her lap. Her honey-colored curls were gathered neatly atop her head and snaked through a crown of platinum leaves that circled her temple. Freckles dappled her nose. I recognized her instantly—the reflection in the lake at Belray while dancing with Emmerick.

The Constable stepped to the side of the room and lowered to one knee. A vision of servitude for his Queen. The Queen's gaze settled on him.

"Sir Emmerick, I am pleased with your work bringing our guests to court."

When Queen Wymark nodded, Emmerick stood. Her attention was now on me and Fenris. I gathered my robes and lowered myself to one knee. The leather of my breeches squeaked against the marble floor. I realized that the guards had not checked us for weapons—which reassured me that we were, in fact, being received as guests and not prisoners.

Fenris knelt beside me. We both bowed our heads, awaiting acknowledgment. Amara had taught me these formalities of the courts should I ever need them.

"Lady Asterie, High Enchantress of the Central Corridor."

I braced as she announced me in my formal title.

"I am honored to make your acquaintance. The Court of Luz welcomes you. Thank you for your service to the lands of Henosis. You may rise."

"The pleasure is mine, my Queen."

I stood. Queen Wymark turned her unflinching gaze to Fenris, who had stayed bowed before her. She contemplated him for a moment.

"Fenris, Destroyer of Phynx. You are here due to a great debt owed." The young Queen's voice showed no kindness to him. *Good.*

"We shall discuss that debt tomorrow morning. I require you and Lady Asterie in my study by eight—no later. Do not make me regret my decision to leave you uncuffed. You may rise."

When Fenris rose to look up at our Queen, he wore no smirk or charismatic expression. "Queen Wymark, I am grateful for your mercy."

The Queen turned to me again. "Lady Asterie—"

"She prefers the informal, just Asterie," Emmerick corrected from the left side of the room.

"Asterie," the Queen said with a smile in her Constable's direction. "Watch over Fenris and ensure he is no trouble to this court. Can I trust in you?"

"You can trust me with your life and court, my Queen."

"I offer you sanctuary here. I understand that your absence from the towers is unwonted, but your presence here is most welcome. This evening, you are both to join our welcome celebrations—my court is very curious about their High Enchantress."

"I am most thankful to you," I answered with a weary smile.

That seemed more straightforward than it should have been. The fact she could celebrate at all was worrisome—my mind raced through all the reasons the Queen should dismiss my presence here.

The darkness in my origins.

The flames flickering in my veins.

The unruly draw toward the insufferable warlock next to me.

Firose's connection to the Wastelands.

A dying immortal King in the North.

Queen Wymark seemed at ease with it all.

"You may call me Sybilla. We will be good friends"—it wasn't a question—"and that is reason enough to celebrate."

My mouth hung open, ready to question her, but when I looked up, she was motioning to the guards at the doors.

"After all—we must seek the brightest moments of dark days," the Queen said.

My gaze landed on Emmerick. A familiar outlook on life.

"The maids will show you both to your quarters."

Sybilla stood and walked between Fenris and me. She stopped momentarily to rest a hand on my elbow.

She leaned in, and her words were quiet and for me alone. "I am truly honored to meet you. I wish the circumstances were different. I insist you find your way through the gardens. They're quite beautiful *at dusk*. Alone." This wasn't a recommendation—it was an order.

Dumbstruck, I nodded with acknowledgment before guards escorted Sybilla out of the throne room.

Chapter 23
Asterie

My assigned bedchamber was light and lofty, with vaulted white birch ceilings. Silver was etched into the floral wallpaper. It was vastly different from my tower's daunting iron points and shadows.

The maid had laid out three gown options for the night's festivities. I cautiously eyed each. The thought of adorning myself in finery was unsettling.

I winced at two of the gowns—one a lacey gold monstrosity and the other a pale blue color that would only serve to make me look sickly.

My fingers settled on the last of the gowns—it was the color of a ripe plum. Visions of burgundy fruit hanging from trees in the orchard lingered in my mind. It had a simple bodice and boned structure—no lace or ruffles that would make me feel like a prized pet. The silk was delicate and soft; *this would do.* The bell sleeves hung long, nearly to the ground, and I hoped there would be no need to use a sword with those.

After bathing, I untangled my hair with a wide-toothed comb before I stepped into the wine-colored gown.

A knock sounded on the door.

"Come in."

A pretty maid with braided chestnut hair poked her head in. "Good evening, High Enchantress. Are you ready for my assistance?"

"Yes, thank you. And you may call me Asterie."

The maid carried an abundance of vials, brushes and hair curlers. She looked slightly disheveled, and her skirts were an inch too long.

"What should I call you?" I forced my voice to be gentle and nodded for her to place the overflow of items in her arms on the vanity.

"Oh..." She seemed shocked that I had asked, and she gathered her composure. "Elsedora. But my friends call me Elsie."

Her eyes dragged down me subtly as if waiting for me to attack.

"Well, Elsie, it will take a while to make me look remotely presentable to a royal court, so I am sure we will have time to become friends. Tell me about your life here."

The girl's shoulders relaxed. Within minutes, she was at work on my hair and enthusiastically sharing information like a tea kettle bubbling over. She grew up in the North Corridor with her parents and brother. When she spoke of them, an air of melancholy hung over the retelling of her childhood. I smiled as she spouted off about her favorite places to visit in the North. She unraveled the curlers from my hair with precision.

"Excuse me for asking, but..." Elsie faltered. "Oh, never mind."

"No, please—I insist. You can't offend me with any question."

Her worried look turned conspiratorial. "The warlock traveling with you. Is it truly him? Fenris *the Destroyer*?"

My lips drew into a line. "Yes, it is truly him." I wasn't sure how much more to share, so I left it at that.

"Is that...safe? And what is he like?"

I sighed. *What harm could sharing my anxieties with a lady's maid do?* "He's here on the Queen's request—as her guest. He hasn't tried anything yet, but I am unsure if he is safe. And he's infuriating. Horrid. Cocky in an oddly enchanting way. I'd advise steering as far from him as you can."

Elsie finished lining my eyes, stepping back to admire her work. "Well, he sounds *terrible.*" Her voice held amusement as though reading between lines I didn't know I'd drawn.

Those lines for her to *stay away from the warlock.* Because he was truly horrid or because the thought of him with any other woman made my stomach hurt?

Elsedora took my hand and guided me to a floor-length pedestal mirror. There was no explanation but sorcery for what she had accomplished. I shook my head, staring at myself a moment longer—my hair hung in sleek, shining curls that cascaded over my shoulders. It had seemed like she painted so much on my skin, but I was pleased to see none of the colors were garish.

"You look beautiful, Lady Asterie." She smiled warmly. "You will surely catch the eyes of that *'horrid' and 'cocky'* warlock looking like this." Before I could correct her misunderstanding, she stepped back toward the vanity.

"Oh! I almost forgot."

Elsie retrieved a green velvet box as I slipped on the heeled shoes left for me. Within it was a rose-colored teardrop gem necklace. It caught the light from the window and created a fractal pattern on the ceiling.

"A gift. Isn't it stunning? This color is such a rarity."

Elsie was already reaching around my neck to clasp it, and I held my hair out of her way. I wasn't one for wearing jewelry, but the simplicity of the cut and elegance were breathtaking. It was as if the Queen knew exactly which dress I would choose, as they paired perfectly.

Elsie stepped toward the door. "Will that be all, Lady Asterie?"

I turned my attention to her. "You have worked nothing short of magic. Thank you, that will be all." I thought for a moment before holding up a finger. "Actually, one moment."

I crossed the wood floor uneasily, adjusting to the heel of the shoes. Luckily, they were not so high that I was wobbling, but they were high enough that each step was calculated.

I reached into the brown satchel I had carried with me from the tower, needing to shuffle amongst the dozens of antidotes and charms. *It never hurt to be too prepared.* I looked for the ones that would be most helpful in wartime.

"I have something for you."

Elsie reluctantly opened her hands as I placed two vials in them.

"The green vial will heal you from almost anything—it will bring down fever and ward away pox. It can even repair tissue damaged by most mortal wounds. The purple vial has two doses of invisibility serum. Drink half of the vial should you ever be in a situation where you don't want to be seen or need to get away without notice."

Elsie's eyes grew wide as she stared at the magical concoctions in her hands. Magic that was banned. Magic the realm held so little of. Magic that could save the lives of the people of Luz.

My fault. This whole magicless world was of my own making.

"This is too kind, my lady." Elsedora extended the potions back to me, but I shook my head and gently closed her fingers around the vials.

"Hard times are ahead of us. It is the least I can do."

I was late. How was I always late for the most important things?

Dusk was upon the gardens—the sun-basked roses smelled lovely. Queen Sybilla Wymark awaited me on a wisteria-arched bench. Her honey-toned curls were pulled atop her head intricately, and she wore a royal blue ball gown with silver laces threaded across the bodice.

"Thank you for coming."

The Queen stood quickly as I'd begun to kneel. She shook her head.

"Fuck the formality. I'm with you on that one. Follow me, Aster-ie..."

I was startled stiff by her crass words and quick demands. She looked over her shoulder.

"I lost my guards, but we don't have much time before Emmerick comes sniffing around for me. So, come on, I won't bite." She waved me along impatiently as she marched across the gardens and toward the crypts.

What in the world was the Queen up to?

CHAPTER 24
SYBILLA

As I unlocked the crypt door, the enchantress' eyes went wide. Her thoughts raced through a million what-ifs. *"What if the Queen wasn't trustworthy? What if walking into the crypts of Luz was a trap? Where was Emmerick?"*

Her worry was loud and tasted bittersweet on my tongue. I shut down my senses, cutting her off. She clearly thought *I* was the threat.

I supposed that I was partly to blame...I should have brought her here sooner. My father had been so reluctant to bring the enchantress to our court. I'd always been fascinated by her. I still was.

"Can you light the sconces?"

Asterie hesitated. "My Queen...I am not allowed to wield magic out here."

I huffed. "Just light the Sourcedamned lamps!"

I regretted snapping at her the moment I'd done it, but there was so little time. I had sent messages by hawk to the rulers of the East, West and South Corridors earlier that day. If my father's timeline was accurate, the attack on Luz would begin in one week. Barely enough time to reinforce our troops.

Asterie only lifted a brow and whispered something in one of the forgotten languages. The sconces along the crypt stairs lit, and we descended. In the underbelly of the palace sat a long stone-walled chamber with ornate marble columns reaching up to support a domed ceiling. Intricate silver-edged paintings of acorns decorated each column. A noble resting place for my royal ancestors—stone coffins were lined up between the center columns.

"My father lies here." The words slipped out with little emotion.

My father had been many things—a respected king, an expert negotiator, an experienced swordsman. And, unbeknownst to Asterie's beloved Sisterhood, a very talented Oracle.

He was also an insufferable prick that I'd spent years of my life trying to impress and showing the utmost loyalty to. *So quickly the tides of love for a parent can turn to resentment.*

Yet here I was, doing his bidding even in his afterlife.

"I am sorry for your loss."

I only hummed acknowledgment at the enchantress' words.

"He had his theories. About you, about the Sisterhood and a great deal of other things. Some since have come true..."

Asterie spun, looking at the marred stone walls of the crypt. Her plum-colored dress caught cobwebs as she swung around. Almost every inch of the crypt walls bore haphazard words carved into the stone. The scratched penmanship looked hurried and was barely legible.

I'd spent months after his death cataloging every word. He'd left strict orders that no one but I should enter the crypts when he died. I had broken that dying wish by allowing Emmerick down here with me to set my father's ashes in the last coffin in the row.

My father's prophecies had been unraveling since the last black moon. Just as he said they would.

"He was an Oracle." Asterie's words were flat as she drew closer to the crypt walls and ran her hands along the etchings.

I nodded.

"These are prophecies," the enchantress mused.

I sighed. *Finally, she was catching up.*

"I didn't realize what he was until toward the end. He died six months ago. Before he died, he was constantly journaling, constantly visiting these crypts. At first, I thought he was making peace with my mother. Writing letters, making amends."

No, why would he tell me he too was afflicted with magic of the mind? Instead, my father reveled in making me feel weak for it.

He was so good at mentally shutting me out—but too weak toward the end.

"Are you also—"

I dismissed the budding question. "No, the gift was his alone. He did not pass it to me." She needn't know that I was cursed with something *far* more taxing. "It's a timeline—it wraps around the whole crypt. Beginning here." I stepped over to show her where the prophecies began. The writing was more neatly etched, a closer reflection of my father's once immaculate handwriting.

On the first black moon after your twenty-sixth year, a star-saved enchantress will request an audience with you...

A warlock of great importance lives in the north woods. Bring them together. They are one.

I'd found maps of where my father suspected the warlock to be in his study.

When Mattock no longer breathes, an attack will come to Luz in seven moons...

I'd received word by hawk this morning that Mattock had succumbed to his illness. The last time I sat in a meeting with the once-powerful Sun King of the North, it was clear his thoughts were scrambled. No longer his own.

The golden sorceress of the North will take the crown. She will come to Luz to capture whatever power she has claim over. She seeks power but not for herself...

"Firose. She will come to claim me," Asterie mused. "She cannot have my power...or Fenris' power. Either of us in her hands would be dangerous."

As death had closed its grip on my father, the prophecies got less logical, less instructional. More riddle than sense. He'd likely only had weeks to etch these words somewhere they could not be burned or misplaced before he was bedridden.

The Wastelands will be known to you...

He will rise and Death will reign...

War will be fought with shadows and light...

We stepped around the crypt as I allowed the enchantress to quietly take in all the ramblings etched around us. It was a long while before she said anything. I was tempted to peek into her thoughts. I withheld that urge.

The star-child will die...

It will not end with her...

Our eyes met across the crypt, and I offered the enchantress a sympathetic smile.

"My father has been wrong before."

I moved toward the tomb where his ashes lay within, and my hand trailed over the cold stone.

"He had journals upon journals of prophecies. He predicted that I would have an heir by now, which I do not. There are so many paths that *could* have been."

Asterie paused on a section of the wall. "This part—*The Waste-lands will be known to you.* It's an odd way to write that they have opened. Fenris confirmed that he saw a tear in the wards—saw defectors leaving with Lynx. Firose is building an army."

That I hadn't known.

My guests had already dropped useful news on my doorstep. I tapped my fingertips against the cold stone lid of my father's tomb. *What prophecies did you miss?* I wished I could tear my father from his restful place and shake him from death to ask him more.

I asked Asterie instead, "Do you know what Firose wants with you?"

Asterie leaned against a pillar, getting dust on the hip of her gown.

"I believe she can claim me, my servitude to her—my mother made a bargain with her over some stolen plums from the Lamore-aux Estate."

I stilled. "Plums?" I couldn't hide the surprise in my voice, and the enchantress straightened.

"Yes," Asterie said uneasily.

Plums, plums, plums.

During my father's final days, he kept yelling about fucking fruit of all things. The nursemaids had found it humorous.

"On my father's deathbed, he kept yelling at his nurses, 'She didn't own the plums.'"

Asterie's brow furrowed, and I let my mind reach out into hers.

"Firose didn't own the orchard. Fen's family did. He still owns that orchard…"

Then I reached further in to watch the interaction between Asterie's mother and the North Enchantress all those years ago. *"My mother's blood oath."*

"I swear to forfeit my firstborn child and her power to the owner of the orchard I have stolen from."

Asterie had reached the same train of thought just as I had. We were both holding our breath.

"I think." Asterie struggled. "I think Fenris is the one who can claim me. If he is the last living Lamoreaux—isn't that how an estate would be passed?"

"Peace Prevail. He can claim me. Sources. We are bound already but he can take it all. All my power, all of his own back."

I nodded. "That is how estate law works, yes."

The enchantress bent at the waist as though someone had dealt her a blow to the stomach. I shut down my senses because her horror was nauseating.

"Are you going to be sick?"

She answered, "No."

"Do you trust him with that information?"

"Also, no."

We stared at each other for a long moment, and I allowed my features to soften. "He doesn't seem so bad," I tried.

She waved my words away with a hand as she straightened.

"I will not tell anyone," I committed. It was not my news to share.

"So, what are we to do now?" The High Enchantress of the Central Corridor's shoulders were held tall, and her eyes were lit with determination.

My smile deepened. "Tonight, we welcome you to your Corridor. *That* is long overdue. My people need to know you, to trust you. I apologize in advance for the grandeur and pomp."

"And tomorrow?"

"Tomorrow, we prepare for an inevitable attack on this city. And *if* that golden-haired bitch truly comes to claim you, claim my city, we will be ready for her. Together."

CHAPTER 25
ASTERIE

Fenris could claim my mother's debt.

I was still reeling from the revelation when I reentered the palace. My hands shook, and my heart pounded.

The halls of the Central Court were decorated with large arrangements of moonflowers—their white petals contrasting beautifully with rich blue wallpaper. Emmerick found me there, dusting the cobwebs from my dress hem too aggressively.

A cacophony of joyful sounds echoed down the hall from where guests entered and greeted one another. The nobles were entering the palace—I was somehow meant to endear myself to them. *"My people need to know you,"* Sybilla had said. Her people needed to know I was no threat to them. I needed to remain calm and not give them a fire show so early in the evening. *Count backward.*

"Asterie." Emmerick's eyes trailed down me, not lingering too long anywhere in particular but looking appreciative. "You clean up nicely."

The tone of surprise made the edges of my mouth rise, and his voice grounded me. "You're surprised."

"I'm sorry. That's not how I meant it. I've just only ever seen you in robes and breeches—"

I asked, "So I was not beautiful in robes and breeches?" I reveled in the hole he was digging himself. This light-hearted feeling while joking with a friend was new to me.

"No! I mean, yes?" He ran a hand through his hair.

"Emmerick, I'm teasing you."

His muscles relaxed before he held an arm out with a sigh. "You and the warlock will be the death of me."

"Well, in your defense, *I* have only seen me in robes and breeches too. I didn't recognize myself when Elsie finished with me."

"Elsie?" he questioned as he took my arm and led me toward the courtyard where the festivities for the evening would begin.

"The maid," I answered.

He shook his head. "Your maid's name is Alice..."

"The other maid."

"There was no other maid assigned to you."

My blood ran cold. Emmerick must be mistaken. "Then I do not know who dressed me tonight. Her name was Elsie."

"You're sure? Tall older woman, gray hair." His head tilted, eyes narrowed as a worry line furrowed his brow.

I remembered the redhead's too-long skirts—ill-fitted as though not her own. Emmerick's jaw jerked when I returned a shake of my head. *The palace walls could have been breached.*

"Tell me everything," he commanded.

I told him every remembered detail of the girl that had spent hours in my bedchamber. "You need to warn the Queen immediately." I swallowed hard, hands still trembling.

He nodded, releasing my arm. "Should we tell Fenris?"

"No," I said too quickly. "He may be involved. We go on as if we know nothing and keep our eyes and ears open."

My throat tightened thinking of the vials I had given her—the first, harmless in the wrong hands. The second, lethal. *I've given an imposter the advantage of invisibility. Fool.*

My hand reached out to catch the Commander by his sleeve. "Emmerick."

He paused.

"I gave her a vial of invisibility serum."

"You did *what*?" The weight of his disappointment was crippling.

"I thought she was a maid—that I could help her survive wartimes ahead. She seemed kind."

He steadied a breath. "You are good-hearted. But we must be more careful. I cannot risk the Queen's life...there isn't an heir. More than likely, the girl was someone curious to meet you, curious enough to impersonate a maid. But we can't be sure."

"I know, I'm so sorry—do not leave Sybilla's side."

He nodded. "You be careful too. Something doesn't feel right."

Then, with a squeeze of my shoulder, Emmerick darted toward the candle-lined path of the courtyard, his steps charged with purpose.

CHAPTER 26
FENRIS

The band played dull, proper music—a string quartet of stuffy-looking stout men. To be among party-goers was numbing where joy should be.

The vine-covered stone walls seemed to meet the night sky above. The courtyard was strung with tea lights overhead. A fountain bubbled by the band's stage and reflected the light overhead. It was charming.

I would have once loved a party like this. The possibilities to woo and charm. Wallflowers swayed in the corners, awaiting someone to whisk them away, something the former me would have enjoyed doing.

Footmen served bite-sized food and endless bubbling wine from trays. Most avoided me—rumors traveled fast in any court, and it would be no surprise that I might put these people on edge.

No one's reaction to me mattered because my eyes were glued to the one person they shouldn't be. The same woman who nearly killed me this morning. That burgundy dress hugged every curve, and it rendered me senseless.

Asterie was a graceful and nimble fighter, but she had no idea where to put her feet while dancing. Men who mustered the *bravery* to dance with an *enchantress of the night sky* under the moonlight lined up one after another.

Too polite to say no to any of the men who requested a dance, Asterie struggled, tripped and stepped awkwardly through the evening but seemed entirely distracted. It boiled my blood to see her with other men in the form of other women. The wives of her partners gushed and giggled to see a vision of themselves dancing across the polished marble—a party trick to them. Proof of their husband's loyalty.

What boiled my blood more was when her features *didn't* shift—men laying their desire out for her so blatantly on that dance floor as if they had any right to her. It was no different than men clawing up the side of her tower. *But what right did I have to be angry?*

Asterie was watching me too, not out of interest, but more out of skepticism. I gave her a knowing smirk, which was met with an aggressive scowl. Irking her with my mere presence had become my new favorite game of the evening. She kept looking around the courtyard like she was casing it for something.

Unable to stand by any longer, I began to approach her.

A handsome noble stepped between us. Asterie looked over his shoulder at me and missed that the fucker was looking down the bodice of her dress. Something feral grew in me. She wasn't a display in a museum...his eyes creeping into such intimate places made me want to break the hand he held out to her.

I'd noticed her beauty long before royalty stuck her in a dress. Even sleep-deprived, with thorns in her hair and Lynx blood across her face, she was more beautiful than any woman I'd ever met.

"May I cut in?" My words were a playful drawl intended for Asterie. The nobleman balked—he recognized me and was about to concede.

"You may not." *Oh, my strange beauty. Challenge accepted.*

Fear-stricken panic settled into the features of the man who stood between us. He dropped her hand.

"I..." The man fumbled over his words. "I shall fetch you a drink, Lady Asterie."

The noble scurried off quicker than a rat caught raiding a pantry. Asterie was left with her mouth agape. That perfect mouth—and that slight gap in her front teeth—on full display. *I wanted to slide my tongue across it.*

For fuck's sake. Why couldn't I just think normal thoughts in her presence?

Her face was flushed with anger. Even that didn't make me want her less.

She took my hand reluctantly, and I led her to a corner with more privacy. I savored the feel of her fingers in mine.

"I couldn't stand to watch you step on any more feet."

As soon as the jab landed, she moved to turn away. My grasp on her hand tightened, and I spun her to face me. She braced her arms against my chest, looking like she might raise them and pound them against me.

I smirked. She'd become so easy to rile. "Humor me—dance with someone who can actually guide you."

The music began with a somberly sweet and slow-paced tune. It would have been wise to put more distance between us. I wasn't wise when it came to her.

She spun gently away from me as we danced silently before her body rebounded and pressed into mine. I had one dance before she would return to wanting to stab or behead me. I'd make it count.

"You're right." She spoke the words softly into my neck.

I leaned back only enough to seek her eyes. "While I love those words, what am I right about, exactly?"

She glanced over my shoulder nervously. "I've been righteous. What happened to the Kruthins, it was my fault—there is blood on my hands too."

She'd grown heavier, as though her knees had gone out. I lifted her up to her feet and swayed.

She continued, "All the while, the moonstone isn't guiding me anymore. It hasn't been for weeks...it still won't show me *anything*. Then there's this connection with you and...I'm not sure what I'm supposed to feel about any of it."

She swallowed hard after pouring her concerns out to me like an open spigot. I held her there against me, forgetting entirely how to dance.

Fuck—tears. All my senses faltered. I could hear nothing of the party around us, see nothing but her. I reached up and wiped away a tear with my thumb.

I whispered, "I shouldn't have told you any of that the way that I did." My mouth pressed against the hair at her temple.

She shook her head, and I finally remembered to move my feet and sway her again before we drew too much attention. "I needed to hear it." She seemed to be assessing the shape of her hand, which rested at my collar, judging whether it was her own.

"It is you that I see. I desire you—no matter how much you hate me. I don't care if it makes me the biggest fool in this room. In this realm."

The truth in my words sobered me.

She let me lead her silently for another few moments.

"When you destroyed Phynx...what happened that night?"

"I can't speak of that." My words came out so quickly, so dismissively, that she braced. But then, a look of determination and realization crossed her face as she pulled back to scan my face. Before I could ask her what she was thinking, something else caught my eye.

A familiar-shaped stone. I drew my fingers to her neck, lacing one finger behind the gem and flipping it to reveal an inscription I knew would be there. M.L.L. *My mother's initials.*

"Where did you get this?"

"It was a gift from the Queen."

It was not hers to give. I shook my head and stepped away, looking around the room. Either Asterie wasn't telling me something, or someone wasn't telling *her* something. *That stone. The last time I saw it.*

"Take it off." The barked demand caused her to flinch. Before she could react, I grabbed the stone again and tugged hard. The chain snapped.

Leaving her stunned, I threw my words over my shoulder with haste.

"History volumes won't tell you everything, Asterie."

Chapter 27
Asterie

An hour had passed since Fenris stormed away with the necklace. His demeanor had shifted so abruptly at the sight of the gemstone around my neck. Incredibly gentle to rigid and moody. Warm to cold.

My hackles remained raised during the rest of the evening.

"History volumes won't tell you everything." What was that supposed to mean? What stories were missing from those pages? So much of my own history had been documented inaccurately. Who was to say there wasn't more amiss in those texts?

Maybe it was wishful thinking—wanting him to be vindicated. But it would make the desire I felt for him more wholesome. It would make his claim over me less terrifying.

It would be simpler if he would just tell me what happened that night. Instead, whenever I approached, he took the hand of a wallflower before beckoning her onto the dance floor or he started a conversation with a group that would prevent me from cutting in.

"I can't speak of it." His words were an echo against my logic. That strained, tongue-bitten and forced tone. He can't speak of it.

Can't.

He'd said it before, but I always took it to mean that he *wouldn't*.

A fork dinged against a glass flute before Queen Sybilla rose to a podium. The band quieted and stepped off their stage, leaving only anticipatory chatter echoing up the courtyard's stone walls. Emmerick came to my side.

He leaned over to whisper into my ear. "No sign of the maid. She was likely a fanatic."

All quieted, all eyes now on the Queen as she began to speak.

"I do like her," I whispered to Emmerick, needing to stand on my tip-toes and hold his shoulder to remotely reach his ear. He smirked in response—his eyes did not leave the young Queen as she addressed her people.

"We come together tonight to celebrate the first time our High Enchantress, Lady Asterie, graces us with her presence at the Court of Luz. I wish our celebrations could continue, but we face troubling times ahead."

My pulse thrummed loudly. The once joyous crowd in the moon-lit courtyard was now so quiet.

"Henosis faces grave times. We are to be tested—our strength, our resolve to band together as one. To maintain a peaceful, prosperous realm. It all hangs at risk."

There was low murmuring—discomfort thickened the air.

"War is coming. It will tear us apart...Lady Asterie has had a prophecy that Luz will fall first. It will fall to the North Corridor."

The gasps and chatter began as soon as the words left her lips. My eyes narrowed on Sybilla. While I had my suspicions, she was filling my mouth with words I hadn't spoken. Her father had that prophecy, and her using me to shield his name from association with his magic didn't sit well with me. Then, she raised her hand to speak again, commanding their silence.

"We received word today that King Mattock has passed—with no heir to his name. Firose Van Gran has stepped in to rule the North Corridor in the interim of securing his replacement."

An uproar of disbelief grew—a High Enchantress seizing control over a Corridor? It had never been done. And yet, I believed the Queen. Ice ran down my spine.

"Quiet!" The Queen's brow furrowed. "What is more alarming, Firose has been bolstering northern troops with magic-wielders from the Wastelands. Lady Asterie has confirmed that the Wasteland wards are compromised. This is why I will allow Lady Asterie and her present company to teach our troops defensive magic."

There were gasps in the crowd.

It would be impossible—teaching those without Source magic to wield even simple charms took months, years. Sometimes the magic didn't respond to them at all.

The nobles grew quiet again as the weight of her words sunk in. My chest rose and fell as I searched the unfamiliar faces for Fenris—he was staring back at me.

His expression was unreadable but brought me no comfort.

When I disclosed to Sybilla that the Wastelands were open—knowledge he had entrusted me with—I hadn't expected her to make a public spectacle of the reveal. We were caught in the web of warring royals, a place I had never been but one that Fenris knew intimately.

I hoped my trust in the Queen wasn't misplaced.

"There will be no questioning this. Magic will return to Luz. The Order be damned, for she who made that decree threatens to approach our gates to draw blood from our people. She approaches our gates on the wings of power that *we* gave her. We will not wait to bleed. Luz will not fall to tyranny."

Queen Wymark knew precisely how to rouse a crowd.

"Luz will not fall!"

They echoed her—men, women and guards all yelling back. Gone was Sybilla, Emmerick's cuss-spewing childhood friend. In her place was a calculated strategist, and she'd just won her nobles' support.

"Luz will not bleed!" she yelled over them, and they repeated the phrase until it was a chant.

Firose had done irreparable damage to trust in the Order. She had intended to claim me like an asset from my birth mother, yet the thought of going head-to-head with her on a battlefield made my head throb and my heart thump loudly. *I couldn't.*

As the nobles chanted, everything seemed to grow cold and slow.

"You must choose now, young starling and young fireling. And choose wisely."

I knew better than to look for the source of that ethereal voice. Only the widening of his eyes told me that Fenris had heard it too. *"Choose wisely."*

He reached out a hand toward me, but he was on the other side of the courtyard.

A scream cut through the chanting—I spun around to face the source of it. A woman had a sword ran through her middle, crimson staining her lavender gown. The blade was removed abruptly and the woman fell to the ground.

My body felt stuck to the spot as a flash of gold and black armor passed my right side.

"Not her!" I heard someone yell.

A clambering of blades sounded as Luz guards attempted to fight back men invading the courtyard from all entrances.

Northern soldiers. Here. Attacking nobles in the Central Corridor. Peace Prevail.

A blade was raised and swung at my neck. I ducked, narrowly avoiding decapitation.

A guard yelled, "You idiot! She said *don't* kill the magic ones. Detain them!"

Firose. It had to be.

Emmerick ran from my side toward the podium.

"You must choose now."

I stared down the guard who had swung his sword at me. Something flashed at his hip—*binding cuffs.* I formed two blue flames in my palms.

"Too bad. No one told me not to kill *you*."

I shot the flame from my palm. In a streak of light, the orb slammed into the guard's armor, searing it and burning straight through his heart.

Fen was right. I had never killed until that moment. My hands trembled, and my whole body felt heavy, like I might faint right there in the fray.

A second northern soldier charged me.

I could not let Firose capture me. Not when my and Fenris' powers were so woven. *What could she do with all of that power?*

I didn't watch the second orb strike the approaching soldier, though the blood-gargled groan told me that I did not miss my mark. That grotesque sound of death would stay with me in my nightmares.

Shrieks wrenched from unarmed nobles being struck down. Some put themselves in front of the podium to block the path to their Queen, facing soldiers in the name of loyalty to their royal line. The smoothed stone ground was now stained red. Fenris was still on the other side of the courtyard with Vangard, protecting a large group of nobles. *Safe.* I tried to cross the courtyard toward him.

More northern soldiers stormed the entrance—at least fifty of them now overwhelmed the Luz guard.

Fury pounded in my temples. My whole body radiated energy that begged to be set free—the stars called for me to unleash them. I'd never felt so charged, so on edge. Something was glowing. I looked around before realizing it was coming from *me.*

It felt like a hum against my skin—exhilarating.

I stepped out into the center of the courtyard in front of the podium.

"Stop, or I will make you stop." My voice was otherly—charged. But the northern soldiers that were storming toward the Queen did not heed my warning.

Closing my eyes, I felt myself tear apart. It didn't hurt. *No,* it felt like I was part of the sky—a homecoming. Each part of me could travel in different directions. It was as though I could see the whole courtyard yet stood nowhere.

A combustion of a thousand glimmering lights swirled through the air...then through the hearts of my enemies. Those who remained standing shielded their faces from the light. But as Fenris watched the fragments of me collide with flesh and bone, he looked in awe and unafraid.

The northern soldiers dropped to the ground in gasping heaps. All of them.

Then I heard a voice, familiar and soothing.

"You must return. You've been here too long, starling. Go back."

"But who are you?"

The names of everyone in the room began to slip away. They were no one. *"Return, young starlight. You are fading."*

"But I don't want to leave."

It was growing painful to be in this form—whatever it was. On the other hand, it felt so right and addictive. Darkness began to cocoon me, and I saw only the light of the stars I had become.

"Asterie," a voice called out. *Who was that?* "Count with me, beauty. Ten...nine..."

The sound of his voice washed over me. He wanted me to return. A feral part of me wanted to fight it, but I listened.

"Eight...seven...six."

He kept counting to me.

I came back together so abruptly that my knees hit the stone. There wasn't enough air—my lungs were gasping for it like I'd been held underwater. It hadn't been water. It was somewhere *else* entirely.

What was that place?

The courtyard was quiet, save for the muffled cries of those grieving and the groans of those wounded. The sounds were heart-wrenching, and tears sprang to my eyes. All the lantern flames had been knocked out, and the moonlight alone captured the horrified faces staring at me. I'd protected them, but the magic they witnessed seemed only to make them uneasy. It made *me* uneasy too.

Fenris worked quickly to throw fire to the lanterns and tea lights that lit the courtyard. Sobs coated the air with melancholy as the nobles covered the fallen with table linens, awaiting healers to arrive for those wounded.

As the feeling in my limbs returned, I was finally able to stand. Fenris approached me at a jog, but I held out a hand against his chest to stop him from embracing me.

"Stop," I snapped. "Do you still have ties to her? Tell me now."

The maid, the attack, his connection to Firose. His connection to me. I wanted to vomit.

"Asterie," Fenris whispered as his arms slackened at his side. "No. How could you think—"

"How could I not?" I let my hand drop between us before turning to gaze up at the podium. "And you." I pointed at Queen Wymark as I approached the podium to speak to her privately.

Emmerick still stood by the young Queen with his sword raised. He was still ready to take on anyone who dared touch her. Including me.

Sybilla stood tall, unafraid.

I continued, "I would prefer if you did not lie to your court in my name." My voice was charged in a way that sounded like static against wool, like some of that glowing power had stuck in me.

"You have my word. I only meant to rouse support. I do intend to be your dear friend in wartimes ahead, Asterie. Accept my apology." Sybilla may have used my prophecy to gain support, but my instincts told me she was the lesser evil. *No,* that rotting evil in the realm had been under my nose for centuries. I'd just been too blind to see it.

"Next time, rouse your nobles with honesty."

A scuffle of feet against the stone had us all turning toward the courtyard entry gates.

"We found her, Sir Emmerick!" A guard shouted as they ran into the courtyard, trailed by three others who held their captive. "She opened one of the Egresses in the tunnels. It is how the soldiers got in."

"I was here for Fen alone—I had nothing to do with this! I didn't even use an Egress!" Elsedora thrashed and spat the words wildly. The guards pushed her to her knees before the Queen at the podium.

"You." My voice boomed, and my skin began to glow again, power thrumming through my fingertips. The maid—the one I'd thought so innocent. *Could it truly have been her that allowed this attack to occur?*

"Asterie, stand down until we hear her out," Queen Sybilla cut in.

"Else..." Fenris burst past me. "It's you. You, you're alive. Is it really you?"

"It's hard to kill a Lamoreaux. You told me that once, brother." Elsie's eyes filled with determined tears as she spoke. "I never believed you were dead. You're far too stubborn for that."

Fenris collapsed to his knees. Elsie tried to reach out to him, but the guards pulled her arms behind her back before she could. Emmerick stepped between them and cuffed her.

"How did you find me?" Fen's words sounded like they were wrenched from him.

"I found a very detailed memorandum. In which I saw you—alive. With a pretty enchantress asking you to help her in Luz. I figured that wasn't something you would resist."

Even through her tears, the girl smiled and chuckled at her own joke.

"There's been a mistake," Fenris desperately reasoned with Emmerick before looking up at Queen Sybilla. "She wouldn't do this."

I wanted to believe Fenris, but the evidence against Elsedora was staggering.

"She broke in and impersonated a maid just before an assassination attempt on our Queen," Emmerick barked as he pulled Elsie up and spun her roughly.

Van stood behind Fen with his head held low as though contemplating attack, but I shook my head.

"Who sent you?" Emmerick snarled.

Elsie met his eyes without fear. "No one you would know." Elsie's words were laced with sarcastic playfulness that only spurred the Commander's rage.

"Liar!" he shouted.

"Emmerick, that is enough." Queen Sybilla stepped down from the podium.

"Your guard dog is quite pretty," Elsedora said to the Queen. *Has the woman no self-preservation instincts?*

Emmerick growled low, which didn't *not* prove Elsedora's point.

Sybilla drew nearer to Elsedora. The Queen seemed to be listening for something that no one else could hear.

"Lady Asterie will use a moonstone and settle this in the morning. For now, lock this woman in the keep. Lady Elsedora is innocent until proven guilty. Fenris, put away that beast before he eats someone."

Was I the only one who had noticed Sybilla knew Elsie's full name without being told it? I'd only told Emmerick that the maid's name was Elsie.

My eyes narrowed on the young Queen...a question for another time.

Emmerick questioned, "Why not the dungeons?"

I'd never seen such lethal intent in the Commander's eyes. Queen Sybilla gave a quick shake of the head before he reluctantly backed down.

"This is war," Queen Sybilla declared as she looked down at the northern crest across the star-singed chest plate of a fallen soldier and then back up to me. The guards led Elsedora away.

"Emmerick, escort Fenris back to his chamber."

"Sybilla, you should not be alone," Emmerick warned.

"I am not. Asterie is going to escort me to the Egress so she can ward it."

"You're not going anywhere near—"
"It was not a question."

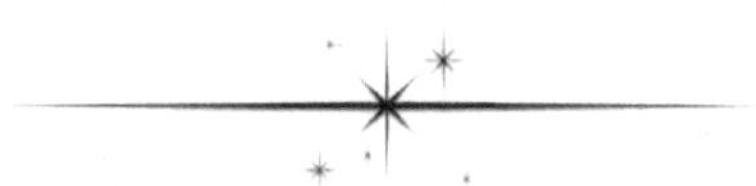

The tunnels below the castle were cold, and spider webs hung overhead.

"No one bothers to clean down here," Sybilla explained. "I fear I haven't been the best host—I've now taken you to two dust-ridden parts of my home."

I huffed a short laugh. "I don't see why you need to accompany me, my Queen."

"Sybilla," she corrected.

"Sybilla, what if more soldiers come from the Egress?"

"They won't."

How does she know?

"The nobles in that room...do you know how many of them have thought about assassinating me?" Sybilla asked as we turned a corner of the tunnels.

That's an odd question. My mouth hung agape.

Some nobles had stood to protect her tonight, but others *had* fled...

"Let's just say—a lot of them. Many did not want me as their Queen—they thought my cousin Haward would be a better fit. But lucky for me, not many of them actually have the gall to follow through, and some even grew to like me."

I stopped as we neared two guards standing in front of an Egress—the stone cut away enough to fit only one man at a time.

"Leave us," Sybilla commanded the guards who stood at the Egress.

Once the guards had stepped out of earshot, I asked, "Sybilla, how do you know what they have thought?"

"The same way you conjure prophecies and paths."

"You are an Oracle?"

"No, I'm an Empath. At least from what I've read of them."

My arms were limp at my sides as I stared wide-eyed at the young Queen who had just openly admitted to having Reverist magic.

"Elsedora did not open the Egress, but someone in that room did. I heard the imposter's thoughts before they fled, but I couldn't figure out who it was. Their thoughts indicated that this attack was only meant to scare us—to frighten my nobles out of supporting me."

She'd put her trust in me, and I would do the same. "I can't use the moonstone tomorrow—it will not answer to me any longer."

"I know—you should really learn to ward your thoughts." Sybilla leaned against a dusty wall. "Speaking of wards, why don't you take care of this Egress, and I'll share what I think we should do next."

CHAPTER 28
FENRIS

Seeing Elsie brought me back to the night Phynx fell—she'd been just seventeen. I had seen her just before I met Firose on the roof. I'd been furious with her for following me and had told her to run. It had been too late. The chaos unfolded so soon after. *How had she escaped that night?*

Hours had passed since the palace was infiltrated by northern soldiers. I believed my little sister. Unfortunately, she'd always had a knack for being where she shouldn't be at the most inconvenient times.

You'll have to trust Asterie to clear Elsie of wrongdoing.

But there was no way Asterie could conjure it from a moonstone, so Elsie's fate would be determined by the enchantress' willingness to lie.

There was no knock at the door, only a creak in the wood frame before it swung open abruptly.

I sprung upright, and the covers fell into my lap as I dumbly watched Asterie cross the room, as if she'd been summoned by my thought of her. She moved so quickly that there was no time to swing my legs over the side of the bed before she climbed into it and knelt in front of me. It might have been an erotic sight if her glare didn't threaten to level me.

Her hair was down and disheveled, and she wore only a white linen nightdress. She opened a leather-wrapped parcel to reveal a raw moonstone. Judging by her mussed appearance and the flush in her cheeks, she'd thrown herself out of bed.

"Take my hands," she said.

I ignored her request and blurted out, "What fate will you condemn my sister to tomorrow if that moonstone does not answer you?"

"She will be proven innocent—Sybilla knows it was not her."

My body slackened in relief. "Thank you, Asterie. Thank you."

"Do not thank me yet. If you can't tell me what happened that night in Phynx, then show me." It was a cold demand. "Maybe your Source magic will help me through this conjuring drought."

"Asterie," I warned, but it was too late. She set the moonstone down before reaching to grab my hands with her long cool fingers. The moonstone rose between us and began to glow, leaving me wide-eyed and uneasy.

Her usually dark eyes grew opaque and shielded, ghostly.

And then I felt it—my mind yielding to hers. Before I could object, Asterie pulled me in and took us somewhere else...or maybe I took us there.

I was in Firose's guest chamber at the Lamoreaux estate. She was at the vanity, combing her long golden hair.

Asterie let out a low growl.

"Is this really what you want me to see? I give you a chance to share the truth, and you take me to your lover's bedroom?"

I couldn't answer. I could only watch as a younger version of me entered the room to make the biggest mistake of his pathetic life.

That bright-eyed version of myself crossed the room to Firose and placed my arms around her shoulders. I looked at her in the mirror before she stood and turned to face me.

"I still have no answer for you," she cooed in the way that had once made me putty in her fingers.

"It was a simple question—will you, or will you not marry me?" I grimaced to watch myself grovel.

Firose made her clear blue eyes so wide I almost believed her again. "It would be too much. Marriage, Fenny? Really? So soon?"

I asked, "You worry about my devotion to you?"

I watched as I got down on one knee with a short blade and opened my left palm, cutting into it. Then I pulled an heirloom teardrop gemstone of my mother's from my pocket. I let my blood drop to the ground. The blood sizzled.

"With this proposal, I vow to give you half of my power. Half of everything I am—you shall wear it in this gem." Half of me—the stupidest grand gesture to offer a woman. And Firose loved grand gestures. *"All you need to say is yes."*

She looked down at me and glanced at the ink on my arm.

Stupid, stupid, stupid.

"Yes—I agree to marry you. To carry the burden of your power with you."

I got up to kiss the lips of the woman who would later rip my heart out and stomp on it. Then I lifted that gemstone necklace around her and clasped it. It was as though, with that moment, my magic strung around her and paved her path toward darkness.

Asterie's voice rasped through that clouded, tormenting memory. "Show me what happened that night in Phynx."

CHAPTER 29
ASTERIE

As we entered the next conjuring, Fen's emotions weighed heavily—regret laced with self-loathing that gave way to despair. It made me want to scream. I'd never taken another person into a vision with me. I hadn't realized what it would feel like, that my feelings would mirror theirs.

Maybe this was a reckless idea...

Then, Fen pulled me into his next memory.

We were at the top of a castle's highest tower. Fenris and Firose were alone there. The blue rooftops of the city below surrounded them, and limestone buildings spread for miles.

White flags were flying on every battlement.

The realization hit me. I hadn't recognized Luz because it had never been the city the prophecy had shown me. The prophecy had recollected the fall of Phynx—then led me to him. It shared the past as a path to my future.

Phynx burned around us, and cries carried through the wind and up the castle walls like tortured spirits. The reality was worse. Those were no spirits. Those were people—women, children, innocent civilians dying below. A red glow was cast against the starless night sky clouded with smoke.

The putrid smell of dark magic lingered in the air and climbed the walls. Death exchanged for power.

Fen collapsed to his knees, his shoulders sunken, and his breath rasped. Firose faced Fenris with her chin held high and the tip of her broadsword pointed at his heart. He was at her mercy.

"What have you done?" He was bleeding from a large laceration spanning from his chin to his torso—a claw mark.

Firose rebutted, "No, Fen, what have you done?"

His sword arm was exhausted at his side. "Firose, please...make him stop. We were here to help. We were here to prevent this battle, not fuel it."

"Why? So that one side might rise above the other? So that this war might rage on? No, Fen—don't be so naive. Both kingdoms will be buried in history as reminders of why a new realm is necessary. I've been chosen. I am the key, Fenris."

"You're not making sense, please...just think about this. Please." Fen's head dropped to rest against the sword's blade as though willing it to end him.

"Think of the world we can create," she hissed with wistfulness in those cold, calculating eyes. She seemed to look to another, but no one stood where her eyes rested. It made my blood run cold.

"You know it is not that simple. Any world created from this will be built on a foundation of darkness."

"That's the thing, Fenny. I do not fear the darkness."

Fen shook his head. "Please, please, Firose. This isn't you."

"Open your eyes. All it took to edge Krait Darvanda's fury was one beheaded princess. These kingdoms were bound to fail...He will rise and Death will reign. I feel it."

The words of a fanatic.

"He will rise and Death will reign." Those words—I'd seen them before. They were on the walls of the crypt, written by the dying Central King.

"Fucking listen to yourself—you leveled a city for nothing. *You are not chosen—the Source of Death will not rise."*

Firose narrowed her gaze. "Will he not? He promised to help me siphon the other half of your power from you in death." Firose played with the gemstone she wore around her neck.

There were footsteps rounding the tower stairs.

Firose's sword lifted to Fen's throat. She could have beheaded him, but she seemed to hesitate. Instead, she whispered the Tace enchantment—one often used on spies to ensure they never spoke their true intentions if captured.

Tears ran through the copper in Fen's beard while she set history against him.

"If by some miracle you live past tonight, you will never reveal what happened here. You will die the mad warlock whose pet destroyed all of Phynx in a single night. Who aided Darvanda's warpath."

"Why?"

Seeing him grovel at her feet broke me.

"Because, Fen, you are weak. And weakness has no place in the world we are building."

It was hard to watch the events unfold before me. I was hot with fury.

Amara ran up to the landing.

"Fen..." Amara was covered in soot and ash. "Fen—what have you done?" Her words were more anguish than anger. He opened his mouth to respond, but his breath caught. He gagged against the blade at his throat, against the spell.

"He lost control," Firose answered. "He would have leveled the whole city had I not found a way to siphon off and bind half of his power to me. I was just about to take care of that thing."

Firose cried out a command to Van. "Come, beast!"

The screams prevailed, but the sound of crumbling brick and mortar grew quieter as a familiar ink returned to Fen's arm.

"He must die," Firose said with her sword still at Fen's neck.

Amara shook her head. "Firose..." Her words cracked in uncertainty. "He is our friend...We cannot kill him. This was not him. It couldn't be him."

Fen said nothing in response to her denial.

"Are you a sympathizer of those who kill innocent people, Amara?" Firose's tone could cut stone. "You smell it in the air, don't you? The stench of what he unleashed on this city. He's been a Brennac ally this whole time. Playing peacekeeper."

Amara knelt in front of Fenris. "You have done so much good for the kingdoms," Amara whispered to him as she pulled Firose's blade away from his neck. Firose let out a low growl but reluctantly let the blade fall away.

Amara took Fen's hands into her lap. "No amount of good deeds will forgive this night, Fen. We don't have many choices...you need to forgive me for whatever comes next."

He looked into her eyes, and anguish soaked his face.

Amara turned to Firose and asked, "What did you bind his power to?"

Firose lifted the familiar rose-colored teardrop.

No wonder Fen had reacted so strongly to it tonight.

"Give it to me," Amara ordered.

Firose stilled. "I will not."

Amara stood with two glowing orbs of gold growing in her palms, ready to take on both of her friends—willing to take on the beast *himself should she have to.* "It wasn't a question. You will give it up, or none of us leave this castle alive."

Firose reluctantly raised the amulet to eye level, looking torn. She finally murmured, "Fine."

Fenris began to shut me out—I could feel him willing away the visions forced upon him.

CHAPTER 30
ASTERIE

When I found my body, the moonstone crackled and fell between us. A gust of wind swept through the room, knocking the light from every candle. Fen's hands were warm in my chilled palms, and my grip tightened on them.

"Fen?"

Had I locked him in those horrible memories?

My hand broke free from him to light a glowing blue orb in my palm. Fen's eyes were glazed over, milky white, and his brow was still crinkled in pain.

"Fen, please...come back to me."

I leaned in to brush the gentlest kiss across his lips, then his cheek. My head dropped into the crook of his neck.

"Please, please..." I whispered there into his skin, running my free hand up through his auburn waves.

What if he didn't come out of it?

"Did you just kiss me?" The vibration of his voice startled me. Relief washed over me as I pulled back to find his eyes had cleared.

"Now that is a beautiful expression, definitely my new favorite." He brought his thumb to my lower lip. Guilt settled a pit into my stomach.

"I'm sorry…I shouldn't have made you show me."

He simply smirked, still looking a bit dazed, and shook his head.

Blue light from the orb danced through his thick lashes. His lips, which I'd once sworn off kissing, were slightly ajar as though mesmerized by the sight of it.

"It wasn't you," I whispered.

I was finally seeing all of him. *The horrors he endured, the guilt, the agony.* It was all laid bare to me.

"It may not have been by my hand. But I gave Firose that power." He reached up for his throat as if expecting pain where there was none. "I can *speak* of it."

Forcing the truth from him seemed to have broken the Tace enchantment.

"I loved her." He swallowed hard. "Until the moment she broke Van free of my arm and used him against the people I was trying to protect. Then, I could never shake the feeling that *I'd* done it to her. I gave her that burden. She descended into a person that I did not recognize—it was as though bearing my power in that gem ruined her. Seeing it on you…"

No. I would not allow Fen to blame himself.

"She was an opportunist," I said firmly. "*Is* an opportunist. She used your love against you like she is plotting to use my obedience against me. You did not ruin her—her actions are her own, and you can not own them for her."

He wouldn't meet my gaze, and I couldn't bear to see him like this. Needing to be rid of the orb in my hands, I raised it over our heads and allowed it to float up to the ceiling, where it broke into tiny fragments resembling the night sky. A trick I'd learned to do as a girl when frightened of the dark and wishing to see the stars above.

It cast a cool-blue glow across the bedchamber.

With my hands free, I took his face between them. His warmth thawed my cold fingertips. *Stars meeting flames.*

"I felt your heart—your intentions. Your pain. I felt everything. You let yourself be vulnerable with her, and she *betrayed* you. It was not your fault. You cannot keep blaming yourself."

I would pull Firose's heart out with my bare hands and not think twice. The hairs on the back of my neck stood at that realization. Maybe it was simply the bond of our magic, but I would do whatever it took to relieve the pain in his expression.

A warm feeling grew in my stomach—*affection*. I realized it had been growing there and budding into something all along.

"In the arena...I said horrible things to you."

I wanted to pull him closer to me, to hold him. Instead, I stroked the sides of his face, trying to will forgiveness into his heart. Forgiveness for me, forgiveness for himself. His breathing grew shallow.

My blood flashed cold—*that half of him that Firose had once possessed. It lived in me.*

His hot and cold affections, his fickle games—they'd been partly his nature, but partly the effects of a guarded heart.

"Don't you dare start apologizing." He pulled my hands away from his face.

"I need to." My voice rasped. "I will give it all back—your power. We will figure out how to unbind it from me. I would never..." I couldn't figure out what to say.

"You would never what?" His words were a soft plea.

"I would never use it against you, against innocent people. I vow never to use your power at all. I'm so sorry, Fen."

His eyelids grew hooded as he looked down at my lips.

"Stop apologizing. You've done nothing wrong." He let a weak smile touch his stiff features. "And if using my power keeps you safe, then so be it. You, my strange beauty...your power mixed with mine scares me half to death. But I do not fear *you* with it."

"What do you mean?"

He placed my hands back in my lap, seeming to notice the thin fabric of my nightgown with a smirk that I'd once found insufferable. Now it heated my cheeks. Now I just wanted to touch him, hold him, and yet he kept moving me away.

"I mean that you are not my darkness, Asterie. You are my light. Stars are meant to guide us home, are they not?"

Home. His—that orchard in Belray. My heart sank for a moment. *Would it change this moment if he knew that he could claim me? Would the temptation of my power get the better of him?* I knew that entangling myself further with him wasn't a good idea.

All good ideas were leaving me.

"It pains me to say this, but it's best if you go now. You look *far* too good in that for me to behave myself a moment longer."

Relieved by the return of his light-hearted flirtation, a smile crept into the corners of my mouth. "I don't think that's for the best. Not at all."

"This morning, you threatened to kill me. You damn near tried."

"This morning, I was a fool." I trailed my gaze down his scar. Every muscle on his toned body called for touching—my hand reached out, but I paused.

That smug smile on his face grew deeper.

He answered as though knowing where my mind had wandered. "Go ahead," he drawled with quiet amusement.

On impulse, my fingers found the scar. Starting at his neck, I traced it down his torso. He made no moves to touch me but didn't ask me to stop either.

"This was from Van that night. That's why it stayed...You tried to stop him." It wasn't a question.

He nodded, and his core jerked as my finger rested on his pelvic bone where the scar ended. His hands gripped the sheets at his sides.

"Asterie..." My name on his tongue sounded like the sweetest temptation. "You're playing with fire."

It didn't feel wrong to want him. Admittedly, it had never felt wrong. "What if I like playing with fire?"

He wore a hungry expression, yet he still fisted the sheets at his sides as though bracing to keep his hands off me.

He had been so forward with me all along. *Why did his confidence wane now? With his truths laid before us, had he grown unsure of wanting me?*

"How exactly did you come to that realization?" he teased.

"I found myself attracted to an infuriating warlock who commands fire."

He let out a dark chuckle, looking at the ceiling where the orb's remnants still stuck, illuminating us in a pale blue glow.

I continued because he needed to hear the words and see himself as I saw him. "An infuriating warlock who would put his own pain aside to help me. One whose words get under my skin more than any other in both good ways and bad. One who has helped me see that there might be more to discover about myself than who I was made to be by others."

I should tell him of his claim on me. But selfishly, I did not want to fill these moments with him with any doubt. *I will tell him in the morning light.* I wanted to forget my fate too—*how could I contemplate inevitable death when he made me feel so alive?*

"What is it you want, Asterie?" A hint of desperation lingered in his drawl as he stared up at those faux stars. The space where his beard met the skin of his neck was shaved in a neat line and beckoned the touch of my lips—I tried to fight that urge but found myself pitching closer to him.

"You asked me once before what I wanted and who I might like to be. I didn't even let myself consider it then. But now, I want...I want a life beyond misguided loyalty. I want to live in a world outside of towers. And...I want you to be by my side for whatever is next. For us to approach it together."

When he finally leveled his gaze into mine, the gold and green there seemed lit from within. *Ferns illuminated by the sun.*

"What happened to the High Enchantress who *shouldn't* want things?"

A weak smile crept across my face again to match his. "She was a fool, so she is hanging up her robes."

"Is that so?" His charismatic drawl returned with an upward quirk of one brow. This time, I didn't mind him toying with me. *Not at all.* "And what about right now? What do you want right now?"

My palms met the planes of his abdomen, soaking in his ragged breaths and his heart's accelerated beating. "You. It has always been you. Despite my better judgment, despite feeling guilty for it. I want *you.*"

"Thank the fucking Sources."

One of his hands found the back of my neck. His other arm snaked around my waist and pulled me to straddle his lap. When our lips collided, I met his kiss without hesitation.

The scent of him was intoxicating—cedar, pine and smoke. His hands were finally where they belonged—on me. His fingers quickly found where the buttons of my nightdress began.

I found the loose edge of his breeches and hooked a hand there—we were a frantic tangle of limbs, lips and breath.

We broke only for air.

He'd finished with the buttons down the back and slid the nightdress down my shoulders, letting it drop around me. The way he looked at my bare skin made me feel worshiped, and it was impossible to be self-conscious under his appreciative gaze. A shiver ran down my spine as his fingers traced up and down my sides.

He kissed me again, this time slowly—as though savoring the taste of me.

I moved to pull back the covers between us and push his waistband down. He chuckled softly between our lips. *Was he reveling in making me wait?* The evidence of his need pressed against the seam of his breeches below me. I wanted nothing between us.

"Impatient?"

"Yes," I rasped the word while I caught my breath.

"I'll give you what you want. But first...what exactly do you like about playing with fire, my beauty?" He was toying with me like he had in the tub. Making me beg, making me stroke his ego.

I asked, "We aren't talking about fire anymore, are we?"

"We are not." He trailed kisses up my collarbone between words.

"Well then, I liked the moment when my body ignited for you like a wildfire raging through pines. When I'm...*alone*, I have felt...that release. That wildfire running from my core to every nerve."

He pressed a kiss so softly to the skin just below my ear, making me shudder. I didn't want to be embarrassed, but my cheeks heated anyway.

"So." His words were quiet and reassuring against my earlobe. "No other man has ever made you come, only by your own hand?"

My cheeks heated more. It was such a silly admission. Fen shook his head softly and traced his hands up my sides before cupping my breasts.

"I'm not teasing you." He traced careful circles around my nipples with his thumbs, which sent my neck inadvertently tilting back to expose more of myself to him.

"But you are teasing me now. Because I've been thinking about your touch ever since. Even when I thought the worst of you."

"If you keep talking like that, you're going to fill my head so much I may float away."

"You think entirely too highly of yourself already." My body betrayed my words as his mouth met the peak of my breast, and my hips responded by thrusting against him. "Please. Please, make me feel it again."

I wanted to wake up coiled in these sheets with him. I wanted to look into Fen's eyes in the morning and allow him to see me and not a beast of my creation when the rays of dawn soaked through the curtains.

He answered my plea. "Gladly."

Flipping me onto my back, he placed a knee between my thighs. I wondered if he could feel what pooled there for him. With a playful growl of discontent, I tried to pull down the waistband of his breeches again. He laughed as he unbuttoned and freed himself from them—his length was swollen for me.

"Wait..." He paused. I whimpered in disagreement. "Has anyone ever tasted you?"

What does he mean? I shook my head, and he smiled wide with hands braced on both sides of my head, looking down at me.

"Good. What I did to you in that tub...it will be nothing in comparison. I want to taste your release on my tongue."

My eyes widened at the brash statement. He inched lower and lower, kisses falling down my breasts and torso.

"Oh..." I grabbed the sheets next to me as he widened my thighs and pressed a kiss to my core. At first, I thought the kiss he placed there felt pleasant enough. *He didn't truly intend to—*

Oh! He did something delightfully wicked—he parted me with his tongue. I gasped and felt him smile into me before he continued. My fists tightened in the sheets as he worked his tongue along the most sensitive part of me. I couldn't stifle the low moan that escaped my throat.

He responded by thrusting his tongue into me, and my hips moved against him. One of his hands reached to take hold of a breast, the other splayed over my stomach, bracing me.

"Fen, I..." I cried out, grabbing a handful of his tousled waves. "I'm on fire..."

Wildfire.

I writhed against him. He stilled momentarily before swiping his tongue over me once more, causing every muscle in my body to jerk.

He smiled between kissing his way back up. I was putty in his hands, gasping for air. *He hadn't been lying.* This surpassed all expectations of what pleasure could feel like.

Halfway up, he spoke into my stomach. "Is that the feeling you had in mind?"

I nodded wordlessly, breathlessly.

"Speechless?" he teased as his lips met my neck.

"More," I breathed. "I need more of you. I want *all* of you."

"I like the sound of that." His tone was amused, but he seemed to be enjoying every moment of my begging. "I also have an admission." He was over me now, and his length was positioned at my entrance.

"What is it?" I asked as his forehead rested against mine.

"I haven't been with a woman in at least four centuries." He paused. "Will you help me end that dry spell, my strange beauty?"

I swallowed and returned his self-assured response as my legs snaked around his. "Gladly."

His eyes turned dark as he reached between us. He pushed into me with a slowness that clouded all of my senses. Every inch of him filling me made it harder to breathe. When he groaned, he tamped down the sound. But I didn't want that. I wanted his fire to tangle with mine—to see all his need, hear it unstinted.

"Don't hide your pleasure from me," I whispered. "I want to hear you enjoy this—enjoy us, together."

"Fuck..." he breathed out between our lips.

He pulled out of me with a rasped breath and then thrust back in up to the hilt with an indulgent groan. I gasped at the sound of him, the feel of him. His pleasure mixed with mine was a symphony to my senses. I was aware of everywhere we touched and still wanted to be closer to him.

"You feel so good, Asterie. You were made for me."

My fingers tangled in his mussed waves as he moved inside of me. He leaned down and grabbed my lower lip with his teeth.

"Faster," I pleaded, on the edge of release. I bucked beneath him with impatience. I didn't want him to be gentle anymore.

His pace heightened with agonizingly delightful groans against every stroke as though trying to hold himself together. But, no, I didn't want that. I wanted ignition, flame.

"Don't stop, please. Never."

"Asterie."

My name on his tongue was my undoing.

"It's been so long, I don't know how long I can..."

My nails dug into the moving muscles of his back before I was unable to hold on any longer. For the second time that night, my vision went starry with bliss. I repressed no sound, letting myself cry out for him.

He ignited—his mouth fell open, and an impassioned cry escaped his lips. He thrust deep and stilled as he pulsed and filled me. His eyes met mine as his whole body twitched above me, and the look of bliss etched into his features made me light up inside.

His body had slackened against mine.

"I…" He tried to find words between labored breaths before giving up and letting his head collapse to the pillow beside my ear.

I reached up to gently rake my fingernails over his shoulders. My touch was met with a pleased noise from the back of his throat, and his body relaxed into me.

"Don't ever stop touching me, my strange beauty." His voice muffled into the pillow.

Biting back a laugh, I took a fistful of his waves and lifted his head to force his hooded gaze back to mine. "Why do you call me that?" I asked.

He fought my grip in order to lean down and kiss me before he spoke. "When I finally saw you in the light of my cabin, you were not just beautiful. You were *strangely* so. I could think of nothing but you, every curve of your body, every subdued expression you offered. I found it strange how compelled I was to kiss you from the moment I set eyes on you."

Though his words were meant to charm me, I grew uneasy.

"Do you think it's just because of your power? That you're so oddly drawn to me just because of the bond?" I winced at the vulnerability in my voice, at the information I was keeping from him.

He quipped, "I'd like to think I'm not *that* self-absorbed."

I leveled a glare at the illuminated ceiling. It tore me to pieces to think this likely wasn't real. *What if it is just his claim over me drawing him to me?*

"I've never felt this way before," he added. "I feel more alive when you're near—you make me feel whole. Maybe some of that is the magic pulling us together...but I never felt this whole."

I swallowed hard. *You will tell him about the claim in the morning,* I reminded myself. *Enjoy these moments now.* "Will you be here in the morning?" I asked.

He pulled his head back to look me in the eyes again. "That depends. Will you have horns and claws and sharp teeth?"

"No." I smiled—my cheeks were beginning to hurt from their lack of muscle memory.

"Well, then, what would be the fun?" he teased, but his smirk faded into a soft expression that made my heart skip. *If this wasn't real, how could he possibly look at me with such unguarded warmth?*

"I'll be wherever you are. Wherever you go. I knew that from the moment I set eyes on you."

The sincerity in his promise settled in my heart like kindling to a flame.

PART THREE

FALLEN FLAMES

CHAPTER 31
ASTERIE

The sun had not yet risen. Fenris slept soundly with an arm slung across me—so soundly that he didn't notice me reluctantly slip from his hold.

Every instinct begged me to stay with him.

He looked so peaceful, with a tousle of hair over his forehead and his face relaxed and lineless.

I slipped into my nightgown and bent over his sleeping form, whispering a Phynnic charm to deepen his sleep so he wouldn't wake when I left his quarters. Before stepping away, I kissed his brow.

"I will be back before you wake," I whispered for my own good conscience, knowing he couldn't hear me.

I grabbed his green cloak from a hook by the door. I'd only need to borrow it. For what Sybilla had requested, it would be best to travel about the palace *clothed*.

Taking one last look at Fen's blissfully unaware expression, I slipped out of his room.

***

My velvet slippers were quiet against the stone of the spiral staircase that led up to the main chamber of the Keep.

Another tower meant to protect, which instead imprisoned the one person Fenris held most dear, his only remaining family. Before he had fallen asleep, he told me stories about his sister, the fiery redheaded girl who loved nothing more than trying to keep up with her older brother. The youngest child—wild at heart and his father's favorite.

When Elsie was born, Fen was already a century older than her. He had hurried home to help his mother since his father had been away on business with the Brennac King. Fenris had cared for Elsie for three long nights as his mother recovered.

I heard the faint sound of snoring ahead.

The first guard of the Keep was asleep on the steps—convenient. I whispered the sleep charm to deepen his slumber before snapping my fingers to cut off the lamp lights in the staircase.

It made sense now why fire always moved toward me—that part of Fenris had touched my heart just like the star.

"Wherever you are. Wherever you go."

Panicked guards scampered down the steps to where the lamps had gone out. Their armor screeched, and one of them barked orders at the other.

I whispered the sleep charm again. Only when the two guards clambered to the steps in a snoozing heap of leather and metal did I snap for the lamps to relight.

Only three of them?

How Queen Sybilla had convinced Emmerick to station so few guards was beyond me.

Familiar purple and green vials stuck out from one of the guard's belts. I plucked them out nimbly and pocketed the once-gifted remedies.

Catching sight of a key ring on the other guard's belt, I unclasped it before approaching the door of the Keep's tower.

It was not wise—what the Queen had asked me to do. But she knew as well as I did that it was a risk to leave Elsedora to the fate of a trial in her court. She could only hold her in the Keep so long before the families of those fallen last night would demand her head.

What would it do to Fen if she was found guilty? When he had seen Elsie, his eyes had lit like the thousands of candles of Belray's summer celebrations.

My hands fumbled with the lock to the Keep's door. The lamplight in the room was dim and dreary. A neatly made bed with plain pressed linens sat to the right, and a fireplace was lit with dull embers to the left.

"It's Asterie."

Elsie's hands were bound—the chain attached to an iron pipe by the window. She didn't look up when I crossed the room, but a sarcastic smirk crossed her face. *So familiar.*

"Come to punish me for trying to kill your precious Queen?"

"No," I said flatly. "I have come to hear you out." Elsie's eyes tracked me with curiosity, but she only answered with a "hmph" of disbelief. "You lied to me. Why?"

"When I learned Fen was alive, I needed to see him myself. I needed to see if he was safe."

"With me," I added, and she nodded.

Elsie's hands wrung together, but she showed no other sign of nervousness. "I didn't trust that you were bringing him to Luz for any other reason than execution. Not after what Firose did to him—I couldn't risk him."

"You knew he was innocent then. How?"

Elsie's jaw tightened. "I saw what happened that night in Phynx. I was just a girl—seventeen. I ran away to follow Fen, determined that I could help him somehow. He had been called there to create mines around the castle. Traps and safeguards against the Brennac attack...he was there to keep the city's people *safe*.

"Fen always saw the world in gray—even when the Phynnic began to condemn people like our parents. He wouldn't let innocent people suffer for a war amongst their rulers. The way that history paints him is all wrong."

Elsedora's hands shook. "I know."

Her shoulders dropped and she let out a breath. "Then you understand my fury."

"I do," I replied. Fenris would never have attacked the people of Phynx. It took me so long to admit that fact, one that should have been so obvious.

Elsedora's shoulders slackened. "I wanted to be just like him. I snuck into Phynx that night after him. He found me and told me to go. But before I could run, the siege began. I was frightened to be captured by either side. So I followed him up to the roof and hid."

Elsie's eyes brimmed with tears.

"I could do nothing to stop it. I was so weak then. I just *watched*. How pathetic is that?"

I'd crossed the room before realizing it, and my hand found the top of hers—it didn't come naturally to offer someone comfort, but I found myself wanting to comfort her. *Fen's sister...his only remaining family.* Yet I didn't know the words to ease her guilt.

She would never work with Firose.

"Who sent you here, Elsie?"

"I work for King Darvanda. Still following in my brother's footsteps, I suppose. He used to work for him too before the Great Wars."

My mind had snagged on the name. *King Darvanda, where had I heard that before?* An excerpt that I'd memorized about Fenris the

Destroyer. King Krait Darvanda was the King to order the attack on Phynx.

"The King of Brennax?"

"Once upon a time, yes. Darvanda rules a different realm now."

The Wastelands. My heart snagged to think that Fenris had left out that very important detail...*Did he know?*

I shivered. The exiled King of Brennax led the Wastelands. And Elsie worked for him. That seemed a bad omen.

"The necklace...where did you get it?"

"The North Tower," Elsie answered with a shrug. "I was on an errand for Darvanda, and while rifling through some things, I came across it—I knew the stone immediately...You see, I'm not an assassin, but I *am* a talented thief."

So Firose had taken the stone back from Amara. *But when?* Last night, Fenris had explained what Amara had told him—of attaching his power to that star, saving him. My guess was she'd given it back to Firose after that, a keepsake that Firose didn't deserve.

"It was a family heirloom. I thought that maybe if Fenris saw the stone, he might know I was there—foolish, really. Men never piece together what you want them to. Or maybe I'm the fool for putting such a horrid memory back into his head."

I asked, "What did Darvanda want in the North Tower?"

"Information."

My lips turned up—she wasn't going to make this easy. "Information about?"

"Firose has angered my lord with her careless pursuit of power—she's weakened the wards to our realm and recruited the lowliest of our forces to her army. You and he have a common enemy."

So it seemed the Wastelands did not answer to Firose, at least not all of them. "How is Firose pulling forces from the Wastelands?"

"Many magic-wielders in the *'Wastelands'* still resent Henosis for outcasting them. Many there are willing to fight for her, to seek vengeance. Ironic, isn't it?"

"I fail to see the irony."

"Our people are defecting to her when *she's* the one who put them there. She's the one that bled Henosis dry of magic, of power, to keep it vulnerable. She locked away all the spell books in those towers and recruited you and your Sisters to do her dirty work. She thinks we do not know what she is up to—but we have been watching ever since the wards were compromised."

A thief *and* a spy. Something told me that Fenris might, in that moment, be proud.

I shuddered to think she was right. For centuries, Firose quelled any unrest, enforced the strictest of policies against magic use and crippled the five Corridors. She was a black widow who carefully built her web, spinning history to her whims before snaring what she desired. *Power.* It had always been power.

Elsedora's eyes widened as I found the key to uncuff her.

When her hands were free, she rubbed at her raw wrists and stared at me in disbelief. Dark red waves were loose over her shoulders. *How had I not seen the resemblance immediately?*

"Why help me?"

"You are Fen's sister. Despite what King you serve."

Elsie's lips creased into a smirk, and she took me in as though trying to size me up. "When I was in the North Tower, collecting my *information*, that is when I found the memorandum on Firose's desk. I thought it might be a trick."

I swallowed hard—*my foolish actions were to blame for the lives lost at the celebration.* My blood ran cold.

When I didn't speak, Elsie continued, "Firose must have sent one of her defectors to open the Egress. She knew you were headed to Luz, knew the Queen was working against her after seeing that memorandum. I believe her show of force was simply to prove how weak the realm is against her. Did you ward the Egress?"

"Yes, I have."

Elsie glanced at her unbound wrists once more.

"So, have you figured a way out of the Keep, then, thief?"

She gave me a confident smile that was so much like Fen's it nearly knocked me off my feet. "Of course. It will be much easier now that you've released the shackles. I was still working on a way out of those. I can scale down to the lower balconies and, from there, make my way out. Easy as one, two, three..."

"Well, this should make it even easier. It belongs to you anyhow—" I plucked the purple vial of invisibility serum from my pocket and held it out to her for the second time. She met my eyes with skepticism that gave way to confusion.

"You're not what I expected..."

"People keep telling me that."

Elsedora let out a faint huff of laughter. "I expected you to be more like *her*. You seem a perfect match for my brother, truly."

I could have ended up like Firose. If not for Amara—if not for being shown what genuine, unconditional love looked like. If not for leaving that tower. "I'm not—"

"Oh, but you are." Her eyes lit with amusement. "My brother has written ballads and poetry for dozens who stomped on his heart well before *she* ever did. He fell often but never very hard. Something tells me that may have changed in our centuries apart."

"He hasn't fallen—" I tried to deny it, but Elsie crossed the room to the window with lethal grace and speed.

Soon Elsie would be gone, into the night. *Free*—just as Sybilla had requested. But I still had one more duty to the Queen.

Sybilla had said, *"Break Fen's sister out of the Keep. Tell her to approach her lord about sending aid."* The Queen had been purposefully cryptic about who 'her lord' was. I should have asked her *far* more questions.

"Wait!" I stopped her. "Tell King Darvanda that if war is waged...we request his assistance."

This was a risky bargain. I wished I could shake sense into Sybilla. Elsie paused as she pulled back the curtains.

I added, "There is no way I can train all of those soldiers to use any useful magic or defense in a week's time. You know that as well as I do. We are sitting ducks. We have a mutual enemy."

"He'll want to know what's in it for him...the price will be steep." She was straddling the window frame with the invisibility serum tipped to her lips.

"The Wasteland wards. We will lower them all. If magic-wielders wish to return, we will give everyone a fair trial. We can reunite the realms." That part Sybilla had not instructed me to say—I hoped I hadn't taken too much liberty.

Elsie lowered the vial for a moment. "The wards are already broken—how do you think Firose got her lackeys here? How do you think I am here? And who says anyone *wishes* to return to Henosis? Who says we won't just come with force and take your lands?"

My heart pounded. "I can't imagine the Wastelands being a pleasant place to live," I reasoned.

"Then you judge a place by its name, my friend. Some in the Wastelands look at those wards as a blessing."

Elsie turned toward the window but smiled over her shoulder.

Darvanda would not come to our aid. Firose would approach with an army of Wasteland defectors—she would possess magic long forgotten by this realm and use it against the people of Henosis. We were fawns sitting in an open field with wolves approaching from all angles.

"Tell my brother we will meet again soon."

Elsedora downed the invisibility serum and silently slipped out the window.

Through the floor-to-ceiling windows, I could see it had begun to rain. The droplets steadily pattered against the palace windows. The sun was just beginning to peek over the horizon, and the mingling of golden light and droplets falling tempted me to go outside.

Cutting through the gardens would be the fastest route to Fen's bedchamber anyway.

I pushed open the heavy silver-embellished door and met the lukewarm, breezy air. A gentle sun shower graced the gardens as the birds began their morning song.

As I stepped out from under the overhang of balconies and spires above, I didn't bother to pull up Fen's cloak hood. Instead, I savored the feeling of the rain that gathered on my forehead and dampened my hair. Rain slid down my cheeks as my legs carried me in a blissful daze toward the maze of hedges that snaked through the garden's center.

Puddles gathered in places where the garden path was worn. It felt childish, but an urge to jump in them overtook me, so I did. My velvet slippers were soaked through. I was too distracted by the scent of wet soil, grass and honeysuckles to care.

Amara used to grow honeysuckle vines just like these along the walls of the South Tower. She taught me to place the sweet nectar on my tongue.

My hand trailed the hedges, which were trimmed below the eye-line. As I walked, my fingers slid over the delicate yellow silk blooms.

"Ouch!" I withdrew my hand—the bushes had transitioned to roses. *Damned thorns.*

Then my mind collapsed in.

"It hurt me, Momma!" A boy no older than four scurried across the South Tower's balcony, holding his right hand. Tears streamed across his tanned cheeks, and dark curls topped his head. He ran to a woman I didn't recognize. She was silver-haired, yet no older than thirty.

"Oh, my dear, let me see. The roses got you, didn't they?" the silver-haired woman said to the child.

Darker fingers than my own stretched out before me. I longed to comfort the child but stopped myself. The unfamiliar woman looked at me with a sad smile as she cupped the boy's head to her hip.

"A prick from a thorn can mean good luck—you can make a wish. Come now, let me have a look." I would recognize that voice anywhere. Amara—I was in Amara's memory. It was as clear as the other prophecies, no—*memories* of the fall of Phynx. *"That will certainly leave a scar—let's get it bandaged up. Now, what will you wish for?"*

I picked up the boy, and he looked at me with tear-soaked golden eyes and said, "All Knights have scars, right, Aunt Amara?"

"Mhm—most of them do." Amara's soothing tone was the same she'd once used to comfort me as a child. "Why do you ask?"

"I wish to become a Knight," the boy said triumphantly, wiping the salt from his face with his sleeves.

Amara's pride and fear of his sweet dream mixed. "You will be one of history's greatest Knights if you choose it, my love. Run along."

The fair-haired woman stepped closer. Her expression grew sadder with each step.

"You're sure this has to be the last time?"

"Yes." Amara's voice cracked in repressed agony. "And we must wipe his memory of me to be safe. No one must know, Angeline. I'll need to erase your memory too. If Firose finds out Mattock has an heir, she will kill him. It's not safe for you if she knows he is ours."

Angeline nodded.

"I will raise him in a way that will make you proud, Amara. He will want for nothing and always be loved like our own."

Amara's heart broke.

When I came to, I grasped my bleeding finger with my other hand.

"Everything alright, Asterie?"

Emmerick had been quiet in his approach. Or maybe I'd simply been too lost in the memory of tear-soaked golden-brown eyes filled with innocence and determination—Amara's son.

I was met with a gaze that held the same determination.

Amara's eyes.

Amara's child.

Mattock's child.

The heir of the North Corridor.

Immortal. And he had no idea about any of it.

"You're walking in the rain, hood down, in nothing more than slippers and a nightdress. And...bleeding. Should I bother to ask?"

He was smiling, but I was frozen, staring at him. I examined every curve of his face, every line.

"I like the rain." It was all I could say.

Emmerick looked at me bewildered.

"Just the two I was looking for."

A noxiously sweet voice hit me like a lightning bolt to the chest. *No. Not here, not now.* "What a strange place to find the Central Corridor's High Enchantress and the Queen's Constable, alone, unarmed."

The sunlight seemed to disappear in an instant, and the bird's song stopped.

Firose stood at the garden archway as six cloaked archers flanked her, donning northern armor. And blackened fingertips—they'd killed to gain access to the gardens, harnessed that dark magic for use on us now.

"I'm never unarmed," I growled.

Blue flames ignited in my palms. Emmerick's arm moved out in front of me as though he could protect me from whatever she had planned.

How had she gotten in? Had she been in the palace all night?

"I need them alive," Firose ordered as she looked under her nails carelessly, as though we were no threat.

I released the blue flames, aiming at two of the northern guards, but the flames bounced off an invisible shield before them and back at us. Emmerick and I ducked in unison.

Warded. Now I knew what they'd used that dark magic for.

"I won't let you go breaking apart to kill these ones too," Firose cooed.

Emmerick and I exchanged glances.

*She won't kill me…*I desperately wanted to believe that. I had no idea what she intended to do with Emmerick.

"Run," I commanded. "Now."

Emmerick shook his head and said, "I'm not leaving you." He did not understand the dire situation he was in. He was the heir to a throne Firose desperately wanted.

The six hooded archers drew their bows from their backs.

"Don't aim for anything vital," Firose commanded.

The archers released their arrows at once.

Emmerick was hit in the shoulder. I cried out as an arrow buried into my thigh—pain shot up my body. The arrow had struck bone.

Every belief that the woman who had once trained me wouldn't harm me vanished. In its place sat a heavy sense of betrayal. This was a political game, and we were all playing on Firose's game board, bending to her whims.

Everything grew clouded, groggy, slow. *Poison.*

"Asterie!" Emmerick's shout reached my ears just before I slumped to the ground.

This was the end of the road.

All the unseen paths that I'd tried to conjure, they all had led here.

CHAPTER 32
FENRIS

I awoke and reached toward Asterie's side of the bed. It was cold and empty.

My head felt groggy, like I'd been willed to sleep. *Has she sleep-charmed me? A lump grew in my throat—maybe Asterie regretted what we'd done. Maybe she was reeling from the intimacy.* That would be the simplest explanation. But it didn't seem like her to leave me jilted after the night we'd spent together.

No, if she left and hadn't returned, then there was a reason. I threw myself out of bed and pulled on my breeches and a tunic so quickly that I stumbled into the wall. As I shoved my feet into my boots, my fingers tried to reach for my green cloak but didn't find it. *She'd taken it...she went willingly.*

Yet something felt irrevocably wrong. My heart wanted her to simply be outside the bedroom door, returning to me with a glass of water or breakfast. The hairs on my arms were on edge.

I pushed the doors open to the hallway—she wasn't there.

Van appeared before me in the hallway as though responding to my panic.

"Find her."

He leaped down the Corridor, eliciting a shriek and a clambering of dropped metal trays from maids passing by. I sunk my fingers into my hair—my throat closed, utter helplessness washed over me. *You are overreacting.*

"Let me see her if you find her," I whispered to Van through the bond.

She likely just got an early start on her day.

"Will you be here in the morning?" she'd asked. I'd thought the question implied that she would be too. *But what had she been up to in the middle of the night? And why hadn't she returned?*

I paced the halls for what felt like hours, yet it was likely only minutes before I felt the press of Van trying to show me something at my temples. I let him in.

Blood.

Vangard's eyes were on a pool of blood staining the rain-dabbled cobblestone of the garden path. My stomach turned.

It can't be hers.

To spill that amount of blood, it could have been a fatal wound. *I'm still standing. She must be alive.* I couldn't breathe.

Vangard sniffed at something else.

There, on the blood-puddled ground, lay a recognizable patch of fabric. An emblem—an eye, a scale and a ring of thorns. The patch that I had ripped from Asterie's robes that awful day in Kullworth and tucked into my cloak pocket.

The once-white embroidered scale was now stained red.

After racing up the palace staircase to the third floor, taking steps in twos, I was out of breath. A cold pit of *emptiness* settled in my chest—that empty feeling that told me Asterie was not near. It was an unpleasant yet familiar sensation that I'd grown numb to for the centuries spent without her. That feeling was now ripped raw.

When I burst through the doors, Queen Sybilla was sitting at her desk—a grand oak piece, more art than function. Her head was collapsed into her hands. *Was she weeping?*

"Where is Asterie?" I hadn't meant it to be a snarl.

I kicked the door closed behind me, hard. My vision was in hues of red. Flames licked from my fingertips—it wouldn't take much to set me over the edge. Just a spark. *Go ahead, say the wrong thing.*

I would burn this palace to the fucking ground if the Queen didn't start talking.

She lifted her head and barked back, "Mind your tone."

Ready to strike, I crossed the room. The Queen didn't flinch as I neared, and though her nostrils flared, tears threatened to fall down her cheeks.

Sources, how I loathed seeing women cry. Fisting my hands, I extinguished the flames on my fingertips.

"Where is she? I'm not going to ask a third time."

The Queen circled the desk to stand before me, hands shaking but otherwise holding her posture.

"Firose Van Gran has taken my Constable and your Source Match." Her voice cracked on *Constable*. My heart cracked at *Source Match*.

The Queen had made an assumption that I should have far sooner. The pain in my chest due to Asterie being in danger—it confirmed what she really was to me.

Every muscle in my body went rigid.

Vangard burst through the door, leaving it swinging on its hinges. The Queen stilled at the sight of Van, but to her credit and courage, her feet didn't move an inch. He stalked into the over-decorated room, flanking me and waiting for my signal to attack. Drool pooled down his curled lip onto the elaborate, woven carpets.

I wouldn't let Van attack—no, if she'd done something to Asterie then I would kill her with my bare hands. That didn't mean I couldn't let him scare the piss out of her first.

Where are the Queen's guards? Who in this court protects her aside from the boy?

Her voice was quickening with explanation. She didn't look at Van, only at me as she continued to explain the conversation she and Asterie had in the crypt. She spoke of etched prophecies, the dead Central King's journals and his dying words.

She needed to get *on* with it.

"What have you done?"

"Nothing! Firose kept Asterie locked away in that tower for centuries. Cultivating her, waiting to use her." She huffed out a breath as Van's furled lip drew close—inches from her face. "Only she must know by now that she can't claim Asterie as she'd planned." The Queen winced when she looked up at Van's bared teeth.

"What do you mean?" I shouted.

She matched the volume of my voice. "The orchards never belonged to Firose! The plums belonged to your family, to *you*."

I hated those words on the Queen's lips—they hit me like a hammer to the chest. *That can't be possible.* "Then why take her and not me?"

She answered, "If you are near, then *you* can claim Asterie—that's a risk Firose isn't likely to take without a plan, now is it? But what do I know? Please just call off your dog!"

An exasperated sound left my lips.

I would never dull Asterie's light. I would never claim her.

I motioned for Van to cease his threatening. He growled one last time before grunting and lying down behind me.

The Queen added, "Asterie figured out that Firose cannot claim her when we spoke before the welcome celebration. If I had known sooner..." Queen Sybilla looked lost for words.

Asterie had known last night. She just hadn't trusted me enough to tell me. It felt like someone drove a blade through my heart.

I'd find a way to be worthy of her—whatever it took.

"We will go find them," I ground out.

"No." It seemed to pain her to say it. "We can't."

Every muscle in my body went rigid. "And why not?"

"I received word that Firose's forces have already gathered along the western and northern borders of the Central Corridor...Leaving now would put the city at risk."

"Then let me fight through them all."

"Think about it, Fenris," she reasoned. "We have no idea where she has taken them. As much as I want to, I can't split my forces and send them on a fool's errand. If I send soldiers with you, it weakens my defense here. I can practically hear Emmerick scolding me for even *entertaining* the thought."

She was right. The world was one giant fucking chessboard for Firose. She had us in checkmate.

It *would* be a fool's choice to go after her knowing that an army of magic-wielders stood in my way.

"How did she get to her?" I asked.

The Queen's shoulders finally slumped. "I don't know. Emmerick left this morning while I was still asleep. The next I knew, there was banging on my door and news that Palace guards were downed outside the garden. By the time additional help arrived, they were gone."

That empty feeling inside of me grew.

The Queen cleared her throat, looking up at the ceiling. She dabbed at the tears under her eyes with her fingertips.

"What do you propose we do then to get them back?" I couldn't believe I was contemplating staying.

"By my scouts' estimates Firose's forces will be here by dusk. So we fight her *here*—when she comes for the gates of Luz. Then I will provide you with whatever resources you need to find them."

Find her.

I needed to find Asterie.

If anything happens to her...

"I'm going to need you to grow a pair now and stop panicking—your fear is literally suffocating me. No man makes good choices when afraid."

"What?" I asked.

She smirked weakly. "I'm an Empath."

Shit. I immediately tried to clear my thoughts.

"Shit, indeed, Fen. Shit, indeed."

"My sister—"

"Is safe. On her way back to the Wastelands. I asked Asterie to break her out of the Keep last night."

That was where she'd gone. That feeling of being pierced in the heart now felt like the blade was being twisted. While she hadn't trusted me, she'd left my bed only to help my little sister.

"Emmerick must have been heading to check in with the Keep guards when he and Asterie were taken. It must have been just before sunrise...I hadn't told him my plan." She let out a defeated sigh.

Emmerick. The boy I'd helped save, Amara's boy. Firose had Asterie and Emmerick. Prince of the North Corridor. The Queen's head tilted in curiosity. *Had she slipped into my mind again?*

Sybilla corrected me, "*King.* Not prince." The Queen's fists clenched. "I'll kill her. If she lays a hand on him—"

"You will need to get in line for that, my Queen."

My Queen.

A new alliance was being built here.

Seeming to pick up on that thought, Queen Sybilla spoke, "Without you, we won't stand a chance against northern forces." Gone was her hardened shell. "The people here—they are completely unprotected against magic. We need you here. Asterie needs you *here.* Firose will not kill them. They are too useful to her."

Despite wanting nothing more than to raise fire to anything that stood between me and finding Asterie, she was right. My strange beauty would want me to fight for the innocent lives in Luz. She would turn away my help instantly if it meant securing the Central Corridor from enemy hands.

"It will be an honor to serve the people of Luz, Queen Wymark." My hand extended to her.

"Please, call me Sybilla."

"Sybilla, then."

She took my hand and gave it a firm shake, squeezing my fingers hard enough to hurt.

We will bring them home safely. Sybilla nodded at that thought.

I tried to find comfort in the knowledge that Asterie had Emmerick and that her powers weren't up for the taking.

So many things called me to Asterie—the blood oath her mother made, my fire within her and whatever strange prophecy kept speaking to us.

She was stardust sweeping through the skies. She was flame cutting through an open field. She was strong—stronger than Firose, stronger than me. No one would claim her, not now and not ever. She would fight, and she would win.

Fight, Asterie. You must fight.

CHAPTER 33
ASTERIE

*W*hat had happened? The iron archways towered above me. *The Central Tower.* I focused on the vining ivy and dark stone of the foyer wall in front of me. This place had never felt so domineering as it did through blurred, poison-induced grogginess.

The bargain in the orchard.

The heir of the North.

Fenris' innocence.

Firose's guilt.

And her hand in the attack on the Queen.

The effects of the poison jumbled my thoughts. My heart ached as every dreadful memory resurfaced up until the moment when a poisoned arrow had pierced my skin.

The arrow was no longer jutting from my thigh. In its place was dried blood caked against my bare leg. The dried blood was the first clue that I had been unconscious for hours. The second was that no sunlight trickled in through the windows. Dusk had passed.

I wasn't one to curse, but I muttered every forbidden word under the sun at the sheer pain coursing down my leg. Immortality might come with eternal life, but it didn't erase pain.

Emmerick was bound and chained to the thick iron door frame of the atrium. The glass pane of the window next to the frame had been punched out, and both of our chains had been looped through it. Emmerick sat slumped over, looking at the floor, his hands bound in his lap.

I cursed again under my breath. He was only a couple of yards away, but in my state, that felt like miles.

"Emmerick," I whispered, but he didn't respond. "Emmerick, look at me."

When his eyes lifted, they were fogged and glassy as though he'd had too much to drink. "Em, are you okay?"

He nodded but said nothing. Dread clutched my chest. He looked helpless—broken.

I shook my head—I'd never imagined Firose would hurt me. Yet, she had. She'd hurt Emmerick.

She'd hurt Fen.

Would he think I left on my own will? Would he look for me? I hoped he would stay far away from here—far from the woman who had once carved guilt into his heart. I feared what she might do with both of us.

What was her plan?

"How long was I unconscious?" I croaked at Emmerick through dry lips.

From behind me, Firose answered, "Oh, all day. I truly thought you'd handle your poison better."

The cool calculation in Firose's words made me see red. I tried to summon blue flames in my palms, but nothing happened. *Peace Prevail*—I'd forgotten she'd cuffed me.

"But it gave me and the Constable some time to catch up. Pity, really, that Amara kept him from me all this time. Such a fine specimen, isn't he?"

A growl roused from my throat as Firose crossed the room and crouched before Emmerick. She took his chin between her polished red fingernails.

"Don't hurt him," I ground between gritted teeth. "Why? Why are you doing this?"

She had her murderous, power-hungry fingers on my friend. Someone who cared about *me*. Not the power running through me.

People were shouting outside—a man barked orders. An army. She'd staged an army in the clearing surrounding us.

"My dear Asterie," Firose crooned. "You have wandered far from this tower. Tell me about your journey."

Did she genuinely believe I would be so easily distracted?

I wouldn't bend to her will this time. She had no claim over the powers that the Stars had bestowed upon me. I would shake the heavens to make sure she never got ahold of Fen's again either.

"Fuck you."

"You leave your tower once and suddenly become a sailor." Firose's eyes narrowed as she rose and stepped away from Emmerick. "Don't be a fool."

She crossed the room toward the hearth and began to prepare something, plucking ingredients from my shelves.

"I won't be your fool, not anymore," I spat. "You cannot claim me!"

Then, crying out from the pain in my leg, I stood and faced the back of the woman who had raised me with all the nurture of a Commander training a front-line soldier. I was merely a piece of her grand puzzle—an asset to use when she had pleased.

Firose braced but did not answer. It looked as though her hands shook as she readied a vial.

"I know and Death knows that too now," she answered, and when she looked at me over her shoulder, I saw the whites of her eyes.

What in hell did that mean?

Firose sucked in a breath. Her gaze returned to cruel indifference once again before she turned back toward the hearth. Emmerick was motionless, steps away from me, but he raised a narrow glare at Firose like a dog on a chain might look at a trespasser just out of its reach.

"What's your move here, Firose? Unbind my powers from me?"

"No, not quite." Her tone sounded removed, calm. "Since a Lamoreaux lives, it complicates things. Once we've taken Luz and eliminated the risk of Fenris the Destroyer claiming you, then we'll figure out how we might work together."

"Work together." That I doubted—she would try to figure out how to use me.

She kept speaking as though she had allies left. My rage carried me forward a couple steps, and I winced through the fire-like spread of pain up my leg.

"Who is 'we,' Firose? I don't see any of our Sisters standing at your side."

She did not look at me, she only said plainly, "In time."

I scanned the ingredients she was using. Lavender, pig's blood and grated birch bark.

The Skei remedy.

She intends to unbind something. Would she try to unbind the powers from me to take them for herself? Would I survive it...would Fen? When had she realized that Fenris' magic coursed through my veins? My heartbeat was throbbing in my ears.

"I learned a lot by listening through the castle walls all night. Enough to confirm my suspicion that part of his magic lives in you. It felt so very familiar. Unfortunate that his powers won't be salvageable." She seemed to be answering the question I had not asked.

Sources. Could she hear my thoughts as Sybilla could?

My blood ran cold. *She intended to kill Fen.*

If she unbound that half of his power from me and destroyed it...*No.*

"Let me guess...he charmed himself right into your breeches, and now you're *in love* with him?"

When she met my gaze over her shoulder again, my expression must have betrayed me. A sad smile crossed her features. "Your potential exceeds his."

All the air left my lungs.

She continued, "He's not coming for you, dear. No one is—but I have always been here, haven't I?"

A lump grew in the back of my throat. She would kill Fen just to ensure he couldn't claim my power. But she wouldn't stop there—she'd find a way to use me. After the awakening of my full power at the welcome celebration, nothing scared me more than my starlight in her hands.

Peace Prevail. She could end it all.

The realm wouldn't just be in political ruin. It would lay in *ruin.*

Finally, I understood for certain why no path led me here, why no conjuring in the moonstone would allow me to see my fate. It would always end in death for me.

A thousand what-could-have-beens raced through my mind.

Living a quiet life with Fenris in a cabin by a riverbed.

Visiting with Emmerick and Sybilla in Luz and watching their children grow.

Dancing through every court.

Seeing every sunrise with renewed appreciation for the light.

I turned my attention to Emmerick. My brother, in a way. The son of the enchantress who raised me with love and kindness that she should have had the opportunity to extend to him. But she couldn't because of Firose. I seethed for him—to lack such a bond.

"And you, heir of the North Corridor." Firose followed my gaze to Emmerick, her elbow leaning against the hearth mantle. "What better Queen to rule with than one who has already been controlling the North Corridor for centuries? You may even grow to like me in time. No one will refute my claim to a crown if you are by my side."

Emmerick stared blankly at Firose—he had reacted to so little. *What horrors had he endured while I was unconscious? What truths had he faced alone?*

The risk of Fen's death, her ending up with my starlight and her rule over the North Corridor made me dizzy. I could only control two out of those three evils. As she returned to mixing the Skei remedy, my mind settled on the solution.

Fighting a groan against every step closer to Emmerick, I finally reached him and knelt. I glanced down at his pant leg, pleading with any Source willing to listen that he had the one weapon he was never without. I felt around for the green vial in the pocket of Fen's cloak—relieved when my fingers found the cool, smooth glass.

"I request the presence of Lady Angeline," I softly said as hot pressure built behind my eyes.

His expression crumbled, realizing what I was asking. Our exchange hadn't caught Firose's interest yet.

I whispered, "Now. Then unbind my hands. Cut them off if that's what it takes."

"Asterie," Emmerick pleaded, but the blood oath caused him to reach for his blade anyway.

I slid the green vial from my pocket, popped the cork lid and downed the tonic. It would not save me, but I hoped it would slow the process enough for me to save Fen.

"Falling by your hand is the most honorable way I can leave this world." I met his eyes with a reassuring intensity. "Em, it's *now* or never."

Angeline's ruby-gilded hilt caught the light of the lamps in the foyer.

"No!" Firose's shriek rang through the tower.

But it was too late. Emmerick used the precision of years of training to pierce my heart and fulfill the awful blood oath he'd made with me.

Firose hesitated to cross the room as though her feet were stuck to the ground.

In another swift motion, Emmerick rose and crushed the cuffs that bound my wrists beneath his boot—my bones broke between the cuffs, but my magic was finally free.

The tonic afforded me only a few moments of consciousness to do what needed to be done.

"You!" Firose was upon Emmerick now, and I heard footsteps on the tower stairs.

The last thing I saw was Firose's hands igniting in flames, she pressed them against Emmerick's chest and forced him against the wall, away from me. The singed smell of his skin and his cry of agony filled the air. *I'm sorry, too. So sorry.*

I willed Fen's power out of me with every ounce of energy that remained.

Release our hands from the ropes that bind us.
Unshackle our legs once twined—allow them to roam free.
Sever the ties holding our bodies together.
Release him.

I called upon Death to save him. *Spare him.*

Lacero, Lacero, Lacero.

It could be done if the Origin of Death was willing to make a bargain. The Lacero curse could be added to any common binding or unbinding—at least, that was what the texts had stated.

Take me, Death. Let him live. Return his power to him. Let him fight. Death closed in, ready to take me in his grasp.

Firose couldn't have me.

She wouldn't have Fenris, either.

Fen's power fought to stay, but I fought harder to force it out. The fire crept through every vein. It felt like my blood boiled as it held on to me. Shards of glass fell upon me, cutting across my face, as every window in the tower blew in from my screams. I was a black hole consuming the sun. For a few moments, I was nothing, and yet I was everything.

Please. Let Fenris live.

Then everything grew very dark and very cold.

CHAPTER 34
FENRIS

The stars shined brightly over Luz. But below their serene twinkle, cannons blared, cutting through the peace of night.

Hours ago, we had evacuated as many civilians as we could. The rest, hundreds still, were secured behind the walls of the bailey and in the tunnels below the Keep. Anywhere we could find a place for them, the innocent lives of Luz had been stowed away.

The siege of Luz had begun.

Firose's troops had stormed so quickly. Hundreds of Wasteland defectors marched at the sides of hundreds more northern soldiers. Cannons were pulled into the city by a cavalry clad in black armor. Sybilla had barked orders to her guard all day and readied the Corridor for attack, yet I'd felt utterly paralyzed.

"Fenris." Sybilla's voice interrupted my worry—she refused to stay up in the Keep despite the guards' pleas. Instead, she was with me on the outer south battlement wall, facing her falling city. Her hair was braided around a thin crown of silver acorns, and she donned war leathers that seemed sharp compared to her delicate features.

Sybilla leveled an arrow at a soldier who was trying to climb over the battlement wall. She met her mark without hesitation. The arrow struck through the soldier's eye—his grip was lost and he fell to the battle below.

"Good work," I mumbled.

"Emmerick taught me," she mused sadly. Then, as my frown deepened, she offered words of reassurance. "Remember, if you are still standing, then it's likely she's still alive. You're bound."

I nodded with a hard swallow.

Fire burned in my palms. It grew and grew until it became unruly, then I unleashed it at the cannons below, approaching the south wall. The cannons burst into flame as intended, three in one strike. *I still had some fight in me.*

There was no fighting dark magic with mortal means. The northern magic-wielders' weapons ebbed only with darkness and, every so often, flashed dark amber against their opponents. Smoke and ash began overtaking Luz—the city looked to be painted in black and amber. The inky, putrid smell of death hung around us.

The ground cracked at a Soil-wielder's hands to create sinkholes for Luz's cavalry. Buildings burned in deep orange hues, and gusts of pale brown wind clouded the air, making sight near impossible in the fray below. Every magic known to the lands was being wielded against the mortal soldiers of Luz.

Each downed central soldier only added to the strength of the northern attack. There were no flames of red, blue flares of the Moon or white streaks of Wind—every Source magic wielded was marred by Death.

In the city below, Van was taking out dozens of soldiers at a time with ease. He spun and snarled in rage—he was half as tall as most of the buildings around him, his largest form possible with only half of my power. *Still a lethal and near-undefeatable opponent.* Soldiers were squashed beneath his feet as they tried to swarm him, and any blood they drew only made his wrath stronger.

The siege neared the outer battlements, dangerously close to where Sybilla and I stood. Only a few soldiers had made it up the wall so far, but it was only a matter of time.

Shrieks rattled my eardrums—they came from above. Dozens of giant hawk-like creatures flew overhead. Air raiders from the East Corridor had arrived. They dropped bombs of saltpeter, sulfur and charcoal upon Northern troops still entering the city, staving off further entry.

Sybilla had written the rulers of all Corridors that morning to alert them of Firose's approaching forces. The East and West Corridor leaders had quickly agreed to send aid, not wanting to give the North a central foothold to continue conquering their lands next. But only the flyers of the East had been fast enough to be of any help.

Even with the beating wings of Griffiths overhead and Van's massive form in all his fury, we still stood to lose. I was no war general, no Constable. I hated to admit it, but I missed the boy Commander. All I could do was stand by the side of the woman he loved and hope that he too would be doing everything in his power to protect Asterie. It felt like an eternity had passed since waking without her that morning.

We will die on this wall.

I will never see her again.

The Central Queen rested a hand on my shoulder as if knowing where my thoughts had wandered.

That's right, she *did* know.

"All hope is never lost, Fenris. I dream of a realm where we can find sustainable peace...and even if we go down in flames today, those who come after us will not bend to enmity. They will remember this day. They will avoid repeating it." She squeezed my shoulder once more. "Asterie is fighting too."

They sounded alike—Sybilla and Asterie. It was admirable. Insane—but admirable. "I hope that we live to see that dream come true," I answered with a weak smile.

Then, a tingling feeling shot up my forearms. My hands were glowing, and red flames shot from my fingertips in an unruly flash. I closed my fists before the flames could hurt the Queen.

"Fenris, are you alright?" Her alarmed question was drowned by the roar in my ears. Every nerve in my body sparked—like a burning sensation sinking into my bones.

The ground shook beneath my feet. My senses hadn't felt this sharp since...*Sources.* It was before the other half of my power had been siphoned from me.

Smoke billowed like molasses above us. All movement around me slowed. Despite the darkness, my vision adjusted to how *bright* the world seemed. Even Sybilla's outreached arm lagged as though she were swimming through mud. Then my heart clenched, and the whole world surged to life—every muscle ached as if my body was readjusting to its form.

Sybilla's mouth was agape as she stared at something over the wall.

Van had tripled in size—he towered over most of the buildings and was taking out dozens of soldiers with a single swipe of his clawed paw. Soldiers were attempting to point cannons at the towering beast approaching them.

When Van let out a roar, it was accompanied by flames that set the soldiers and their cannons ablaze.

My flames had returned to him. How?

I looked down at my hands. *Fenris the Destroyer...whole again.*

Whole.

But, if I was whole, that meant the other half of me had returned. I paled as Sybilla grabbed my wrists.

No. That wasn't possible. Not without...fuck.

A memory flashed of a peculiar volume on Asterie's desk the morning we fought in the Central Tower's arena. I had thought then that she would try to unbind herself from me out of anger. She'd been reading about the Lacero curse—a type of magic you need to make a deal with Death to wield.

"She's unbound my power," I shrieked.

Sybilla's grip on my wrists grew tighter. Rage simmered in me. I wanted to rip the Central Queen's throat out for convincing me to stay, to not go after Asterie right away. Sybilla met my gaze with cold determination and a lack of fear.

She grew still as she listened to things I could not hear. "I am not your enemy, Fen." She glared before her expression cracked. "I can feel Emmerick again—he's near. He's in pain."

If Emmerick was near, that could mean Asterie was close too. *She couldn't be dead*—my mind raced for any other explanation for how she might have been able to return my power to me.

If Firose never possessed part of me in the first place, if I'd never loved her, then none of this would be happening.

"You are not my enemy," I numbly repeated.

Sybilla forcefully let go of my wrists before grabbing her bow. An arrow whipped past me, and I turned in time to see it catch a northern soldier between his chest plate and shoulder armor before he fell to his death.

I stepped to the battlement wall and looked down.

In the chaos in the city below, I spotted a large figure illuminated by the light of the burning city. Stepping through the smoke, a form of pure muscle, brute strength and short black hair. Emmerick's ankles were chained. My blood boiled when his captor's golden hair caught the wind below the northern crown.

Firose held the chains like she was leisurely walking a dog through a battlefield. Lynx and northern guards flanked her as she made a show of it. *It was probably a trap.* She was looking for a reaction, and I was ready to give her just that.

Then my attention caught on a lifeless figure in a familiar green cloak lying in Emmerick's blood-soaked arms. Her body was limp and her fingertips, blackened from the magic she'd wielded, hung toward the ground.

Asterie.

"No…" I had no breath. "No, fuck—no!"

"Fenris, don't…" Sybilla tried to catch my arm, but her hand slung back with a hiss as my skin ignited. I'd burn anything between me and Asterie. "Fenris, wait!"

Her words blurred behind the roar in my ears as I launched through one of the crenels of the south wall and began to scale my way down.

Down to kill the bitch that dared to lay a hand on the most precious thing to happen to me.

Firose would pay for whatever she had done.

CHAPTER 35
SYBILLA

That crazy motherfucker was going to kill the newly appointed *Queen* of the North. As Fenris scaled down the jagged stone wall with adrenaline-fueled precision, all I could do was watch in horror.

I was on the upper south wall—I'd requested to be alone here. If the palace was to be sieged, it would be among the first walls to fall. With me dead, or captured, I hoped the attack would relent and soldiers would not kill those in the Keep behind me or the tunnels below.

My breath hitched and my heart clenched at the sight of Emmerick in the chaos below. Seeing him chained made me seethe. It made me root for the warlock even more. *Let him set her aflame.*

Emmerick's rage felt like cold tacks dragging along my spine. It tasted metallic, like blood slipping between a split lip. He looked at the tower and pushed through my carefully built mental blocks. It wasn't hard to focus on his thoughts alone—*they were so loud.*

"*My Queen.*" His voice soothed me. His next thoughts made my heart stop. "*How long have you known?*"

All that bitterness wasn't entirely aimed at his adversary. *No,* some of it was aimed at *me.*

Shit. Emmerick knew.

"*Since the first time that I kissed you.*" I pushed that admission into his head.

My father would have been proud of me for not disclosing a truth that could have threatened our Corridor—for holding it from Emmerick all these years.

"*Come here and sit.*" *My father pulled me by my hand to sit on the sofa beside him. It was our first moment alone since traveling to the North Corridor. He'd been furious with me for inviting Emmerick along—but I'd needed a groom for the horses. At sixteen, I'd entered the age that selecting my own staff for long travels from home wasn't out of the ordinary.*

There were so few of them whose thoughts I could endure.

My father and I awaited King Mattock, our Corridor's long-time ally. We sat in his study in the Castle of Helos. The walls were weighted with so much gold it burned my eyes. The Sun King. *Every inch of his study reflected the sun's rays. The castle was built atop the highest peak of the Hussa mountain range—the closest point to the sun in all the realm.*

"*The stable boy. It is okay that you are friends, but you must promise that it is friendship alone. It can never surpass that. He has work to do. And you have a Corridor to rule.*"

Was he seriously lecturing me about Emmerick before we were to meet with the North King?

"*Father.*" *I rolled my eyes.*

"*Sybilla.*" *His tone was serious and gruff. He wasn't fucking around, and I knew he could make this visit a miserable one. Since*

I had not earned any bruises on this trip yet, I conceded to choose my battles. "I mean it."

My father had always liked the stable boy, allowing him to teach me how to use a bow and arrow. Emmerick had access to me that no other boy two years my senior would be caught dead with.

Suddenly, the reality of that set in. He trusted Emmerick with me more than he trusted me with Emmerick.

"I'm offended by your insinuation that I lack self-control. Have you asked this of him too?"

"He understands his place in my court. And it is my *court until my dying breath—"*

He was interrupted by his own fit of coughing.

Mattock entered, cutting my father's cough-filled tirade short.

"Old friend!" Mattock grasped my father's shoulder tightly. "You look like hell," he joked jovially. There was something different about the North King—dark circles below his eyes, a faint sadness that emanated off of him.

My father braced at Mattock's observation of his health. He had been ill for some time and often hid the blood coughed into his napkins. The maids in Luz talked, and even if they didn't, I'd hear them thinking about it.

Mostly, the court's staff thought me incapable of ruling, worried that if my father was gone too soon, the Corridor would descend into chaos.

The immortal North King was exuberant, a presence at over six feet tall. Broad-chested and handsome with a mop of brown hair and hazel eyes. He regarded me politely with a bow and a kiss on the top of my hand.

"Princess Sybilla. You have grown—you were yea high last time I was in the Central Corridor." He held his hand a few feet from the ground.

After exchanging pleasantries, my father and Mattock launched into political negotiation—amicable, standard topics. Trade routes. Avoiding famine this winter. Nothing out of the ordinary.

My mind was occupied—my father brought me along as education, but I learned nothing from the conversation. I was too busy studying every detail of King Mattock's face. The strong line of his chin, his almond-shaped eyes, the way he grabbed the back of his neck when concerned. It was all so familiar.

Then Mattock asked my father a peculiar question.

"He is here?"

My father nodded but shifted uncomfortably as though not want-ing to speak freely in front of me. Or think *freely.*

"I should like to meet him. But she *is present, and it isn't safe. Next time." There was sadness in the Sun King's voice.*

My curiosity peaked.

I opened my mind to my father's thoughts. He was careful never to think in words. He knew better around me, but he wasn't as talented at guarding his visual thoughts. A vision of Emmerick flashed—wearing a crown. The very one on Mattock's head now.

The familiarity suddenly struck me, and I nearly spit my tea, choking on it.

"Are you alright?" My father's voice sounded like a warning. Caught. I was caught.

"Yes!" I exclaimed too quickly.

I steadied my hands, allowing my mind to push into Mattock's. It was clouded with worry, worry for a son he didn't know. But then a cold, dark feeling gripped my mind. It was like my very thoughts were being pressed together.

A vicious snarl that did not sound human, not like Mattock at all, shouted, "Get out!"

I gasped, and my father elbowed me, hard.

"Sybbie, please give me and King Mattock a minute to speak privately."

I rose without question, but my father caught my arm with a commanding grip that would later bruise. So much for leaving Helos without bruises.

"But carry a message to Emmerick. Tell him to stay in the stables. He isn't to enter this castle, and he isn't to be seen on the grounds. Understand?"

With a terse nod, I curtsied to the North King and stepped away from the two rulers, feeling as ill-prepared for this life as the maids and footmen thought me to be.

As soon as the doors behind me clicked shut, I hiked up my skirts and ran down halls and passageways of the North Court. Crossing the courtyard, I trudged through puddles and mud and rocky terrain. When I arrived at my intended destination, I'd managed to lose all of my guards and *the bottom hem of my dress.*

Bursting into the stables, I looked for the boy who'd taught me everything—how to play a game of cards, sharpen a blade and curse like a sailor when no one was listening. He was alone, grooming a massive draft horse. He hadn't noticed me right away. My breath was labored, but I crossed the stables to him instead of stopping to regain it.

He turned to me with wide eyes. I stood on my tip-toes and took his face between my hands. He was completely still, but his face slackened with a traitorous look of need while his shoulders relaxed. My father should have known better—telling me what not *to do had never worked for him.*

"Sybilla." My name escaped Emmerick's lips in a reluctant warning. But he leaned down toward me.

I kissed him. He returned the kiss for a few brief moments of bliss, snaking his hands around the back of my neck and into my hair.

I was lost in that kiss. My first kiss.

Then he grasped my wrists and pulled my hands from his face to push me away. When he put distance between us, his brow creased in a pained expression. He shook his head, and fear crept up my spine. Not my own—his fear.

It was then I realized it—he was on my father's payroll in more ways than he let on. There was a reason my father trusted me with him. He was no groom or stable boy.

"How long have you been one of my guards?"

"Since you were twelve."

A low gasp escaped me as he pushed my hands back down to my sides—that was their proper *place when interacting with one's guard, after all. He pulled his hands away from me, as though he'd touched hot iron.*

Emmerick had always seemed to take any job my father gave him without complaint. He had spent years mucking shit from stalls and acting as a servant. He could blend in seamlessly, aside from his size.

"You shouldn't be wandering around the North Court alone," he said.

I gave him a flat, sarcastic smirk which he countered with a deep sigh. "You kissed me back," I tried.

He shook his head of now disheveled black curls—his infuriatingly beautiful face hardened into a resolute frown. "You can't do that."

"What?"

"You can't just come in here and kiss me out of the blue, Sybilla."

"Why not?" I asked.

"Just promise, don't do that again. It isn't fair."

I allowed myself only a glimpse into what he was thinking—he was afraid to disappoint my father, afraid to be made a fool by me. "So your loyalty is to him then?" I knew it was an unfair question.

He winced. "Sybilla..."

I glared then—his rejection sitting heavy on my heart. But, instead of wallowing in sadness, I saw red. "Fine then." My tone turned icy as I began to storm out of the stables. He didn't follow me, which only ignited my fury as words tumbled coldly over my shoulder. "No guard of mine is to shovel shit and carry bags. You are appointed full-time as a Knight of the Central Court and my personal guard. In a permanent capacity. For now, it has been requested that you stay in the stables and avoid being seen. The King of the North does not like outside staff on his grounds."

If he was going to outright reject me, he deserved a front-row seat to every suitor that came knocking, every horrible match that my father tried to push. If he couldn't love me back in this moment, could he ever?

He stared me down with a stubbornness I'd grown to love about him—but at that moment, I loathed that part of him. The part that would put duty above wanting me.

Pissed off, dejected and raging at him for not chasing after me, I decided not to tell him the one thing I'd learned that could change his fate.

My father would later convince me it was for the best that he didn't know—a bastard son of the North King did not make a match for me. Plus, it put Emmerick in danger of being outcast to the Wastelands, or worse.

I made the first mistake toward losing him that night in the stables and had kept making it every night since.

After my father succumbed to illness and a crown touched my head, nothing but the Corridor mattered. Not even my selfish, misguided heart. I would not become my mother—drunk, sidelined, bruised and betrayed.

I would never marry a man who could weaken my position. I may have married Em the stable boy but never Emmerick the King.

Royalty has a way of being poison to one's character, allowing all the rotten bits to rise to the surface and leaving a shell of the person you used to be. It was a blessing from the Sources that Em was not raised that way.

In the fray below, Emmerick's rage was roiling, but beneath that rage was ash-tasting, curdled heartbreak. I was so deep in feeling his turmoil that I nearly missed my opportunity to down a soldier as he rounded over the battlement wall.

Stepping back, I lost sight of Fenris, Emmerick and Firose in the commotion unfolding below. The Griffiths' cries as they took arrows from archers and spiraled to the ground made my hands shake. Every flash of power used below was an assault on my nerves.

Then, a roaring sound began to cut through the night air coming from the gates of Luz—hoofbeats. So many horses that they created a thundering effect on the ground. The cavalry approached the city with whooping shrieks, ready to attack. Thousands of lanterns flickered from the horsemen, but as they neared, I realized the lights were not coming from lanterns at all.

No, the horses *themselves* wore flaming armor—each mount looked as though they were made of steel.

My throat closed.

White flag.

Firose's army was about to decimate the city my family long promised to protect. It would all end with me and my fucking stupidity in thinking my father's deathbed ramblings could possibly save us. It was doomsday for Luz.

I was about to drop my bow and light the flare that signaled defeat.

"They're quite something, aren't they?"

A deep, rough voice with a melodic accent came from the shadows to my right.

Spinning on my heels with an arrow drawn, I found a tall hooded form approaching, seeming to slip from the shadows. Ash-blackened fingertips pointed down at the flaming horses approaching.

How the hell did he get up here? I was so very screwed.

Behind him, Elsedora trailed from the shadows. They both wore dark rust-colored robes with a rattling serpent symbol embroidered across the chest. A symbol of the Wastelands, perhaps.

"Elsedora," I greeted calmly, not dropping my bow but knowing that between myself and the two of them, I didn't stand a fucking chance. "And your friend?"

The man lowered his hood to reveal dark stubble across a strong jawline, dusky skin and a striking grave expression—he wasn't the type of man I imagined ending me. I'd never thought I'd stare down death and find him attractive, but this grave, harsh-looking man was admittedly stunning.

His face was hardened into an effortless glare. He seemed to have permanent frown lines, and his dark brows creased downward.

"Krait Darvanda." His voice was gruff. My bow lowered only slightly in surprise. "Yes, the wisest choice is to lower that. And *look.*" He pointed out to the battlefield below. Men were dying below, and he looked sadistically amused.

Fucking pig.

The last Brennac King himself had come to see our downfall.

I should have known no good would come of having Asterie request his aid.

What did I expect from the man responsible for killing my Phynnic ancestors? The man had obliterated the city of Phynx centuries ago—his troops had mercilessly attacked with Vangard on that world-shattering night.

I'd thought for sure after hearing Elsedora's thoughts that we had a common enemy.

It took fighting every instinct to peel my attention away from Krait and Elsedora and glance over the wall. I braced for the bloodshed of my men. But the flaming mounted soldiers were fighting *alongside* them.

The Warhorses and the Central Corridor troops worked to fight back Firose's men. Only then did my bow lower completely; the wooden grip fell from my white-knuckled grasp, and the weapon clattered against the stone.

They weren't here to end us. They were here to help. It had worked.

I could have laughed. I could have cried. I did neither—I just stood there with my mouth agape and watched what felt like a miracle unfold below.

In my peripheral vision, I saw Elsedora whisper into Krait's ear, setting a hand on the King of the Wastelands' shoulder with familiarity. She didn't seem to fear him, and he gripped her fingertips momentarily before he nodded.

The cold sting of fear escaped Elsedora's mind despite her confident strides toward the wall. *"Fen, please be okay. Please be okay."* Her thoughts echoed on panicked repetition.

"Be careful," Darvanda barked. "Don't do anything stupid."

Elsedora smirked as she bounced over the battlement with defiance. "Oh, where is the fun in that?"

"Wait—" I held up a hand to stop her. "Fenris is okay. Or he was just minutes ago." I could feel the relief ricocheting off her like a wave of warm water rushing over my skin. "But Asterie isn't—and he's gone after Firose. I lost sight of them in the fray."

Elsedora nodded a brief thank you before quickly sliding down a drainage pipe.

No words found me as she disappeared over the wall, leaving just me and the King of the Wastelands. The King of a forbidden realm—of shadows, nightmares and all the things we'd been warned against letting in because they would *ruin* Henosis. Yet here he was, helping to keep it whole.

"Why?" I asked.

Iron gray eyes met mine. There was no kindness there, just cold calculation and underlying amusement as though none of this mattered to him. Even more reason to make me wonder *why*.

"I received a message from an enchantress that made a compelling offer."

Standing as tall as Emmerick, he didn't carry the same muscle mass, but he *felt* like raw power, like darkness and shadows.

When I tried to peer into his mind, I realized, other than the ebbing power, nothing else was coming from him. For the first time, no feelings were being thrown over my mental barriers, no slipping of emotions into the depths of my mind. He was just...blank.

"I can't..." I almost admitted it before biting my tongue.

He sighed as if war was a minor inconvenience to his week.

My brow furrowed. "*What* offer?" I'd only asked for his aid—I'd never set terms with Asterie.

"We are to remove the wards and unite the realms—isn't that what was proposed? I see certain benefits to that plan." He stared at me like a predator waiting for his prey to run. "I took the liberty of breaking down those wards to get here. More efficient than waiting, don't you think?"

My nostrils flared. I didn't like his arrogance. *What right did he have to tear those wards down?* "I made no such offer to—"

All air was suddenly cut from my lungs as shadows crept around me. It felt like the darkness was trying to find a way in, as if assessing me down to the core. My hands found my throat—I didn't even have the breath to choke. It felt like being encased in nothing. My mind clouded into a numb, cold, blank space. When he dropped the shadows, air abruptly returned, and I gasped out from that horrifying void as though I'd surfaced from deep water.

"What the fuck? You barbaric asshole—what was that for?" My glare met his.

There was no doubt this warlock aimed to scare most people shitless, including me. *It was working.* My whole body trembled, and from his point of view, I guessed that I looked like a pathetic, sickly girl ready to cower in a fetal position.

But that didn't stop me from thinking about six different ways to kill the bastard.

"Charming. I've been called worse," he grumbled. There was not an ounce of apology in his tone. "Unfortunately, since the wards are already lowered, your offer won't be enough. I suppose we'll think of a way you can repay me soon enough."

Darvanda turned to look over the south wall at the wreckage and warring soldiers below.

"Care to join our people below before they start their victory songs?"

When I glared at him again, his brow quirked upward before the darkness crept into my mind again like tentacles pushing their way in. That gruff voice grated against my thoughts.

"Your move, your majesty."

A bone-chilling realization—he knew exactly what I was and had been shielding this whole time.

A snarl of defiance huffed from my lips.

He might be saving my people, but he held my tail under his thumb like the mouse he deemed me. No doubt, whatever it was he wanted out of this arrangement would be a price I did not care to pay.

"There's someone we need to see first," I ground out through clenched teeth.

CHAPTER 36
FENRIS

In my all-consuming desperation to reach Asterie, I left Van to do what he does best—destroy. The flames escaping his mouth were unruly. He was able to push back the attacks of a hundred northern soldiers. Yet the troops kept coming, along with Wasteland defectors that slung shadows and devoured and devastated Luz's defenses.

I'd followed Firose around to the barbican—it was the one area of the castle grounds still being held by Luz troops. Her Lynx attacked anyone in her path.

When I reached them, Asterie was limp in Emmerick's arms.

I was on fire. Physically, mentally.

And the one that started it all was before me.

"Nice to see you, old flame." Firose's words hit my ears like a detonation. I would burn her limb by fucking limb. She stood behind her guards, looking at me with an expression so cocky that it shook my resolve. For a split second, I was back on that rooftop in Phynx four hundred years ago. I was nothing.

"Put her down—let him see what you've done," Firose commanded.

Emmerick knelt to rest Asterie on the ground before me—guarding her body with his own. His tunic was burned through, and blistering burns marred his chest.

Blood coated Asterie's chest and soaked through my green cloak. The lifelessness of her slackened features made the world stop. My vision tunneled. I wanted to crumble there—to hold her to me, to scream at the heavens to bring her back. I'd let flames engulf everything around us until this version of reality was nothing but ash.

None of it really fucking mattered anymore. *It could all burn.*

My Source Match was dead—it had never been clearer what she had been to me. There would be an eternity to grieve. There was only this moment for vengeance.

"You're are dead, Firose." I spat the words at the woman who had taken so much from me.

My wrath burned toward her. Renewed fire whipped from my form, licking the air and threatening to ignite anything that came near.

Don't burn the city. Asterie would want it standing.

Don't burn the boy. Asterie cared for him.

Emmerick did not step back. I could see the flames licking his skin, singeing his facial hair. His shoulders were slumped, and his eyes filled with tears.

"Fenris, I'm sorry, I'm so sorry. She *made* me, she made me." He was breathless and groveling. "I couldn't stop—"

I raised a flaming palm to silence him. My anger wasn't for the boy.

No, there was a singular focus for that rage. Firose had snuffed out the light that Asterie offered the world. She controlled, manipulated and caged her in a tower. She had raised her to be a weapon, and when her weapon fought back, she discarded her like nothing more than a dull dagger.

"You killed her!" I shrieked through the flames.

I was ready to fight fire with fire.

Though my fire couldn't burn her. *Damned Source magic never harming like Source magic.* There were plenty of other ways I could end her with my bare hands. *Or sword*—I pulled my broadsword from my back.

"No, I wouldn't have killed her—that plan was her own." Firose's voice sounded numb. She stilled as if listening to something in the wind. Her brow furrowed.

I bent and grabbed the chains around Emmerick's ankles—it took only moments to melt through the metal and release him. The molten shackles pooled in my hands for a moment before the liquid steel dripped from my fingers. I flicked it away.

"Take her. Run as far as you can," I commanded him.

I couldn't look at her lifeless on the ground any longer.

Firose turned to Emmerick with a tilt of her head as though still dazed.

"Let those two go. He'll be back for you, heir." Her haunted words made my blood run cold—they were so similar to the night I found her on that roof in Phynx.

Emmerick didn't hesitate—he lifted Asterie gently. I strangled a sob as the boy began to run toward the bailey. Reaching an arm out, I created a wall of fire between him and the approaching northern soldiers.

Firose seemed to return to herself, her arms crossed over her chest. A dozen Wasteland defectors flanked her, along with at least a dozen Lynx, who stalked me from all angles. The magic-wielders were growing orbs of amber darkness in their palms.

"Do you plan to burn me, Fenris? You will only stoke my embers, old flame. Have you forgotten how that feels?"

A ring of fire roared to life around me—anyone who dared approach would be set aflame. The guards threw orbs of darkness at me.

I blocked most, but one hit my shoulder, tearing at my skin. "Fuck!" I didn't let it stop me and kept stepping toward her.

She was gravely mistaken if she thought it would be easy to cast me aside. The guards that met the flaming ring screamed and writhed on the ground. The smell of singed Lynx fur and skin only heightened my appetite for bloodshed.

Firose began to walk away, toward the palace entry—as though unworried.

"I will kill anyone who stands between us. Stand down!" I barked at the guards and Lynx that trailed her, allowing flames to engulf more of them as I approached.

The fleeting satisfaction of revenge was so close to being within my grasp.

Lynx prowled around the ring of fire, skeptically assessing it for weakness after watching members of their pride fall.

Guards still surrounded her. *Idiots.*

They burned. Nothing, no one would stand between us and live.

Two guards approached her from the entrance, dragging someone between their arms.

When Firose stopped and turned, my fiery blood ran cold. She held a sword's blade to the soft skin of a cloaked woman's neck. The two guards still restrained the woman by the arms. A rust-colored cloak covered a lithe frame, and long chestnut hair had loosened from its braid.

The remaining Lynx surrounded Firose...and Elsie.

I ate my words—I *wouldn't* kill anyone that stood between us.

"You know." That sickly sweet tone felt like poison finding its way into my ears, paralyzing me with fear. Firose was poised to take Elsie's head—it would only take one well-aimed swing. "You would think by now that you would learn. You cannot win, Fenris—you will lose everyone, everything. So now, we make a bargain. Because I do love a bargain."

Firoses let the blade draw a trickle of blood from my sister's neck.

"I take her life...or I take yours."

Elsie looked at me without fear. Only cold determination brimmed in those familial hazel eyes. She mouthed the words. "*Kill her.*"

She would die for me—that determined look told me so.

I stood torn. Even if I got to Firose through the guards, there were still the Lynx circling Elsie. If I burned the Lynx, Firose would have time to strike.

I heard a familiar growl approach behind me. Van's shadow cast over me.

"Stand down, boy." My words were strained through gritted teeth. *If he attacked, I couldn't be sure he would get to Elsie before Firose.*

"Put that away," Firose commanded.

"Come to me," I told Van. He growled in disagreement before the ink appeared on my arm.

No good moves were left.

Checkmate. Again.

She knew it. Not even the most potent flames in the realm could save my sister if I made the wrong move.

"The choice is simple. Yield, and she goes free. Or fight, and she dies."

The choice wasn't hard. She was right about that at least.

No one else would fall because of me.

"Fine."

"Fen, no! Don't you dare!" Elsie's shrieks of defiance cut through the battle-filled night.

"In blood." Firose pulled Elsedora's head back by her braid to expose more of her neck. The trickle of blood ran faster, prompting me to use my broadsword to cut a slit across my flaming palm.

My blood hit the ground with a sizzle before I dropped the broadsword and lowered my flaming ring. "I'll surrender willingly, but I owe you nothing more than my life."

Firose removed the blade from Elsie's neck and threw her to the ground in front of me. Elsie spun and scrambled to pull a blade from her hip.

Firose blew a cloud of fine dust, causing Elsie to freeze mid-motion and fall, appearing paralyzed. My sister's throwing blade never left her hand. Her body slackened against the ash-covered ground.

Firose commanded her guards. "Restrain him, leave the girl."

No, Sources—Elsie couldn't be left here defenseless.

The guards began to drag me away.

"No!"

"That doesn't sound like you willingly surrendering to me," Firose said.

Northern soldiers swarmed us, blocking my view of Elsie. The wretched blood oath compelled me forward. They were taking me into the palace, away from the battle. Away from my little sister, lying helplessly frozen on the ground.

A rumble shook the ground, and a roar of sound seemed to come from all directions. Fire was everywhere. Flaming horses.

The Warhorses were *not* attacking Luz. The rush of flaming soldiers began slaughtering northern soldiers in droves.

A coarse laugh left my lips as Krait Darvanda's cavalry descended upon Firose's troops. Warhorses had been a creation of his centuries ago—one that I helped him attain the magic for. *Full circle, wasn't it?*

Crazy bastard. What would his price be for this stunt? The price for his aid was always steep. I would know.

Firose let out a frustrated growl at the approaching Warhorses. "Hurry!" she commanded her guards.

The blunt end of a sword struck me down with force, and a boot met my ribs for good measure.

As the guards beat me, I couldn't stop laughing.

"You are so fucked." I gasped the words through a chuckle. Krait wouldn't let Firose live for what she'd done all those centuries ago. For her deceit, for her hand in his lost love.

The guards pulled me into the palace. They dragged me through the halls and into the throne room, where I hit the cold white marble hard. Looking up, the cerulean ceiling of stars greeted me.

Asterie...I will find you. Wherever you are.

My breath heaved against broken ribs. Firose crossed the throne room, pulling a royal sword off the wall, sapphires encrusting its pommel. It was likely a Luz heirloom blade that she would soon defile with my blood.

"This will do. Bring him here. It's time we cut the beast out of this one."

I was pulled up by my arms and made to kneel before her. I'd told her once a story about a tomb, a mummified prince and the curse of the beast in his skin...she remembered.

Firose cut deep into my bicep, peeling away the skin where the ink housed Van. I writhed and screamed as they cut him from me.

My battered body was picked up like a rag doll and thrown forward. Palms flat to the stone, I was at her feet, bleeding out, beaten, heartbroken and ready to meet my end.

Fuck. I hoped there was something more after this. Some way to find Asterie. *Please, let me find her.* I pleaded to Sources that I barely believed in.

I forced myself to think of Asterie's face, of her lips parted and ready for me to press my own to them. I wanted her to be the final thing I saw.

"Hold on, Fenris." Otherly, but familiar. *So familiar,* yet blurred against the sound of chaos just outside the palace walls.

My arms shook beneath me. *Was that her voice in the afterlife, guiding me toward her?*

Asterie had told me that our story would not end happily. Happily ever after was for fairytales—our story had ended when a blade pierced her heart.

I spent my last moments imagining what could have been.

We would wake next to each other for an eternity.

I would show her every square mile of the realm, reveling in seeing her expression light up with each new place.

"Wherever you are. Wherever you go, I will be there." Asterie's voice reached out to me again.

With that whispered promise and a blade held high over my neck, I prepared to die.

CHAPTER 37
ASTERIE

A wave of relief washed over me after everything grew dark—the pain was gone, it was over.

Yet when I came to, I was somewhere else. It was cold, so very cold. Only the sound of my sloshing footsteps against black puddles surrounded me.

Taking a few more steps forward, I spun on my heels, looking around at the abyss. *Nowhere.* I was in a giant nowhere. Darkness spanned as far as I could see.

A single blue light formed in the void. It seemed to erratically flit, flicker and wind toward me from an immeasurable distance away. Maybe it would take minutes to reach me, maybe hours. *What was time really in death?* I existed then in a million moments of never and always.

When the light grew closer, it became a silhouette—almost human but longer and without a consistent form. Instead, it ebbed, seeming to break at the seams. I stood completely still as a caress of energy touched my cheek like a mother might console a crying child.

Golden eyes. So much sorrow in them.

An ache grew at the memory of them. *Who had that been? Why were they so sad?* Everything blurred together in that dark depth of space and nothingness.

"You have done well, young starling."

That voice.

That voice guided me before. It guided me here from out there.

Where was out there?

None of it mattered in that depthless space. With grace, the silhouette grew closer, its amorphous head tilted as though assessing me from all angles.

A warlock. A Queen at war. A bargain. It was returning to me in fragments, snapping at my essence.

"Did the bargain work? Are you Death?" My voice sounded unrecognizable, otherly, and beautiful.

"Worry not."

That didn't answer my question. Hope beat within me that I'd accomplished what I aimed to do.

What had I been doing?

The warlock. He needed to save them. Who was he saving?

"Hold on, Fenris," I whispered into the void.

Fenris—why did that name sound so familiar.

"Where are we?"

The blue-ebbing silhouette seemed to stretch its limbs across the vast space around us. It wiped away the inky ground. With every swipe of its limbs, dark clouds cleared the way for a bright midnight sky and stars began to shine all around us.

We were suspended there within it—nothing below, nothing above—just the glow of starlight.

"You are among your own, child. You are here with me."

Whatever it was, it was very good at providing nonanswers. Another question grew on my tongue.

When I reached out toward its shoulder, I expected to see my arm, but in its place was sparkling blue light. My shock stubbed the question out—*my body was not my own.* I spun to get a better look at my glowing limbs. The stars rippled around me as though responding to my movement.

"What—" My breath caught with the beauty of it. "What is this? What am I?"

"The Source Origins once walked among mortals, young starling. I will not walk again, but you can."

Kneeling, I tried to capture stars in my hands. They only rippled away from my touch, but the sensation and the shimmering power in my veins felt like a homecoming. "Are you saying that I am a Source Origin?"

The illuminated figure seemed to close its hands in front of itself, patiently watching me. "In part."

"Will I stay here then?" Finally righting myself, my gaze wandered around the endless space and over my mesmerizing limbs. The allurement of this place made me feel anchored, a safe harbor.

The figure shook its amorphous head slowly, and despair threatened to rear within me. This place—it was so endlessly radiant, entrancing.

"Let me stay."

I wanted to stay through the rest of eternity. I couldn't leave this place to move on to whatever came next.

Was there anything next?

"You are not made to be here—you cannot survive this place for long. Your place is with the fireling and sunling. You must return to them."

Unwilling to give this place up, I shook my head heartily like a petulant child.

But then images of two figures—one aflame and one made of golden light—filled my head. It was as though the Stars showed me the Origins of Fire and Sun themselves. They both felt so familiar.

Fenris. Emmerick.

"They need you, my starling. You must show them the way. The Origins bestow a great duty upon you."

What had happened before my body and essence split?

It all flooded back. *Emmerick in the clutches of Firose. Fenris' bed left cold where I should have been.* He would know by now that something was terribly wrong. My only hope was that he wouldn't blame me for the choices I'd made or Emmerick for the choice I made for him. Or worse, blame himself. My heart suddenly ached to be with them.

Fen's words the night before Firose had taken me flooded my mind like a dam breaking. *"I'll be wherever you are. Wherever you go. I knew that from the moment I set eyes on you."*

But he couldn't be where I was.

I needed to be where he was.

"Please, please." I knelt before the illuminated form and bowed. "I want to return."

A cold wisp of a finger picked up my chin.

"Young Asterie, I did not give you life for you to waste it. Try not to make Death more than an acquaintance. He is difficult for me to negotiate with."

I nodded and spoke to Fenris, who I hoped awaited me in a faraway place.

"Wherever you are. Wherever you go, I will be there."

Then everything went dark once more.

CHAPTER 38
SYBILLA

With Darvanda at my back, the steps down to the bailey took a century to climb down. I had felt vulnerable the moment he'd held his arm out to motion for me to go first. The King of the Wastelands didn't press for any conversation as we rounded the stairway. He was a domineering presence with nothing but severity in his gait. The levels crawled stone by stone, step by step.

Emmerick's anger led me down into the bailey. His rage and despair roiled in the air in a way that made me brace once we hit the landing.

The scene was chaotic. Guards were racing to help Emmerick place Asterie on a bedroll. A healer was checking her vital signs with a grave expression that told me all I needed to know. *My High Enchantress, the woman I'd summoned here to help us, was dead.*

My heart raced, and it was difficult to hold my posture straight as the guilt raked through me.

Stupid. I was so fucking stupid. I felt sick to my stomach, and I bent at the waist for a moment, wishing it away.

Would she be dead if I'd allowed Fenris to look for her?

When I rose, King Darvanda glanced at me with a quirked brow. My feet were planted, trying to capture Emmerick's eyes with my own—his anguish and resentment still hit me like a punch thrown to the gut. Winded and devastated, I finally managed to speak.

"Emmerick."

When he looked at me, I wished he hadn't. The blindly loyal boy who had accepted my father's terms to protect me was gone. What stood before me was a destined King, dejected because of a Queen who had held him at arm's length for a decade. *How could one explain such selfishness in words?* I'd likely spend the rest of my life trying.

Emmerick knelt over the downed enchantress. My eyes fell on Asterie's still, lifeless body, and the lump in my throat grew.

"This is King Darvanda of the Wastelands," I explained. "His troops are fighting for Luz. The Warhorses—"

Emmerick just stared at me with an intensity that caused my hands to fidget.

"She is not dead," King Darvanda said from beside me. "I don't see her in the shadows yet. But she doesn't have much time."

"Can you help her? Can your magic help her?" Emmerick stood to face Darvanda. He ran his blood-soaked hands over his breeches to no avail.

"Careful, Em. Asking for this bastard's aid comes at steep costs."

I slipped my fingers into my loosened crown of braided hair. I wanted to plead with him to soften, to be my Emmerick—the stable boy, the friend.

My Constable ignored me.

Darvanda grunted before huffing. "Charming...such a fowl mouth on such a pretty face." He stepped close enough to put me in his shadow. "Mind you, *this bastard* just saved *your* people tonight. I suggest you remember that."

Emmerick visibly braced, and his hand found the hilt of his sword. *He still cared.* There was hope.

As Darvanda watched Emmerick's reaction, it was the first time anything resembling a smile had touched his face since I had met him.

"Oh—how predictable," he mused darkly. "A Queen warming her bed with those on her payroll. Leash your dog. If I wanted to kill you, I would have done so already."

If my powers were a two-way path, I'd make him see every creative way I was thinking about killing him. Darvanda watched me now. His smirk only deepened the more violent my thoughts grew. *Could he hear me? Did he* like *it?*

I shivered then asked, "What do we do?"

Hurried footsteps across the stone of the courtyard interrupted any answer to my question. A woman with dark curls, pushed back with a golden band, approached. Emmerick's gaze softened as it landed on her.

"No additional forces approach by sea. The northern fleets stood no chance against the southern navy."

My brow furrowed in confusion as she spoke to me, as though awaiting my commands. I felt utterly ill-prepared for this.

I pushed into Emmerick's mind, pressing against his mental shields. He fought it, but I pushed in anyway against his learned defenses—like picking a lock. He hated when I did it, but I needed to know how to help him.

"Amara. She's my birth mother. Now, get the fuck out of my head, Sybilla. Lead your beloved Corridor."

Emmerick's mother stood expectantly. *The High Enchantress of the South Corridor.*

My mind raced for what to do. Then Amara's eye caught the lifeless form on the bedroll that Emmerick still leaned over.

Amara closed the distance between her and her fallen Sister and collapsed to her knees. Her dark eyes welled with tears as she ran her hand over the younger enchantress' pale, cold, blood-soaked face. Emmerick reached across Asterie to take his mother's hand.

"No...Asterie, no. This cannot be." Grief wrenched out of Amara so strong that it began to suffocate my senses. That pain hit me more intensely than any I'd felt before. Even Fenris' pain, in the moments he had climbed down the wall, had been laced with wrath, which had covered the foul taste and feeling of despair.

Darvanda stepped up and crouched next to Amara. He said nothing, but he placed a hand on her shoulder. So, he *was* capable of compassion, at least for someone. Emmerick fought his own tears.

I felt numb. It was always difficult to not shut down completely when emotions in a room were strong. I needed to cut them off, but it was so damn hard when their pain tore at my seams.

"I killed her. I fucking killed her. It's all my fault. I should never have agreed. I did this."

I wasn't prying this time. Emmerick's mind was warring with itself, and thoughts snapped out of him uncontrollably. My feet couldn't move. I was stupefied and helpless.

There was no way to get him through this.

"She knew," Amara breathed out to Emmerick as if feeling his pain too—a mother, even though estranged, able to read the horror in her child's eyes. "She knew she was going to die—she told me." She squeezed his hand firmly.

Emmerick finally looked at Darvanda, who still kneeled with a hand on Amara's shoulder.

"She isn't dead, Amara," Darvanda said plainly. "Not yet."

Amara looked over her shoulder. "Krait...you can't bring her back, can you?"

He smiled with a softness seemingly reserved for only her. *How do they know each other?* The Enchantress of the South Tower had friends in high places. They were both ancient, so it wouldn't be surprising for their paths to have crossed.

"No—I can't raise the dead. That is a rumor. Only the Death Origin was capable of that. But your loved one isn't gone yet. I can't find her among the shadows here."

Amara was upright at once.

"Someone, please explain." The words burst from my mouth, and all three of them stared at me.

Amara ordered, "Queen Sybilla, go get me salt, bones—any type—and a blade made of silver."

I momentarily braced at the commands—not used to being *ordered* about. But these moments could count for my prospective friend's life, for Emmerick's *sister*. Without argument, I took to the stone staircase of the Keep at a run.

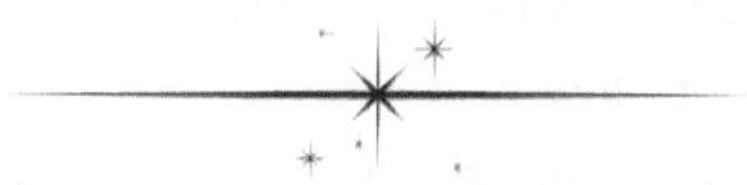

Minutes later, everything requested had been retrieved. I'd barked at no less than a dozen guards to help me gather turkey bones and salt from the kitchen before ransacking the royal armory for a blade made of silver.

When I returned, Emmerick still would not look at me, and King Darvanda was helping him position Asterie in the middle of the courtyard facing up toward the night sky.

Amara circled Asterie in salt and placed the bones in her hands. Then Amara sliced a cut in each of her own palms with the silver blade and passed it to me to do the same. When each of our palms ran warm with blood, she set the blade at Asterie's feet and extended one hand to me and one hand to Emmerick.

I tried to explain. "I don't have magic, I can't—"

"You do. Now isn't the time to hide it," Emmerick snapped at my reflex to deny it.

"And apparently, I might too." His thought slammed into me like he'd shouted it. I flinched. He'd be angry, but he'd get over it. *He had to get over it.*

I took Amara's slender hand in mine as she began speaking to Asterie.

"The night you were reborn, my dear…I called upon the Stars to save you. We plead with them again tonight. Let them answer. Let them bring you back to us—"

Amara's voice filled the air as cannon blasts and war cries grew further away. Darvanda took my other hand. His hand was massive compared to mine but warm and oddly comforting.

"Everyone, please close your eyes and relax," Amara calmly instructed. "Let me in. I'll be siphoning from you all to make my plea to the Source Origins of the Sun and Stars."

My magic was different than theirs. I wasn't sure how the Source magic would respond to me. My nerves skyrocketed, and my arms trembled, but I closed my eyes and tried to relax.

It wasn't working. My mental barriers were coming down—everything outside was flooding in. It made it impossible to relax.

Darvanda's finger began to trace quick circles on my palm with his thumb. The sensation centered me, like a tether to reality. There was no way to pick the lock of his mind. *Was it an act to comfort me or a show of impatience?* Likely the latter, with how much disdain he showed for me.

A charge filled the air like the feeling before lightning striking the ground. The hairs on my head began to rise, but my eyes stayed tightly closed. Those barriers started coming down again. My throat closed; my heart raced.

"Breathe." Darvanda's voice was gruff, but his cadence was gentle.

Comforting. He was trying to comfort me. The King of the Wastelands was cruel, unforgiving and infuriatingly cocky. Yet he wanted this to work—he wanted to save a friend of my Corridor. One he had never even met.

I wondered what the price would be for this.

My body slackened and became a vessel for use—opening myself for Amara to pull whatever magic she needed from my veins.

"Allow her to come back to us." Amara's voice was ethereal and unnervingly distant despite her proximity. We stood there for a few long minutes. An intense hum of power sounded deafeningly loud around us.

Then everything stopped. I dared to let one eye open only to see an amorphous form of light towering over Amara next to me—I gasped when its glowing head seemed to turn toward me. Snapping my lids closed once again, I squeezed Darvanda's hand tightly.

Sources, she's summoned a Source Origin.

Darvanda returned my grip as the wind kicked up around us and threatened to knock us down.

"I understand," Amara seemed to answer, yet I hadn't heard the being speak.

Then the wind died, and Amara released my hand abruptly.

When I looked upon Asterie, her eyes fluttered open. There was a milk-white coating over her once-dark irises.

Asterie's hand shot up toward the sky with a look of longing. The stars in the sky were swirling, and she was beginning to glow like one of them. Her whole body was radiant, blue effervescence ebbing off of her.

"No, you cannot join them," Amara whispered as she stepped to Asterie's side. "Call them to you, my dear."

The swirling stars caused me to feel off-balance, like the world was tilted on its axis. Then, one by one, hundreds of stars fell into Asterie. It looked violent at first, the way those blinding lights kept hitting her chest and jolting her body. Amara jumped back into the circle with us—narrowly avoiding being hit by the light.

When the night sky returned to its usual gentle twinkling, and no more stars fell, a gasp burst from the center of our circle. Asterie shot upright. Blood still caked her clothing, but the wound on her leg was healed, along with the stab wound to her heart. She was whole, alive, breathing.

Emmerick's glare narrowed on The King of the Wastelands and my linked fingers. I hadn't realized he still held my hand. I abruptly pulled away, and didn't let the wicked smirk on Darvanda's face make me blush. *Prick.*

We all joined Amara in kneeling at Asterie's side. The enchantress' irises had returned to their dark hue, only rimmed with a blue ring, as they searched us wildly.

She grasped Emmerick's shirt collar.

"Where is he, Em? Where is Fen?"

CHAPTER 39
ASTERIE

A cannon sounded in the distance, and I flinched.

Ten...nine...eight...

"We're at war." My own voice sounded wrong. *Where was the ethereal thrum it had had in that beautiful place?*

Amara nodded slowly.

"I'm not dead." Another flat statement.

Seven...six...

They still hadn't told me where Fenris was. Emmerick's pained expression struck me. One of my hands found his cheek.

"You have done well, sunling..." The words did not feel like mine as they left my tongue. That phrase seemed so familiar.

Emmerick swallowed hard.

"I'm sorry for asking that of you."

"If you ever ask me to make that oath again, I'll kill you." At his words, my lips curled upward before I scanned the other faces surrounding us.

"Where is he, Em?"

"I don't know…I left Fen to get you out of there. He told me to go…He was standing off against Firose. He had it under control. I-I think."

My chest tightened. *No. I needed to get to Fenris.* When I stepped forward, my balance faltered. This body felt sluggish, and the ground seemed to tip beneath my feet, unlike walking through the starlight just minutes ago. Emmerick held my elbow firmly, not allowing me to topple over.

Amara, Sybilla and a dark-haired stranger stared at us. Strange shadows seemed to ebb from the stranger, edging around the young Queen as though they would suffocate her—*or protect her?* I couldn't tell.

"Who is he?" *Propriety be damned.* I needed to find Fen.

This would all be easier if my vision would clear and my body would stop glowing. They were squinting just to look at me.

"Krait Darvanda, Chief Prick of the Wastelands," Sybilla quickly answered. "But—he came to our aid, and for that, we are indebted. I'm glad to see you back, Asterie."

"You came…for a price," I mumbled to Darvanda, knowing all too well what I'd done. The domineering man's brow quirked with curiosity. "We'll come to an agreement later."

The King of the Wastelands only grunted in response, and Queen Sybilla shot him a glare that would have raised the hairs on the back of my neck. He looked unaffected.

A powerful gust overhead drew my attention upward.

A single Griffith sailed gracefully through the air and landed just a few yards away. Its beak opened, letting out a cry. I winced at the shrill sound. Everything felt new, louder, brighter.

I couldn't see her face, but only one person I knew had war leathers worn down so much they had holes in the knees. The rider's brown hair was pulled back into neat braids.

Cassidee dismounted. Another woman slumped against the saddle horn on the back of the Griffith. My vision finally snapped into focus—chestnut hair, robes that matched Darvanda's. *Elsie.*

She looked drowsy but awake and unharmed. She mouthed his name, "*Fen.*"

"Elsie, where is he?" I stepped closer to them, reaching up a glowing hand to take Elsie's in mine.

"*She* has him," Elsie groaned. Every nerve in my body sparked. The light under my skin flickered so bright that those around me winced.

I looked at Cassidee. "You helped her? She's from the Wastelands."

Cassidee shrugged. "I saw a pretty redhead in need of help."

Emmerick helped pull Elsie down from the Griffith, lifting her easily with one arm under her knees.

"I can walk," Elsie snapped at him, but he merely shook his head impatiently.

"You can barely keep your neck from lobbing back." His words only showed a hint of annoyance.

Elsie mumbled expletives and a tear flowed down her dust-covered cheek.

"Where is Fen?" That ethereal voice was back...otherly, commanding and charged by whatever energy coursed through me.

Every star in the sky would rain down on Firose if she touched a hair on Fen's head.

Emmerick gently lowered Elsie to the ground and propped her against the bailey wall, steadying her with a palm on her shoulder so she wouldn't fall forward.

"She was leading him toward the east entrance," Elsie choked out.

"Take me." I was already stepping toward the Griffith at Cassidee's side. Cassidee looked hesitant at first but then gave me a leg up to propel me into the saddle. *How much different could riding a Griffith be than a horse?*

"Asterie." Amara approached and put a hand on my leg. "Be careful."

"Something tells me she's going to be just fine. I worry for Firose, though," Cassidee said as she mounted the beast behind me. "You were always my bet. I knew you'd be the best of us. Now, you even sparkle."

I wanted to be able to laugh, to be grateful that not every kind moment between me and my Sisters was a lie. My expression remained unaffected.

"Hurry," I commanded.

When Cassidee kicked the beast into flight, my back hit her chest with force. The powerful creature pounded its wings around us.

This felt nothing like a horse.

Amara watched us ascend before yelling up to us. "Make her pay!"

I held on, hoping Fenris could do the same for a few more moments.

From the height of the Griffith's flight over the palace, I could see the grounds, and the city was in shambles. Fire sprung from shop windows, walls crumbled and bodies of the fallen lay scattered in the streets. The repugnant smell of dark magic hung heavy in the air.

Horns of retreat were sounding in the distance. Cassidee landed the Griffith in front of the barbican. The northern soldiers were beginning to retreat.

Luz was not for the taking. Neither was Fenris.

"Here." Cassidee handed me a sword from a sheath built into her saddle. We dismounted and headed for the palace entry.

Cassidee guarded my back as I pushed open the large white-oak double doors.

Where would she take him?

Firose would wish to defile a place sacred to this Corridor.

The throne room.

"Down the hall," I called over to Cassidee.

Cassidee flanked my left. A group of northern guards approached from the hall, shouting for reinforcement. Dark amber orbs grew in their palms, but Cassidee sheathed her blade and clapped her hands hard in front of her. The men were blasted back by a gust of wind so strong they were left unconscious. But more soldiers swarmed us, wielding Death.

We blocked the magic with our blades as orbs were slung at us. Cassidee used her shield to push our way toward the long hall. We were still outnumbered.

Wyeth burst through the castle doors behind us, shouting Phynnic charms that pulled vines through the windows. The vines grew thick like tree roots before winding around the ankles of guards that approached Cassidee.

Cassidee paused to marvel at the magic Wyeth spun. Her mouth hung open but edged up at the sides.

"How did you find me, love?" Cassidee asked.

Wyeth answered, "The trees...they whispered. I hate you for worrying me." Wyeth's black hair flashed green, but with her command over the soil, she wasn't lying about the trees.

"Your left!" Cassidee shouted to me as she turned to meet the sword of a mortal northern guard. Wyeth held off the entryway by cracking the marble ground beneath her feet. The stone gave way, and the dirt opened to swallow enemy forces in a sinkhole.

Blue light grew in my palms, and I launched it at the two guards approaching from my left. To my surprise, instead of throwing blue flame, it left my hands as a constant stream of light and seared through the soldiers. It burned holes in the hallway walls behind them before I fisted my hands to stop it.

"Go! I'll hold the door," Wyeth shouted at Cassidee. She'd cleared a path to the throne room.

I didn't wait for Cassidee. Instead, I ran down the hall before throwing the silver-trimmed doors of the throne room open.

"Firose!" My voice boomed.

My whole body stilled at the glint of a blade being drawn up toward the sapphire ceiling.

Fenris was on his knees, his head bowed. He lifted his head, and his eyes widened as he reached out a hand toward me.

No. The blade was coming down.

Where was Van?

"He has some of his own free will. He just chooses to listen to me." I remembered Fen's words.

"Vangard, come!"

The blade was falling, and Fen was not moving. *I was too late.*

No, no, no.

A familiar gust of wind and dust enveloped the room. Vangard appeared over Firose. I'd done it—bond or no bond, I'd drawn the beast out. Van's black fur was matted with blood, his lip curled and his eyes raged with no mercy.

Firose had a path for a clean strike, yet she cried out as though straining against something as the blade came down.

When the blade struck the marble floor, my heart stopped.

No blood. Fen was alive. The sword had only nicked the collar of his shirt.

She missed. How could she miss?

I couldn't risk her striking again. I shouted, "Van, stop her!"

Firose met my gaze—the whites of her eyes showed, and her jaw slackened. My arm reached out to her as she attempted to turn the blade on Vangard.

The beast swiftly took Firose between his giant jaws and chomped twice. Her screams wrung out, filling the throne room with agonized pleas.

Firose shrieked, "Stop, please!"

I tried to convince myself there was no death more fitting for Firose's cruelty. Death at the jaws of a beast that she could never tame and the prodigy that she'd once hoped to wield against this realm.

Van snapped his head violently from side to side—his hackles raised with a rage-filled snarl. The sapphire-encrusted blade fell from Firose's hand and clambered to the ground.

"Shit…" Cassidee muttered from behind me as she entered the throne room. She let out a soft whistle of approval. I hadn't realized how weak my knees had grown until she steadied me by my elbow.

Despite her evils—Firose was my mentor.

She'd helped to raise me.

What had I done?

Vangard tore Firose limb from limb, beginning with her head. I gasped and looked at the floor to avoid the gore of it.

"Van, drop her." I was breathless. "She is too foul to eat." The words escaped me in exasperated relief.

It is over. She cannot harm anyone else. She can't hurt Fen.

Van dropped a headless torso onto the throne room floor.

I whispered, "Go help protect the palace." Blood pumped cold through my veins.

Van lowered his head before he trotted out of the throne room as though he hadn't just torn Firose apart. It was odd that the bond seemed to have a residual effect. *He should not have listened to my commands.*

"I need to check on Wyeth," Cassidee said before she stalked after Van.

My knees continued to shake; my body still glowed brightly, reflecting off the shined floors.

Fenris got to his feet, facing me. It looked like it took all his strength to lift himself. I'd been so close to losing him. But it was over. *Fen was safe.* He stared at me in disbelief, breath ragged. We took each other in from across the throne room for only a second.

Then, I ran to him. My feet couldn't carry me fast enough. It wasn't until I could hold him that I'd be sure he was real. That he stood there, alive. I threw my arms around him.

He winced.

Oh my Sources—the skin on his arm where the ink used to lay was ripped away. My hand paused over it, tears welling at the sight of such cruelty.

"What has she done?" I sobbed. "I'm sorry...I never wanted to leave you. I love you, Fen."

Fen's undamaged arm snaked around the small of my back, pulling me tightly to him. He was trembling, or maybe it was me—our pounding heartbeats met.

"I lost you," he whispered into my hair. "When I saw you...I couldn't bear it. The thought of you—"

"I'm here."

He lifted my chin. Both of our cheeks were streaked with tears. "How?"

I shook my head. "I don't exactly know. It doesn't matter. I'm *here*. You're here."

"Elsie?" His voice sounded pained, as if bracing for bad news.

"Safe, safe—she is in the bailey with the others. Cassidee found her on the grounds. Amara and Emmerick are unharmed too."

Every muscle in his body slackened as he brought both his hands to my wet cheeks. Then he leaned down and caught my mouth with his. His hands found their way into my hair, deepening the kiss.

I finally felt like I could breathe—he was the air that I'd needed.

Our magic collided with a force akin to fire meeting the cold expanse between the stars. A star rupturing, igniting to life. We shared no magic, no bond, and yet his nearness—it felt right. I felt a pull toward him. Bond or no bond, his fire mingling with my starlight made me feel whole.

"You are here." He kissed me between words. "And you love me?" I caught a glimpse of that light-hearted smirk.

"Yes, I do," I managed through tears. "Do you still—"

"Don't even ask that question." He buried his nose into my neck, seeming to not mind that the skin there was still *glowing* an eerie iridescent silver-blue.

"We're no longer bound," I reasoned. "Nothing is drawing you to me."

"I don't believe it ever worked that way," Fenris answered. "I'm yours, Asterie. I want you to be mine—but that is your choice. No one will ever own your choices again."

"Given a choice, it will always be you," I said.

He held me tighter as his tears ran down my neck. "I love everything about you. Horns, claws and whatever this starlight under your skin is—I love that too. I didn't know you could glow, my strange beauty."

"I don't know how to stop it." I laughed through my tears.

He drew away only enough to examine me from head to breast before he dipped his chin down to kiss my forehead. "I'm a fan...I just wonder if you glow *everywhere*. I think we need to find a bathtub so I can properly investigate before it burns out."

I grabbed his face gently between my hands. "You are always going to be a hopeless flirt, aren't you?"

"Only with you." He sealed his answer with a kiss, and my worries melted away. *He was safe. The battle was coming to an end. We'd face the aftermath. Together.*

"Soon enough we will get out of these soiled clothes." The insinuation in my words brought a devious smile across his face. "But first—we find the others and see what help is needed."

"Must we?" His voice vibrated in a light and teasing way across my brow as he placed a kiss there.

I would happily never leave his arms again, but we had a realm to rebuild. We walked out of the demolished palace halls, into the battle-torn night, hand in hand.

CHAPTER 40
ASTERIE

It took three Phynnic healing charms to mend Fen's arm and broken ribs. There was still bruising that would require time to heal. But he was *alive*.

My skin still glowed in an iridescent shine. I had begun to wonder if the magic used by the Source Origin of Stars had made this permanent, but the glow was slowly fading. The added light had been quite handy as we had searched the ruins of Luz for survivors.

The city lay in shambles around us—even with my light, the darkness of night masked the reality of the devastation behind a veil we'd need to face at dusk. The battle was won, but rebuilding would be a long, grueling process.

"We should head back to help with healing the others," Fen said, ushering me forward with a hand on the small of my back. I nodded, reveling in the feeling of his touch.

We passed three horsemen from the Wastelands. I'd been told that those horses could ignite into flames, but they looked like average armored mounts now. The riders pressed their index and middle fingertips to their lips and then toward me.

"It's a Brennac gesture of respect." Fen leaned in to whisper to me. "You return it."

I kissed my fingers and pointed back at the soldiers, who nodded as their Warhorses clopped away on the cobblestone.

What a strange new world we would usher in—opening the Wastelands. It was hard to know what came next. *Would the northern rebels rebuild their forces? Could the realm return to peace after mutiny? With the Sisterhood dissolved, what consequences awaited us?*

Vangard trailed behind us with his head hung low. He'd been hard at work digging for the fallen who had been stuck below collapsed buildings and debris. Wyeth had helped him by reshaping the ground, making it easier to rescue as many as we could—there were no longer shouts for help. Just a silent, dark, ruined city.

I let my hand slip into Fen's as we neared the palace gates. Neither of us had let the other out of sight. Though it was unspoken, I imagined his fear mirrored my own.

We stepped through the palace gates, into the now-destroyed entry gardens. The grounds were transformed into a makeshift infirmary. Cassidee and Amara were patiently teaching Emmerick a Brennac healing charm to help with abrasions and minor wounds on his guards. Between the rips in his tunic, I could see that the Commander's burns had been healed, but in their place, hand-shaped scars remained on his chest.

Emmerick, my friend, the heir of a divided Corridor. My throat constricted to think of the challenges that lay ahead of him. Since he looked to be a fast learner, it confirmed one thing—he possessed Source magic. Cassidee repeated the charm, and Amara showed him where to place his hands on a soldier with a laceration across his shoulder blades.

What had the Star Origin said in that dream-like place?

"'The Origins bestow a great duty upon you,'" I mumbled into the night air.

Fen tilted his head toward me. "What's that?"

I shook my head. "Nothing....at least I think nothing. When I was *gone.*" My words made Fen visibly brace. "I went somewhere *in between.*"

Fenris' eyebrows rose. "Does that have something to do with why you are glowing?"

I managed a weak smile and nodded. "I believe I spoke with my namesake, Asterie. Though she was in no mortal form. She said that to me before letting me return."

Fenris drew out a breath. "Leave it to the Sources above to be cryptic. Are you sure it was real? That they truly exist somewhere?"

"Can we be sure *anything* is real?" I teased while squeezing his hand. But in my heart, I knew it had been Asterie of the Stars.

I didn't have time to think about it any longer. King Krait Darvanda appeared from the shadows themselves. He barked orders at his men to assemble on the south lawn.

"Krait." Fenris curtly greeted him as the Wasteland's King passed.

Darvanda simply glared at Fen as he stormed away with a bearish growl. He snapped at a young boy to gather two loose Warhorses, calling him no less than five surly-delivered slights in the process.

"Friendly," I murmured under my breath to Fenris.

He let out a low chuckle. "You have no idea..."

I didn't.

But I wanted to learn about every part of Fen's past—including his history with the grumpy King who had saved Luz. I wanted to let Fen unravel every piece of his life to me for centuries to come. We had that chance now to truly *know* one another.

Queen Sybilla approached us, looking flushed and carrying a stack of quilts from the palace. It was the first I'd seen her since waking up in the bailey, and we exchanged smiles. Emmerick was right—I did like the young Queen.

I needed to work up the nerve to ask her if I could stay to serve her court as she rebuilt.

Fen asked, "My Queen—where is my sister?"

Sybilla balanced the quilts in one hand and pointed up to the tower of the Keep with the other. "She still temporarily can't walk—and cursed me up and down for locking her in the Keep again. Only so that she wouldn't *drag* herself around trying to help. She was more of a tripping hazard than she was a help."

Fenris stifled a laugh. "So—visitation?"

Sybilla chuckled back. "I might give her some time—last thing she said was 'tell my hair-brained, fuck-all of a brother that I'm going to kill him for trying to leave me again.' Amara sleep-charmed her and said she'll be right as rain by morning."

My attention lingered uneasily on the King of the Wastelands.

"Why is he still here?" I asked her, careful to keep my voice low as I nodded toward Darvanda.

The Central Queen huffed. "Fuck if I know—I believe he's sticking around to discuss the terms of his bargain. Thank *you*, very much." She eyed me with a faux glare that returned to warmth nearly instantly. "I told him we won't be discussing anything until tomorrow. The rest of the Corridor leaders arrive in two nights. It gives us time to think through what comes next and how to present him to others without them waging war on us too. His troops leave here and head back to the Wastelands tomorrow."

So Darvanda's men would return home to the Wastelands. Which begged me to wonder—*why was he here?* The last Brennac King was still a mystery. *Still a threat.*

"You're sure that we should not rebuild the wards?" I asked.

Sybilla sighed. "I don't know."

The young Queen looked as though she might lay her head down on the quilts in exhaustion. Fen's brow furrowed.

He asked, "Can't you...hear if he's up to no good?"

"Apparently not," Sybilla grumbled under her breath before straightening her posture. "To be safe, I've told the civilians to remain in the bailey and the tunnels below for tonight—I don't want to risk northern soldiers returning, and I want the Wasteland soldiers to leave prior to our people returning to the city. Also, I don't want the children seeing..." Sybilla motioned to the gore all around them. "They're panicked, and many grieve as we identify the fallen. I'm off to see that they're alright and maintain some semblance of order down there."

We nodded a solemn goodbye as Queen Sybilla followed a group of soldiers carrying water jugs and kitchen maids carrying dozens of food trays toward the stairs to the tunnels in the belly of the Keep.

Vangard nudged his nose into my back with a whine, begging.

"You can come back and rest." Fenris urged the beast. Van only huffed in response and nudged me again, nearly knocking me off my feet. I turned around to greet him with a weak smile.

"Oh, stubborn animal." Van bowed for me to scratch between where his horns and ears met. The beast tilted his head in a blissfully satiated way while his back leg kicked up involuntarily. "Return to your master, Van."

A familiar cloud of dust kicked up around us as Van disappeared, but Fenris looked confused to not see the ink etch down his newly healed bicep. I grabbed his arm and gasped. There, from my inner wrist to my inner forearm, was an inked image of Vangard.

"Return to your master."

My eyes widened. Fen wore a smile as he ran his fingers down the ink on my arm. A smile that held no resentment, no regret, just surprised joy.

"I suppose when he was cut from my arm, he decided he liked you better. Who could blame him? But *that is* now your problem, my strange beauty."

He placed a kiss to the soft space just below my ear before he trailed his lips down my shoulder and forearm.

Wyeth approached, interrupting the heat growing between us.

"Hello, shiny one and...*friend?*" She looked between me and Fenris with a fox-like smirk. Her short black bob was pinned aside, and her hands were coated in blood from healing the wounded. "Care to help us?"

My cheeks heated. Fen and I nodded in unison.

"Of course!" I chirped out.

Fen and I helped the others and went from bedroll to bedroll, healing as many of the wounded as we could until our bodies were as exhausted as our magic.

We began to hear roars of applause and cries of joy from the ground below as soldiers were reunited with their families in the tunnels. Emmerick's words at the lakeside in Belray returned to me.

"Look for the brightest sides of your darkest days."

I felt the first glimmer of hope for the future of Henosis and my place in it.

CHAPTER 41
FENRIS

My mind left the battle-torn grounds behind. We had done all we could, and thoughts of rebuilding the city would still be there in the fast-approaching morning light.

The only thing that mattered in this moment was Asterie's hand in mine, the way she looked at me without reserve and the curve of her body pulled tight to me as she guided me up the palace stairs. *Asterie, my guiding light. The beautiful star that led me home, for home would be wherever she was.*

She pulled me along, into my bedchamber. She ran a bath, stripped me down and sat me on a stool in the shower—a luxury only royal residences had. I reveled in the feeling of the water hitting my back.

Asterie rubbed healing salves, which she'd gathered from palace healers, over the bruises on my ribs. She cleaned away all evidence of the pain I had endured that day—it seemed to be restoring her as much as me.

Her brow was still creased with worry. I wanted to kiss that crease away.

"You're fretting over me…" I teased as she rubbed dirt from my chest with a rag. I grabbed her wrist and gently pulled her toward me. "And you're wearing entirely too much while doing so. That is my only complaint."

When she joined me in the stream of water, my bloodied green cloak grew wet and heavy on her frame. Asterie hadn't bothered to undress, too busy tending to me. Her scowl was replaced with a half-hearted smile that could knock me dead. She braced her arms on the shower wall behind me, her lips just inches from mine. Our breath mingled, and my heart pounded.

"I almost lost you." She whispered the words into my mouth as her eyes welled.

"I can say the same to you. But we are here."

"Just let me tend to you. It is helping to keep me grounded—helping to convince me it is really over."

I answered, "Let's tend to each other. Alright?"

She nodded, resting her head on my forehead.

I stood and backed her out of the stream of water only long enough to undo the buttons of the wet cloak and let it fall. Beneath it was that damned nightdress, which clung to her wet body, showing me her peaked breasts. I'd have peeled it off with my teeth if she hadn't begun to unbutton it herself. The evidence of where she'd been harmed remained caked in blood over her heart and down her thigh. Her skin still glowed that iridescent blue, though it was fading, and her color was returning.

So close. I'd been too close to losing her too. *Never again.*

"My fallen star—I'm forever yours. Let me rinse you off, and join me for a soak in that tub because there are things I'm too tired to do while standing right now."

She dropped the nightgown and stepped into the stream of water in front of me. As I ran a cloth over every inch of her, blood rinsed away, coloring the water a rust hue as it ran down the drain. When I was finished, she led me by my elbow to the tub, finally passing an appreciative look over my bare body as I stepped in. I smirked, biting back a comment.

When I sunk into the heat of the water, a hiss escaped my lips.

I leaned back to take her in as she stepped into the tub. Water ran off her naked glowing form like rain sliding down a lit window pane. *Sources, she was devastating.*

"I love you, Asterie. I mean that. I can't say it enough."

"You barely know me." It wasn't denial. Her softly stated words were vulnerable as she met my gaze. I needed to find a way to prove to her that she could trust me.

"So are you saying that you don't love me after all?" I teased.

"That is not what I said," she responded sternly before pausing there over me. "I am serious, Fen. What if this is fleeting or just the aftereffects of our brushes with death? There are plenty of logical explanations that could feel like love."

Taking her hand, I shook my head. That type of doubt gracing her lips was not allowed. Not now when my mind was so sure that she was everything to me.

It still pained me that she did not bring up my claim over her power, that she might feel a need to hide it. But I didn't want to talk about a stupid fucking blood oath now.

"Love often isn't logical. I plan to spend eternity proving my devotion to you."

I pulled her down abruptly and caught her as her knees buckled around me with a splash. The whole tub lit with her presence. A laugh escaped her lips as she slipped into my arms, and the water rippled over the tub's edges. That laughter, a sound more beautiful than any music, anything nature could create—it made everything we'd endured worth it.

"Does this feel fleeting?"

She shook her head as her hands found the back of my neck, and she let her lips brush my temple in a kiss so gentle it nearly brought me to tears. She quietly answered, "Not in the least."

Her resolve removed the final weight of worry.

She added, "I think you might be stuck with me for a very long time, Fen."

"Good," I said. "I didn't want to have to chase you around the realm begging on my hands and knees."

"I might enjoy that," she teased back.

A groan escaped me as she shifted her weight in my lap—positioned exactly where I needed her. "We'll save that for another time."

The feel of our bodies sliding against one another was pure bliss. She ground against me, and that was all it took for me to lose all self-control.

I devoured her mouth, running my tongue over that delightful gap in her teeth and biting at her lower lip.

"I need you." The words were a desperate plea spoken into my mouth. "Now. Forever too...but now."

She didn't need to ask twice. I was ready at her entrance. "Take what you want, siren. I'd sooner drown than make you wait."

She took my length in one hand between us, positioning me where she needed me. When I thrust up, deep into her, she gasped and stilled as though she might break right then.

The water around us glowed brighter. Its luminescence seemed to respond to her arousal. *Interesting theory to explore later.* Every thought of debauchery and position in the book ran through my mind at the sight of her riding me.

I wanted to bend her over the side of that tub and see what she felt like from behind. I wanted to let her hold me underwater between her lush thighs so I could taste her again as she found her release. I hadn't been lying—*I'd lose air for her.*

There would be time for all of that, so much time.

In that moment, I needed to feel her with me, gentle, gasping the same air. I needed to see the look in her eyes when her flames lit. Her legs wrapped tight around me; her nails dug into my back.

When she finally cried out and her warmth contracted around me, she looked flushed and wilder than I'd ever seen her before. It was my new favorite expression of hers. One I intended to get very acquainted with.

The sensation of her tightening around me was too much to bear as she writhed above me, seeking the remaining waves of her climax. When I could no longer hold out, I slammed into her to the hilt. My body seized—I ruptured with her name on my lips.

Wildfire.

All the fire within me stoked to life—she made *me* spark to life. If I had to do it all over again, I'd happily wait another four hundred years in that damp, dark woodland for even a minute with her.

Our eternity would be made from the brightest fires and most vivid stars.

CHAPTER 42
ASTERIE

We didn't leave Fen's bed for hours, though neither of us slept.

Instead, we spent the night stealing kisses and exploring each other's bodies in between tearful explanations of all we had learned over the past days apart. Fen shared everything that happened after his powers returned, about nearly losing Elsie.

He hadn't appeared to be breathing when I told him everything that had happened in the Central Tower, of my time spent in that *in-between* place, of waking up to the sight of stars over the bailey and wanting nothing more than him by my side.

We'd both felt so helpless in those moments.

He rubbed the back of my hand, which was splayed over his chest. The sun from the window created a golden glow over his freckled features.

"Queen Sybilla told you, then, about your claim over me?"

Fen stiffened. "She did," he answered hesitantly.

"So, will you claim me then?"

He made a pleased sound in the back of his throat. "I've already claimed you twice," he teased.

"That is *not* what I mean." I playfully swatted at him. "And you know it."

Fen reached to the side table where a letter opener sat. He quickly cut a small line in his thumb and let his hand fall to the side of the bed. "No. I vow to never exercise that claim over you. The debt owed to my family for those stolen plums is null."

As a drop of blood fell from his thumb, so did my heart. *He didn't want our fates tied.*

My disappointment must have shown in my expression. He flipped onto his side, reaching for me.

"You misunderstand me," he said as he cupped my cheek. "We could be re-bound—on our own terms and timeline. Not that you need my power. You command the stars above and a beast that used to be mine. What good do you have with some flame-throwing tricks? But that decision will never be mine. I would have never claimed you under that blood oath."

I felt light again, like he had just breathed air into me. For so long, I'd belonged to others, for so long, my choices seemed to be made for me. "When we are both ready, I would like that. Being re-bound to you," I admitted. Something saddened me about having no bond with him now.

He cleared his throat. "Well, we'd need to be married first—and the wedding would need to be the gaudiest, most over-the-top affair this realm has ever seen. Three cakes, multiple bands, released doves."

I burst out laughing.

"You wound me." He held his heart playfully. "I *mean* that."

"You would want to marry me? How very mortal." My face grew serious. "I don't know the first thing about *living* out here. I'd make a terrible wife. I don't even know how to cook...an egg."

"I hate eggs." He rolled me on top of him, nipping at my neck. "Plus, I have all I could ever want to eat right here."

"Be serious."

"Oh, but I am." He met my eyes with hooded intensity. "I look forward to spending the rest of my life teaching you every mundane thing about living out here. We'll travel the whole realm—every Corridor. You'll see it all. Every mind-numbing monument to mortal arrogance, every shore, every court."

My heart swelled—*life.* I'd never dreamed of my own life the way he promised it.

"And when we are bound again you will have no doubts that I am irrevocably committed to loving you. We are already Source Matched. It would be no different. Plenty chose to be bound and married to their Source Match if it is also a love match."

I pushed up on my arms abruptly. "Source Matched?"

"Oh, did I leave that part out?"

It was an ancient principle that I'd thought was a myth. When Source Origins walked the earth, they created pairs—magic-wielders whose magic called to one another for protection.

Because the Origins were fickle and liked the entertainment of it, it was said they often did not interfere in helping those matched find one another. Leaving it to chance.

"How do you know that we are Matched?" I stared into those irises flecked with green and gold.

He smiled up at me. "I just do."

Somehow, that explanation was enough. I'd felt the same realization as that blade came down upon him—that same crushing weight of impending loss.

That dark feeling was chased away by the sun peeking further through the window. The bustling sounds of civilians leaving the Keep cut through the sounds of the birds chirping. The fall of hundreds of feet crossing the courtyard carried up the palace walls.

Guilt stung me as hooves clattered along the cobblestone. We needed to return to Queen Sybilla and face the day.

As the people of Luz left the palace grounds, they *sang*. It was a solemn tune but one filled with forlorn hope.

"Her lips grew blue, but the stars brushed her heart.

"And made it beat anew."

I paused, tapping Fen gently to let me rise. "Are they singing about me?"

Fenris smiled mischievously before releasing me to slide off of him and get out of bed. "Why shouldn't they?" he asked.

When my brows scrunched, he rolled his eyes playfully.

"Your actions *saved* them, Asterie. The sacrifice of your life to give me my powers back saved them. Your journey here, your prophecy. Sybilla has clearly spread the word."

A lump grew in my throat as I approached the window. Their faith in me seemed so misplaced—the actions that led me to Luz were ambling and graceless.

The volume of their voices rose, and more of them sang, learning the simple chant. Verses were added. They sang of me, they sang of Fenris, they sang of their brave Queen, of the enchantresses that stood against one of their own kin to save them, of the King of the forgotten realm who sent aid, of a new North King who would herald peace in the Corridor.

"Now." Fenris sat up and watched me. "Will you have me on my hands and knees begging for you one more time before we go and face the music?"

I couldn't help but smirk. "We'll need to be quick this time."

He would never have to beg for me. Claim or none, bound or not, I was his.

Sybilla had sent a maid up to our rooms with fresh clothing and a note that said: "*We will be meeting for breakfast in the dining hall.*"

The palace was bustling with staff cleaning up as much of the wreckage and blood as possible. Fen and I passed the throne room. I squeezed his hand to remind myself that the night's horrors were over.

To my relief, the doors were closed.

When we entered the dining hall, a meager spread of meat and cheese was sitting untouched on a silver tray. All eyes were turned to Queen Sybilla, who sat at the head of the long white-oak table. To her left sat King Darvanda and Elsedora. Elsie eyed the Queen like she wanted to actually try to assassinate the royal now.

"The other rulers of all the Corridors will arrive tomorrow." Queen Sybilla explained to them before her attention caught on us.

My remaining Sisters sat in a row to Sybilla's right—Amara faced away from me, but her posture was relaxed. Cassidee sat with an arm slung over the back of Wyeth's chair and one boot up on an empty chair beside them.

"Good morning." My voice cracked, not prepared to face them. Fen's hand squeezed mine.

The Queen's face lit with an exuberant smile. "Welcome, sleep well?" she asked with coyness.

Upon seeing Fen, Elsedora launched from her seat and bounded over to throw her arms around him. Fen grunted as his sister tightened the embrace. She loosened her hold only to punch his arm—*hard*.

"You fool!" Elsie exclaimed.

Fenris bristled with a huff. "It is nice to see you again too, Else."

Elsedora's arms crossed tightly in front of her. Then she rolled her eyes with a smirk. "I never could stay mad for long." She squeezed Fen's arm before returning to Darvanda's side.

Interesting. Elsie loved Fenris, but her devotion to the King of the Wastelands seemed strong...a problem for another day.

I scanned the room.

Emmerick was standing, leaning against the far wall's door frame and looking like he'd rather be anywhere but here. Yet his lips curved into a trace of a smile as he watched us.

Fenris pulled me over to where the Commander stood. "I should burn you on a spit for what you did to her."

The entire room stilled and went quiet.

Emmerick's smile waned with Fenris' words, and his brow furrowed. Then, before he could answer, Fen released my hand to take Emmerick's and pulled the Commander into a bear-like embrace.

"Lucky for you, I know she can be convincing when she wants something to go her way." He released the Constable with a wink. "And she came back to me. So you're safe. For now."

Tears threatened. *When had my body become so leaky?* I turned to the table.

"She's not glowing anymore," Darvanda mused darkly—as though it was a disappointment.

I reluctantly stepped over to my Sisters, who rose at the table, turning to me. Amara embraced me first. She still smelled of salty air, honeysuckle and sunshine. The familiarity of it made the threatening tears finally fall.

"My girl." Amara said nothing more.

Wyeth lingered near. I felt Cassidee's rough hand on my shoulder before she pulled me into an embrace, picked me up off my feet, shook me and squeezed me like a rag doll.

"You all should have seen it—Asterie had that wolf-demon tear Firose to *shreds*. It was the most hauntingly beautiful, gruesome thing I have ever witnessed, and *that's* saying something."

"Enough, Cass." Wyeth swatted at Cassidee to put me down. Wyeth had never been a fan of being touched. However, when I hit the ground with a huff, she offered me a smug smile and said with quiet sarcasm, "Must you make death such a hobby?"

I was so weepy now that I had to catch tears on the sleeve of my freshly pressed tunic. Finally, after our reunions were settled, we all found our seats at the table.

Sybilla continued whatever news she had been sharing upon our arrival.

"We can discuss plans when all six Corridors are represented tomorrow." She was looking at Emmerick, but he refused to meet her gaze. A pang tugged at my heart to see them at odds.

"Six?" Darvanda interrupted with amusement.

"The Wastelands are to be included," Sybilla reasoned.

Darvanda leaned back in his chair, kicking his feet out under the table with a look of defiance. "Ah, but that is the problem. We are not a *Corridor*. We are a realm of our own—and will be respected and negotiated with as such."

Queen Sybilla's face grew red as she sucked in her cheeks, but she nodded.

"My mistake...I see that semantics matter greatly to our friends from the forgotten *realm*," she corrected. "All five Corridors' rulers and the ruler of the Wastelands will meet tomorrow."

"Sahlmsara," Darvanda interrupted again.

Sybilla tried to hide a glare. "Excuse me?"

"The Wastelands are what *you* call it. Sahlmsara is the realm's name. We refer to that land informally as the Sahlms." He sighed and tilted his head as though egging her on to disagree.

This dynamic was going to be interesting.

"Well, we will deal with priority concerns for Henosis and *the Sahlms*, first—defense, fighting blight of our crops and opening the Egresses to enable trade reform. We must rebuild a stronger partnership. We'll have council meetings twice a month."

Krait Darvanda ran a hand through his hair, looking entirely unimpressed. "We can negotiate around a table all day and hold as many council meetings as you desire. But this realm, and your Corridor, still owes me a debt for my aid. So why don't we settle that today? Then maybe I'll engage in your little game of monarchy."

Fen's hand gripped my knee beneath the table. *How long would it take before these two royals tore each other's heads off?*

At that thought, Sybilla glanced at me with a smirk as though to say *not long.*

"Imports of water in the summer months," Darvanda demanded. "Also, a decree to allow those who would like to return to their families in this realm the right to do so and..."

Darvanda paused as though looking around for one last thing.

"As collateral, her." He pointed a finger toward me. Bile rose to the back of my throat. "My people need reassurance of your *cooperation*. She'll be unharmed, so long as things go well."

Fen growled and shot up, rattling the table. I caught his arm before he could launch at the Wasteland's King. Darvanda rose, and so did Elsedora, who stood tall beside her King, but worry crossed her expression.

"I'd like to see you try, Krait." Fen's skin seemed to shift to burning embers beneath my hand.

Darvanda chuckled darkly. "Ah, so you *are* Source Matched. Elsedora suspected." The serpentine smoothness of his Brennac enunciation fell on my ears like nails grating steel. *Source Matched.* It still felt odd to have the feeling explained. "Your little show of arms and disobedience four centuries ago got us exiled, old friend. Give me one good reason not to take your precious Star away?"

Elsedora's back stiffened at the King's words. Emmerick stalked toward the table with fists clenched.

"Stop this!" Elsie boomed. "It wasn't him, Krait. He did not betray you or Brennax."

Krait Darvanda looked between Elsie and Fen before leveling a glare at Fenris.

"Explain," Darvanda growled. The man was terrifying. It seemed he was used to getting his way—right now, his way would have me shipped off to the Wastelands with him. I shuddered.

Fen explained what happened that night four centuries ago. About Firose's deception, her wielding his power and his ultimate surrender.

"So, you weren't following Commander Stygian's command to attack?" Darvanda was piecing something together. I didn't know who Stygian was, but by the wrath in his eyes, it was likely better that way.

"No. Because I never attacked...Firose used Van." Fen ran a hand down my ink-covered arm. "Before I knew it, Stygian had given the order for the Brennac attack. At your command."

"I never gave the command to attack past the city gates. It was meant to be a coup, not a massacre," Darvanda answered.

Then he spun on Elsedora.

"You never told me. Why?"

I'd hate to be under the scrutiny of that dark glare. But Elsie looked unaffected as she cocked a hip, like dealing with a petulant child. She had nerve, Fen's sister.

"Would you have believed that I wasn't just protecting him? I was broken—you gave me a job. A purpose. I thought my whole family was dead when you took me into the Sahlms."

Darvanda rose from his seat, jaw tightened and fists curled. He leveled a look between Elsie and Fen.

"I'm sorry, but you both know I don't renegotiate without a better offer once I've set a price. She is coming with us. My people will need assurances."

Just as Fen was about to launch over the table, a voice interrupted.

"You will take me instead."

All eyes shot to the head of the table. Emmerick took two steps toward Sybilla as if knocked forward, while Sybilla stood and rounded the table to Darvanda.

"What better way to provide your people assurances than to have the Queen of the Central Corridor of Henosis in your custody?"

"Fuck that. Sybilla—are you serious? Offering yourself like a prized pig at auction?" Emmerick stormed to her side of the table before his hands slammed down on the oak in front of her.

"Emmerick—you are speaking to your Queen." Sybilla's voice invoked respect, but her words had a waver that dripped with veiled pain. Emmerick's face turned bitter and twisted.

"Funny. Based on what I've learned in the last twenty-four hours, you were *never* my Queen. Not really." The words landed precisely as he'd intended, and Sybilla visibly reeled back as though struck.

I turned Fenris toward me and away from the table—he was still heaving with anger.

"Count..." I reminded him in a whisper.

This meeting couldn't turn violent. We needed to remain calm no matter what Darvanda did to provoke us.

Amara chimed in, "You should hear Queen Sybilla out, Emmerick. I am sure King Darvanda would swear in blood to do Sybilla no harm. This could be a positive move for our realms—we can hold trials to ensure anyone who wants to leave Sahlmsara and return to Henosis has that chance. But when the trials end, she will be released back to Luz. There needs to be a timeline. Krait—you cannot just pluck a Queen from her kingdom. You, of *all* people, know that." Amara's tone was political and placating.

Queen Sybilla nodded along, agreeing with Amara's sentiments, but Emmerick looked bewildered.

"Should we share blood on that?" Darvanda asked with a curled lip that was part smile and part scowl.

"Sybilla, don't you dare!" Emmerick's shout rang through the room as guards approached him. They reached him and hesitantly restrained their own Constable.

Wyeth and Cassidee remained seated, glancing at each other with a look of slight amusement.

The Queen's attention never left King Darvanda as if she was sizing up her opponent as she extended her hand to him.

Darvanda gruffly took it along with a blade from a belt sheath. The Queen's hand seemed small in his as he sliced his own palm and then hers. Sybilla barely flinched.

"I agree to your demands. I will go willingly to the Sahlms so long as no harm shall befall me or my Corridor until the trials end," Sybilla promised.

"Why are you doing this?" Emmerick shouted as the guards pulled him back by his arms. He wasn't a match for the four of them, though they still struggled to remove him.

Darvanda huffed in amusement at Emmerick's outburst then said, "No harm will come to the Central Queen, or her Corridor, so long as she is an ally to Sahlmsara in all negotiations with the rulers of the Corridors." He glanced over at Emmerick with a quirked brow.

Darvanda and Sybilla let their blood fall to the ground. The magic sizzled—acceptance of the blood oath. My throat constricted—that oath seemed one-sided. While we owed the Sahlms a great deal, I feared for my friend.

"We leave tomorrow after our first *council* meeting." The icy sarcasm bled through Darvanda's tone.

Emmerick was swearing and kicking against the four guards that dragged him from the room. My heart pounded as Amara followed them out.

"I missed being with you in the courts," Cassidee whispered into Wyeth's hair. The room had fallen so silent that I could hear their exchange.

"I did not." Wyeth's hair flashed a shade of green.

"Look at the bright side—now if anyone calls you my sister, I can acceptably knock their teeth out," Cassidee joked.

Wyeth gave her a warning nudge with her elbow, but an underlying smirk gave her affection away. "I *have* always enjoyed watching you fight for me," she playfully noted. "We should leave them to this and see that Amara has *that* handled."

Maybe their relationship should have surprised me, but instead, it clicked into place like a missing puzzle piece. Even if I hadn't always understood it, there had been an example of love under my nose my whole life.

"Down, boy..." Darvanda taunted as he observed Fen's still clenched fists. "It looks like your little Star gets to stay after all. Pity."

Sybilla met my gaze with a nod of reassurance.

Fenris and I sat across from the Queen in her study, the weight of her words still echoing in my ears.

I was to become the Chief Advisor of Luz.

Me and Fenris were to be interim rulers of the Central Corridor.

Fenris was tense but gripped my knee to ground me.

"Asterie?" Sybilla was tapping her delicate fingers on the table as though against the keys of a piano.

"I'm sorry." I mustered a response. "Are you *sure*? Surely there is someone in your court more *qualified*, more worthy of—"

"I've made my choice."

Fenris still hadn't said a word.

"I—" Intaking a breath, I was still unsure. "I would be honored to accept. But will your people accept us? A High Enchantress and a warlock, once condemned for destroying a kingdom?"

Sybilla smiled with a tilt of her head. "My people trust in me. And I trust in you. They will accept you, and you will serve them well until I can return." The Queen paused. "I won't lie, I would have entrusted this to Emmerick, but with the North Corridor needing support now more than ever and our current...strained relationship, I need rulers who will put the people first. Who will try, who will be unafraid to face hard times."

Fenris cut in, "I, too, would be honored to handle matters of rebuilding and setting up a sanctuary for those who would like to learn to wield magic."

His confidence helped ease my worries, but only slightly.

The road ahead would be a long one. Queen Sybilla was entrusting us to enact all of her plans while she was deposed and in the Wastelands. The rebuilding of Luz, creating a sanctuary for magic-wielders, handling the political fall-out of a realm overcoming an attack. *There had to be someone who could do this job better than we could.*

"Have you no advisors, no relatives?"

Sybilla flinched as though I had hit a bruise on her very soul. "None that are helpful."

I pressed on. "What of the nobles you spoke of that do not approve of your ruling? Will they rise against us?"

Sybilla smirked and responded, "Well, speaking of family—those would be my cousins. After seeing you burst apart and kill men in a fit of stars, I doubt they would dare try. But you will need to be careful. We *all* need to be careful...I can't trust this with anyone else."

I suddenly felt sad for the young Queen. *She had no one.* Her own family couldn't be trusted. Even I had Fenris and Amara and could work on connecting with Wyeth and Cassidee in the way I'd once wanted to as a child.

"Don't pity me, Asterie. I have you two. And from what I've seen of you—I stand firm in that we will be good friends."

I'd forgotten the Queen would be able to feel my uncertainty and hear my thoughts. I tried desperately to reel in all of my doubts and feelings of inadequacy. *Why us?*

Sybilla simply smiled and asked, "The stars and flames—what do they both have in common?"

Fenris leaned back in his chair and looked over at me as though I was the most marvelous being in the realms.

When I could not think of a relevant similarity, I shrugged and shook my head in defeat.

Sybilla answered, "They both light the way."

EPILOGUE

ASTERIE

I was awake just before dawn again and sat at our bedchamber's vanity. I'd let Van out to frolic in the gardens—the staff were growing used to him, and the kitchen maids often snuck him cuttings of meat.

A month had passed since the attack on Luz. The realm seemed calm, yet something stirred in my magic still. Dreams visited me of that *in-between* place, of conversations among the Source Origins that were muted and inaudible to me. They were not unpleasant, but I couldn't shake that Origin Asterie was trying to warn me of something.

The night prior, Fenris had shared a quiet worry while our limbs were tangled together.

He'd whispered into the dark between us, "It feels as though it is not over."

Now Fenris slept soundly in bed behind me with one arm slung over his eyes. His dark auburn waves caught the light of the sun as the light began peaking through pale blue curtains, and his free arm stretched to my side of the bed as though subconsciously searching for me.

Fen's words, paired with my strange dreams, had compelled me to unpack the moonstone that had been sent from the Central Tower. I unwrapped it from the velvet.

Setting the white stone down on the vanity in front of me, I tapped my fingers against it. I hadn't attempted to use a moonstone since that night in Fen's bedchamber. Part of me feared it may still not respond to me at all.

Placing both hands on the cool stone, I watched my dark irises grow milky in the vanity mirror before everything went black.

Are we safe? I focused on the question and thought of that place I'd visited in death.

In that void, a blue light flickered in the distance. *I'd seen this before...*

Then, I heard a whisper. "This is your path, starling. You must live it now."

This time, the blue light did not grow near. Instead, it winked out like a dying star. I swallowed hard, contemplating what that might mean.

"Asterie?" Fen's voice pulled me back.

His brow creased in concern as he looked at me through the vanity mirror.

"Are you alright?" Fen asked.

The corners of my mouth lifted. Every new day got better with him being a part of it. He was still hopelessly flirtatious given any chance, as though he needed to keep winning me over.

Yet I was wholly won.

I answered, "Yes, I'm fine."

"What did you see?"

"Nothing that I understand yet, unfortunately," I admitted.

"Come back to bed," he urged.

"I need to go through our correspondence."

"Mmm, if your dedication wasn't such an attractive quality, then I'd be far less distracting," he teased sleepily.

I huffed a laugh but forced my attention from Fen to the neatly stacked letters addressed to my new title. *Asterie Bennett, Chief Advisor of Luz.* A new identity—one that tethered me to a new reality, a new realm.

Queen Sybilla had left for the Sahlms. I wondered, and worried, about her journey to those unwelcoming lands. I shuffled hopefully through the envelopes until I found one with a royal blue wax seal and the initials SW and quickly cut the letter open.

Asterie,

We have arrived in Sahlmsara. The settlement here isn't as awful as I imagined—charming even, in a way. I'm safe, mostly comfortable, aside from the heat, and I'm alive. King Darvanda has not yet killed me despite constantly looking like he wants to. I do think he will read my correspondence—and he can fuck right off if he does. No hawks are allowed in or out of this place, so my letters may be delayed. They travel by horseback and post comes weekly.

Do check in on my Sun King. I hate to ask you to step into the middle of our dispute, but I hope you would tell me if you were worried about him.

Tell Fenris that his sister is an endless pain in my ass.

Though I am anxious to return to my people, there are no better hands that I would entrust them with in the meantime.

Yours,

Sybilla

P.S. I have negotiated with King Prick to allow you and Fen to Egress in for weekly dinners so that I can advise you. More impor-

tantly—to speak amongst friends. I will send word when the Egress is built.

I smiled at her mixture of kind and vulgar words. There was a wine stain on the page—I am sure that if I were stuck in the Wastelands, my letters and lips would be stained with wine too.

Fen's scent of smoke and cedar enveloped me as his arms slipped around my stomach. I hadn't heard him rise from bed, but all my anxieties were melted away by his touch.

"I'd pay good coin to have seen that negotiation." Fen read over my shoulder before pulling my hair aside and pressing a kiss to the soft skin of my neck. He *was* a distraction—but one I delighted in.

"Do you think he'll harm her?" I asked.

"He's a man of his word. Plus, he made a blood oath. You can't lose sleep worrying, my beauty. She will be alright."

Beside her letter lay a few pieces of parchment that the Queen had left behind, covered in her hurried penmanship. Sybilla's instructions for us. I re-read them as I gathered ink to write her back.

Care for the families impacted or unhoused by the battle—they will need shelter, food and supplies.

The Central Corridor is to provide refuge to magic-wielders as they reenter Henosis. If you agree, turn the Central Tower into a sanctuary for them.

Cassidee Arkwright is to be appointed Constable to the Army of Luz, should she accept.

Wyeth Winnow is to be appointed Head Healer, should she accept.

The Order against magic in the Central Corridor is no more. The conception ban for immortals dies with it.

The Egresses are to be re-opened in Luz, allowing easier trade and travel between Corridors. We shall build one in Sahlmsara.

<u>Do not</u> let my cousins within a foot of this palace. Trust me.

Fenris, do not burn the palace down while I am away.

I will see you soon.

Unless an Egress was built sooner, we would see her in a few weeks' time when meetings among the rulers of Henosis began along with the trials to allow reentry into the Corridor. The realm's trust would need to be rebuilt brick by brick, one meeting at a time. Righting the wrongs of a falsified history of injustice would not be easy.

Fen slipped a hand down my stomach and to my core, teasing over the light silk of my nightdress. My toes curled at the feeling, somehow already wanting him again even after he'd wrung release out of me three times last night.

When Fen was not away, working on plans for the Central Tower's sanctuary, he was here with me in Luz. Doing devilishly grand things to my body.

I looked into his eyes in the vanity mirror. "Do you think this will fade?" I tried to hide the fear in my voice.

He tilted his head before resting his chin on my shoulder. His hands stilled, and I almost whimpered in protest. "Will what fade?"

My sigh was met with a knowing smirk.

He knew exactly what I meant.

"I keep waiting for your interest to wane," I admitted.

He looked alarmed. "I can assure you that will never happen."

He bit at my earlobe playfully.

"It might feel different over time, a deeper connection, less physical *desperation*." He waggled a brow to which I rolled my eyes at. "But the way I care for you is not something that will ever wane or wither. That I am sure of."

I took his hands in mine, and he tightened his arms around me. With time away from those woodlands, from the past betrayals that haunted him for centuries, Fen was growing lighter.

The last time I saw Amara for weekly tea, she had commented to me in private that she hadn't seen Fen look so happy, so himself, in a very long time. My body warmed at the thought that I was able to dull the ache in his heart, at the notion that somehow I had given him something he needed.

There was so much that required our attention, but under the glow of the morning light, with him near, it felt as though it would all be alright. One of his hands slipped from mine to return to where my nightdress ended, meeting my bare thigh.

"We have work to do," I warned despite craving his touch. When he slid the silk fabric upward an inch, I whimpered.

"Do we?" he drawled into my neck.

"I suppose that I could spare a *few* 'fleeting moments' of distraction."

In Helos...

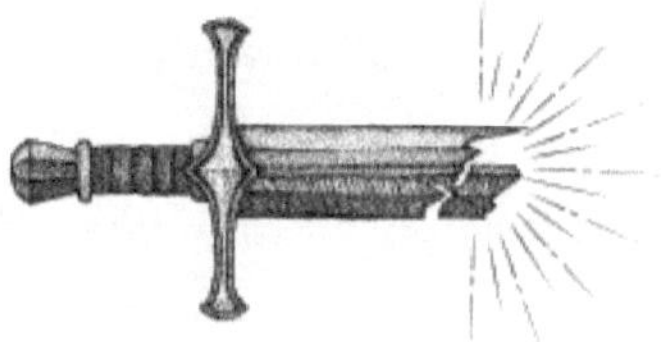

The bell tower above sings.

The rage of Mattock's heir hits my tongue—tangy and metallic. He is crowned on the abbey steps, and the people cheer. That rage could easily be turned lethal. *Yes*, the new Sun King would live long enough to see that anger through, unlike his father.

I lick my lips, thinking of the sweet taste of Corric's agony as he maddened to death in that high castle above me as a crown is placed on his son's head.

If only the golden-haired enchantress had been easier to mold, I could have been freed sooner. She'd been so desperate for purpose, so full of that same rage that radiates in the new King as he accepts a crown he does not want.

The bell tower continues to ring a sound of hope. As the crowd cheers for their new King, I look down at them. I see what they all might look like with the skin rotting from their bones.

When the Star Origin had come to bargain, the taste of the starling's death had been so sweet. I almost hiss at the memory of it, forgetting what body I am in. To absorb her death...it would have been pure bliss.

"Let her live," the Star Origin had demanded.

I had answered, "Release me, and she shall live."

"That is not a fair bargain. We will release you. But upon your freedom, you will return the full power of the Origins to our descendants."

"I beat you all once. What makes you think your younglings can defeat me now?"

When I accepted her terms, she'd snarled.

They might try to stop me. But now I walk the lands again while they lay dormant in that world in between. I will grow strong enough to finish what I started—if only with a little help.

King Emmerick Mattock turns to me. "I'm ready to return to the castle."

ACKNOWLEDGEMENTS

If you've made it this far, I first want to say thank *you*. When I decided to write *Born of Starlight,* it was an outlet at the end of hard days, an escape into what my brain was capable of and just plain fun. If only three of you have as good of a time reading this as I did writing it, then I'm immensely happy!

To my husband, Dan—despite losing nights and weekends with me, you've remained so supportive of this budding dream. Thanks for forcing me to take breaks when I needed them and for not freaking out when I told you I was going to write some magical sex stories.

Mom, thank you for loaning me all those urban fantasy romance novels as a teenager. Or did I steal those? However it went, I'm grateful that I get to share this story with you in a genre that you love.

Lois, keep reading! You are just not allowed to read this until you're eighteen. Okay fine, seventeen. But don't tell Mom.

Those of you who made this book possible—we did it! I hear that self-publishing is always tough, but it was made a lot easier because of the team on my side. Just to name a few of you...

Britney Waldrop, thank you for seeing this story through every stage of editing. It wouldn't be what it is today without your thoughtful critique and feedback. Can't wait to work with you on the next one!

David Gardias, I'm still gushing over the cover design. It's remarkably beautiful. Alyssa Hurlbert, the map you drew totally brought this world to life. Both of your artworks are getting framed and hung in my office.

To my lovely beta readers, cheerleaders and critique partners: Tiffany, Holly, Ashley, Shalini, Shantell, Megan, Tina, Britney, Kim, Kirsten, Maddi, Jan, Eve, Lena, Britt and Amber. Gosh I sincerely hope I didn't forget anyone. Those of you who touched this story are all amazing—you gave this book your time when it didn't *quite* deserve it yet. For that, I'm so grateful.

Thanks to Barley and Candi for the snuggles and for being my not-so-ferocious sidekicks.

Oh, and thank you to wine and chocolate—you got me through the tearful moments of imposter syndrome.

THE ADVENTURE CONTINUES...

In the next installment of the Legends of Henosis series, *City of Snakes*, we follow Queen Sybilla Wymark into the city of Sahlmsara.

Her people are safe, but an oath sealed in blood demands payment.
Now, she must settle the debt.

Sybilla Wymark has one choice—sacrifice her friend to King Darvanda's realm as collateral or go in her place. As Queen, the answer is simple. Sybilla will go. Wary of his realm's magic, her allies question her safety, but where they see trouble, she sees opportunity.

Krait Darvanda smells death in the air. Time runs thin to claim his destiny, so he drags a headstrong Queen back to the Sahlms. The only way Krait can prevail is to fight alongside his spoiled, foul-mouthed new ally. He has no choice; she holds a key to the ultimate weapon and his people's salvation.

Want updates on what's to come? Subscribe on marietkay.com for news, exclusive bonus content, and more!

About the Author

Mariet Kay is a fantasy romance author who lives in Phoenix, Arizona, with her husband and a pack of rescue animals. She loves writing steamy love stories set in make-believe places. Mariet has a decade-long career in digital marketing and has always possessed a passion for digital media and content creation. For more information visit marietkay.com.